MURDER IN THE TELEPHONE EXCHANGE

MURDER IN THE TELEPHONE EXCHANGE

June Wright

DARK PASSAGE

All names, characters and incidents are fictitious.
Description of the Telephone Exchange
and its working is partly imaginary

DEDICATED TO
'CENTRAL'
AND TO ALL WHO HAVE WORKED THEREIN

A Dark Passage book
Published by Verse Chorus Press
PO Box 14806, Portland OR 97293
info@versechorus.com

Cover design by Mike Reddy
Interior design and layout by Steve Connell/Transgraphic
Dark Passage logo by Mike Reddy

Country of manufacture as stated on the last page of this book

Library of Congress Cataloging-in-Publication Data

Wright, June, 1919-2012.
   Murder in the telephone exchange / June Wright.
      page cm.
   ISBN 978-1-891241-37-6 (pbk.) — ISBN 978-1-891241-96-3 (e-book)
   1. Women detectives--Fiction. 2. Murder--Investigation--Fiction.
   3. Melbourne (Vic--Fiction. I. Title.
   PR9619.3.W727M87 2014
   823'.912--dc23
                        2013043859

PREFACE

The crime novels written by June Wright have been unjustly forgotten both in Britain, where they were published between 1948 and 1966, and in her homeland of Australia. They are distinguished by finely drawn settings in and around Melbourne, Victoria, feisty female protagonists and credible social situations, and in my opinion they thoroughly deserve a contemporary reappraisal.

She was born Dorothy June Healy on the 29th of June 1919 in Malvern, a leafy suburb southeast of Melbourne; and Catholic educated at Kildara College in Malvern and Loreto Mandeville Hall in the adjacent posh suburb of Toorak. She first showed literary promise as a schoolgirl; the respected Australian journalist P.I. O'Leary (1888-1944) awarded her a prize in a children's writing competition run by *The Advocate* newspaper in Melbourne. But writing was in June's blood; her grandfather John Healy (1852-1916) was a well-known Melbourne writer who wrote under the name "The Onlooker." After leaving school and briefly studying commercial art, June got a job as a "hello girl" or telephonist at the Central Telephone Exchange in Melbourne (she is pictured overleaf operating a switchboard). In 1941 she married Stewart Wright, a cost accountant. They had six children: Patrick, Rosemary, Nicholas, Anthony, Brenda and Stephen.

When June's first child Patrick was one year old, she began writing her first crime novel *Murder in the Telephone Exchange* (1948), which was set in her former workplace. Sarah Compton, a supervisor at the Central Telephone Exchange in Melbourne, is bashed to death with a "buttinsky," a device used by telephone mechanics to butt in on or interrupt telephone conversations. June considered it to be "unique in the history of murder instruments. Just imagine the mess that sort of [thing] would make of anyone's face," she gleefully told the author of "Murder on the Brain" (1952). Maggie Byrnes, a spirited young telephonist at the exchange, who June emphatically denied was modelled on herself (I didn't believe her!), narrates the Dorothy L. Sayers–style whodunit. (At the time, Sayers' *Gaudy Night* (1935) was June's favourite detective novel.)

A Telephonist operating a position on a C.B. multiple switchboard.
(Note the correct adjustment of the outfit and the approved method of handling keys and plugs.)

June Wright in 1939: the model telephonist

While wrapping up vegetable scraps in an old newspaper, June happened to see an advertisement for an international literary competition run by the London publisher, Hutchinson. She entered *Murder in the Telephone Exchange* in the Detective and Thriller category of the competition, which was to be judged by Anthony Berkeley Cox (1893-1971), the author of the Roger Sheringham murder mysteries; John Creasey (1908-1973), the author of the Toff crime novels; and Dennis Wheatley (1897-1977), the author of the Gregory Sallust spy thrillers. "Unfortunately, in the Judges' opinion, no novel was of sufficient merit to justify the award of a prize of £1,000," Hutchinson informed June in 1945. "It has been decided, however, that certain manuscripts are deserving of publication, and to those authors who submitted entries considered to have the greatest merit we are prepared to offer an advance commensurate with the standard of the book. As your novel, *Murder in the Telephone Exchange,* is one of these, we have great pleasure in offering you an advance of £154 [...] with an option on your next two novels." June was thrilled.

June claimed "*Murder in the Telephone Exchange* was the first detective novel set in Melbourne since Fergus Hume's (1859-1932) *Mystery of the Hansom Cab* published in 1886." Whether she was correct or not, Melbourne certainly does feature a lot in her book. June saw no reason why Melbourne's Russell Street police headquarters should not become as well known in crime fiction as Scotland Yard, she told the Australian magazine *Woman's Day;* and at a swish lunch to promote *Murder in the Telephone Exchange* ("Oysters au Natural, Lobster Newburg, Chicken Maryland and Bombe" were on the menu), Sir Raymond Connelly, the Lord Mayor of Melbourne (1945-1948), thanked June for publicising the city in such a fashion. The setting of the murder mystery had to be "a real place, somewhere I knew and knew well, not an imaginary place," June told me almost 60 years after her crime novel was first published.

Most book reviewers were full of praise for *Murder in the Telephone Exchange,* often singling out its quirky local setting, which June described in the kind of telling detail that only an insider could provide. For example, U.M.C., the author of "Have You Read These?" (1948), remarked: "Perhaps it was the Melbourne setting that gave a new freshness to the form. (One almost expected to meet the characters walking down the streets, to hear their voices over the phone.) But I think there were other factors, too: the atmosphere, the plot, the characterization, all are good." June energetically promoted *Murder at the Telephone Exchange* in the press, on radio and at a number of literary events. The book was a bestseller, which according to *The Advertiser* newspaper in Adelaide, South Australia, "outsold even Agatha Christie [(1890-1976)] and other world-famous authors in Australia" in 1948. The ensuing royalties didn't make June rich by any means, but she was able to buy herself a fur coat and pay for the remodelling of her kitchen.

Many people were intrigued by June's ability to effectively juggle crime fiction writing and motherhood, which was reflected by the titles of several magazine and newspaper articles, such as "Wrote Thriller with Her Baby on Her Knee" (1948) and "Books Between Babies" (1948). June believed that housewives were extremely well qualified for writing novels, because "they are naturally practical, disciplined and used to monotony—three excellent attributes for the budding writer," she told *The Sun* newspaper in Melbourne. She liked to hold up as an example Harriet Beecher Stowe (1811-1896), who wrote *Uncle Tom's Cabin* (1852) when the mother of 10 children.

June's second book, *So Bad a Death* (1949), which also features Maggie Byrnes, was "possibly the best Australian thriller yet written," reported the author of "Brilliant Writer in Magazine" (1949). The book was serialised on ABC radio and also in *Woman's Day*. By now, June had four children—Patrick aged seven, Rosemary aged five and the twins, Anthony and Nicholas, aged three—and two bestselling crime novels. How did she do it?

"With washing to do three days a week, I never get up later than a quarter to seven," June told *The Australian Women's Weekly* magazine in 1948. "On Monday, the biggest wash day, I rise at 5.30, light the copper, and have the washing on the line before breakfast. The twins are dressed in time for their breakfast at 7.30. Then come the other two, who have their meals with us. Monday is kitchen-cleaning day, Tuesday bedroom day. On Wednesday I scrub the back verandah and bathroom, and clean the two play rooms. On Thursday the lounge and study are done. Friday it's back to the washtub, and the front verandah gets scrubbed. I cook an especially nice hot meal on Saturday morning, but like to sew or garden in the afternoon. Oh yes, I have to spend one night ironing, but I write on the others."

June took up writing to make her domestic life more tolerable. "Marriage, motherhood and the suburban lifestyle were not enough—though one would never have dared to voice such sentiments then," she confessed in 1997. By the same token, she never hid her frustration with domestic family life either. For example, at one stage, *So Bad a Death* was called *Who Would Murder a Baby?* When F.M. Doherty of *Australasian Post* magazine asked June why she had named it that, the then mother of four frankly declared: "Obviously you know nothing of the homicidal instincts sometimes aroused in a mother by her children. After a particularly exasperating day, it is a relief to murder a few characters in your book instead!"

Hutchinson rejected June's next book *The Law Courts Mystery*. Undeterred, she tried a different genre, a psychological thriller called *The Devil's Caress* (1952). According to the author of "Oven Fresh" (1952), it made her first two books "read like bedtime stories," however it was generally not as well received as its predecessors. For her fourth crime novel *Reservation for Murder* (1958), June created a truly inspired character, the unassuming but strong-willed Catholic nun-detective Mother Paul, who in many respects is a female equivalent of the Catholic priest-detective, Father Brown, created by G.K. Chesterton (1874-1976). Hutchinson turned down the next book that June submitted, *Duck Season Death* (published for the first time by Verse Chorus Press in 2013). It seems that her publisher wanted more Mother Pauls because her final two crime novels *Faculty of Murder* (1961) and *Make-Up for Murder* (1966) both feature the inimitable nun-detective.

When June's husband Stewart suddenly fell ill and could no longer work, she gave up writing crime fiction altogether to earn a regular salary. This was a great pity as I believe she could have written many more first-rate detective novels in the same vein as *Murder in the Telephone Exchange*, which not only tests the reader's wits, but also is a wonderful evocation of post-war Melbourne. Nor had she exhausted the possibilities of Mother Paul in my view, a detective identified as "special" by a number of crime fiction reviewers. For example, according to J.C. of *The Advocate* (1961): "Mother Paul is indeed a most attractive personality, worthy to rank with the great sleuths of fiction, even if devoid of the eccentricities possessed by most of them. We shall be very disappointed if we do not meet her again."

June passed away on the 4th of February 2012 aged 92. "Maybe I'll never write a classic," she once told Lisa Allan of *The Argus* newspaper in Melbourne. "Maybe that isn't my role in life. But vegetable I'll never be, and neither will I toss out any God-given talent simply because 'I'm only a housewife'."

DERHAM GROVES

CHAPTER I

This is John's idea, not mine. It will bear my reluctant signature and is a record of my impressions of the various incidents which occurred during the heat-wave of last February, but the inspiration is John's. I think his suggestion sprang from the desire to give me something to do besides count the days for my stay in this shameful place to end.

The whole project fills me with revulsion and the lethargy of one who has survived a crisis only to find another ahead. For that is what I have experienced. I have been through some terrible moments of suspicion, fear and misery. Heaven knows what other words there are to describe the emotions which accompanied me step by step into this room, so bare and expressionless except for the sinister barred window. I reached the peak of those emotions two weeks ago. Now, another summit is waiting to be scaled; for climb it I must, if I wish to survive the results of my own errors. Perhaps this is the way I can do it.

It is so hot again. The cool change which followed the thunderstorm was only a temporary respite. Even in this stone building I can feel the heat. The bars at the window seem to waver against the hard burning sky. As I reached for the jug of water on the table a moment ago, a bird perched itself on the ledge with its beak slightly open. We stared at each other with envious eyes.

It was hot then. The newspapers printed paragraphs about record temperatures and bush fire warnings, filling up picture space with snaps taken of bathers, ice vendors and children drinking lemonade. That was before we hit the headlines. But it was during the same heat-wave that crime, as it was so melodramatically phrased, held the upper hand at the Telephone Exchange, so I daresay they went on printing things like that. I didn't notice them. But I do remember the heat. It seemed part of the whole ghastly business. A background, just as much as the Exchange buildings were themselves.

I find it difficult to know where to start, and how to express myself in the way I was then. I didn't feel lonely, embittered and miserable a few weeks ago. Life was full and intriguing.

My perspective and sense of values were totally dissimilar to the distorted vision from which I am now suffering. Maybe I'll be able to see straight once I get this off my chest.

Did you read about the Telephone Exchange murders in the papers? There wasn't much chance of anyone missing them. Just in case you were not one of those numerous sightseers who parked themselves outside the building and gaped like landed fish, I will give you a brief description of where the crimes took place.

The Telephone Exchange, which comprises two buildings standing back to back, runs half a block in length. But the frontage being comparatively small renders it a rather inconspicuous place. The old Exchange, facing Lonsdale Street, is a two-storied establishment with Corinthian pillars and other arcanthus decorations, containing aged apparatus for the dwindling manual subscribers in the city and some country stations. At the back of "Central," like a modern miss shielded by her anxious grandmother, rises the eight-story red brick building which houses the most up-to-date Trunk Exchange in the Southern Hemisphere. We telephonists who have worked there, while dubbing it a "madhouse" or a "hell of a hole," will always be proud of it.

Eight floors with a basement, a flat roof and one lift, which had the rather trying tendency to break down on occasions when one was running late, the switchroom and cloakroom being on the sixth and eighth floors respectively. This only happened at odd hours, as by day it was run by old Bill, one of the nicest men who ever lost a limb in the First World War. He was intensely proud of his lift, and would hear no word against it.

I am trying to remember when I first became conscious of the changed atmosphere in the Trunk Exchange. It was so gradual that its beginning was almost undetectable. The strange behaviour of the Senior Traffic Officer can provide a point from which to start. That was the first significant item that penetrated my consciousness.

Albert James Scott, or Bertie as he was spoken of except to his face, was in charge of the two Exchanges, Central and Trunks; a dynamic little man with the sense of humour that usually goes with a rotund figure, who changed before our eyes almost overnight. It was his custom to trot about the room, throwing cheery words at traffic officers, monitors and telephonists alike, or to mumble under his breath other words, that began more often than not with the second letter of the alphabet, if any of the Departmental heads had been tedious. Either he would bang the handset telephones about on his desk, or swoop down to the boards and toss the orderly piles of dockets into disarray if he considered the delay on the lines was too high. But that was his way. Those sorts of thing did not worry anyone. Indeed, if one had been connected with the Exchange for as many years as Bertie such behaviour was normal and quite to be expected.

Then one day arrived when he did none of those things, but spent most of his time quietly at his desk in the centre of the room, the single line between his eyes obliterated as his bushy brows met in one unbroken bar. I heard Sarah Compton, the monitor in attendance at the Senior Traffic Officer's table, comment: "Poor old Bertie is getting very grey. I wonder what he is worrying about?"

He was staring moodily in front of him when, going off duty to my tea one evening, I asked if I could change my all-night shift with the girl Patterson. John Clarkson, a traffic officer, was talking on one of Bertie's telephones, but he found time to wink at me. He was rather a lamb, with the figure of an athlete and the wrists of a golfer. As a matter of fact I had played with him several times, as the whole Exchange now knew thanks to Compton, who was a regular snooper. I would not have put it beyond her to be jealous. Clark had a very attractive personality.

Bertie came out of his trance with a sigh.

"What did you say, Miss Byrnes?"

"May I change with Miss Patterson on Friday? She is working from four until eleven. I am on all-night."

It was quite a normal request. Changing shifts and their ensuing pay-backs occurred every day. As I started unbuckling my headset, the pencil that I had slipped over my right ear caught and then fell with a tiny clatter to the floor. Bertie started like a shying horse.

"Change!" he said loudly. "No more changing until further notice. Miss Compton, tell the staff, please, and get me the Sydney Traffic Officer."

He indicated dismissal still further by scribbling out the booking on a docket.

I departed without a word, completely baffled. As a rule relations between Bertie and me were very friendly, bordering almost on the mildly flirtatious. I concluded our Senior Traffic Officer was feeling the weather and decided to reopen the subject at some later and more suitable time.

Two flights of stairs, a long corridor and into the telephonists' cloakroom with its rows of lockers and racks. It was cool and dim as the lights had not yet been switched on, but with the ease of long practice I located my own locker without difficulty, and put my telephone set away. The ebonite was sweating slightly from my long session at the boards. We were always busy at that time of the year. Now, in this February heat, there was a bushfire or two thrown in for good measure.

Voices floated through the half-open door that connected the cloakroom with the telephonists' restroom. Recognizing one, I strolled in, kicking the door shut behind me. Five girls were seated around a table playing cards.

"Bertie won't let us change, Patterson," I said, as a fresh hand was dealt. "What's got into the man, does anyone know? I'd go misère if I were you," I added as Dulcie Gordon tilted her hand up for me to see. "You won't get through, but it's worth a try."

"Shut up, Byrnes. No help required," one of them ordered.

"Yes, be quiet, Maggie," said Gloria Patterson. "It spoils the game if you give hints. Why won't Mr. Scott give you permission? Not that I mind overmuch. I loathe all-nights."

"It was to be a pay-back," I reminded her.

"Was it?" she queried vaguely. "But I can't on Friday. I am going to the Embassy that night with an American fellow I met the other day."

"What are you wearing, Gloria?" I asked, instantly diverted, and giving the others a wink. "The gold lamé or the marquisette model?"

Patterson was always telling us of her extensive wardrobe and many boy-friends. There were those unkind souls who considered both were myths. Certainly she was looking very snappy now,. with a cyclamen orchid pinned to the lapel of her sheer black suit, and I had seen more than one seedy-looking individual waiting for her outside the Exchange. But she was quite unabashed and serious as she told with a wealth of detail, incidentally allowing the little Gordon girl to get her misère, what she was going to wear. Presently she got up to leave.

"Take my hand, Maggie, will you? I'm due at the 'Australia' for a cocktail in five minutes."

I took her place.

"Only one hand. I must have my tea."

I saw an easy solo and declared it. We played a quick hand in silence. Ormond snorted as she paid me for two over.

"Cocktails at the 'Australia'! Oh yeah! And how does she manage to dress on our miserable screw? That's if she has all the clothes that she says she has, which I very much doubt."

"Shut up," I said softly. The door into the cloakroom was ajar. Yet I was sure a click had registered itself on my brain as Gloria had left. When I opened it suddenly and looked out, the shadows cast by the light summer coats seemed to waver as though someone had just passed. There was no sight of Gloria, however, and Mrs. Smith, one of the cleaners, was there dusting the lockers.

It was a puerile impulse to try to catch Gloria. I still don't know what prompted it or what result I expected. But it manifests the state of nerves everyone was in at that time. I noticed several others had been suffering from similar futile and unreasonable impulses. There was definitely something wrong in the Trunk Exchange, for no one is so sensitive to atmosphere as a crowd of females; especially when those females are telephonists.

"What's up, Maggie?" said one of the rota from the restroom. "Are you going to play this hand? Diamonds are trumps."

I turned my head, still standing on the threshold.

"No. I'm going to have my tea. The fair Gloria has gone."

"Did you think she had been listening at the key-hole? Talking about listening at key-holes, someone around here has been doing a spot of prying. A couple of the girls complained that their lockers had been tampered with, though nothing was actually taken. And I'll swear that someone was listening in on that call I made yesterday from our phone in here."

"How sinister!" I replied in a light tone. "Probably it was Compton. She seems to find out a lot of things."

"Meaning you and Clark, Maggie? I say—"

"I am going to my tea," I repeated firmly. "So long."

As I made a pot of tea at the boiling urn in the lunchroom across the passage, I tried to put my finger on the cause of my sudden and unfounded apprehensions. Perhaps it was the heat, a close humid blanket of it enough to fray the already taut nerves of any telephonist. But Bertie with the jumps and now all this poking and prying were facts that could not be ignored.

"Oh, blast!" I thought, trying to dismiss them. "I need my leave."

The lunchroom is long and narrow, with a cafeteria at one end divided off by a grille reaching from the roof to the counter. At the special table reserved for the traffic officers and monitors, Sarah Compton was talking in low tones to John Clarkson. She was leaning forward, with her pale eyes looking earnestly and compellingly into poor Clark's. He appeared to be slightly discomfited. I caught his eye as I went to sit facing Compton, and the expression of relief that came into his face was almost ludicrous. Presently he lounged over to my table.

"Hullo, Maggie," he said, then added softly, "How good it is to see you after yon desiccated old maid. She has been holding forth. Like the bridegroom, I couldn't get away once she fixed me with her eye."

"What was she holding forth about?" I asked, exploring the contents of a sandwich.

"Usual stuff. You know—honour and glory and the noble tradition of the Telephone Exchange. And a bit of polly-prying about you."

I muttered under my breath, borrowing a phrase or two from Bertie.

Clark laughed and glanced at the clock above my head.

"I must go. Wait for me to-night and we'll have a bite of supper some-where. I am going back to the trunkroom, Sarah," he called on his way out.

Compton raised her eyes slowly from the piece of paper over which she had been poring, her arms stretched either side of it protectively. Her eyes meeting mine gave me quite a shock. I tried to analyse the strange combination of emotions that they held. Usually pale and dull, they were gleaming not only in excitement, but also with a certain degree of surprise. She stared straight through me. Not with the idea of ignoring my presence. She just didn't see me.

After my evening meal I sauntered up to the flat roof. If there was any stirring of air anywhere it would be there, and I was not due back in the trunkroom for another quarter of an hour. As I mounted the concrete stairs that wound around the lift-well, I noticed that old Bill had gone off duty. The lift was stationary at the eighth floor.

Situated on a hill with no very big buildings near, a view of remark-able distance and beauty can be had from the roof of the Exchange. On that particular night, the mountains in the east seemed to rise straight out of the suburbs. They were dark blue, which coupled with their apparent nearness usually meant rain. But although the sky was heavy with clouds, no breeze stirred to break them into action. It was more likely that a blus-tering north wind would start the following day, bringing the dust and hot breath from the Mallee district to make us limp and exhausted until the wind swung round to the south bringing relief and rain.

I struck a match for my cigarette without bothering to protect it, and the first plume of smoke hung blue and still around me. Leaning over the waist-high rail that ran around the low parapet, I could see far below the glass roof of the basement annexe. It was a foolish thing to do, for like the majority of people, heights always made me giddy. Immediately I started to imagine myself falling. It was so real that I could feel the force of grav-ity tearing at my body and knew exactly the splintering crash of glass I would make on the annexe roof. It was insanely tempting to see if my ideas were correct. It was here that I was dragged from the last sickening thud by the most extraordinary sound. There was a small cabin set on the roof, containing the lift paraphernalia, the walls of which provided shelter for a few garden seats. From the other side of it I could hear a voice repeating: "Peep you, peep you . . ." At least it sounded like that.

'The madhouse has claimed another victim,' I thought, going to inves-tigate. It was Sarah Compton, sitting hunched on a bench and staring at her slip of paper again. Her sandy head jerked in rhythm with that absurd "peep you." The look of complete satisfaction on her face vanished when she saw me. She tried to cover a certain confusion by asking sharply: "Why aren't you back in the trunkroom?"

"I was a few minutes late coming out. Anyway," I added sarcastically, "aren't I working the same time as you? Four until eleven?"

Compton ignored this, and glared at my cigarette.

"You're smoking again," she remarked, rather obviously, I considered. Belonging to the diehard set who began their telephonic career when Central had but a few subscribers, she resented any forward behaviour which might, as she thought, cast a slur on the fair name of the Telephone Department. I told her that that sort of idea went out of fashion in the early twenties.

"It is not prohibited out of the building," I retorted gently. "In fact, it is now permissible to smoke in the restroom, so—er—put that in your pipe and smoke it!"

Compton grew very flushed. "I shall report you for your rudeness."

"Nonsense!" I said briskly. "I am off duty now, and so are you. We are just two females, suspended up here more or less like Mohammed between heaven and earth. Come, come, Miss Compton," I went on, putting just a nice shade of pity in my voice. I detested the woman and felt I owed her something. "Let us forget that you are a monitor and that I am a telephonist, and enjoy this beautiful evening amicably."

My flow of eloquence must have stunned her. Without speaking she turned to where the sun was settling for the night behind the bay, making the ships anchored around the Port appear black-etched against the sky. She was so quiet that, as I glanced casually at her profile, I knew that she had forgotten my existence again. Her head was raised slightly. With her rather hooked nose and thin wide mouth she reminded me of a bas-relief plaque I had once seen of a Red Indian brave. In fact, although it must sound incredible to those who knew Sarah Compton, she looked both noble and dignified.

The Post Office clock down town struck. I took a last draw before stamping on my cigarette.

"Well, duty calls," I said brightly. For some unknown reason, I was feeling as though I had behaved rather badly. "Are you coming, Miss Compton?"

She stirred with a sigh and turned towards me. Her pale eyes shone full of tears in the twilight.

'Heavens! How awful!', I thought, aghast. But she seemed to control herself. We walked slowly together over the asphalted roof to the stairs. It was just as I had opened the door that she grabbed my arm so fiercely that I let out a yelp.

"Hush!" she whispered, staring over her shoulder. "Someone went into the lift cabin!"

I peered fearfully through the gloom to where the cabin was now a black box against the sky. Compton's nervous condition was infectious. We stood very still, her hand still on my arm. There was no movement from the lift cabin. No light shone from its tiny window. I shook myself free of Compton's grasp and said bracingly: "Rot! The door is closed. Come on, or we'll be late. Anyway, why shouldn't there be someone in the lift cabin? It may have been one of the mechanics going in to oil up the works."

I was beginning to have had enough of Compton and her histrionics. She followed me obediently and without a word down the single flight of stairs. The lift was still standing at the eighth floor. Sliding open the doors, I continued in my brisk tone of voice: "This will be quicker than walking. Hop in."

I knew Compton was one of those not uncommon individuals who hated riding in an automatic lift. While there was a special attendant, she was fairly happy, but to trust herself to a telephonist she disliked must have taken all her will-power. The lift was worked by a lever when Bill was on duty. Now, after hours, I pressed the button marked sixth, thinking how silly it was of Compton to be nervous of lifts. She was very still in her corner. I could see the pale blur that was her face. A pleasant draught of cool air came through the open emergency exit in the roof as we settled gently at the sixth floor. But when Compton put her hand on the doors ready to slide them open we started to move again, upwards. That was a thing that happened every day, although I must admit that it gave me quite a fright. I heard a gasp from Compton and told her shortly not to worry, at the same time jamming my thumb hard against the emergency button and bringing the lift to a standstill between the seventh and eighth floors.

"Blast!" I said, as nothing happened when I pressed the sixth button again. It was very quiet and warm in that dark cage, lighted only by the small red globe above the indicator board. But for that first gasp my companion remained as still as a corpse. My imagination started to leap, so much so that I found it hard to suppress a scream when some object whistled past my ear. It fell to the floor and lay white. I bent to pick it up, reeling clumsily in my fright against the apparatus board. In some perverse and mysterious way the lift began to move again. By the dim red light, I opened my hand to disclose a small stone wrapped roughly in paper. Two words written in pencil caught my eye, and made me turn to Compton.

"Look what someone has been throwing through the roof at us! A letter! It has your name on it, so I suppose that it is meant for you."

We were descending very jerkily, as I pondered on the childish trick. I thought that that sort of thing went out with one's school-days. Compton was standing quite close to me trying to read her note by the light from the indicator board. I was forced to quell a most unladylike impulse to share it over her shoulder. Oddly enough I was to know what it contained very soon, but I did not dream of that possibility then.

The lift had stopped again, and I made a mental vow never to ride in one again. I was badly shaken. Rather strangely, Compton seemed quite calm. Her very placidness disturbed me. I wanted to break the unnatural silence.

"Miss Compton," I began, but broke off as she lifted her face towards me. It was clear enough to make my heart jump with a sickening fright, as I saw her lips drawn back from teeth that appeared bloody in that red glow. Her eyes were staring and horrible to look into as she crouched there like an animal about to spring.

I don't know how long I stood there, watching her. I felt like a bird fascinated by a snake, paralysed and numb. Then an instinct as old as time asserted itself. The instinct of flight. A voice seemed to shriek in my brain: "Run! Run for your life!"

But how? Where? Dragging my fascinated gaze away from that bestial form, I saw a white light shining through the lift windows. The lift must have been at a floor landing for some time; precious moments, when I could have been far away from this mad, fearful thing that was hunched beside me. My fingers bruised dragging at the doors. I pulled them to behind me to give myself a chance to escape down the long passage outside. I had no idea where I was. The corridor was deserted and dimly lit. I hurried on with the vague hope of finding someone sane and solid and sensible. But the doors along the passage remained unopened to my knocking. The whole floor appeared to be empty. My only plan would be to make for the back stairs and chance my speed against Compton's. Then the sound of footsteps, light and running, made me stop and press against a door in the wall. My throat was parched by my panting breath.

'I'd love a drink of water', I thought idiotically. The door handle turned under my fingers but did not move inwards. Locked! The footsteps came nearer. Round that bend in the corridor, and she'll see you in that light frock. Run, you fool!

But where? My senses seemed distraught and unreliable. 'This is a dream!' I told myself, starting to edge along the wall. 'Soon I'll come to a precipice, and then I'll wake up.'

I screamed lightly, once, as a dark figure loomed up in front of me. A hand closed tightly on my arm.

"What on earth are you up to, Margaret?" asked a familiar voice in my ear sharply. This was better than the back stairs; even better than someone sane, solid and sensible. My fingers gripped the lapels of Clark's coat. One arm crept round me protectively, drawing me closer until I could feel his heart racing against my temple.

"What are you doing on this floor?" he demanded.

"The lift—it got stuck," I explained in jerks, "and that horrible woman—"

"What woman?" he asked quickly.

"Sarah Compton. She—she looked evil. She's insane. I'm certain she's insane."

Man-like, Clark patted my back without speaking. I became calmer. Meeting Clark like that made me feel as if I had exaggerated the whole affair.

"Someone threw a note down the emergency exit in the lift."

I went on. "It had Compton's name on it. She read it and then—then her face changed. She looked like an animal." I shuddered involuntarily. "I got out at once and started to run, but I didn't know where I was. What floor is this, anyway? Then there were footsteps, running"—I raised my head to look into his face, wonderingly—"but that must have been you."

The suspicion of a frown gathered between his brows. His arm slackened, and I moved back shyly.

"I must go. I'll be terribly late."

I could see Clark smiling. It did things to you, that smile; reducing the younger telephonists into simpering idiots, and making even Sarah Compton come all over girlish. Having reminded myself thus of my last encounter with that woman, I said resolutely: "I'm not going back by that damned lift, John Clarkson, and don't you think it for one minute. I suppose the back stairs are just around the corner? Anyway, it will look better if we don't enter the trunkroom together."

He caught me by the shoulders and pulled me towards him again, laughing, "Why, Maggie?"

"Because—you know quite well what I mean."

"Right you are, little prudence. On your way." He bent his head swiftly and kissed my cheek as I passed. "That might satisfy the scandalmongers."

"You revolt me!" I declared over my shoulder, as calmly as I was able. On top of my unnerving experience with Sarah Compton I felt doubly shaken by that careless kiss. I kept thinking about Clark as I started to climb the concrete stairway, and incidentally to regret my decision about the lift. He had taken me to a few shows in the city, and had entertained me several times at an exclusive and expensive golf club of which he was a member. As he kept a very comfortable bachelor flat in South Yarra, I concluded that his parents, whom I knew were dead, must have had money. In fact, Clark seemed to have everything the praying maiden could wish for. I knew several lasses in the Exchange who were pursuing him hopefully.

After some solid climbing, I arrived at the glass doors that opened into the trunkroom, slightly breathless and with the backs of my knees aching. Although every floor in the Exchange is architecturally the same, there is something unforgettably familiar about the sixth. You can feel a unique atmosphere, one of telephones and telephonists working flat out to serve a public, which for the most part remains ungrateful. Just as a 'wowser' seeing an intoxicated person thinks that everyone who drinks is a drunkard, so the person who, by chance, gives the responsibility of their call to a careless telephonist considers that all Exchange employees are rude and haphazard.

I have seen girls, beaded with perspiration from hot apparatus, putting calls through every minute for hours on end during bad bush-fires and crises in Europe and the Pacific, until they collapsed from sheer nervous exhaustion. I know that strained concentration which is needed to complete connections, with half a dozen lines under your tense fingers, that must not make mistakes.

I can honestly say that the greater majority of telephonists endeavour conscientiously to answer the oftentimes outrageous demands of the public. Here is an excellent example, when an unnamed man was located in one of our larger country towns for a very urgent call. He was a traveller for an engineering firm in the city, but for some inexplicable reason his name could not be supplied. He was tracked down through thirteen hotels, half a dozen garages and hardware shops and three clubs. I know this for a fact, because I found him myself!

However, we to whom the Exchange means our bread take the romance of the telephone very casually. So it was that buckling on my apparatus in obedience to the rule before entering the trunkroom, I resigned myself to a hot and tiring night.

The trunkroom is a T-shaped room covering the whole of the sixth floor, except for the front and back stair landings and a telephonists' toilet and washroom. Gone are the days of the plugs and cords more familiar to others than telephone employees. In their place are highly polished rows of boards about three feet in height, and worked by keys, lights and automatic dials. These boards occupy the larger part of the room together with booking, inquiry and information desks, and the Senior Traffic Officer's table. In one arm of the T-shape stands the sortagraph, which brings dockets to the operator from the boards by means of air-pressure tubes under

21

the floor. In the other is an immense delay board, another marvel of this mechanical age, which manifests the waiting time on the various interstate and country lines. The room is lighted and aired by windows on all sides for the hundred or more people working therein at the peak period.

At night the Senior Traffic Officer was not on duty, so John Clarkson was head man. I could hardly expect a rebuke from him for my tardy return, though he was a great stickler for punctuality as a rule. He was sitting at Bertie's desk, his head bent over his writing. And there was Compton fluttering around him as normally as ever. It was as if I had last beheld her plain face in an absurd nightmare. She even had the audacity to say accusingly: "You're very late, Miss Byrnes," as I approached her to learn my position. I glanced at her keenly to observe any recognition of our last meeting, but the pale eyes that met mine were quite blank.

"You can start the relieving," she told me.

If there was one job I loathed more than another, it was that. In the hour before the rush half-fee period, those telephonists working more than three hours on end were entitled to a ten-minute break. I suspected Compton of spite in allotting the relieving to me, though to give her her due, it was usually the job of the late telephonist. Where all the other telephonists would go off duty at 10.30 p.m., I had to wait until the all-night girls who worked the interstate positions came on at 11 p.m. Just as the late telephonist on the country positions on the far side of the room would gather all working country lines on to a couple of boards and operate them all, so I would have to do the same with the interstate lines. Although traffic was cleared up rather well by 10 p.m., two telephonists to cover the work of sixty meant all your concentration and ability. I have always hated that last half-hour.

To-night there was no late country operator. It had been arranged that Gerda MacIntyre, the sortagrapher, would transfer there when her own position closed down at 10 p.m. Mac, who was by way of being a particular friend of mine, was one of the most versatile telephonists I have ever known. She had a lovely voice, unroughened by many years in the Exchange, and tiny hands that dealt with any amount of work with the most amazing competence and ease. John Clarkson would probably take us both down town somewhere for supper after work. There was a time when I was afraid Mac was taking Clark rather seriously. However, everything seemed to have cleared up, and I was somewhat relieved, though I could never put my finger on the exact cause of my relief.

I started on my tour of the interstate positions; ten minutes here, and ten minutes there. No two telephonists work alike. By the time you got the lines working your own system the original operator returned to say rather acidly: "You seem to be in a bag."

'In a bag' is an expression peculiar to the Melbourne telephonist; it means that you are in a muddle or so confused that you can't straighten things out. In Sydney, the girls say that they are 'overboard.' As a rule Mac was sent for when anyone got in a bag. It was a delight to watch those small hands of hers pass rapidly over the board from key to dial and from dial to docket, a pencil always between the first two fingers but in no way hindering the clearance at which she arrived so quickly.

I plugged my flex on the main Adelaide board, waiting for Gloria Patterson to slip out of the position. Patterson was what I call a genteel telephonist, and one to whom Mac often rendered assistance. She was more concerned with keeping her rather high-pitched voice refined, like those of our local socialites to whose calls she delighted in listening, than speeding up the tempo of her connections. She ought to have been shot for eavesdropping of course; one day she'd be reported and would most deservedly get it in the neck.

"That's there, and I was just dialling this out, and that's been on for two and a half minutes," she said, pointing at the dockets clipped under the three Adelaide lines she was working.

I could hear Adelaide saying: "Waiting, Mel., waiting," rather querulously. I concluded that Patterson must have been super-refined to-night.

"That's just grand, Gloria," I replied gravely, "most lucid. Now, run along, dear, and I'll have it all nice and straight for you when you return."

She gave me a cross look, as I transferred my attention to the patient girl in Adelaide. I knew her rather well.

"Thank goodness it's you, Byrnes," she declared with a sigh of relief. "Who is that awful mug?"

"One of our shining lights," I replied, picking up a docket. "I'll have L3178 for U7173, not a personal call, here. Give me your country line to Salisbury on number 3. How are you going? Has the weather changed yet?"

"Wait for a minute." She went off with a click of her key to dial out my number. Presently she said: "No! It is still as hot as ever. Perth have had a change; the girl there says that she is wearing a woollen cardigan. Salisbury on three."

"Thanks, Ad.," I said, dialling my caller quickly. "That means that we won't get a cool change for at least another three days."

"Stop gassing, Maggie," nudged the girl next to me. "Ob. is hovering around."

Ob. is observation. About two or three monitors of Sarah Compton's vintage patrol the boards to see amongst other things, that we behave ourselves. Their listening post was situated on the third floor. It is considered a matter of honour to warn your neighbour when she is approaching. Presently a voice said coldly in my ear: "Who are you, Trunks?"

When I had replied M. Byrnes, the voice went on: "I shall be observing your work for the next quarter of an hour for a time check." It was very decent of her to let me know. As a rule Ob. doesn't make her presence known. The first you learn of her presence is a report on the Senior Traffic Officer's desk with an immense "Please explain" at the foot of it.

"I am only relieving," I warned her. "I will be off in a few minutes."

"Very well, then. Thank you, Miss Byrnes. I'll come back presently," and the voice departed as quietly as it had come. I could see the telephonists farther down looking startled, and then giving their names. Ob. gets you that way.

Patterson came back late. She had cribbed an extra five minutes. Compton followed her down to her position, the look of malice on her face reminding me of the lift episode again. Although I didn't care much for Gloria, I felt sorry for her when Compton had her claws bared as now. What a beast that woman could be! I was becoming more and more convinced that she must be mentally deranged.

"You're five minutes late, Miss Patterson," she said. "You will not be allowed to go until 10.35 p.m. I was timing you."

She would be, I thought. Patterson replied: "I couldn't help it. I had to go to the other building to ring up. The restroom door is locked."

Compton looked surprised.

"Who locked it?"

"I don't know," said Patterson. "And the key is missing. Are you ready, Maggie?"

I slipped from the chair, explaining how the work stood until Compton moved away.

"I quite agree with you, Gloria," I said, as she muttered angrily under her breath. "Are you sure the door was locked? It might have just jammed."

"I tell you it was locked," she replied crossly. "If you don't believe me, go and ask your friend MacIntyre. She was with me."

"All right, keep calm," I said soothingly. "But I'll take your advice and ask Mac."

Mac had been talking to John Clarkson and Compton. I walked down the room with her.

"I've just been reporting the mystery of the locked door, Maggie. Did the girl Patterson tell you about it?"

I nodded. "Our Sarah jumped on her for being five minutes late. Has the key been found?"

"No. And as far as I can make out there is no duplicate. It will have to stay locked until the morning."

"I wonder who could have done it, and why," I said thoughtfully.

"Anyone, I suppose. The key is usually in the door. Did you go back there after your tea?"

"As a matter of fact, I didn't. I went up on to the roof for a cigarette. I met Compton there, so she can vouch for me, which I'm sure she won't. Bless her kindly heart!"

Mac adjusted her mouthpiece to the regulation inch from her charming mouth. I remembered how Clark had once said, with mock sentiment, that a telephone set was a privileged thing. "By the way, Maggie, do you know what is wrong with Compton? She's like a cat on hot bricks tonight."

I leaned towards her. "To give you my candid and unprejudiced opinion," I said softly, "I think that she has gone crackers."

Mac looked at me, mildly surprised at my earnestness.

"I'll tell you why, later. I must get back to the relieving at once, or she'll jump on me the way she did to young Gloria. So long."

I finished the job about five minutes before the rush period. An atmosphere of tension is always felt at this time. To-night, with the oppressive heat, the strain seemed augmented. I felt hot and weary, but my brain was keyed up and alert to take the burden of the next two hours. I will never forget that night. The main Sydney board was given to me to work, and there was a two hours' delay on the lines. I could not give my whole mind to the operating, as the brush with Compton and the subsequent event of the lift and even the locked restroom door were playing around in my brain in a jumble. Still further back, in the recesses of my subconscious mind, something was trying to thrust itself on to my notice. Making rapid connections was not conducive to recapturing an elusive thought, even if it had registered itself on my brain in the first place. During a respite when I had all my lines covered, I came to the conclusion that it was something peculiar that I had either seen or heard. But when and where, my memory failed me.

After that, I settled down more peacefully to the business of breaking that pack of dockets, so much so that by the time the last call was put on, I realized with a jerk that I had forgotten all about those odd occurrences that had taken place earlier in the evening. I felt strangely loath to summon them again, and kept telling myself that I was imagining the premonition of disaster I was experiencing. But the whole building and its occupants including myself seemed to be on tip-toe waiting for a climax. There was that solo hand that I had played in the restroom and Dulcie Gordon's conviction of an eavesdropper on the telephonists' private phone; also her knowledge of the rifled lockers, and presently that unnaturally ajar door after Patterson's departure; even Mrs. Smith, the cleaner with an ever present familiarity about her that I could never place. Then I considered Bertie, a mass of nerves, and Sarah Compton with that evil look on her face, full of malice and triumph.

Compton had been dodging around the boards, querying dockets and taking inquiries in her usual fashion all night. That was one of her habits that I deplored most. She would ask you questions when you were in the middle of booking with the other telephonist. Her sharp voice, which reminded me always of someone using a steel file, sounded in your uncovered ear demanding futile explanations.

As I shifted my hot earpiece on to my temple and leaned back in my chair, I noticed that she was not in the room. John Clarkson still wrote at the Senior Traffic Officer's table, but I did not suppose that he had been doing that all the time for the last two hours; anyway, I had heard his voice behind me during the night.

"All clear, Maggie?" asked Gordon, who was sitting next to me. "Whew! What a night! Do you think a cool change will ever come! I am nearly dead."

"Think of icebergs," I advised. "Dulcie, when you and the others left the restroom, what time was it?"

She reflected for a minute.

"About twenty-five to seven, I think. We were all due to go back."

"Did you see anyone go in after you left?"

She shook her head.

"What about Patterson?" I asked quickly. "She is on your rota. Was she with you?"

"Gloria was coming up in the lift, as we passed to go down the stairs to the trunkroom."

So that was how the lift came to be at the eighth floor.

"Did she say anything to you?"

"Only that she'd made some new conquest at the 'Australia,'" replied Gordon with a grimace. "What a liar that girl is!"

"No, she isn't," I corrected. "She really believes all she says. She's a romancer. She appeared much as usual, then?"

"I think so. What is all this, Maggie? Why the cross-examination?"

I said: "Since I'm certain to be accused of locking the restroom door, I thought that I had better dig up some other suspects."

"As a matter of fact," Gordon confessed. "I thought that it must have been you. After all you were the last, and that's what they are saying on the boards."

"Oh, are they?" I returned viciously. "You can just inform all the little gossipers from me that I didn't go near the restroom after my tea. I didn't even go into the cloakroom."

"What about your telephone? Didn't you put it in your locker?"

"I took it out again on my way to the lunchroom," I said. That unknown something jerked in my brain once more. I tried to follow it up, but Gordon interrupted.

"What did you do after tea?"

"I went up on the roof, and—" I stopped suddenly. Somehow I didn't want to spread the facts of my meeting with Compton. Once a fragment of information got to the boards, it would grow like a snowball.

"What did you do up there?" asked Gordon. "Was there anyone with you?"

"I had a cigarette," I answered, somewhat lamely. "There was no one else." Sometimes I think now that if I had told Dulcie exactly what had happened on the roof perhaps at least one of the terrible events that took place might not have occurred. But how was I to know then? I did what I thought best at the time, and John says that it would not have made the slightest difference.

"There you are!" she declared triumphantly. "You have no alibi."

"Oh yes, I have," I said to myself, "providing Compton will back me up." On the other hand, she might be only too eager to forget those adventures we had shared. I wished that I had forgotten my sensibilities and taken a good look at that note, which was thrown into the lift so dramatically.

A couple of dockets came to the boards. I handed them to Gordon to complete. She sniffed audibly.

"Be a good girl," I asked. "I want to think."

"What with?" she asked in a silly way that made me want to slap her.

I closed my eyes in an attempt to bring back the details of the letter. I felt myself pressing the sixth-floor button, and then that rush of cool air that came through the emergency exit.

"That was it!" I thought, feeling very clever. "Someone was watching for Compton to enter the lift, and then threw down the note." It must have been the person Compton saw entering the lift cabin on the roof; in fact, it was quite conclusive that it was, because that was the only place from where one could look on to the lift roof, as we were at the top floor. But it was quite another thing to name that person. Who it was and why write a note to Compton I could not understand. The more I thought of it, the more I wanted to see what that letter of Compton's contained.

The 10 p.m. girls had signed off and gone long since. Dulcie Gordon was shifting impatiently in her chair; it was a minute after the half-hour, and Compton whose duty it was to release the staff was still absent. Suddenly John Clarkson laid down his pen, rose, and walked down the room. Several girls said plaintively: "I'm supposed to be off, Mr. Clarkson."

"Where's your monitor?" he asked, looking round the room swiftly.

"Miss Compton has not been in for some time," said Gordon. "I didn't see her go out."

"You'll have them all claiming overtime if you don't let them go," I murmured, as he bent over my board to see if there were any dockets. I thought his hand touched mine for a second. He straightened up and said clearly: "All right, all you 10.30 girls, just drop out. Couple up these boards, Maggie."

"Now for the rush," I thought, replacing my earpiece and picking up a light from the panel. On these modern boards when an interstate or country telephonist is wanting attention, her ring on the line brings a light flashing in a panel on the Melbourne boards. To transfer that line for working is accomplished by merely pressing a button.

I heard Korrumburra yelling her head off, demanding service, and re-leased the line to let Mac deal with her on the far side of the room. I had both my boards covered, and more lights were flashing in the panel, waiting to be picked up. As a rule, the late monitor gives assistance during this half-hour, and I wondered again, irritably, where Compton had got to. She was never around when you wanted her.

John Clarkson passed on his way to dismantle the delay-board at the other end of the room.

"All right?" he asked.

"Quite," I retorted. "Absolutely nothing to do.

He grinned. "I'll give you a hand in a minute. Where's that blasted woman?"

I didn't have time to conjecture about Compton's whereabouts. The lasses across Bass Strait were being neglected shamefully. I gave Sydney the go-by, and picked up Launceston. A blistering diatribe greeted me. I listened patiently.

"Sorry, dear," I said in a meek voice. "My attention is all yours from now on."

That was the only apology I gave during that hectic half-hour. I cut the standard phrases originated by some leisurely Department official in his nice quiet office to the minimum. Once I wondered how Mac was faring over on the country boards behind me. The Senior Traffic Officer's telephones rang for a while and were silent, so I supposed that Clark was as busy as we were. Book, dial, connect and a swift glance at the clock to complete the docket with my numerical signature. I felt the perspiration trickling down my ribs, and the wire band of my headset was cutting into my skull.

"Mel., book please."

"Your particular person is waiting, Mel."

"Mel., take a through call."

It came at me from all lines; all those telephonists throughout Australia with the same metallic crisp voice.

On with those calls.

"Sorry to keep you waiting."

"Three minutes—extending please?"

"You're through—go ahead."

Mentally I threw up my hands in despair, while coaxing slow callers to start their conversations. The perpetual 'Hullo's' and those bad telephone voices, with their unenunciated consonants and flattened vowels. They all wasted precious seconds of the three minutes that most subscribers declare that they do not get, not realizing their own extravagance.

Five minutes to eleven! Out of one corner of my eye, I could see Clark grappling with lines with a spare telephone set from Bertie's table. His face was in profile, but I thought that he looked angry.

"Sarah will get it in the neck for landing us in this bag," I thought. "She deserves boiling in oil."

Three minutes to eleven, and a couple of the all-night girls came in early. Bless them! May all their children have curly hair! I stayed on for a while helping to straighten things out. It was amazing the difference one or two extra telephonists made. At ten past eleven, I rose wearily from ray chair and stripped off my outfit.

"And so to bed," I said. "Sweet dreams, my dears."

"I believe you have been locking doors, Byrnes," remarked the girl Billings with a grin.

"I am too tired to defend myself," I answered, "so let it stand that I was the culprit until the morning."

"Giving yourself time to think up a good one," another called after me as I went to sign off. Mac's neat signature was the last in the book, made at 11.5 p.m., while above hers with many flourishes was that of Gloria Patterson at 10.40 p.m. She must have been afraid that Compton would see her if she had gone with the rest of her rota.

I found Mac outside on the lift landing, studying the notice-board.

"I'm down for a late on Sunday," she said as I joined her. "What a bore!"

"Did you see my name?" I asked, scanning the list. "I worked last Sunday, but you never know what fast one they'll pull next."

"I'm afraid you've got the dog-watch with John. Compton is working late, too."

"That'll be great!" I said bitterly. "Especially if Sarah does the disappearing trick again. I'd like to get my hands on that woman."

We had started walking up the stairs together. At the eighth-floor landing, Mac paused to light a cigarette; at this late hour we should be able to dodge a reprimand, so I followed her lead.

"Having supper with John?" she asked with a sidelong glance that made me wish that I knew more about her late 'affair' with him.

"And you," I said in a firm voice.

"I don't think so. I don't want to butt in, Maggie."

"Shut up!" I said loudly.

We entered the cloakroom and parted company. Mac's locker was against the wall, while mine was in the centre aisle facing the restroom door. It was still closed, and no light showed through the glass pane at the top.

"That blasted door!" I said, tossing my telephone into my locker.

"What's that, Maggie?" called Mac.

"The restroom door! Someone locked it, and everyone seems to think that I did, since I was the late telephonist."

I heard Mac laugh softly.

"Yes, I heard something about that. Perhaps it is not locked but jammed after all. It has happened before to better doors. Try it for yourself and see."

"I will," I said, advancing with my cigarette between my lips so as to have both hands free.

"Well!" I declared. "What do you know about that!"

"What?" Mac asked, appearing around the corner of the lockers, lipstick in hand. "What's the matter?"

I pointed to the door in amazement.

"Why, it is not locked after all. I suppose someone must have found the key," she added, rather obviously.

"Someone is going to pay for this," I said, putting my hand around the door to switch on the light. "The idea of accusing me!"

Mac was amused.

"I think things look rather black for you, Maggie. After all the door is locked, and you are the last one to be near the restroom."

"I wasn't," I protested.

"And then you come off duty, and lo and behold the door opens. Very, very ominous!"

"Rot! A dozen others could have done it. Oh well, at least we can make up under a decent light." I returned to my locker to get my handbag. "I look a hag. I say, Mac, I must tell you about our Sarah."

"Sarah!" I heard her repeat in a horrified whisper. "Sarah!" I swung round quickly. Mac was standing in the lighted doorway of the cloak-room, swaying slightly. I was beside her in a second. She turned towards me and tried to push me away. Her face was close to mine. I could see the pigment of her pallid skin, and the dilating iris of her eyes. They both spelled terror.

"Don't go in, Maggie," she whispered imploringly. "It's—it's horrible." But I pushed her roughly aside, and went into the restroom.

I think I almost expected what I saw. It was as if I had dreamed it all before, but the stark reality of the scene froze my blood and parched my throat. Mac was leaning against the wall, panting; her normally pale skin had taken on the bluish appearance of alabaster. We heard someone walking down the corridor outside, whistling the 'Destiny Waltz.' Suddenly hot sweat started to flow down my icy body, and dark mists crept up from the corners of my eyes. I heard Mac shriek like a madwoman: "John! John! John!"

'Fancy knowing that those footsteps were Clark's!' I thought, as I slid to the ground and remembered no more.

* * * * *

I was in a floundering boat on a rough sea. I could feel the icy water on my face. Then a pair of oars appeared in some mysterious fashion, but I did not seem to be able to manage them. They kept hitting my hands and eluding my grasp. Presently I heard a man's voice say: "She'll be O.K. in a minute, sir," and wondered about whom he was talking. I was quite comfortable now that the sea was smooth. I wanted to stay quiet, but a strong light was shining through my eyelids, forcing them open.

I knew where I was immediately: in the sick-bay on the eighth floor of the Telephone Exchange building. I had tried that hard bed before.

'That's funny!' I thought. But I must have spoken aloud, because the man's voice said: "What's funny?"

I struggled to sit up. "I thought I was in a boat."

A strange man stood over me, and another figure was in the back-ground. They swayed a little before my puzzled gaze. I put my head down to my knees automatically. They spoke over my head.

"We'd better leave her until the last, Sergeant."

"Very well, sir. What did they say her name was?"

I raised my head.

"M. Byrnes," I said clearly.

The first man seemed amused. "What does the M. stand for, Miss Byrnes?"

"Margaret," I replied, embarrassed. Ob. was to blame for my slip.

"How do you think you will stand up to a few questions, Miss Margaret Byrnes?" he asked.

"It all depends what they are about," I answered, swinging my legs over the side of the bed.

The two men gazed at me so keenly that I began to feel uncomfortable. I looked at them inquiringly, but they remained silent. Then a wave of horror started to sweep over me, and Mac's tragic whisper seared my brain.

"Sarah Compton," I breathed in answer to my own question.

"Precisely, Miss Byrnes," said the second man crisply. "I am Detective-Inspector Coleman from Russell Street Police Headquarters, and this," indicating his companion, "is Detective-Sergeant Matheson. We are inquiring into the murder of Sarah Compton, late monitor at the Melbourne Trunk Exchange."

I gripped the edge of the bed, hard.

"Murder!" I repeated, still whispering. Something seemed to have gone wrong with my voice-box. Detective-Inspector Coleman nodded in silence. The sick-bay room was so quiet that I could hear the thudding of the dynamo many floors below.

"Surely, Miss Byrnes," he went on, "as you saw the body, you realize that Miss Compton has been the victim of foul play?"

I stared down at my clenched hands.

"I only looked into the room for a minute—a second," I replied jerkily. "It—she was a shocking sight, but—murder did not occur to me. It doesn't seem possible. Those sorts of thing," and I threw my hands out helplessly, "murders—only happen in mystery novels, not in a Telephone Exchange."

"They happen in real life," said inspector Coleman quietly, "only too frequently."

I stared at him, trying to absorb the fact. Sarah Compton—murdered! Someone had killed her; taken from her the most precious thing we own. And Mac and I had found her, lying face down in her own blood. At once I realized what it meant. We would be mixed up in this ghastly business, no matter how repugnant we found it. But would I find it so distasteful after all? It was horrible and frightening finding Compton like that. I was not likely to forget the scene in the restroom in a hurry. But I had never cared much for the woman. I felt no personal grief on top of the horror.

The situation might prove exciting and intriguing. I wondered if Mac, who had always been indifferent to Sarah, was thinking the same.

"Where is Miss MacIntyre?" I asked abruptly.

"In the next room. I am just going to take her statement. Sergeant Matheson here has a few questions to ask you. I hope that you will give him every assistance."

I nodded dumbly and watched him depart. He was a big man, but as light as a cat on his feet; later, I learned that he was an enthusiastic amateur boxer. Sergeant Matheson switched off the bright overhead light, leaving only the shaded one on the table aglow. I supposed that he thought the powerful light would only aggravate my aching head, but it had the effect of making me feet very nervous. It was as if he was setting his stage. When he sat down beside me, notebook in hand, I lost all my fears. He looked shy and ill-at-ease, so much so that I wondered if this was his first important case. It took me a long time to realize that this appearance was only part of his stock-in-trade, and that he was considered one of Russell Street's most able officers.

However, just then I thought he was bashful, and to break the ice I remarked lightly: "Why is it all you policemen only have blunt stubs of pencils with which to take your notes?"

His smile was infectious. It lit up his plain face, and made his eyes twinkle under their sandy brows.

"You seem to know a great deal about policemen, Miss Byrnes," he remarked, writing carefully in his book.

"Here! I hope you're not putting that down to be used in evidence against me."

His mouth was closed firmly, but his eyes still danced.

"No, just your name. Margaret Byrnes," and he repeated it slowly.

"That's quite correct," I said tartly. "Now what is it you want to know?"

"Your address, please, Miss Byrnes."

"15 Lewisham Avenue, Albert Park. I board there. My real home is in the country. You've probably never heard of it. Keramgatta."

"About twenty miles from the north-east border?" he queried.

"That is right," I agreed in vexed surprise.

"I used to work in that district," he said apologetically.

I kept what I thought was a dignified silence.

"Now, Miss Byrnes—you knew the deceased?" I nodded.

"What sort of woman would you say she was?"

"She was a—" I shut my mouth quickly. Sergeant Matheson looked up from his writing.

"You were saying?" he prompted.

I thought for a minute. "She was a very difficult woman to work with," I said lamely.

He gave me a direct glance. "What were you going to say originally, please, Miss Byrnes?"

"I don't think that I'd better tell you," I parried. "It was something very rude, though rather apt when applied to Sarah Compton." I was sure that his eyes twinkled again, as he let the matter pass.

"I believe that you were the first to find the body," he continued.

"The second," I corrected. "Miss MacIntyre saw Compton a few seconds before I did."

"Miss MacIntyre is a particular friend of yours, Miss Byrnes?" he asked quickly. I looked at him speculatively.

"A friend, yes," I answered, "but not an accomplice."

"I did not suggest it, Miss Byrnes," he said, appearing uncomfortable and ill-at-ease again.

"No, but you were thinking it," I retorted, and had the doubtful reward of another infectious grin. He shrugged his shoulders slightly.

"We seem to be getting nowhere, and taking a long time about it," he remarked. "Perhaps it would be better if you told me in your own words exactly what happened."

"No interruptions?" I asked, and he raised one hand solemnly.

"Not unless strictly necessary."

"Right!" I said briskly. "Have you a cigarette? I don't remember finishing my last one. Thanks. And a match, please?" I drew a long breath. "Are you ready? Shall I go fast or slow?"

"Medium," he suggested. "I'll take it down in my own particular brand of shorthand, but I want to absorb all the facts."

I looked at my cigarette a moment in silence, mentally gathering myself together.

"I'll begin by answering your first question more fully," I began. "Sarah Compton was a prying old busybody. Hundreds of people, not only in the Exchange but outside, that is if she behaved anything like she did here, must have had her in the gun. But I don't know of anyone who would want to murder her for her inquisitiveness. You see, I have provided you with a motive for the crime already." I flicked the ash from the cigarette and drew again. "I disliked her intensely myself; why, I won't tell you. That's my business! But I will say that the reason I detested her was not enough to make me even want to, murder her. I might have scratched her face, considerably, but bashed it in, no!" I wished I had not said that now. My stomach felt squeamish, and I fought against nausea. "When did it happen and how?" I asked, desiring a breathing space.

Sergeant Matheson looked up from his notes.

"That's for you to help us find out, Miss Byrnes. Medical evidence is rather vague as to the time. The body was still warm, but then it is a hot night. We dare not give an accurate time. As to how—two blows were struck with some heavy instrument, as yet undiscovered; one on the temple, the other directly in the face. What time did you last see Miss Compton?"

I frowned in concentration. "The last time that I actually saw her," I said slowly, "would be about five minutes to eight. I had finished the relieving—letting different girls have a short break," I explained in answer to the question in his eyes, "and then Compton sent me to work the principal Sydney board. We were very busy. In our game you rarely lift your head during the rush period, but I can remember her querying me about various dockets. I think that the last I heard of her would be about twenty to ten. I can check up with the time on the docket, if you like."

He made a note in his book.

"However," I continued, "someone else is certain to have seen her after that. I was only one of many in the trunkroom."

"Can you think of any reason why she left the room?" he asked. "Surely it is not usual for a monitor to absent herself during the busy time?"

"Yes," I said promptly. "I told you that she was a busybody. Someone had locked the restroom door, which is quite against the rules. I'll bet you anything you like to name that Compton had her nose on the trail, trying to find out who it was. As a matter of fact, I was the chief suspect in that little affair; being the late telephonist, everyone jumped rashly to the conclusion that I locked it."

"Why rashly, Miss Byrnes?"

"Because I didn't go near the blasted room after 6.15 p.m. I kept my telephone outfit with me while I had tea in the lunchroom, so that there would be no need for me to return to the cloakroom. After tea I went up on to the roof for a cigarette. Oh!" I ejaculated, pausing.

"Go on, please," said Sergeant Matheson quickly. "What time would it be?"

"About a quarter to seven. What I was going to say was that I had an alibi concerning that door, but not now. She's dead," I finished blankly.

Sergeant Matheson looked interested.

"You met the deceased on the roof?"

"Don't use that word," I said in an irritated voice. After a gruelling night's work, to be kept from your well-earned rest by a murder inquiry was a little trying on the nervous system. Heaven knew what I would feel like in the morning!

"I will tell you in detail," I said resignedly. "I was smoking a cigarette and enjoying the hot night air, when I heard someone in a corner playing games with me."

Sergeant Matheson looked at me sternly.

"It's quite true," I protested. "I'm not trying to be funny. Compton was playing 'peepo's' with someone, and I was the only one on the roof. At least I thought that I was. I'll tell you more about that in a minute. Compton was sitting at one side of the lift cabin. You'd better go and inspect that later, by the way. When I went round it to see what was up, she was reading a piece of paper. There's no use asking me what it was," I interrupted, observing him take a breath. "It was nearly dark. You'll probably find it in her handbag. She put it there when she saw me. Then we talked for a bit."

"What did you talk about, please, Miss Byrnes?" asked the Sergeant, writing furiously.

"This and that," I answered airily.

"Was the conversation friendly?"

"Most. She barely said a thing, while I pursued an amiable discourse on the view. After a while, we started to go back to the stairs. Here is something that may be of interest to you. Just as we were at the door, Compton said that she saw someone go into the lift cabin."

I paused for effect, but the Sergeant only asked in an expressionless voice: "Did you?"

"No," I said, feeling unreasonably annoyed. "I thought that she was imagining things. But there must have been someone, because a note was thrown down into the lift at us."

"The lift?" he asked, puzzled.

"We took the lift down to the trunkroom," I continued impatiently, "only we didn't arrive. It got stuck or something. Anyway, some fool of a person hurled this letter at me. I gave it to Compton."

"Why did you do that. Miss Byrnes?"

"Because," I said, raising my eyes to heaven, "it had her name on it."

"Did you see what it contained?"

"No, but I wish I had. The note will probably be in her handbag, too. I caught the words 'spying' and 'Compton' on it before I handed it to her."

Sergeant Matheson looked at me thoughtfully.

"Why did you say that you wish you'd read the letter?"

"Because," I replied, speaking very slowly, "it had the effect of changing her from a very insignificant, commonplace telephone employee into a snarling animal. She looked insane. I was scared stiff when I saw her face.

The lift had stopped at some floor, so I got out and ran like mad. But I don't think that I need have worried. She had forgotten my existence."

A slight smile flickered across the Sergeant's face.

"There was nothing amusing in the situation at the time," I remarked crossly. "If I hadn't bumped into Mr. Clarkson, I'd be running still."

"What floor were you on during your marathon, Miss Byrnes?"

"I haven't the faintest idea," I confessed, and his brows rose. "Clark will be able to tell you. What's the time? Can't I go home now?"

"No, not just yet. You must finish your statement first."

"I'll miss my last train," I complained, "and I suppose, murder or no murder, I'll have to be on duty to-morrow."

"Arrangements will be made to get you home. Now, Miss Byrnes, what did you do when you met Mr. Clarkson?"

I pushed my hair back, and sighed. "I clung on to him as though he was the proverbial straw. I tell you I had got a terrible fright. He soothed me down, and after telling him about Sarah I walked up the back stairs to the trunkroom."

"Did Mr. Clarkson go with you?"

"No. He went to look for Compton."

"Miss Byrnes, what made you walk up the stairs instead of going with Mr. Clarkson?"

"I was too damned terrified to travel in that lift. I wouldn't go in it again if it was with a policeman."

The Sergeant laughed. "We must try it one day," he suggested. "Did you find out what floor you were on, when you started to walk up the stairs?"

"No, but it must have been a long, long way from the sixth. I arrived at the trunkroom about 7.25 p.m., and Sarah Compton was there as bold as brass to reprimand me for being late. In fact, she was as normal as ever. If this murder business had not taken place, I would have thought that I had dreamed everything that I have just told you."

A long silence fell. Sergeant Matheson tapped his notebook pensively with his stub of a pencil, which had become blunter from its long use that night. I stared vacantly at my creased, linen skirt, and wondered if I would be let go home now. I felt limp from all the mental and emotional strain of the past few hours, though somehow the horror of the whole business seemed diminished. It was as if I had begun a tedious job, that must finish sooner or later. I could even think of that horrible scene in the restroom without feeling squeamish. My brain was so sodden and weary, that if anyone had asked me then if I had been responsible for the locked door, or even the murder itself, I would have agreed quietly just for the sake of a bit of peace.

Sergeant Matheson got up unhurriedly, and put a hand under my elbow. "That's all," he said gently. "Home you go, and I advise a couple of aspirins before you go to bed."

"I won't need them," I answered, stretching. "I'm nearly asleep now."

"Better take them," he advised. "It'll be worse to-morrow. You'll need all the rest you can get tonight, or rather this morning," he added, glancing at his wrist. "It's nearly one."

"What!" I shrieked. He grinned at me.

"Don't forget that you were rowing around in a boat for a considerable time, while Inspector Coleman and I were trying to revive you with the good old-fashioned methods of cold water and slapping your hands."

"Was that what it was?" I asked with the air of one making a great discovery. "I fainted! Well, well, I've only done that once before in my life—running a mile to school without my breakfast, when I was a kid."

"At Keramgatta?"

I nodded.

"Good place," he declared, opening the door and standing aside to let me pass through. The narrow passage outside ran down the walls of the cloakroom and restroom and into the main corridor. There were several small rooms opening from it. Outside the closed door of one stood a uniformed policeman. It opened as I came up. Mac and John Clarkson came out, followed by Inspector Coleman.

"Fixed things up, Matheson?" he asked his subordinate. "Right! Now, all you people, go home to bed. There is a car waiting outside for you. One word of advice before you go. Carry on with your normal duties, and the less spoken about all this the better. We don't want any unnecessary rumours starting. Do I make myself clear? Good! Mr. Clarkson, will it be possible to interview the night telephonists immediately?"

"I should think that it would be all right. Mr. Bancroft is the traffic officer on duty. He should be in the trunkroom at this moment. Just say I sent you down, Inspector. He'll fix things for you."

"Many thanks. You can come along with me, Sergeant."

"Wait a moment," I said. "Can I go into the cloakroom to get my coat and bag?"

The Inspector swung around. "That's quite a reasonable request. Roberts! Take these young ladies into the cloakroom."

Mac put a small hot hand into my cold one, and I squeezed it gently. Poor little Mac! If she was feeling anything like I was, she would be pretty bad. Even Clark looked pale and stern. Roberts took a ring of keys from one of his pockets, and fitted one into the lock.

"You'll find several duplicates of that one," I informed him.

"I'll tell the Sergeant," he replied, swinging the door open. "Thank you, miss."

I could see the half-open door of the restroom, and caught the glimpse of a trailing dust-sheet as two men moved across the opening. Advancing to my locker, I realized that I was probably treading in the very footsteps of the murderer; that shadowy, brutal figure which was to hold us in its fearful influence for days to come. For never, until the Exchange building is razed to the ground—and I believe that it is built to stand the strain of many years—will that evil shadow be removed. My hands were shaking as I took my handbag from the locker and unhooked my light summer coat. I noticed a burnt-out cigarette on the linoleum-covered floor near the door, and remembered that it was the one Mac had given to me on leaving the trunkroom. "I hope they won't think that it is a clue," I thought, pulling myself together.

Mac said gently at my elbow: "Ready, Maggie? John is taking us home." Her face was pale, but very calm; only the still dilated iris of her fine eyes showed any remembrance of horror. I slipped my hand through her arm without a word. We went out.

Clark stood in the corridor, a raincoat over his arm. I thought, in a detached fashion, of how we all must have thought that it would change that night. Rarely in our damnable climate does one venture forth without being prepared for a taste of several seasons during the day. Clark was very gentle and understanding with us. He held my arm firmly as we descended in the lift. I felt grateful, as I could not resist the impulse to glance at the emergency exit above us. He kept his torch alight all the way down, and it softened the memory of Sarah's hideous grimace in the red glow of the apparatus board globe.

We walked in silence along the narrow passage of the ground floor in single file, Mac leading the way; passed the power-room and into the old Exchange building, where the only entrance to both Exchanges was guarded day and night by an ex-serviceman with a revolver on his hip. To get by him into the Exchange, you had to produce a special pass issued only to Telephone employees. He bade us a cheerful good night. Clark answered for us all in a quiet, even voice.

A Departmental car was at the kerb. Mac and I got into the back, while Clark slipped into the driver's seat.

"Home, James," I murmured, leaning back and closing my eyes.

Clark let in the clutch, and swung the car around in a big semicircle.

"Listen, you two lasses," he said presently, driving swiftly through the deserted streets, "you're coming to my flat for five minutes before you go home. I want to give you a dose of medicine that'll fix your night's rest."

"I've already been advised aspirin," I said, without opening my eyes. "What's your prescription, Clark?"

"Aspirin!" he said scornfully. "Who said that? The flatfoot who poured water all over you? Just you wait and see what I've got for you, my children."

"I must say I'd be glad of something stronger than aspirin," Mac remarked, with a faint smile.

"All-in, Gerda?" asked Clark, glancing at her in the mirror over his head.

"Just about. What about you, Maggie?"

"I'll make that five minutes, but no more. You must be rather fagged yourself," I added to Clark. I could only see his profile but guessed he was frowning.

"You're quite right," he replied briefly over his shoulder, and then remarked on what was uppermost in our minds. "What a hell of a business!"

"Perfectly bloody," I agreed with accuracy.

"Shut up, Maggie," said Mac, with a shudder. "Don't be so callous."

"I'm not," I protested. "It's just that if I let go one minute I'll have hysterics, or something equally idiotic."

"Don't repeat your fainting act," said Clark with a grin. "I think I'd be even clumsier at reviving you than our friend, the Sergeant."

"What happened exactly? I know that I went off into a genteel swoon, while Mac was yelling like mad for you. Then I came to after some time to find two strange men ministering to me. Don't tell me that you let me stay unconscious until the police arrived without doing something!"

"No," said Mac, smiling faintly again at the recollection. "He pushed you aside from the door, so as you wouldn't be in the way."

"What!" I cried, leaning over the driver's seat. "I'll get even with you for this, John Clarkson."

He put up one hand to pat my check. "Sorry, my sweet. But what else could I do? Besides you in a swoon, as you term it, Gerda was still yelling her head off, trying to explain what had happened."

"I was speaking quite clearly," interrupted Mac, "but you were saying 'what' so many times that I thought you couldn't hear me."

We were turning off the highway into South Yarra, as Clark spoke jerkily: "It was rather difficult to grasp the situation."

"You were great, John," said Mac in a soft voice. "As soon as he saw Sarah was—what had happened, he pulled me out of the room and locked the door. By the way, you'll be interested to know that the key was in the lock on the inside. John carried you into the sick-bay, while I went back to the trunkroom to ring the police. They arrived in less than no time.

John had to deal with the situation alone, as I was being violently ill in the washroom."

"I'm glad that it affected you in some way, and that I wasn't the only weak-kneed person." We had drawn up outside a block of flats, and Clark said as he got out of the car: "I wasn't so marvellous. I nearly followed Gerda's example a couple of times. In fact I wish you'd shut up about it until I have that medicine."

I had been in Clark's flat several times, but never by myself. That was one of the many things I liked about him; in spite of his air of a gay Lothario, he was, in the correct meaning of the word, a gentleman. The lounge room where Clark left us was furnished with a taste for which it was hard to give a man credit. A plain mulberry-coloured carpet covered the floor, and the misty chintz that hung in the windows matched the deep lounge chairs where Mac and I had seated ourselves. A rather lovely mahogany escritoire stood in one corner of the room diagonally opposite a low table with slender, curved legs. On the cream-textured walls were two or three charming water-colours depicting Australian bush scenes.

Clark came back presently with a tray of long, frosted glasses. He put it down on the table by my chair, and took one to Mac.

"Hold your nose, my pet, and swallow it down."

"What is in it?" I asked, peering into the amber depths. It tasted delicious, cold and fragrant.

"That is a very guarded secret," said Clark gaily. "Only through many years of careful experiment has this drink been discovered. It's my own invention," he added, White Knight fashion.

Mac fished for the floating lemon ring, and started to suck it.

"I can taste soda water."

"A very minor ingredient. How do you like it, Maggie?

"It is delightful, but I'm very glad you're taking us home," I confessed. "I won't trust my legs by the time I reach the bottom of this glass."

"You'll be all right. Have a cigarette?"

"That'll put a few more minutes on to our stay. How I'll get to work to-morrow, I don't know. What say we drop out, Mac?" "Drop out" is another Exchange expression. Its obvious translation is to stay away from work on the excuse of illness.

"I wouldn't mind," Mac agreed, "but what about John? In his responsible position, now that he knows our plans, he will be compelled by his conscience to report us."

"You wouldn't give us away, Clark, would you?"

" I'd send someone out to your boarding-house to see if you were faking," he threatened.

"Dirt mean!" said Mac. "Sarah Compton used to have that job."

"And didn't she love it," I cut in. "I'll always remember the day she came to see me, prepared to be very triumphant, and ran into my doctor. It was the one bright moment of my illness."

"Hush!" said Mac, looking troubled. "Don't forget that she is dead, Maggie."

"I don't care," I said defiantly. "She was an abominable woman; everyone thought so."

Clark sat down on the arm of my chair, and swung one leg.

"All the same, sweetheart, I don't think you'd better go around saying how much you hated her. People, including the friends we made to-night, might start thinking things."

"The police? You mean that they might suspect me of killing her?" I asked scornfully. He nodded through a cloud of cigarette smoke, watching Mac turn an empty glass in her small, nervous hands. "But that's ridiculous! I told that Sergeant person that I didn't hate her enough to kill her. Anyway, I've got an alibi. We all have for that matter. We were all in the trunkroom two floors away from the murder."

Mac got up to collect the glasses.

"Did Sergeant say when it happened?" she asked over her shoulder.

"Not exactly," I said slowly, frowning. "As the night was so warm, they didn't like to make a definite time. But what does that matter? We were working all the time, and Sarah was actually in the room at least until a quarter to ten. I can prove that with a docket of mine that she queried. You probably saw it, too, Mac. I sent it along to the sortagraph."

Mac gave a tiny laugh, though she seemed far from amused. I thought it held a note of embarrassment, perhaps fear.

"Maggie," she said gravely, "would you swear that I was in the room all the time until 11 p.m.?"

I looked at her in complete astonishment. "I didn't actually see you, but I presume that you were there all the time. Weren't you?"

She made a pretence of arranging the flowers in the low bowl on the window ledge. Her head was turned away from us. Clark was very quiet. I glanced at him uneasily and then at Mac's straight, slim back.

"What is all this nonsense?" I asked impatiently. "Did you go out of the room or didn't you? What story have you told the police?"

Clark got up leisurely and strolled over to her.

"You are making yourself appear very mysterious, Gerda," he said lightly. "There is a very simple explanation, which in no way impairs the alibi that Maggie has supplied so blithely." He turned to me. "I let Gerda shut up the sortagraph at ten to ten, so that she could have a few minutes' relief before taking over the country boards."

"Is that all?" I asked, relaxing in my chair. "Why have you been acting so strangely, Mac?"

"I saw Sarah," she said in a low voice.

"You mean when she was dead?" I asked, feeling a trifle sick. "Before we found her?"

She turned quickly. "No! Oh no, Maggie. You don't think that I was pretending up there in the cloakroom?"

"Hardly," I lied, for the thought had occurred to me. "What do you mean, you saw Compton? When and where?"

"Entering the lift just as I came out on relief."

"That must have been about eight minutes to ten," said Clark swiftly. "Did she say anything to you? What floor was she going to?"

Mac twisted her hands together, and swung around to face us. "I don't know. She just glared at me. But she must have gone past the fourth floor because I remember glancing at the indicator before I went up the stairs."

"I wonder where she was off to?" Clark said thoughtfully. "There is only apparatus below the fourth floor."

"Observation," I cried, inspired. They looked at me blankly for a minute. Then Clark slapped his knee with his hand.

"Maggie, you're a marvel!"

"But observation closes at 9.45 p.m.," argued Mac.

"What was to prevent her from wanting to observe herself," I retorted. "Not her job, certainly, but quite in her line."

"But the room is always locked when the observation officers go off duty," Mac still protested.

"Another damned locked door!" I said, determined not to be put off from my brilliant idea. "She'd find a key from somewhere. In fact, I'm even beginning to think that she was responsible for the restroom door."

Clark interposed. "The point is, my dears, whom or what did she want to observe?"

"Anyone," I declared airily. "I said that it was in her line."

Mac was looking thoughtful. "She had a docket in her hand. I do remember that."

"There you are!" I said in triumph. "She was going to follow it up, and try to catch someone doing something they shouldn't, I'll bet."

Taking no notice of my solution, Clark asked Mac if she saw Compton at any later time.

"Not alive," she replied, and a shudder passed through her small figure.

"Why didn't you tell the Inspector all this, Gerda?" asked Clark gently. She gave that small laugh again.

"It sounds very silly, but I forgot all about it."

I was sure that she lied. Mac was too honest and straightforward to be able to deceive anyone. It was not in her nature to be subtle that way. Why lie about seeing Sarah Compton alive at 10 p.m., or rather at eight minutes to ten, I couldn't understand.

"Mac is playing a dangerous game," I thought with anxiety, resolving to find out what it was. A silence had fallen. Mac was staring at her entwined fingers, and Clark was whistling softly, flicking his cigarette for ash continually. I hauled myself up from the deep chair in several stages.

"Stop that noise," I ordered irritably. "We must go at once, Mac."

Clark removed his gaze from his swinging foot and grinned. "You're very cross, Maggie."

"I know I am," I snapped. "Who wouldn't be with all this murder business keeping me out of bed, and Mac here acting the fool."

"I'm ready, Maggie," said Mac, putting an arm through mine. "Don't be angry. I didn't mean to put on an act." Her eyes were clear and candid, as I looked down at her.

"Let's go home," I said gruffly, ashamed of my irritation. Clark turned off the lights and we returned to the car in silence, Mac still holding my arm.

"Goodness knows what my landlady will think of me coming in at this hour," I said, trying to speak lightly.

"You'll be the star boarder when she reads the paper in the morning."

"Of course!" said Mac suddenly. "I can just imagine the headlines. I suppose we'll sweep the world news from the front page."

"I bet our glamorous Gloria has her picture waiting for the reporters when she hears all this," I remarked. "By the way, she was off late. I wonder—"

"Shut up," interrupted Mac wearily.

"Seconded," said Clark in a firm voice.

"All right," I said huffily. "I was only wondering."

"Sit on her, Gerda, for Heaven's sake! I'll be glad to say good night to you two women."

We all seemed to be behaving like tired, cross children. I forbore any correction regarding the time that I might have made about Clark's remark. The car sped through sleeping suburbs, passed jangling milk-carts. I stayed silent in my corner until we drew up outside Mac's boarding-house.

"Don't get out, John," she said, as I opened the door. "Good-bye, Maggie, and sleep well. I'll call around to see you in the morning."

"Come to lunch," I suggested, drawing up my knees to let her pass, "but not earlier. I mean to stay in bed until late."

"Very well, then; about twelve-thirty. Good night, John." Clark, ignoring her request, held the gate open and patted her shoulder as she passed. He waited there until we heard the click of her key in the door, and then came back to the car.

"Cut down the right-of-way," I advised. "It will be quicker." I lodged only two streets away from Mac, but there was no cross road, which made the distance quite considerable if one went by the main streets. Clark steered the car carefully down the narrow lane, bumping a little on the uneven paving stones.

"Very exhausted, Margaret?" Clark's voice was oddly gentle. It gave me a shock hearing my proper name; rarely do people call me that. I remembered suddenly that it was the second time that night that he had done so.

"Completely and utterly," I replied. "Do you think it will be bad tomorrow—John?" His name came to my lips with difficulty. I could not share Mac's ease with it. I continued hurriedly: "Questions again and the like, I mean."

"It'll be pretty grim. Be a big girl and you'll get through. I'll try to stick around as much as possible if that is any help."

"It will be," I said gratefully, "but do you think that you'll be allowed?"

"No, probably not." He stopped the car precisely opposite my gate, and leaned over the back of the driver's seat, chin on his clasped hand, to gaze at me intently.

I avoided his eyes and said in a desperation of shyness: "What was it that Mac had on her mind?"

He relaxed and shrugged his shoulders slightly. "Heaven alone knows! But what about you? Is there anything worrying you?"

"No," I replied slowly, trying to concentrate. "I don't think so. But I'm tired now. My brain refuses to function. Good night, Clark, and thanks for being the proverbial rock."

"I'll take you to your door," he said, getting out.

"No, better not. If my landlady sees you, she'll have a fit."

"Rot," he replied, taking my arm. Suddenly he swung me round to meet his gaze.

"Listen, Maggie," he said earnestly, searching my face. "Are you sure there is nothing worrying you; something perhaps that I could help you fix?"

I stood still in his grasp under the hot, hazy stars. His eyes were keen and bright on mine. Presently I said with difficulty: "It's ridiculous, I know, but I feel as if there should be. There was something on my mind earlier, that I was trying to remember—before the murder, I mean. But I can't think what it was."

He gave me a little shake. "Try now," he commanded. "Think hard." I shook my head.

"It's no use," I said wearily. "I've tried and tried. I don't think that it could have registered in the first place." He let me go and patted my shoulder as he had done to Mac.

"Never mind, my sweet," he said softly, "just forget everything and have a sound sleep. But remember, Maggie, if there should be anything worrying you now or later, tell me. I would be glad and—honoured to help you." We had reached the doorstep and I turned to look at him wonderingly. I could not think of any way to express my gratitude, so I just repeated Mac's phrase: "You're great, John."

He smiled a little before his face became serious again.

"No, Maggie. It's just that I—well, perhaps we'd better leave it for to-night. Good night, my dear."

Again that night I felt his lips on my cheek. I put out a hand to hold him. But he had gone, striding swiftly down the path to the gate. He did not look back, though I was ready to wave a last good-bye.

CHAPTER II

John Clarkson's "medicine" must have done the trick, because I slept very deeply for several hours. I don't recall having had any vivid dreams as perhaps I should, and awoke, prosaically enough, feeling refreshed and active. The burning sun was seeping through the brown blind at the single window of my bedroom. I stretched out a hand to the bedside table, that I had bought a month previously at a sale, for my watch. It was 11 a.m. About twelve hours since Mac and I had stumbled into that horrid affair; plenty of time before I need shower and dress before lunch. I had missed breakfast altogether. I kicked off the sheet that I had used through the night as a protection against mosquitoes, and hunted for some fruit. Chewing an apple, I lay back on my pillows to reflect.

The day was promising to be another scorcher, and mentally I selected the frock I would wear. Then my eyes roamed around the little north room which I had made my home in the city. The green linoleum on the floor belonged of course to Mrs. Bates, my landlady, but the couple of sheep-skin rugs came from my home in Keramgatta. One was at the side of my divan bed, the other in front of a chest of drawers, both pieces of furniture being made in some uninteresting hardwood. My eyes dwelled appreciatively on the folk-weave curtains, striped in green and white, that

I had bought and made up myself; presently the bed on which I lay would be disguised with a cover of the same material. The walls had been covered with some hideous wallpaper. This, with Mrs. Bates' reluctant permission, I had stripped off only to disclose stained plaster. The marks were minimized by tinting the walls a faint pink and a cunning arrangement of furniture. I had put a very bad water-colour of the old homestead into a rather good frame, so that it had a blended effect on the observer. This hung opposite the flattering, pink-tinted mirror that Mac had given me. For this room and three meals a day, I paid a substantial amount from my fortnightly pay envelope. But I was comfortable enough, and my fellow boarders did not worry me.

Only Mrs. Bates, a follower of some obscure religion, ever pryed into my private affairs. To do her justice, I think that she considered herself responsible for the ignorant country girl whom she had occupying a front room on the first floor of her boarding-house. I had heard her light switch on and the bed creak as I crept past her door the previous night. I fully expected a visit from her to learn why I was so late, so I was not surprised when a tap synchronized with my thoughts.

"Come in," I called, pulling the sheet over my pink silk pyjamas. Sure enough, it was Mrs. Bates. When I first set eyes on my landlady I had the impression she was too unreal to exist. She was more a product of the imagination; the type of character Dickens would have created and revelled in. She was fairly tall, clad always from head to bunion-swollen feet in respectable black, with a surprisingly enormous bosom pushed high to her chin by old-fashioned corsets. Her face was long and narrow, and there was something wrong with her tear-ducts. She was compelled to wipe her pale blue eyes continually. It gave her the appearance of a mastiff dog, which was rather apt. According to the saga she had told me in serial form over a space of months, she had had a dog's life. This canine career included a drunkard of a husband, who, having deserted her many years previously, turned up frequently demanding money. I often heard Mrs. Bates haranguing him when I was hanging stockings over my window-sill to dry. Her Billingsgate, or perhaps I should say Fitzroy language, to make it more local, must have been totally at variance with the weird religious creed to which she was always trying to convert me.

In addition to the affliction of her eyes, she had had an operation for goitre, which had in some way impaired her windpipe. This caused her to wheeze every few words she spoke. It held Clark fascinated the first time he met her. She carefully inspected all the men whom her young ladies, as she called us, brought to the house, and later issued gloomy warnings as to the general infidelity and unsteadiness of the male sex. Clark had had a bad start. He was too good-looking to be trusted at all, though I had seen Mrs. Bates relax a little under his infectious smile.

"Good morning, Miss Byrne," she said, as usual omitting the "s" from my surname and thus rendering it completely insignificant. I could see that I was in for a bad time, and tried to brazen it out.

"Hullo, Mrs. Bates," I said brightly. "Have you come for your rent? I don't get paid until tomorrow, you know."

She hated any direct allusion to money, and disliked the word rent. When I did pay my board, she would write out a receipt quickly and hand it to me, so as to forget the disagreeable occurrence immediately. I often wondered what would happen if I didn't see her each fortnight in my honest way.

"There are two letters for you," she said, putting them on my table and ignoring my question. "The telephone has been ringing all the morning. I said that I wouldn't disturb you, as you were so late last night."

"Here it comes," I thought, before saying aloud: "Yes, I was rather late, wasn't I? Sorry if I awoke you."

Mrs. Bates was one of those people who say that they hear the clock strike every hour. I pondered as to the best way to attack her. I was feeling physically at a disadvantage lying in bed lightly clothed, while she was standing on one of my sheepskin rugs, thickly upholstered. Presently she came to my assistance.

"Here is the morning paper," she said, handing it to me folded.

"Are you sure that you've finished with it?" I asked, not attempting to open it. "Any special news?"

"You'd better read and see," she said grimly.

I spread the front page on the bed, hoisting myself to a sitting position. The first thing that struck my eye was a photograph of myself. One in profile taken at the boards some weeks ago for publicity purposes; not this type of publicity, however. I didn't bother to read the caption below, but grinned up at Mrs. Bates.

"Not bad, is it?" I asked, surveying the picture again with my head on one side. "It makes my nose look rather long, don't you think?"

Mrs. Bates wheezed several times in a visible effort to control her indignant curiosity. "Miss Byrne," she demanded, pointing a trembling finger at the paper, "what is the meaning of all this?"

I leaned back on my pillows again and closed my eyes.

"It means, dear Mrs. Bates, that you are harbouring in your respectable house a suspect of murder."

Her wheezing was so loud that I opened one eye anxiously. Her pale blue eyes were filling and being emptied in such rapid succession that unkindly I wanted to laugh. She was as curious as a cat and was trying not to appear so.

"Is that why that man has been ringing all the morning?" she asked.

"What man?"

"Sergeant someone or other from Russell Street. But I told him that you were still asleep."

I sat up with a jolt and swung my legs over the side of the bed. Mrs. Bates transferred her gaze to my solitary picture.

"What did he want? And why didn't you get me up? Where's my dressing-gown?"

Mrs. Bates got it from a hook, and held it out in front of her face.

"Thanks," I said, slipping it on and tying the girdle. "All right, Mrs. Bates, I'm modest now. What did Sergeant Matheson want?"

She sniffed audibly. "He said that he'd call back, and he did again and again until I said you'd let him know when you were up."

I made for the door. "I'd better ring him at once. It may have been important."

Mrs. Bates moved after me, wiping her eyes again. "Get dressed first, please, Miss Byrne. I can't have one of my young ladies walking down the hall in night attire."

"Don't talk rot," I said irritably. "There is no one around at this hour, and what does it matter? We are all females here, worse luck!" I dashed along the hall and slid down the banisters under Mrs. Bates's mortified gaze.

"Russell Street—Russell Street," I muttered as I ran. "I should know that number. What the devil is it? Do you know the number of the police station?" I called to Mrs. Bates, as she came down the stairs after me.

"I've never had any dealings with the police, so I can't tell you," she returned virtuously.

"Never mind, Mrs. Bates, dear," I grinned from the telephone book. "I'll tell you all about it in a minute. Just be patient."

I dialled quickly, and sat down on the edge of a table. Mrs. Bates passed to close the front door, not because of any draught that might be blowing, but in case anyone should pass and see me in pyjamas.

I got on to Sergeant Matheson without any difficulty; it seemed as if he were waiting for me. He sounded as ill-at-ease as he appeared the previous night, so much so that I was glad television was still considered impracticable.

"What's the matter?" I asked quickly. "Anything new?"

"Only routine stuff, Miss Byrnes. I rang to ask you to be at the Exchange at 2 p.m. this afternoon."

"Is that all?" I said in disgust. "Do you realize that you've got me out of bed?"

He gave an embarrassed murmur.

"My landlady is just as scandalized," I assured him. "What do you want of me at 2 p.m.?"

"Inspector Coleman wants to ask a few questions."

"What, more?" I interrupted.

"Can you get hold of Miss MacIntyre. We want her, too."

"She's coming to lunch with me. We'll arrive together. Is that all you want?"

"Yes, I think so. Er—how are you?"

"Pretty fit, thanks."

"Did you take those aspirins?"

"They worked like a charm," I answered mendaciously, not wishing to disillusion him. "Do you mind if I go now? I must get dressed, or Mrs. Bates will be fainting with outraged modesty." I thought I heard him laugh softly, and wondered if his eyes were twinkling as they had the night before. He was quite a lamb, but of course not in the same street as Clark.

"Very well, Miss Byrnes. We will see you and Miss MacIntyre this afternoon."

"We'll be there," I promised, and hung up the receiver. I started up the stairs, but paused halfway to say over the banisters: "By the way, Mrs. Bates, will it be all right for Miss MacIntyre to come to lunch?"

"I suppose so," answered my landlady in a grudging tone. "Did you find your number?"

"Yes, thank you. Sergeant Matheson wants Mac and me to be at the Exchange at 2 p.m. for further questioning."

She digested the information in silence and then asked suddenly: "What exactly happened last night?"

"Last night," I answered softly, "a very inquisitive, prying old woman was found dead with her face bashed in. A very nasty sight! If you want to know more, read the papers again. They always seem to know everything."

Mrs. Bates looked offended. "I'm not being merely curious, but I have the tone of my house to think of."

"Don't worry, Mrs. Bates, they won't arrest me. I've got a watertight alibi."

"I wouldn't dream of thinking that you committed such a dreadful crime," she said indignantly. "You are one of the quietest young ladies that I have ever had."

"Thank you," I replied dryly, thinking how uninteresting I must be. "Were there any other 'phone messages?"

"Mr. Clarkson rang," she said, looking very sour. "I believe that it was he who brought you home at such an unearthly hour."

"You asked him, I bet," I accused her, grinning.

"Well, what if I did? If you only knew how I lie awake at night worrying, when you girls are out with young men."

"Who else rang?" I cut in with impatience.

"Miss Patterson, and it isn't often that I run down one of my own sex, but that girl is an out and out liar."

"I find her most entertaining. There is no need to tell me what she wanted. I can guess."

"What did she want?" asked Mrs. Bates immediately.

"Didn't you ask her?" I inquired in mock surprise. "I imagine that she wanted to hear all the gruesome details, much the same as you do."

Mrs. Bates ignored this. "She says that she is coming to lunch."

"What!" I shrieked. "Who said she was? I haven't invited her. Well, if she comes, she'll have to pay for herself, for I'm damned if I will. The nerve of the wench! She knows I detest her."

"Please, Miss Byrne," said my landlady, looking up at me with earnest eyes. "You must not hate anyone. It should be all love and truth between souls."

"Not between Gloria's and mine. Anyway, you just called her a liar yourself."

"Then I did a great wrong. Miss Patterson probably has her good points."

"Don't talk such rubbish," I said irritably, continuing on my way. "If Miss MacIntyre comes, send her up to my room."

I took a hot shower and then a cold one, but they were much of a muchness. The sun had been beating down on the water pipes all the morning. Back in my bedroom I began to tidy things up, clad only in a slip, when Mac walked in. Her face gave me what Mrs. Bates would have termed a "nasty turn." It was ghastly, so white that it seemed almost blue as though with the cold, which was impossible that hot morning. Her brown eyes, which did not meet mine, were heavily ringed, and there was a line between her delicate brows that I had never noticed before.

"Well!" I said slowly, tucking in the bedclothes. "It doesn't look as though Clark's medicine did you any good."

"I slept on and off," she shrugged indifferently. "Want some help?"

"Yes, round the other side, and toss over the bedcover," I replied, following her lead. Whatever Mac had on her mind, she most obviously did not wish me to know. I felt hurt, of course, but what were friends for if they didn't respect each other's moods?

"Inspector Coleman wants us at the Exchange at 2 p.m.," I remarked presently, and saw those small hands pause a second in their smoothing of my folk-weave spread.

"Oh?" said Mac casually. "What for, do you know?"

"More questions," I answered, trying to observe her surreptitiously. She turned aside to dust my chest of drawers.

"What is it like out?" I asked, as Mac for no reason at all inspected an absurd dog that I had won at a charity fair in the city.

"Hot as hell!"

"No stockings," I decided. "Do you think that I'll pass all the old diehards?"

"I'm not wearing them. Anyway, the only one who objected to bare legs was—"

"Sarah Compton," I supplied gently. There was silence.

"Mac," I said pleadingly, but she did not look around. The silver pin-tray that she was dusting fell to the floor.

"Blast! Sorry, Maggie, I've scratched the wood."

"Doesn't matter," I replied mechanically, bending with her to retrieve the tray. Our heads bumped.

"Out of my way," I commanded flippantly. At last her eyes met mine. Kneeling there on the floor I caught hold of her shoulders.

" Mac, you silly, silly fool," I said, shaking her gently. "What is the matter?" I looked deep into her eyes and thought that I could read fear. But they seemed so full of misery that I wondered if I had been mistaken. She shook her head without speaking.

"All right," I said, getting up, "if you won't tell me, won't you at least let Clark try to help you. He is a very nice person, Mac." As I thought back on the previous night, I wondered if it were possible that she was jealous.

'Damn this thing they call love,' I said to myself, 'if it divides such good friends as Mac and I have been.'

She jumped up quickly, trying to smile. "Don't be so imaginative, Maggie. I'm tired, that's all. I didn't sleep too well. Can you wonder after last night?"

"No, indeed," I said truthfully, omitting to tell her of my own sound slumber. As I took out a navy sheer frock from my wardrobe she started to chatter inconsequently.

'My lamb,' I thought anxiously, 'you wouldn't deceive a baby.' I lent only half an ear to her story about Mrs. Bates and the salad she said she was 'throwing together' for our lunch. I ran a comb through my hair, and hunted in a drawer for lipstick.

"By the way," I cut in. "I have another guest arriving, but not at my invitation. Our cherished friend, Gloria."

"Patterson?" repeated Mac in genuine amazement. "What on earth does she want?"

"I seem to have answered that question before," I said with difficulty as I was concentrating on my lips. "I suppose she wants to be in on the news. I bet she was wild when she saw my picture in this morning's paper."

It did my heart good to hear Mac's laugh. "Don't be too hard on her, Maggie."

"She's a little fool," I said, shutting all the drawers that I had delved into, "with no brain above clothes and boy-friends."

"Both of which are most necessary."

"I don't agree," I declared firmly. "Look at Mrs. Bates. Not a male around the place, and the same old black garment year in and year out. A worthy example to all."

Mac laughed again, and I made a mental vow to pursue this banal conversation to its utmost.

"Maggie, you do talk the most utter rot. Come and see what she has got for lunch. When I last saw her she was chopping lettuce and singing the most awful songs."

"Those are hymns," I corrected, opening the door, "all based on truth and love. She even loves Gloria."

"She must be mad," said Mac frankly.

We walked down the hall to the stairs.

"Is that you, Maggie?" called a voice from the lower hall.

"Oh, lord!" I said softly, as we went down. "She is here already. Hullo, Gloria, to what do I owe this honour?"

To my horror, Patterson started to weep. Her round babyish face broke up in typical fashion: mouth awry and tears pouring out of wide open eyes. I threw Mac a resigned look, and tried to speak kindly.

"What's the matter? Do you feel sick?"

She continued to sob, but burst out presently: "Oh, Maggie, I'm so scared."

It sounded like an act. I raised one eyebrow at Mac who shook her head gently. As I considered Mac a shrewd judge of Gloria's emotional performances, I inquired in what I thought was a sympathetic but firm voice: "What are you scared about? And why come and tell me about it?"

"I thought that you'd be able to help," she sniffed, lifting her head. "You are always so—so sensible."

What a vile epithet! First Mrs. Bates practically informed me that I was like a cow in a paddock, and now I was sensible!

"You speak as if I wear skirts six inches below the knee. Come on now, what's the matter?" I asked briskly.

Gloria looked around her, throwing Mac a rather watery smile. "Do you think," she whispered, "that we could go some place where we can't be overheard?"

"There's only Mrs. Bates in the kitchen," I said impatiently.

Everyone else is at work. But we can go into the lounge-room."

I led the way down the hall to the first door on the right.

"Now," I said, as we seated ourselves on Mrs. Bates's fat leather settee. Gloria looked at me earnestly.

"Will you swear that you won't tell anyone about what I'm going to say? You too, Gerda?"

Mac nodded, but I said with caution: "That all depends on what it is."

Gloria became very agitated. "Oh, very well," I agreed, "I swear."

Gloria settled herself comfortably. She seemed quite happy now that she had our attention. I thought grimly of all the things that I would do to her if this was just an act.

"You remember last night," she began.

"Will I ever forget," I declared, closing my eyes.

"Maggie, please listen. I don't mean the—the murder, or rather I do, really."

"Just what do you mean?" I asked. "Now take a deep breath, and start at the beginning, but don't take too long. I want my lunch; which reminds me, I hope you realize that the cost of yours is not going on my bill."

"Of course I do," she said indignantly. "Let me tell you that I cancelled an engagement to have lunch at Menzies' to come and see you."

"I have already said that I was honoured. Get on with your story, and see that it's a good one."

"Maggie," she said, raising one hand solemnly, "I swear that everything I'm going to say is the truth." I forbore any comment in the hope that she would get to the point more quickly.

"Last night," she continued, "Compton abused me for being late back from relief, and said I was to work overtime. Do you remember?" I nodded briefly. "When 10.30 p.m. came, and all the girls on my rota went, I thought that I'd better stay just in case Compton saw me. So, by the time that I left the trunkroom, all the others had gone home. There was not a soul in the cloakroom, and the restroom door was still closed."

"Was it locked?" I asked quickly.

"I didn't try it. But there was an atmosphere in the cloakroom that I can't describe. As you know, I am considered psychic, and I felt then that something was going to happen."

I heard Mac sigh, but frowned myself. Although I did not wish to couple my brain with Gloria's, I had to admit to sharing that feeling all night.

"What time was this?" I inquired.

"It couldn't have been much after 10.35 p.m. That was when I signed off."

"Yes, I noticed that. Go on."

"Did you?" asked Gloria, as if I had done something particularly bright. "Where was I? Oh yes, I was just getting my orchid out of my locker. That beast Compton, though I suppose I mustn't say that now that she is dead, told me not to wear it at the boards. Then I heard someone coming down the passage. Who do you think it was?" She paused dramatically. Mac and I sighed together. Gloria was that type of person who, when she rang anyone, invariably asked: "Can you guess who is speaking?"

"Well, who was it?"

"Sarah Compton!"

I sat up with a jolt and heard Mac's quick indrawn breath.

"Now look here, Gloria," I said sternly. "You're not making any of this up, are you?"

She seemed so frightened that I believed she was in earnest. Sarah, alive at 10.35 p.m.! Mac, Mac, what was worrying you?

"Continue," I said, trying to be calm. She looked a little shamefaced.

"I hid behind the lockers, and she came into the cloakroom."

"Why did you hide?" Mac asked. It was the first time she had spoken.

"I didn't want her to see me," Gloria answered defiantly.

"That," I remarked, "is obvious. But why didn't you want her to see you? You'd worked your overtime."

She remained silent, looking sullenly down at her hands. "Good Heavens! another mystery," I thought.

"All right, we'll let that pass. What happened next?"

"I stayed where I was. I thought that I'd slip out later when she had gone. But she didn't go. She went into the restroom."

"Did she just open the door, or did she have to use a key?" I demanded. That restroom door had me puzzled.

"I don't know," Gloria confessed. "I didn't actually see Compton go in, as I was hiding behind the lockers. I only heard."

"Well, think! Do you remember hearing a click? Anything like a door being unlocked?"

She shook her head. "I wouldn't like to say."

"Go on," I repeated.

"Well, that was all," she replied. "As soon as I knew that the coast was clear, I left."

"If that is all," I remarked practically, "what are you so scared about? All you have to do is tell Inspector Coleman everything you have told us."

The tears welled into her eyes again, and she looked genuinely upset. "Oh no, no, I couldn't do that," she whispered.

"Why not? If you don't, I will."

"Maggie, you wouldn't. You promised."

"Pull yourself together," I advised. "I don't see why you are making such a fuss. It all seems perfectly simple."

She gazed at me piteously, "Don't you understand?" she whispered again. "They'll think I murdered Compton."

"And did you?" I asked brutally.

Her eyes met mine, wide with horror. "Maggie, how can you? I don't know anything about it."

"You seem to have been hanging around quite a bit," I pointed out. "I just wondered. Furthermore, my pet, as a statement your story appears to have a few gaps. You'd better fill them in when you tell it to the Inspector."

"I tell you—" she began, but I waved her aside and got up.

"Not interested, are we, Mac? All we are concerned with now is food. Come along, my children."

"I don't know how you can bear to eat," declared Gloria with a shudder, "I didn't have any breakfast after I saw the headlines."

"Are you sure that it was the first you knew of it?" I asked, bending to retie my shoe-lace.

"Shut up, Maggie," interposed Mac.

"I'm glad that someone sticks up for me," said Gloria, gratified.

"I wasn't," answered Mac in her calm way, "but all this bickering spoils my appetite. Are Mrs. Bates's salads as good as ever, Maggie?"

We went down to the dining-room. Gloria, despite her protestations, made an excellent meal. But Mac barely touched her plate, and I started to worry again. I knew that I had absolutely no chance of persuading her to confide in me. Mac, for all her sweetness, could be as obstinate as a mule. However I comforted myself with the reflection that Clark might be able to do something. Gloria seemed to have forgotten her worries, confident that I would not break my promise. It was absurd that she would not tell Inspector Coleman the truth at once, as they would be certain to find out sooner or later. Her story was very thin, to say the least.

She had started chattering about our charity dance which was to take place the following Saturday. I roused myself to inform her that quite likely it would be cancelled now. Her eyes widened in surprise.

"Why should it be? They can't stop it now that all the tickets have been sold."

"I daresay," I said, annoyed that I had started another argument. "But don't forget the slight disturbance that we had last night. Those policemen have come to stay; that is, until the truth has been discovered. We might dance over important footprints."

"Don't be so silly. No one would want to go near the restroom."

Mac raised her eyes quickly, her small fingers crumbling at some bread. "Why do you say that?" she asked in a quiet voice. I looked at her in astonishment, wondering at what she was driving. Gloria seemed surprised, too.

"My dear Gerda," she said loftily, "who would want to go near a room where a murder has been committed?"

"You can stop the 'my dear'-ing," I interrupted. "What's up, Mac?"

She was leaning across the table. I could see her eyes boring into Gloria's.

"How do you know where the crime was committed?" she asked, her voice suddenly clear and hard.

"Good girl," I thought, "you've got something there."

Patterson looked confused. "Why—why, I just heard."

"Where did you hear it?" I put in quickly.

"I read it in the papers."

Mac sat back again. "I read two morning papers before I came out, and in neither of them was there any mention of the exact place where the body was found."

Gloria's eyes darted around the room. "You told me yourselves," she whimpered.

"We most certainly did not," I declared emphatically. "Now think up another one."

"Leave her alone," interrupted Mac, passing a hand over her face wearily. "It's not our job to try and trap her."

"You're not trapping me," Gloria cried. "I've got nothing to hide. I remember now. One of the girls rang and told me."

"No good," I said, shaking my head. "They wouldn't know any more than what the papers printed. Who was it rang you, anyway?"

Gloria got up from the table. "I—I won't tell you."

I shrugged indifferently and folded my table-napkin. "Have it your own way, my pet," I said, "but if you are a wise person, which I very much doubt, you'll take my advice and go straight to Inspector Coleman."

She turned towards the door sullenly.

"Surely you realize that once the police know you were late off, they'll question you. Then where will you be? If an untrained person like myself can see through your flimsy yarn, how will you fare with experts? That is all I have to say. You came to me for advice, and I have given it to you.

Have you finished, Mac? I'll dash up and get a hat. You two can start on ahead, but don't you forget to see Mrs. Bates first, Gloria."

* * * * *

They were nearly at the station when I caught them up. I hadn't bothered to look up a train. Having travelled for years on that particular line to attend different shifts at the Exchange, I practically knew the time-table by heart. Mac and I both had monthly tickets, but we had to wait at the barrier for Patterson, who lived in the eastern suburbs, to buy a single to town. I found a vacant carriage, but the short journey was unbroken by any conversation. Gloria seemed subdued, and neither Mac nor I felt inclined for any more talk. It was only when we were crossing the river into the city that I asked Gloria: "Have you made up your mind? You can come with Mac and me to see the Inspector."

"I've nothing to say to him," she muttered sulkily.

"You're a silly little fool," I told her roundly, wondering why I bothered. "You're certain to be found out, isn't she, Mac?" I saw the strained look come back into Mac's eyes. She nodded and turned to the window. I watched her averted head in silence.

"Mac, Mac," cried a voice in my brain, "why don't you tell me what it is? What has filled your eyes with inexpressible sadness and lined your lovely skin?"

We lost Gloria when we got into town. She must have slipped away in the crowd at the station. I was rather thankful. After all, whatever foolish game she was playing, it was none of my concern. I had vindicated myself of any responsibility that she might have thrust upon me by appealing for my advice.

We boarded a west city bus that would take us right to the Exchange door. It was too hot to walk for pleasure, although the usual lunch-time crowds were milling at the street corners waiting for the green light. Wet or fine, city workers always take a constitutional down town between the hours of 1 p.m. and 2 p.m.

I always think that the Exchange buildings look different by day; perhaps because of the continual stream of telephonists tripping up and down those few steps, passes in hand. By night, it is a gaunt, lonely place, situated on a hill away from the heart of the city. As we entered, I saw a summer-helmeted policeman sitting with our usual guard. I supposed that this was to be expected. I nudged Mac significantly as I fumbled for my pass. We walked by a group of Central girls who were talking together in the hall. They stopped to look at us curiously, and I noticed Mac's chin lift a little. I gave them a brief nod as we went through the swing doors to the new building. The stuffy atmosphere of air-conditioning enveloped us. As we passed a block of apparatus, the continual click of the automatic feelers warned us that it must be after 2 p.m. and that afternoon work had commenced all over the city.

Bill was on duty, so I entered the lift with but few qualms. He gave us his usual cheery greeting, perhaps a little kindlier than was his wont. I inquired mechanically after his vegetable garden.

"Do you know where we can locate Inspector Coleman?" asked Mac, as Bill managed the lift dexterously with his one hand. We learned that the police had taken over the room next to the sick-bay to use as a temporary office. It was there that, some years previously, higher officials of the Department had sat mapping out operational instructions. In the opinion of the majority of telephonists, these instructions were all very well in theory, but put into practice with four lines buzzing on your board and a pile of dockets to break, were well-nigh impossible to obey.

We were informed by a man in uniform outside the cloakroom that lockers and coat-racks had been moved to another room off the corridor. We retraced our steps to the telephonists' classroom which had been fitted up as a temporary cloakroom. A quantity of telephone sets were neatly laid out in rows on a table. The powers that be must have authorized someone to go through the lockers with a duplicate key and remove them before the police closed up the rooms. A number stamped on each chest piece coincided with the numerical signature with which we signed dockets. But I recognized mine immediately by the small chip in the mouthpiece. Telephonists are very jealous of their sets. They become as attached and accustomed to them as a child to a doll. It is only with extreme reluctance that they are loaned, and any criticism by the borrower as to the quality of the telephone is strongly resented.

I balanced my cartwheel hat on top of a dummy pedestal telephone and observed casually: "I hope that it won't change to-night. I didn't bring a coat."

I was slightly apprehensive about the forthcoming interview. There was Gloria's semi-confidence that had fallen on my unwilling ears that morning. Not that it worried me overmuch. She could stew in her own juice for all I cared. But Mac's tragic eyes troubled me. There seemed neither rhyme nor reason for her secretive manner. She appeared placid enough now, a small cool figure in a printed crepe dress with her dark hair brushed up from her temples against the heat. Together we went down to the sick-bay passage.

The solemn-faced Roberts opened the door, and I heard a familiar voice say: "Here they are now."

It was Bertie Scott, the Senior Traffic Officer. Somehow his existence had gone out of my head completely, so that it came as a surprise when I saw him seated with Inspector Coleman and the Sergeant. His appearance was shocking. The gradual disintegration of his face and bearing that we had observed had risen to a climax. He looked an old man.

"I suppose that you would like me to go now, Inspector," he said, getting up slowly.

"I'd rather that you stayed, Mr. Scott; that is, if your duties are not calling you urgently. There may be a few questions for you to answer in collaboration with these young ladies."

Sergeant Matheson placed chairs for Mac and me opposite the wide desk, from behind which the Inspector had half-risen when we entered. Then we all sat down together in a rush as though we were playing musical chairs.

That little room was almost unbearably hot. The close atmosphere and the nervous anticipation that I was feeling made me perspire in a most unladylike fashion. I wiped the palms of my hands on my handkerchief and cast a covert glance at Mac who was sitting very straight. She still looked calm and cool, but I considered that her fine eyes were more than naturally alert and wary. Beyond Mac's profile, I could see Bertie. He was clad in his alpaca office coat and was sitting slackly with his hands hanging loosely from his knees.

The Inspector hunted on his desk until Sergeant Matheson put a single sheet into his hand. His big frame fitted badly into the dark suit which most of our city men seem to wear in all seasons. Only the Sergeant had compromised with the heat. With unreasonable irritation, I saw that he was wearing a thin, fawn-coloured outfit without a waistcoat. In spite of a glaring tie, he looked all one colour, with his sandy hair and skin. I had had plenty of time for these observations. A long silence had fallen as Inspector Coleman read through his paper, frowning. I sighed and transferred my attention to a solitary fly buzzing about his head. It settled on his broad wet forehead, and he brushed it away with an impatient wave of his hand. At length he raised his eyes, and the three of us—Bertie Scott, Mac and myself—were compelled to run the gauntlet of his keen scrutiny. It took me all my control not to fidget my feet like a guilty schoolgirl. Up to that moment I had a clear enough conscience, but I began to wonder if perhaps there was not some little thing that I was trying to conceal. I think it was then that I realized what a very formidable body the Police Force was. I made a mental vow never to get mixed up with them again.

"Miss MacIntyre," he began and I saw Mac's eyelids flicker. "I understand that it was you who discovered the body. According to your statement you last noticed the deceased about 9.30 p.m. Wednesday night, that is yesterday evening, when she approached the sortagraph position where you were working."

"That is so," said Mac in a low voice. "She put a docket in the file at the side of the sortagraph."

"Did she speak to you at all?"

Mac frowned. "I don't think so."

"Come, Miss MacIntyre, my question required only yes or no."

She looked at him directly. "She muttered something. Whether it was meant for my ears or not, I don't know."

"Did you catch what she said?" asked the Inspector. Mac hesitated.

"I am not sure," she replied cautiously, "but I thought she said 'that'll fix it' or something similar."

"H'm," said the Inspector, "it may or may not be significant. Was it an unusual phrase for Miss Compton to use?"

A slight smile crossed Mac's lips. "I have heard stronger remarks made during the rush time," she said.

I coughed suddenly, noticing at the same time Bertie's hand crossing his mouth for a moment. Mac's answer could tickle the risible faculties of telephone employees only, although I observed Sergeant Matheson lower his eyes quickly to the papers on the desk. Only the Inspector remained grave.

"That was the last time that you noticed her in the trunkroom?"

"Yes," answered Mac, and I felt almost happy. The form of the Inspector's question had not necessitated her lying. I looked around the room benevolently, and caught Sergeant Matheson's keen eye fixed on me. As he leaned over and whispered to his superior, I cursed myself heartily for not keeping a poker face. The Inspector nodded. and turned again to Mac.

"Have you anything that you wish to add to your statement, Miss MacIntyre?"

There was another pause, while Mac stared at her hands. Presently the Inspector stirred impatiently.

"Well, Miss MacIntyre?"

"I was thinking," she remarked coolly. "Perhaps it would help if I could see my statement?" She held out one small hand for it.

"She's playing for time," I thought anxiously, as Mac's eyes travelled down the single sheet to her signature at the bottom. Only her left hand pleating a fold of her floral skirt betrayed her nervousness.

I said to myself: 'You're no good at deceiving people, Mac, my sweet.

Why don't you tell them that you saw Sarah later. They'll soon find out about the relief you had.'

"That is quite in order," she said, returning the sheet, "I have nothing further to tell you."

It was my turn next.

"I believe that you can swear to Miss Compton's presence in the room at a later time than Miss MacIntyre can."

"Correct," I answered without hesitation. "I remember she queried a docket with me about a quarter to ten. A Windsor number was the caller, so it should be easy to trace."

Bertie spoke for the first time: "Dockets are filed under the calling number, Inspector. I'll have it looked up for you. Any query on a docket is always noted on the back and signed by the person handling it."

"Thank you, Mr. Scott," said the Inspector. "Perhaps if I could have that call at once?"

Bertie rose with alacrity. He seemed to be anxious to be up and doing. "A Windsor number you said, Miss Byrnes?" I nodded. He trotted out of the room in his fussy manner.

"Now, Miss Byrnes," continued Inspector Coleman, as Roberts pulled the door shut. "That was definitely the last time that you saw Miss Compton?"

"I didn't see her," I corrected again. "Working at top speed you don't see anything but the board and dockets that you are handling. But I'd swear that it was Compton who made the inquiry. I'd know her voice anywhere."

Sergeant Matheson whispered to the Inspector again, who smiled a little.

"No, that is a little too subtle," he answered, and added to me: "Sergeant Matheson suggests that it may have been someone imitating her voice, but I think that we will trust to your judgment."

"You can rely on it," I said firmly, directing a withering glance at the Sergeant. He reddened a little.

"You don't know if the deceased was seen by anyone else at a later time?" I was asked. I felt Mac stir beside me and closed my eyes for a minute thinking: 'Now what do I say? It is obvious that Mac doesn't want me to mention her meeting, and then there is my promise to Gloria.' Of course it would be me who came up against the difficult part. I crossed my fingers and lied bravely, hoping that I was a better actress than Mac.

John told me later that it was the silliest damn thing I did throughout that dreadful time. He adheres to the opinion that if I had told the truth, the case might have been broken then and there.

I sighed with relief as Mac drew their attention by suggesting that they query the all-night telephonists as to whether they saw her. The Inspector did not seem pleased with the advice. He probably did not like being told his business, and on any other occasion I wouldn't have blamed him. However he made a note on his pad and asked at what time they came on duty.

"At 11 p.m.," I informed him. "We usually went when they relieved us, but last night it was so busy that we stayed on helping to clear things up. I signed off about 11.10 p.m." I glanced at Mac inquiringly.

"11.8 p.m.," she said, meeting my eyes calmly.

"You can check that up with the time book," I bit my lips, suddenly remembering Gloria Patterson. 'Oh well, what's the difference?' I thought, 'Bertie's certain to have suggested them seeing it.'

"How many all-night telephonists were there?" asked Inspector Coleman.

"Four. Two of them came into the trunkroom a few minutes early, for which I was very glad."

"Were you and Miss MacIntyre working near each other?"

"Have you seen the trunkroom?" I demanded, but they shook their heads together in a way that was almost comical. "The country boards, which Miss MacIntyre was working, are on the west side of the room. Pillars, inquiry posts and booking boards separate them from the inter-state positions where I was on duty last night."

"When these girls came in, did they make any mention of having spoken to Miss Compton?"

"You didn't talk to Sarah Compton unless you had to," I retorted. "In spite of Miss MacIntyre's suggestion, I consider that it would be very unlikely if they saw her at all." Mac knew what I was getting at, just as I had realized that her interruption had been to divert the two officers' attention from my untrue statement. They appeared puzzled, so I went on to explain: "The all-night telephonists take it in turn to sleep. There is a dormitory on the seventh floor which they use instead of the cloakroom."

"You mean that none of them would go near the eighth floor?"

"They might have," I said carefully, "but it would not be usual. They generally leave their headsets in the dormitory all day, so that there would be no need to go up to the cloakroom when they came on duty at night."

Inspector Coleman turned to Mac. "You knew this, Miss MacIntyre?" Mac nodded. "Then why," he went on sternly, "did you suggest that the all-night telephonists may have seen Miss Compton?"

Mac was silent, and I cursed the Inspector for his acuteness. I realized it was going to be very difficult to continue deceiving him, but having gone thus far I could not retreat now. But it was obvious that he knew that we were both withholding something, and I was surprised that he did not press for further information. Later I learned that this was not his method, and that in spite of his calling, he was a soft-hearted man, as far as his duty would allow him.

However, he gave us a severe warning.

"Last night," he began, punctuating his words with a tap of his pencil, "you two girls stumbled on one of the foulest crimes that can be committed. A middle-aged woman was battered to death by some person whom we only know now as a coldblooded fiend. The time of her death is uncertain, and the weapon used still undiscovered. You see, I am laying the facts before you in the effort to make you realize that this is a very serious affair, and one in which you should endeavour to render the police every possible assistance. The motive for this unfortunate woman's death is, we imagine, due to her curiosity."

'I told you that,' I thought indignantly.

"But what knowledge she held and over whom is still unknown. Therefore I ask you two girls to think, and think hard, whether there is not something more you can tell us, Miss MacIntyre?"

I gripped the edge of my chair with my wet hands. I was glad that he had asked Mac first. At least I could get my cue.

"No, nothing," she replied in a low, tired voice.

The Inspector turned towards me, I shook my head slowly, trying to appear as if I were searching my brain.

"Very well," said Inspector Coleman in an expressionless way, I thought that his eyes were as hard as granite. "One more matter. As you know, the Exchange building is not the accessible place it was once." I knew what was coming. It had been in the back of my head ever since we left the building the night before, but I had tried to close my mind to it.

"Everyone," continued the Inspector, "who wishes to enter the Exchange has to pass an armed guard, and present his or her identity pass. Therefore unless the murderer got by on a stolen pass, which we shall consider in due time, this terrible crime was perpetrated by an employee of the Telephone Department. I want you to realize that we intend to bring that person to justice even if it means questioning every single inhabitant of the building, and you have several hundred people working with you. This will make our job long and tedious, and will allow the criminal to cover his tracks and perhaps-who knows-strike again in the same cold-blooded way."

I shivered in spite of the heat, feeling suddenly cold at the thought of an unknown killer walking freely in our midst. If the Inspector had expected some return for his dramatic speech, he was doomed to disappointment. Mac was as silent as a tomb, and I had vowed to myself that as much as I distrusted it, I would follow her lead only.

"To continue with your statement, Miss Byrnes"—I started as he spoke my name, and looked at him inquiringly—"you informed Sergeant Matheson that earlier in the evening you were accused of having locked the door of the room where the crime took place."

"I wasn't accused directly," I declared. "Some busybody had conjectured it, because I was the last telephonist to be near the restroom. The rumour was spread to the boards."

"Do you know who that person was?"

"Not the faintest. To be quite candid, I didn't hear of the accusation until about 10.30 p.m. Even then I didn't pay much attention to it. The girl Gordon, who was sitting at the next board, told me what everyone was saying. It was then that I noticed Compton was not in the room."

Inspector Coleman delved amongst his papers again.

"When was the locked door first known?"

I concentrated on the events previous to the murder. It was rather difficult to assimilate them, overshadowed as they were by more major happenings.

"Miss Patterson," I said suddenly. "I was relieving her and she came back late. I remember now that Compton rebuked her and said that she was to work overtime."

It was then that I saw the trunkroom time-book under the Inspector's hand, and felt a slight admiration. They had probably checked up on our statements already.

"G. M. T. Patterson, 10.35 p.m.!" read the Inspector, and looked up. "Is that the girl?"

"Yes," I answered, feeling maliciously pleased. They were on to Gloria's trail now. How like her to have three initials!

"She was the last telephonist to be off before you two," stated the Inspector, keeping his finger on her name. "What time will Miss Patterson be on duty this evening."

"3.30 p.m. this afternoon," I replied promptly, almost exultant. This new fact which had come to their notice would probably take their attention from Mac and me. I was a little tired of being number one suspect. They appeared to have disregarded our admirable alibis. Perhaps they were considered a little too water-tight to be wholesome.

The Inspector glanced at his watch. "That is very soon."

"Can we go and find her?" I asked hopefully. "She may have arrived already."

He threw me a cold glance, and my heart sank.

"That will not be necessary. We have not finished with you yet. Roberts!" he yelled. The solemn-faced policeman put his head round the door. "Find G. M. T. Patterson—she's a telephonist due on duty at 3.30 p.m.—and tell Mr. Scott that we will not require him for a while."

Roberts withdrew his head without having said a word. If he hadn't spoken to me the previous night I would have had doubts of his ability to do so.

Inspector Coleman turned his attention once more to his desk. He was in truth the most untidy man that I had ever seen. I often said to John afterwards that it was a miracle that he ever solved the case. I came to realize that the more haphazard the Inspector appeared, the closer he had his nose to the right scent. At length he produced a small, grimy piece of paper. This was handed to me without comment. I gave him a surprised look and glanced at the document. Sudden excitement tingled my nerves as I knew at once that it was the mysterious note that had hit me in the lift the night before. I have, like the majority of telephonists, developed a good memory, so I can give you its contents word for word. Printed in block letters, obviously disguised, it ran:

SARAH COMPTON, UNLESS YOU KEEP YOUR SPYING NOSE OUT OF OTHER PEOPLE'S BUSINESS, YOU'LL GET WHAT HAS BEEN COMING TO YOU FOR A LONG TIME. YOU TRIED TO BREAK UP MY LIFE ONCE, BUT I WON'T LET YOU DO IT AGAIN.

There was no signature of course, but the tone in which the letter was written gave no doubt that Compton would have recognized its author. I re-read that grimy sheet several times, until the Inspector held out his hand impatiently. As I gave it back, I saw Mac looking at me curiously; I had forgotten to tell her of my adventure in the lift. It was her own mysterious behaviour that had made it slip my mind, and this morning there had been Patterson to deal with. I dropped my sodden handkerchief to the ground, and bending near her to retrieve it, breathed: "Later."

Again I saw Sergeant Matheson's keen scrutiny, and smiled gently at him. Much to my annoyance, he grinned back.

"Well?" asked the Inspector.

I replied cautiously: "I should say that it was the letter I told the Sergeant about. The two words I noticed, 'spying' and 'Compton" are there, so that makes it rather conclusive."

The Inspector smiled a little. It was amazing how it changed his big, rugged face. "Again we will rely on your judgment. Will you give us your opinion on the matter?"

"The letter?" I queried, pleased, though rather surprised. It was very flattering for a Russell Street Police Inspector to ask my advice, but I went carefully, fearful of some trap that might lurk behind the Inspector's expressionless eyes.

"I haven't any idea who wrote it, if that's what you are getting at." He did not seem disappointed and waited for me to continue. I began to feel helpless, not knowing exactly what to say.

"Let me see it again," I requested. After gazing at it closely and turning it over in my hand, I observed: "I should say that it was written by a well-educated person. I mean the grammar and all that sort of thing. The paper itself—the paper," I repeated slowly with growing excitement and raising my eyes to look at the two men. I saw their faces alight with eagerness. "It is a sheet from an inquiry pad. Look! You can see that a piece has been cut off the side. As a rule there are headings there to facilitate inquiries—number required, calling number, and so on."

Inspector Coleman studied it carefully, holding it up to the light. Presently he gave it to the Sergeant, who perused it in his turn.

"Look, sir," he said. "There's a watermark. It should be easy enough to trace."

"It is from an inquiry pad," I assured him with asperity. "I have seen those forms many times in the past few years, haven't I, Mac?"

She nodded. Her eyes were candid and bright once more. I told myself: "Mac doesn't know anything about this, anyway."

The Inspector put the paper carefully into an envelope. "Who would have access to these pads?"

"Anyone and everyone," I answered, gesturing broadly with one hand. "First of all the printing people who send them to the Stores Department down town, who in their turn send certain supplies up here. A limited amount of stationery arrives at a time, in the hope to make us economize with it."

The Inspector observed: "I consider it more likely that it was used by someone here on the spot."

"That's true," I remarked thoughtfully. "After all, it was someone in the building who threw it down into the lift."

"Miss Byrnes, and you, too, Miss MacIntyre, can you tell us of anyone who might, in your opinion, write such a note to the deceased?"

Mac and I exchanged hopeless glances. But contrary to her former remoteness, Mac seemed eager with suggestions.

"That's very difficult to say, Inspector," she said in the frank manner that became her best. "Miss Compton was a very trying woman, to say the least. Numerous people might have written that letter, which, by the way, I have not yet seen. I am just presuming that it held come sort of spite."

Inspector Coleman took it out of its envelope, and passed it to her. Mac's tiny hands were quite steady as she held it. I felt a surge of relief.

"Thank you," she said calmly, placing the note on the desk in front of the Inspector. "I agree with Miss Byrnes who suggested that it was written by a well-educated person, but I think also that it is someone who had known Miss Compton for a long time."

"Quite so, Miss MacIntyre. The mention of a previous brush with Miss Compton manifests that, but have you any idea at all—"

"Not the slightest," interrupted Mac with a faint smile. "We all had some sort of grudge against Miss Compton, but I know of no one whose life she had once tried to break up. Our differences with her were minor affairs. She tried to stop smoking being allowed in the restroom, and—a criminal offence in the eyes of a telephonist—never permitted anyone to leave work before time, even if there was no traffic on hand."

"They are certainly small grudges," agreed the Inspector, 'but with a certain type of character, those petty annoyances might assume alarming proportions. Have there ever been any other anonymous letters written in the Exchange?"

"Hundreds," I cut in promptly. "Some weak-kneed person is always trying to make a sensation."

The Inspector looked very interested. "When you say hundreds, Miss Byrnes," he asked, "just how many do you mean, exactly?"

"Sorry," I replied, grinning. "Feminine hyperbole! On and off, someone gets the bright idea. I should say about two or three a year; when it was the fashion, it used to be that many a day."

"Do you know if Miss Compton received any of those letters?"

"Her mail was the largest. She must have quite a collection, if she kept them all."

"She probably did," remarked the Inspector surprisingly. "It sounds entirely in keeping with her character. If she has," and here he tapped the envelope in front of him significantly, "that collection may throw some light on this. By the way, I can trust you two girls not to say too much about all this."

"Don't worry," I assured him. "We won't. I must confess, however, that I told John Clarkson about the lift business. You know that," I added to the Sergeant.

"The traffic officer on duty last night?" queried the Inspector, turning over papers. "He is a man of authority, so that will not matter."

"Men are usually very discreet," I conceded honestly. His eyes twinkled for a moment.

The phlegmatic Roberts appeared once more. "Mr. Scott wants to know if you're ready for him yet?"

I felt amused at Bertie's humility; as a rule, he was a most independent person. He peeped around the door like a frightened rabbit.

The Inspector arose. "Come in, Mr. Scott. You have arrived at a very good time." Bertie handed him a docket, and he glanced at it, puzzled. "Oh, yes, many thanks. We will go into that matter a little later on. Just now, I want to know if I can borrow one of these young ladies?" I looked from Mac to the Inspector in amazement. "I'd like one of them to accompany us to the home of the deceased; a little matter of identifying some correspondence. Now which one can you spare?"

"Neither," answered Bertie promptly, who imagined that he was always short of staff, "but I suppose that it is a command."

"That's quite correct," said the Inspector firmly.

"You go, Mac," I urged, rather reluctantly. I wasn't anxious to miss anything that might happen. I felt jubilant when she shook her head, frowning.

"No, I'd much rather not, Maggie," she replied with sincerity.

"You'd better make it urgent leave," Bertie declared in a resigned fashion. "Make out an application, and I'll see if you can get it with pay."

'I should think so,' I thought indignantly, as I thanked him.

"We'll have those rooms cleared for you by to-night," Inspector Coleman told Bertie. I presumed that he meant the rest- and cloakrooms. "We've done all the work we wanted on them. But if we might keep the use of this office for a while, I should be glad."

"That'll be quite all right, Inspector. I'll fix it up with the Department. We are only too glad to be of any assistance. The sooner that this horrible business is cleared up, the better. The traffic is worse than usual to-day, busybodies ringing up and trying to find out details."

"The general public has the mind of an insect," agreed the Inspector. "Are you ready, Matheson? Just leave those papers; we can lock the door."

"Are you sure that you don't mind going?" whispered Mac, as we went into the corridor.

"No fear!" I said stoutly, "I think that it's all rather fun."

As she shuddered a little and turned away, it occurred to me with amazement that Mac was developing sensibilities.

CHAPTER III

We drove towards the east of the city in an open patrol car. Sitting in the back seat and holding my big hat safely on my knees, I received quite a thrill when a policeman on point duty saluted as we passed. How Mac would have enjoyed it; that is, if she wasn't in her present distrait mood. We had had a lot of fun together, Mac and I. Our personalities seemed to harmonize, which was remarkable because I am not overfond of my own sex. I suppose that comes from working amongst females—a hundred of them to one male. Fortunately, chattering is strictly forbidden in the trunkroom, and after work the quicker one gets away from the place the happier one is.

I already knew where Sarah Compton lived. When I first came to town, a rather shy and awkward country girl, I'll admit, she approached me to rent one of the furnished rooms in her East Melbourne house. Luckily someone intervened, and gave me some sound advice as to what type of woman I was up against. I was told that she made one pay "through the nose" under a legal arrangement that did not permit one to back out of the proposition if dissatisfied. I used to pass on this information to any new girl who came to the Exchange, when I saw Compton's eyes alight on her.

I believe that it was her old home that she had turned into small flats. It was one of a terrace, overlooking the gardens. A very excellent position, but I was told that the house itself was terrible: small, poky rooms badly lit and ventilated, and smelling always of mice. She must have been doing excellent business just lately, because every room was taken. But with the present housing shortage, I should imagine that people would be only too glad of any type of dwelling.

Inspector Coleman ran his finger down the cards in the harrow hall, and we mounted the steep stairs to the first floor. Compton had kept one of the front balcony rooms for her own Use. I was agreeably surprised. Though full of hideous, old-fashioned furniture, it was neat, clean and cool. I dropped my absurd hat on to the spotless counterpane of the brass-knobbed bed, feeling a little sacrilegious. Although prying into other people's business had been the spice of life to Sarah Compton, it did not seem quite the thing to be rummaging amongst her belongings when she was not alive to protect her own.

'Heaven knows what they might find,' I thought, wishing that I hadn't come after all. But I comforted myself with the reflection that Sarah herself would have been only too glad to assist in the discovery of her assassin. I sat down in the one lounge chair that her room held to watch the two policemen at work. They were so methodical in their search that I was amazed after having observed the Inspector's untidy desk and creased appearance.

On one side of the room Sergeant Matheson had started with the wardrobe, and was working round to a marble-topped washstand and bedside table. Inspector Coleman was tackling the dressing-table and a masculine-looking desk. The latter was locked, and he glanced around frowning. Without a word, he began to finger the contents of the pin-tray on the dressing-table. I watched him, fascinated, as he selected a good-sized hairpin and slid it carefully into the keyhole of the desk. There was a quick turn of his wrist and a click. The roll-top slid up under his hands.

"Are those the Inspector's usual tactics?" I asked Sergeant Matheson softly. He grinned.

"The hairpin trick? He learned that from an old friend of ours, who is staying out at Pentridge for an indefinite period."

"Nice company you keep," I observed acidly, but he missed my remark. The Inspector had beckoned him over with a jerk of his head. Together they thumbed over a couple of packets of letters, held by rubber bands.

"On the bed, Sergeant," said Inspector Coleman, "The light is better."

I leaned my chin on the arm of the chair and watched. I was longing to ask them what they had found, but their business-like demeanour bade me stay quiet. They went through the letters systematically, until they were tossed in an untidy heap on Sarah's snowy bedspread. But I could see that at least three had been separated from the rest. Inspector Coleman glanced through these again, and then stared thoughtfully out of the window. I coughed gently to remind him of my presence. His eyes came slowly round to mine. After a moment of frowning silence, he looked down at the papers in his hand. Selecting one, he passed it to me. I received it eagerly, and saw with some surprise that it was dated April 1917. What a magpie Compton must have been to keep a letter all these years! Unless, I thought suddenly, she had been using them to some financial purpose.

The note was quite short and written in an ordinary sloping hand, It began abruptly: *I know that you have been trying to set Dan against me. You had better stop, or I will do something desperate. You're only jealous. Dan trusts me, and nothing you can do will change our plans.*

The letter was signed "Irene." I looked up at the Inspector wonderingly. He handed me another letter in silence. My eyes went to the date immediately, June 1917. It was longer than the last one, but written in the same hand on faded blue notepaper, which must have been quite expensive in its day. The name "Sunny Brae," engraved on the top right-hand corner in a deeper shade of blue, was the only address.

My dear Sarah.

I want you to thank all the girls for the charming gift, and to tell them how much we appreciated it. The vase looks so well in our drawing-room. You must come out and see it some day. What a pity you could not come to the wedding. We missed you very much. Dan sends his regards. Many thanks to everyone again.

Irene Patterson (nee Smith).

I had seen that type of letter dozens of times in the past years. Girls who had left to be married were always made some presentation. It is the custom at the Exchange for their "thank-you" letters to be pinned to the notice board for all to see. I examined the pale-blue paper closely, but could find no pin mark. Either the letter was shown around the Exchange, or else Sarah had just passed on the thanks by word of mouth. I was inclined to consider that it was the latter. After the first note, written two months before, this one smacked of malicious triumph. Could it be possible that Compton had had a disappointing love affair? Somehow one could never connect such things with her. She seemed to have been born an old maid.

I stretched out a hand for the third note, and was jolted back to the present time. This one, undated and unsigned, was written on a slip from an inquiry pad. But in this instance the headings had not been cut away like the original anonymous letter. It was certainly printed in a disguised hand, but somehow the two letters did not seem to match. I frowned as I read:

WE WARN YOU, SARAH COMPTON, THAT IF YOU SEND THAT MEMO-RANDUM INTO THE DEPARTMENT, WE WILL MAKE THIS PLACE TOO HOT TO HOLD YOU!

I drew my brows even closer together in an effort at concentration. There was something about that last note that was very familiar.

I looked up. Inspector Coleman was still staring out of the window. The Sergeant had propped himself against the end of the bed, and was whistling softly. They both appeared preoccupied, so I bent my mind to the task of tracing that sense of familiarity to its source. Of one thing I was certain. It had not been written by the same hand as the one thrown into the lift. That had been a more personal note, one that could be related to the first two that I had just read; that is, if Sarah Compton had not gone around trying to break up other people's lives a dozen times a day. My last thought seemed so feasible that I tarried with it, until I came to the conclusion that as the Inspector himself had gone through a pile of letters, he was not likely to select these three that had no bearing on the case. I would rather have seen the rest of the notes myself to make sure, but I doubted whether the Inspector would have permitted me. In fact, as I said to John later, if a few more crumbs of information had come my way, I would not have found myself where I am now.

But that is neither here nor there. My present job was to assist these two policemen in identifying anonymous mail. It was then, quite suddenly, I remembered. I knew who had written that last letter. But I felt a little dubious about informing the Inspector. As far as I could see, it had no connection whatsoever with the business in hand, and I might only stir up unnecessary unpleasantness. So I resolved to hold my tongue; at least until I had consulted its author.

The Inspector spoke at last. There was a twinkle in his eyes as he asked: "Well, Miss Byrnes? What is your opinion on the letters that I have given you to read?"

"I feel very flattered to think that you are asking for my advice." I hedged, playing for time while I thought out my reply. As usual, I had underestimated my opponents.

"Keep to the point, please," said the Inspector coldly. "You were not brought here for the drive, but to assist us."

"Sorry," I replied, with what I hoped was a disarming smile, "but until now, you have been treating me as a suspect. It is no wonder that I am not quite sure of my role."

Inspector Coleman melted. The twinkle returned to his eyes. "We regard you with suspicion, inasmuch as you seem to have an unbreakable alibi."

"I guessed that. It stands to reason. However, the letters!"

"Yes, Miss Byrnes. Try to be brief and to the point. Time is an important factor in this sort of case."

'And me a telephonist,' I thought, casting him an indignant look. 'You can't know much about our game, my man.'

"The first two," I began briskly, "are most obviously written by the same person. You consider there is a possibility that the person who sent that note down into the lift last night might be connected with them; otherwise, why pick them out? Am I right?"

His eyes narrowed. "You're very shrewd, Miss Byrnes. You are correct in your supposition."

"Nonsense," I complimented in my turn. "It is you who are acute. However, I don't want to dampen your idea, but it is quite on the cards that our late monitor tried to break up many a life."

"I have taken that into consideration," he announced calmly. "Of all that rubbish that we went through," pointing to the bed, "these two seemed best to suit our book."

"You're probably right," I agreed reluctantly. "Judging by the second letter, I should say that this Irene person was a fellow-telephonist of Compton's. She herself was one originally, you know, before she passed the monitor's examination. At least, I presume so. She had been a monitor for as long as I can remember, but we all start from scratch. Sorry," I added, taking a deep breath. "I'm wasting time."

Inspector Coleman shook his head. "No, go on."

"There's the name, of course," I said slowly. "That gives you something to go on."

The Inspector perched himself on the edge of the bedside table. It creaked ominously. "This morning," he remarked, examining one huge hand in a casual manner, "you mentioned a Miss Patterson."

"Her Christian name is Gloria," I said quickly. "Patterson is quite a common name. Anyway, she couldn't have written those letters. She is only in her twenties. You'll have to look among the monitors and supervisors to find anyone near the fifty mark."

"An odd coincidence," observed Inspector Coleman. "Is there anyone else by that name working in the Exchange?"

"There is another girl, but I believe that she spells her name differently from Gloria." I don't blame her for wanting to differentiate, I added to myself.

"How old would she be?" asked the Inspector.

"About forty or so. It is hard to say. But she has been at the Exchange for years. You could find out easily enough through the Personnel Branch. They know all our most guarded secrets." I caught Sergeant Matheson grinning like an ape, and longed to tell him that I was only twenty-five.

"Do you think," I asked Inspector Coleman, "that Irene Patterson murdered Compton?"

"It is a possibility," he admitted cautiously, "but don't bank on it." I had no intention of doing so. "You must remember," he went on, "that it is almost certain that this crime was committed by someone on the inside."

"You mean someone who works at the Exchange?" I asked. He nodded. "Well, all you've got to do is to find out under what name Irene Patterson is working, and there you are."

The twinkle grew into a smile. "It all sounds perfectly simple to you, doesn't it?"

"It does," I agreed candidly.

"It is amazing," he declared to the room at large, "how tenacious people are when it comes to giving away information," I felt myself reddening guiltily, and began to put on my hat to hide my embarrassment. He looked down at me a little grimly. "Everyone I have interviewed since the beginning of this case has been withholding some information, from your Senior Traffic Officer down. I can tell when people are not giving me the whole truth; read it in their faces. Usually I find that if they had told me everything they knew, the mystery would have been cleared up sooner. Am I not right, Sergeant?"

"That is certainly our experience, sir."

There was silence. I sought for something to say.

"It rather appears to me," I remarked presently, "that Irene Patterson and Sarah were both after the one man, and that when the former succeeded in hooking him, she wrote a very nasty letter to Compton to rub salt into the wound, so to speak."

"Quite so," said the Inspector. "We'll leave that for the moment however, and concentrate on the last letter that I gave you to read. Compared with the others, it seems to have been the most recently written."

I tried to put on my most guileless expression. "That's just what I was going to say," I declared. I knew that he was gazing at me searchingly, and attempted to meet his eyes.

"I think you know who was responsible for it," he said.

I fell to playing with the ribbon on my hat. "When I saw it first, it certainly seemed familiar," I admitted truthfully, "because of the word 'memorandum.'"

"And why is that, Miss Byrnes?"

I explained, glancing from one man to the other in the hope that they would swallow my half-truths, and not press for more.

"Although sending memorandums to the Departmental heads was one of Compton's favourite pastimes, I fancy that I know what this one was about. It created a bit of a stir at the time, more so than usual. The staff felt very hostile towards her. A few months ago—October, I think—Sarah Compton brought forward the suggestion that telephonists on duty on Sundays should not have their day off during the week. That meant, of course, that we would work two or even three weeks without a break. Quite often we are down on the sheet for alternate Sundays. Our higher Departmental officials," I added bitterly, "have no idea of what that would have meant to us, and would quite likely have favoured her idea. The part that made us mad was that it was to be limited to telephonists only, not monitors. You can understand the reason for our hostility. That was not the only anonymous letter that Compton received about the matter."

"Did you have any hand in them yourself?"

"Certainly not," I said indignantly. "I don't like that method of attack at all. As soon as I heard what was in the wind, I went straight to the woman and told her in no uncertain terms what I thought of her notion. She reported me to Bertie—Mr. Scott, that is—for rudeness. But it didn't cut any ice with him."

"Why, Miss Byrnes?" asked the Inspector, interested.

"He's a sport," I replied, "He is always fighting for us over different matters. That's why the staff work so well for him. Psychology!" I added vaguely.

There was another pause. I was congratulating myself on diverting them from the subject in hand, when I was jolted out of my complacency by the question I had most feared.

"Can you tell us, Miss Byrnes, who wrote that last letter?"

"No," I said promptly, and waited for the worst to happen.

But the Inspector turned away without a word, and started to clear up the papers on the bed. The three letters that he had selected were put carefully away in his pocket. I could see that they were getting ready to depart so I arranged my hat at the dressing-table mirror. It was sheer waste of time as the north wind which was threatening the previous day had started blowing its hot dusty breath from the desert. I would not be able to keep it on for five minutes.

'If it changes to-night,' I told my reflection gloomily, 'my hat will be ruined—not that I care much.' It was a ridiculous creation that I had got some seasons ago, when Clark took me to Henley. In a detached fashion I saw my eyes soften as his name entered my head. It is always difficult while looking in a mirror to reconcile that reflected person with oneself. Often I feel as if I shouldn't appear like that at all. Somehow my spirit does not blend with the rather square-faced fair girl that I see. My eyes met the amused stare of Sergeant Matheson. I spun around feeling annoyed and more than a little foolish. Goodness knows what he thought I was doing. Blast him, anyway.

As the Inspector locked Compton's door carefully, he asked: "Last night, you mentioned to the Sergeant about another letter that you saw the deceased reading."

I looked at him blankly for a moment before I remembered. "You mean on the roof?" I queried. "I don't think that was a letter. It might have been, of course, but it didn't strike me that way. It was too small."

We started down the narrow stairs. "Didn't you tell Sergeant Matheson that you saw Miss Compton put it into her handbag?" he asked from behind me.

I felt for the banister and glanced over my shoulder. "That is what I saw. Didn't you find the paper?"

"No," he said, opening the front door and standing aside.

"That's odd. I am sure that she put it into her bag. Someone must have stolen it." I added brightly.

"That is highly probable, Miss Byrnes." His voice was stern.

"Do you think," I asked, "that the murderer wanted that bit of paper?"

"More than likely," he agreed. I nearly stamped my foot with impatience.

His continual noncommittal replies were getting on my nerves. However, I didn't dare voice my annoyance. We got into the patrol-car again.

"I want to go to Headquarters, Matheson," said Inspector Coleman, as we drew away from the kerb. "Will you take Miss Byrnes back to the Exchange? Stay there until I come. I want to question that guard who was on duty at the door last night. Make arrangements to have him relieved and ready for me."

"Very well, sir."

The car stopped at Russell Street, and the Inspector got out. We watched him disappear into the tall modern building before the Sergeant headed the car down town. Waiting for the traffic signals to change, he said: "What about a cup of tea?"

"I'd love one," I answered with real gratitude. "This detecting business has given me a thirst."

He glanced at me uneasily in the driver's mirror, "Would you rather have a spot?"

"I would not," I said firmly, and then hesitated. "Will it be all right for you to take me—I mean—"

He was staring at the car in front of us, but I could see that he was smiling. "Quite. Anyway, I know of a nice quiet place, where it is unlikely that anyone will know us."

"Don't you believe it," I declared emphatically. "I've yet to go any-where that I don't see someone from the Exchange. I went on a trip to Port Moresby some years ago, and sure enough I met a girl from the Central the first night out."

He laughed as he ran the car into a park. "Come along," he ordered, holding out his hand. "I can guarantee this place to be private." He lead me through an arcade that opened into a right-of-way. A few yards along, an enchanting bow-window set with small lead-rimmed panes bulged out.

"And I thought that I knew all the tea-shops in Melbourne!" I declared, as we entered a tiny black-beamed room. "I've never even heard of this one."

"It's most exclusive," answered Sergeant Matheson, pulling out a chair. "It is run by two very genteel ladies of the old school. They are rather characters. One of them does the cooking. The other does the books. Gentlewomen fallen on hard times, I should say."

"It's charming," I said, looking around me appreciatively as I stripped off my gloves. The room reminded me of a painting of a Dutch interior. Although the furnishings were only imitations, they were not aggressively so. A black and white squared linoleum covered the floors, while the curtains that hung in the bow-window were of crisply starched muslin. A row of brightly coloured pottery stood on the low sill, filled with different specimens of geranium. Even the hard-wood chairs and tables were unusual in design, with slim twisted legs. Red checked cloths covered the tables set with simple white tea things. There was no raucous radio to spoil the digestion. The atmosphere was quiet and peaceful, while from one corner of the room a canary whistled cheerily. The single waitress, who had approached us as soon as we entered, wore a lavender-blue dress with a snowy lace collar. She was a comparatively middle-aged woman with a sweet, serene face.

"Tea and—?" Sergeant Matheson looked at me with brows raised.

"What is there?" I asked practically.

"Make it the usual," he said to the waitress. "I promise you will not be disappointed," he added across the table.

"They know you here?" I asked, leaning my chin on my hands.

"Yes, I'm an old customer. That woman who attended us is some sort of cousin to the two old ladies."

"She looks terribly nice. May I have a cigarette?"

He drew out his case and sprung it open. "She is," he agreed, striking a match. I glanced at him inquiringly over the flame.

"It sounds like a story. Am I right?"

He put the match to his own cigarette. Blue smoke made a veil between us. "I don't think that you'd be interested," he said, and I felt snubbed.

The light repast, which arrived with lightning service, was as delightful as the room in which we sat. From the steaming tea-pot I could detect the fragrant odour of a china blend. I was interested to see what "the usual" was; golden balls of butter nestled in gleaming lettuce leaves to be used on crescent-shaped bread rolls. At least they looked like bread, until I took a bite, and discovered that they had more the consistency of a scone. Whichever they were, they were delicious when spread with butter and creamed honey.

"Nice?" asked Sergeant Matheson with a smile.

"Very," I answered politely, trying to revenge the snub. He looked a shade disappointed, and perversely I felt mean.

The tea-shop was cool and dim, and almost empty of customers. It was past the afternoon tea hour. Soon we had the room to ourselves.

"Would you like more to eat?" asked the Sergeant, as I poured out a second cup of tea.

"I don't think that I'd better. Otherwise I won't be able to eat the three-course dinner that I left at the Exchange." He seemed puzzled. I went on to explain: "Sandwiches, cake and fruit served in a brown paper bag. Most palatable!"

Sergeant Matheson laughed. He seemed so like an ordinary man, and not the representative of the law who had taken my statement the previous night, that I asked coaxingly: "Tell me, how is our murder going? Is the inspector anywhere near solving the mystery, or shouldn't I ask?"

"You shouldn't," he answered, relighting the half-smoked cigarette that he had butted economically before tea. "He has his own ideas, but there is a lot of spade-work yet to do."

"You being the spade," I pointed out.

"I suppose so. But after all he is directing the case. He has all the responsibility."

"The Inspector seems to be an able man," I said disinterestedly and the subject was dropped.

"Do you play golf?" I asked suddenly.

"No, I'm afraid not. Are you a golfer?"

"A very humble one. What about tennis?"

He shook his head. I stared at him in surprise.

"Don't you play anything with a bat and ball? Cricket?"

His mouth was quirking up at the corners. "I am afraid that I don't play anything with a bat, but I am rather keen on basketball."

"I beg your pardon?" I asked faintly. I had always imagined that that was a game relegated to one's schooldays. I had memories of myself, clad in a short tunic, with the knee out of one black stocking, tearing around after a leather ball. The Sergeant looked quite enthusiastic.

"Best game in the world," he declared. "Fast and interesting. I used to play for the University team."

"Are there actually teams?" I asked, awed.

"Certainly," he replied, looking puzzled again. "You're not thinking that I play that tame pat-ball as kids do at school? You were, I can tell. Just let me take you to see the real thing, and you'll soon make up your mind as to whether it's a good game or not.

"Thanks, I'd love to," I lied politely. I couldn't see myself going out with a policeman, let alone to a basketball match.

"You haven't been quite frank with Inspector Coleman, have you, Miss Byrnes?" he asked abruptly. I wondered whether he had hoped to catch me unawares.

"Why do you ask that?" I parried, pulling on my gloves.

"You know who wrote that last letter. Are you protecting someone?"

I avoided his eyes, and answered lightly: "Yes and no. Is all this out of office hours, or will you use it in evidence against me?"

"I'll use your confidence with discretion, and to the best advantage," he said gravely.

I hesitated, playing with the clasp of my handbag. "Did the Inspector choose that letter as a sample of the latest of its kind, or does he think that it has some bearing on the case'?" I was trying to steer a straight course. When I heard him laughing, I looked up suspiciously.

"You are to be congratulated, Miss Byrnes, on your shrewdness. Although he has not said anything definite to me, I think that he considers that it has not the slightest connection with the crime. A sample, as you observed, for there must have been a dozen others like it written about the same matter. I might add that they all showed distinct unoriginality. The letters could have been written by one person."

"If it has no significance, why are you so anxious to find out who wrote it?"

The Sergeant looked a little sheepish. "The Inspector told me to."

I felt indignation rising up inside me. "So that's the meaning of this tête-à-tête," I declared scornfully. "You brought me here so that we could get all confidential and matey, and you could weed information out of me. Well, you're wrong, Sergeant whatever your name is. It's nearly ten years now since I came to town, and that is the lowest trick that has been played on me." I leaned forward, and said softly: "If you had been a shade more patient, and not given your game away, I would have told you what I know; but now I won't. That is, not until I have consulted the writer of that letter. Then it depends on that person whether I do or not. So you can go back to your superior officer, and tell him that his little idea did not go over so well."

He sat unmoved by my abuse, though his eyes seemed troubled. "Look here, Miss Byrnes," he said with a frank air. "I admit that it was a cad's trick, and I'm sorry that I was so clumsy. Apart from my job I really did want to take you to tea." I snorted, and pushed back my chair to get up.

"No, wait a minute," he commanded. "Do you remember what Inspector Coleman said to you this morning? To you and Miss MacIntyre? This is a dangerous business. Whether you disliked Miss Compton or not, it is up to you to help us find that person who battered her to death."

I rose to my feet in contemptuous silence.

"Please," he said, and I caught an urgent note in his voice. "This is not another act. Good Heavens, girl! Do you think that I want to investigate another death at the Exchange? Yours, perhaps? It could happen, you know."

I shivered at his words, but kept my face passive. He came round the table to my side.

"You fool, you hopeless little fool," he continued, gripping my arm. "Don't you realize that you may be holding in that silly brain of yours some half-forgotten fact that may make your life a danger to this inhuman creature?"

My eyes swept his face. Some half-forgotten fact! Last night I had been trying to remember something when I was switching at the boards, and I couldn't. Was the Sergeant right? Was that semi-conscious thought a necessary thread of evidence? Then I remembered Mac and her big tragic eyes. I couldn't speak. I wouldn't, not until she had given me my cue. Mac knew something; of that I was certain.

"You're hurting my arm," I said coldly. "Can we go back to the Exchange now? Thanks for the tea."

Sergeant Matheson removed his hand. He looked at me in a helpless way. "I could shake you," I heard him say breathlessly, as I led the way between the tables to the door.

* * * * *

He appeared so stern as we drove up town, that I began to think that I had behaved idiotically. I felt almost frightened of him. "After all, he is an officer of the law, not a shy boy," I argued with myself. "I suppose that I should tell him." But some instinct made me hold my tongue. "I'll wait until I have seen Dulcie." I thought.

Sergeant Matheson parked the car without a word, and took my arm as we crossed the street to the Exchange door. "Please tell me everything you know soon, Miss Byrnes," he begged. His voice sounded anxious. I shook my head wretchedly. What a nuisance one's loyalties could be!

The Sergeant stopped at the door to speak to the guard, but I continued on my way. A different knot of telephonists was gathered in the hall, but they gazed at me with the same curiosity as the others had that morning. I felt a strong temptation to put my tongue out at them, and was compelled to use all my will-power to pass them in silence. It had more effect than any vulgar gesture I could have made, and they dispersed rapidly. I found old Bill making his last trip for the night before switching the lift over to the automatic, and felt inexpressibly relieved. I hadn't fancied a walk up eight flights of stairs. I would never have ridden in that lift alone.

"Well, little lady?" he asked in his kindly way. "Have you had a trying day?"

"Not so little," I retorted. "Yes, I'm worn out even before I start work."

"Terrible business," he said abruptly, banging one of the indicators shut.

"Very," I agreed. Then a thought struck me. "Look here, Bill, you must know a lot about this place one way and another, driving this box up and down all day. What did you think of Miss Compton? What sort of woman would you say she was?"

He ignored a signal from the third floor and I could hear someone calling out indignantly.

"I knew her when she first came here to work," he said slowly. "I was a mechanic in the old power room at Central; before *this* happened, of course," and he took his hand from the lever to indicate his empty sleeve. I felt touched. He was probably an excellent mechanic; the way in which he looked after the lift proved that. Now, because of that bloody debacle of over a quarter of a century ago, he was reduced to the inanity of his present job.

Bill glanced at me smiling, as though sensing my sympathy. "You mightn't believe me," he declared, "but Sarah Compton was quite a good-looking girl when she was young. Not unlike yourself, as a matter of fact. Tall and fair."

"Good lord," I said blankly. "Will I look like her when I reach middle age?"

"Quite likely. I see 'em all fade as the years go by."

I gazed at him curiously, as we stopped at the eighth floor. "You've been with the Department for a long time, haven't you?"

"Since before the First World War," he nodded. "I was down on the Post Office lifts until this place was built a few years back."

"Did you ever know an Irene Smith? She was a telephonist about 1917, and married a man called Patterson."

There was a pause. He bent forward to open the doors. "Yes, I knew her. She and Sarah used to work on the same rota if I recollect properly."

I began to feel excited. "What did she look like?" I demanded. Bill pursed up his mouth. "She was of medium height, I should say, and dark-ish. Attractive, but not like Sarah, who had the most arresting face that I have ever seen. Blondes always fade quickly," he added, so regretfully that I made a mental vow to buy some more cold cream, and to use it lavishly that very night.

"Was Compton well-liked in those days?"

Bill closed the doors and sat back in his chair. "You're keeping me from going home," he reproached me. "What is your interest in Miss Compton? You'd better leave these things to people who know how to handle them," he added in a serious voice.

"So I've just been told," I remarked dryly. "Let us say that I am merely curious."

"I don't like it," he said, shaking his head. "But I'll answer anything you like to ask me."

I repeated my question. He considered it in a careful manner before he replied. "I wouldn't say Sarah Compton was very popular even then. She was the possessive type, if you follow what I mean. She would attract people, women as well as men, by her strong personality, and then hang on to them too hard. No one likes that, even nowadays. When the break came Sarah would get madly jealous and spiteful."

I nodded. "Love turns to hate, as it were. Was she friendly with this Irene Smith I was asking you about?"

"I imagine that she was," he answered, frowning. "There must have been some attachment between them. I recollect one day I overheard them quarrelling violently. It stuck in my mind because they had been insepa-rable. They were on Central positions, and I was behind the boards with a buttinsky fixing some wires."

A buttinsky, for the information of those who might think that it is some sort of Russian musical instrument, is a telephone receiver, transmit-ter and dial all in one piece. Mechanics and linesmen generally use them a great deal, for "butting in" on the wires.

"They didn't quarrel noisily," Bill went on. "They couldn't, because they were on duty. But the abuse that those two girls hurled at each other, and in such soft voices, nearly made my hair stand on end."

I laughed. "No wonder you never married."

Bill looked at me queerly. "How do you know that I am not married?" he asked. "As a matter of fact, I have a son and a daughter. My boy would be about your age."

I was frankly astonished when he told me that. Somehow it had not occurred to me that he might have a family. To cover my surprise I asked if he remembered the nature of the quarrel between Sarah Compton and Irene Smith.

"Some man, I think, but don't forget that it is over twenty-five years ago, and I've been through a war since then."

"I'm sorry," I said gently, touching his shoulder for a brief moment. "Go home now, Bill, and have your tea. How are the tomatoes this year?"

He pulled open the doors again. "They're just fine. Would you like some?"

"Would I what?" I declared enthusiastically as I stepped out.

"I'll bring some in to-morrow," he nodded through the grille. He lifted his one hand from the lever in good-bye. I waited on the landing until the lights above the lift door winked one after the other and then stopped at the ground floor.

The eighth floor seemed deserted. I walked wearily down the corri-dor to the cloakroom. It was the hour when telephonists had either gone home, or had not yet been relieved for tea. I noticed that my stolid-faced friend, Roberts, was absent from his post in front of the cloakroom, and wondered where he was, until I remembered Inspector Coleman telling Bertie that we could use the rooms again.

'I suppose all the sensation-mongers will be pouring in soon, and asking me questions,' I thought gloomily, as I opened the door. I glanced involuntarily over my shoulder, thinking that I heard a footstep. I waited a moment with my hand on the knob, my heart beating a little faster than usual. I was beginning to regret not waiting for the Sergeant to accompany me. I might have known that the eighth floor would be as lonely as a grave at this hour of the evening. I took a grip of myself and walked in boldly, even trying to whistle a little. As I opened my locker, my hand paused again. I stood frozen to the spot, straining my ears. I could have sworn that someone was moving about in the restroom.

'Pull yourself together, my girl,' I said severely. 'This is pure imagination.' But I wasn't game to have a look round the half-open door of that restroom. Then, as I was pulling my telephone out, a voice behind me said loudly and suddenly: "Boo!" I dropped my apparatus and spun round with a hand to my mouth to stop a semi-materialized scream.

"John Clarkson!" I cried furiously. "What on earth are you doing? What do you mean by giving me such a fright?"

He stood in the doorway, grinning. A look of concern came into his face as he realized that I was in earnest.

"Poor little Maggie," he said anxiously, coming forward and taking my hand. "I'm sorry I was such a brute. Do you feel all right?"

"No, I don't," I choked. "You nearly scared me out of my wits." He slipped an arm around my shoulders comfortingly, and I felt a kiss dropped on my hair. I pushed him away.

"I feel better now," I declared, turning aside to hide my embarrassment. "Just look what you made me do!" The mouthpiece of my telephone had a large piece missing out of it. I got down on the floor to look for the broken-off ebonite. "It was a rotten transmitter, anyway. You'll have to find me another. It was your fault that it broke."

"You will have the best available," Clark promised in a big-hearted way. "Are you coming to revisit the scene of the crime?"

"You talk as if I was the murderer," I protested, walking gingerly into the restroom. "It looks just the same." I stared around in surprise. Unconsciously I must have expected some change. Clark was so quiet that I glanced up at him, and saw his face was very grim.

"Yes, just the same," he repeated.

"Anyway, what are you doing here? Don't tell me that you are playing amateur detective?" I asked sarcastically. Clark walked into the centre of the room, gazing about him in frowning silence.

"Looking for clues?" I inquired in the same vein, as I caught his eye.

"Just mooching about," he answered airily. "Where have you been all day, my girl? I rang this morning, but that old battle-horse of yours said that you were asleep. Then I called in this afternoon only to find that you had left."

"I have been hunting with the hounds," I said, seating myself deliberately on the chair at the foot of which I had seen Sarah Compton sprawled in her own blood the previous night. "I'm not too sure if I'm not a hare," I continued, staring fascinated at the damp patch at my feet. It seemed the only visible link with that horrible scene I remembered so vividly.

"In with the cops, are you, my pet? What happened?"

I shrugged indifferently. "They got the bright idea of going through Sarah's papers at her room. You remember the letter that I told you about last night? They wanted to see if I could identify that with other letters she had. You'd be surprised at the amount of mail that woman got."

"I wouldn't," he said with emphasis. "She was pretty poisonous, though I suppose one shouldn't talk ill of the dead."

"That's what Patterson said this morning," I remarked absently.

"What was that?"

"Gloria Patterson. You know; the wench who thinks that he has 'oomph' or 'it' or whatever it is. She came to see me this morning with a long tale of woe that reeked to high heaven with suspicious circumstances. I told her to take it to the Inspector, and see what he would make of it. Like the majority of us, Gloria seems to have something on her mind."

Clark came to stand over me, looking very large. "Have you?" he asked swiftly. "I asked you last night, Maggie. What is it?"

"Not my hidden thought," I dismissed with a gesture of my hand. "It's just—Mac." I gazed up at him earnestly. "Have you seen her to-day at all, Clark? I can't make head or tail of her attitude. I wish you'd try to win her confidence."

"How can I, if you can't? You know how close-mouthed Gerda can be on occasions."

"You used to be pretty matey," I said in a gruff voice, examining my finger-nails. He laughed and caught my hands to pull me to my feet.

"Maggie, you funny kid!"

"Why?" I asked, still gruffly and staring at his tie. He always wore the most original ones.

"Never mind for the moment," he replied, dropping my hands abruptly. "Things are too serious just now. What happened at Sarah's place to-day?"

I strolled over to the windows, not that I could see anything from there. They were always kept tightly closed on account of the air-conditioning. I told Clark about the letters Inspector Coleman had selected and the latter's subsequent interest in Gloria Patterson.

"But she couldn't have written them," I pointed out. "I consider that it is just the long arm of coincidence. The same names, I mean."

"Maybe," he agreed briefly. "Have the police seen Patterson yet?"

"I shouldn't think so. I have just left Sergeant Matheson, and we dropped the Inspector at Russell Street. He gave me some tea," I added inconsequently.

"Indeed," said Clark in a peculiar voice. "Is he falling for our Maggie?"

"Don't talk rot," I retorted, turning to face him. "I think that he's just a low skunk. Do you know the real reason why he took me to tea? To pump information out of me, if you please. Luckily I saw through his game early in the piece."

Clark laughed gleefully. "Did you tear him limb from limb, my sweet?"

"Only verbally. It was a little too public for anything else. The pair of them—Inspector Coleman and the Sergeant—think everyone is withholding something; even including Bertie. I don't know what he can have on his mind, but I will say that during the last few weeks he has altered a great deal. I don't consider him a well man. What is your opinion?"

Clark thrust his hands into his pockets, and walked around the room moodily. "I'm as much in the dark as you. I have noticed him ageing too. I have been at him to take his leave, but he won't hear of it. He veers away from the subject, and says that he never felt better in his life."

"It's a wonder that his wife doesn't make him take a holiday. I understand that he's married," I said with a sigh. I was a bit tired of all the mysteries; Bertie, Mac and even Gloria. Not that she worried me overmuch, but I had a genuine admiration for the Senior Traffic Officer, and Mac was my best friend.

"Perhaps the Exchange has got him at last. It seems to affect people after a while. Take that Gaynor woman, for instance. Forty-five if a day, and she behaves like a giggling schoolgirl. Just plain simple. Do stop fidgeting, Clark, or you'll have me going berserk."

He came to stand near me again. "Poor little Maggie. Things getting on your nerves?"

"Everything," I declared emphatically. "You and I seem the only normal people mixed up in this business. Which reminds me. I must find Dulcie Gordon. I want a word with her."

"What about?"

"There was a letter of hers amongst Sarah's correspondence. Unsigned, but I think that she wrote it. I don't see any connection between it and this affair," I gesticulated to the wet carpet, "so it's only fair to give her a chance to tell the Inspector herself."

"I'll let her go for tea when I go back," promised Clark.

"You can thrash things out then. By the way, do you intend working at all to-day, or have the police claimed your services for the rest of the night?"

"I hope not," I said in alarm. "I'd much rather work the busiest board in the trunkroom, I assure you. Hasn't Bertie gone home yet?"

He shook his head. "He won't until I return, so I'd better get going. You can come on after your usual tea-time. What's the matter?" I had been staring over his shoulder at the door. It opened slowly, and a head came round the corner. It was Bertie Scott.

"There you are, Mr. Clarkson. I thought that I heard voices. Dear me, they've made a thorough job in here. It looks much the same as usual."

'What did you expect?' I thought sarcastically. 'Bloodstains left spattered on the walls?' I forgot for the moment that I had made the same remark.

"Will you take over in the trunkroom now?" Bertie asked Clark. "The Inspector wants to have another talk with me. Come in, Inspector. We were just talking about you," he called through the door.

'Just as we were when you came in,' I thought inwardly, wondering if he had heard me call him by his nickname.

Inspector Coleman entered with his light tread. His eyes, that passed from one to another of us, were still expressionless. Over his shoulder I could see the plain face of Sergeant Matheson, looking distinctly worried. I wondered if he had told his superior about our brush over afternoon tea, and his ultimate failure to discover the information the Inspector wanted. In my perverse habit, I felt a little sorry that I had used him so roughly. Inspector Coleman looked the type of man who would brook no mistake from his subordinates.

He motioned us to seat ourselves, saying casually: "This is a cooler room than the other. May we stay here, Mr. Scott?"

"Certainly, certainly," answered Bertie, rising a little from his chair, and then reseating himself. He looked like a little grey rabbit, lost as he was in the depths of one of the gay chintz-covered lounge chairs. "Perhaps if you lock the door, we will be quite undisturbed," was his suggestion.

"One moment," said the Inspector, taking a bunch of keys from his pocket. He selected one and put it in the inside lock. I was very glad to see that he had charge of that damned key.

"Mr. Ormond," he called out. I recognized our night guard as a burly individual entered. He had not discarded his leather holster. The hilt of his revolver peeped from his unbuttoned coat.

"This is Ormond, the night guard at the Exchange door," introduced the Inspector unnecessarily. "You may sit down, Ormond." He did so, facing our circle.

"Mr. Scott," began Inspector Coleman. Bertie jumped. "I regret to inform you that we have come to the conclusion that the crime was committed by someone who has access to this building; that is, by a telephone employee."

"Surely—" began Bertie, but Inspector Coleman cut him short.

"There is absolutely no doubt," he said curtly. "Now Ormond, I want you to tell me as far as you can remember those persons who entered and went out of the Exchange between the hours of ten and eleven."

The night guard twisted his cap nervously in his hands. He kept glancing at our Senior Traffic Officer timidly.

"Well, sir, I had just relieved Mr. Parker a few minutes before ten, and we were chatting for a while before he went home, when a man came in, showed me his pass and continued on through the old power-room passage to this building."

"Did you recognize that man?" Ormond hesitated. "Come on, man, who was it?" asked the Inspector impatiently.

"He had his hat pulled low over his face," continued Ormond, "but I could swear that it was Mr. Scott, here."

I gasped with surprise. I hadn't remembered seeing Bertie in the trunk-room the previous night.

"Is that correct?" asked the Inspector, turning to Bertie who was sitting fidgeting in his chair, with his head bent forward. Presently he raised it, and his face and bearing seemed oddly dignified and assured.

"Really, Inspector, is there anything so unusual in my entering the Exchange?"

"I think that there is, at that hour," replied Inspector Coleman grimly. "Especially as you have so far omitted to inform us of your presence here last night."

Bertie sat up very straight and stiff. I could see that he was longing to get up and pace around the room. Such vitality as he possessed must have been hard to curb.

"Have you ever returned to the building after your usual office hours before?" asked the Inspector, motioning to Sergeant Matheson, who took out the eternal note-book and pencil.

"Er—no."

"Yes, you have," I interrupted so unexpectedly that I was surprised to hear my own voice. I wasn't going to sit by and let those two men have their way all the time. The Inspector directed a very cold glance in my direction, as I continued: "You were here late that night of the bush-fires a few years ago, and then that Sunday when war was declared. I should imagine," I declared airily to Inspector Coleman, "that Mr. Scott would have every right to return if anything untoward had occurred."

As soon as I had said this, I knew that I had done wrong. The Inspector leaped on to my faux pas immediately.

"Quite so, Miss Byrnes," he agreed ironically. "According to last evening's papers, the world and local news were both entirely satisfactory. So much so, that the untoward occurrence, as you so lightly term it, has almost stolen the headlines. I should like to suggest, in complete corroboration with you of course," and he bowed slightly before my indignant gaze, "that that is just the reason for Mr. Scott's presence here last night."

John Clarkson got up angrily. "What are you hinting at?" he demanded. He was the same height as Inspector Coleman. Perhaps it was the Inspector's bulk that made him appear the bigger of the two.

"Mr. Scott," Clark continued, indicating Bertie who was still sitting as straight as an arrow, "is a well-known man, and one highly respected by all who come in contact with him. Such an accusation as you are making is completely ludicrous. I am sure that he had some perfectly good reason to come here last night."

Inspector Coleman had transferred his cold look to Clark. "Perhaps you will sit down, Mr. Clarkson, and permit Mr. Scott to give us that reason."

Clark came over to share my lounge, muttering in a way that would not have disgraced Bertie at his best. I was slightly astonished at his swift championship. I had not realized before that he held the Senior Traffic Officer in such high esteem.

Bertie had not moved at all during the tirade, although a shadow of a smile had crossed his lips, loosening the tight lines from nose to mouth. It was only a movement of the facial muscles, I thought, trying to analyse it; almost a grimace, but definitely without mirth.

"Thank you, John," he said. It was the first time that I had heard him call Clark by his Christian name. "Well, Inspector?"

"Really, Mr. Scott!" said the Inspector with an impatient gesture of his huge hands. "Haven't you understood the meaning of all this? We are waiting for your statement."

Bertie shot him a wary look. "And if I refuse?" he asked quietly.

Again Inspector Coleman moved his hands in aggravation. "If you refuse, my dear sir, you leave us with but one thing to do. But I hope that you will not be so foolish."

Bertie turned to Ormond, who had been staring stupidly from one face to another.

'A dozen murderers could have got by you,' I thought savagely.

"What time did you see me go out?" asked Bertie. Ormond thought for a minute or two. I could have sworn that I could hear his brain ticking over. The dolt!

"Cup of tea at 10.15 p.m.," he murmured to himself. "Then a smoke—about 10.25 p.m., sir," he declared suddenly. "I could swear to that, Inspector. Mr. Scott was carrying his hat in his hand, and the light fell right on to his face."

Bertie turned towards the two policemen. "What time do you say that the crime was committed?"

"Between 10 p.m. and 11 p.m. is the nearest the doctor will give us," answered Inspector Coleman. "But you don't seem to understand your extremely serious position, Mr. Scott. Unless you can give us some explanation of your movements during that hour, we shall be forced to detain you. Now, sir! Why did you come back to the Exchange after hours, when it was not your wont?" The Inspector had evidently ignored my futile interruption.

Then Bertie dropped his bombshell. I could see that the scene was working up to a climax and gripped my hands together.

"I returned," he said quietly, looking Inspector Coleman straight between the eyes. "I returned to keep an appointment with Sarah Compton."

"Get this down accurately," flashed the Inspector to Sergeant Matheson. "Go on, Mr. Scott."

Bertie threw out his hands. "That's all," he said simply. The two men stared at him blankly. At any other time I would have laughed at the frustrated expression on their faces, but just now I was concerned about Bertie. He seemed to be sailing too close to the wind for my liking.

I was certain that I saw the Inspector swallow hard. "What do you mean-that's all? What happened? Did you see Miss Compton? And, if so, at what time?"

"Certainly I saw her," Bertie said in a dignified voice. "I told you I had an appointment. It must have been about three or four minutes after ten. She was waiting for me."

"May I be permitted," asked Inspector Coleman, heavily sarcastic, "to ask where this meeting took place?" But this sarcasm went over Bertie's head. Years in the Exchange made one immune to such a figure of speech.

"Certainly," he repeated. "Miss Compton asked me to meet her in the observation room on the third floor."

I closed my eyes as an overwhelming surge of relief passed over me.

This removed Mac even farther away from the setting. Sarah must have been on her way down to the observation room to keep her appointment with Bertie when Mac saw her.

'Exactly where I said she was going,' I thought triumphantly, closing my mind to the fact that at the time it had only been a wild guess. I felt Clark's shoulder press mine for a minute, and knew that he was thinking the same as I.

Inspector Coleman continued with his questioning. "You say that Miss Compton was waiting for you on the third floor. Was she alone?"

"The observation position closed at 9.45 p.m., so that it was a good place to talk undisturbed."

"Did Miss Compton arrange this meeting?"

Bertie seemed to hesitate a minute before he nodded. "She rang my home earlier that evening, and asked me to come to it. She wanted to see me about something of the utmost importance, she said."

"Was this an unusual request, Mr. Scott?"

That peculiar smile flickered on his face again. This time I thought that he appeared a little amused. "No, I'm afraid Miss Compton was always imagining that she had matters of great moment to divulge. In fact, had she not almost implored me to come, I would have let the matter rest until the morning."

"So you sneaked into the Exchange, hoping that you would not be recognized. Why, Mr. Scott?"

"I've just told you," replied Bertie, a little irritably. He had not liked Inspector Coleman's phrasing. "I came in answer to Miss Compton's request."

"Don't quibble," said the Inspector in an icy voice. "I am asking you for the reason for this meeting."

"Miss Compton wouldn't tell me her reason over the phone," Bertie began hopefully. The Inspector cut him short, looking rather angry.

"Mr. Scott, you are wasting our time. Unless you can give us a satisfactory explanation of your conduct and at once, I must ask you to accompany us to Russell Street Headquarters."

There was dead silence after this ultimatum. Presently Inspector Coleman, rather red in the face, glanced at his watch, saying: "I'll give you thirty seconds in which to think the matter over. Then we must act."

I could guess that Bertie was already thinking furiously, and wondered what was happening behind his expressionless face. He got up from his lounge chair to take a turn about the room. I noticed the Sergeant move nearer the door; an instinctive, almost imperceptible movement. 'Quite unnecessary,' I thought scornfully.

Stealing a glance at Clark, I saw him watching Bertie's pacings with a puzzled look on his face. He felt my eyes on him, because he turned his head and frowned warningly. He must have thought that I was going to burst out with another faux pas. He need not have worried. I had cut my dash, and was quite willing to be a passive onlooker from now on.

Finally, Bertie came to stand directly in front of the Inspector; an absurd little figure beside all that bulk.

"How much information are you giving the Press?" he demanded.

"That depends," was the cautious answer. "So far the papers have only the bare outline of the crime. With such a well-known place as the Exchange, the utmost discretion is being used to protect the good name of the Department."

Bertie looked grimly amused. "If I tell you my story, there will be more good names than the Department's to save."

"I will treat your information with as much confidence as I am able," promised the Inspector.

Bertie looked round to the lounge that Clark and I shared. I thought he appeared more embarrassed than anything else. "I suppose that I can rely on the members of my staff to say nothing about what I am going to tell the Inspector?"

"Certainly, Mr. Scott," said Clark promptly, and I inclined my head without speaking.

Bertie gazed at Inspector Coleman, as if he was sizing up his opponent before he struck.

"Well, Mr. Scott?" asked the latter, with scarcely curbed annoyance. My sympathy was partly with him. Bertie could be very trying at times.

"I told you that I came here to keep an appointment with Sarah Compton," he declared slowly. "It was not the first time. We have been meeting for several years now—clandestinely."

CHAPTER IV

I closed my eyes as the room reeled a little before my gaze. I doubted my own ears for a moment, so amazing was the confession that the Senior Traffic Officer had made. The mere idea of middle-aged and seemingly respectable Bertie carrying on a love affair with a faded spinster like Sarah Compton was appalling. Having held him in such high regard for so many years, I felt shocked and more than a little disgusted. It is all very well reading about such things and feeling broad-minded, but on coming into such close contact with an *affaire* my only reaction was a strong desire to be violently ill. I fancied that Clark must have shared my emotions, because his face was blank as was its wont when his contempt was aroused.

If the Inspector had received a similar shock, he concealed it admirably. I presumed in his game nothing would surprise him.

"Are you informing us," he demanded, after blunt facts, "that the deceased woman was your mistress?"

I looked at Bertie immediately, but his face, like Clark's, was enigmatic. He answered Inspector Coleman's question in a prim voice: "Really, Inspector! Must you be quite so frank before a young unmarried woman?"

Again I felt a surge of disgust. Must he add hypocrisy to his other misdemeanours? Why couldn't he be quite open about it, now that I had discovered his clay feet?

"Perhaps Miss Byrnes would like to go," said the Inspector coldly, without taking his eyes from Bertie. But my first instinct to flee had departed.

"No, thank you," I replied, attempting to sound careless, "but I will if you want me to." I hoped that he would not dismiss me. As far as I could see the case was working up to a sordid solution with Bertie as the chief figure. Although I had had some interest in the Senior Traffic Officer's defence, my main concern had always been Mac. I could not see my loyalty to her wavering, no matter what she had done.

Inspector Coleman had started asking questions without a glance in my direction, so I concluded that he took my presence for granted.

"How long have you been—on such familiar terms with the deceased?" he asked presently. The delicate phrasing was on account of my maiden ears, I supposed.

"A matter of some years," answered Bertie promptly. "I knew her a long time ago, when we worked together as telephonists."

"As far back as 1917?" Inspector Coleman inquired in an odd voice. I pricked up my ears. This was definitely going to be interesting.

"Why, yes, I suppose so," Bertie replied in some surprise.

"She was not a—?" began Inspector Coleman hesitantly.

"No," came a firm answer cutting him short. I considered it time to stop such idiocy, and interrupted them. "You needn't spare my ears. I am twenty-five years of age; not a child, you know."

I think that they were both grateful, although neither looked around at me as I spoke. The Inspector continued: "Do you remember a telephonist about that time called Irene Smith?"

"Irene Smith," repeated Bertie slowly. "Yes, I knew her. She was a friend of Miss Compton's for a time, before they had some sort of a quarrel."

"Do you know what that quarrel was about?"

"No," he answered promptly again. And I wondered if I should tell the police about Bill's story. "Miss Compton had an unfortunate temperament, which was difficult for those of her own sex to tolerate. However, she seemed to be well-liked by men. I suppose that there was a little jealousy."

"Did you ever see Irene Smith after she left the Exchange to be married sometime in 1917?"

There was an almost imperceptible pause before Bertie answered. "Not to my knowledge," he said.

The cautious reply had the effect of making the Inspector ask: "Why do you put it like that, Mr. Scott? Did you or did you not see her again?"

"There is a possibility that I might have seen her after many years, and not recognized her," explained Bertie in his precise manner, that his inquisitor must have found excessively irritating.

"There is no need to be quite so accurate," declared Inspector Coleman dryly. "A negative answer would have been sufficient. However, we will leave that for a moment and come up to the present. Are you quite certain of the time that you left the deceased last night?"

"It was before 10.30 p.m.," said Bertie emphatically. "I can't tell you more exactly. I found Miss Compton waiting for me in the observation-room, and after—" he hesitated for a moment "we had talked for a while—say, about a quarter of an hour—I left, going down by the stairs. Miss Compton took the lift."

"Did she tell you where she was going?"

Bertie shook his head. "I presumed that she was returning to the trunkroom."

The Inspector made a sign, and Sergeant Matheson put his note-book into his hand. With his eyes on the writing before him, Inspector Coleman said: "You say that you left the deceased alive between 10.20 p.m. and 10.25 p.m. Did she seem agitated or upset about anything?"

"On the contrary, Miss Compton appeared very pleased and satisfied about something."

"Do you know what about?"

Bertie stared thoughtfully into space. "No, I don't think that I do."

"You have some idea, Mr. Scott?" But he couldn't have heard the question. Presently his eyes came wandering back. He glanced inquiringly up at the Inspector, who repeated the question. "No," said Bertie again. Almost mechanically, I considered. "I have no idea at all."

He had nothing further to add. The Inspector had demanded an explanation and he had received it. Whether Bertie could have enlarged upon his meeting with Compton, or those were all the facts he could present to the police was for the Inspector to decide. The latter seemed inclined to let the matter rest for the moment. I think he was after a more exact time of the actual crime, and did not wish to press a point until that knowledge was his. I had also observed it was his system to encourage each suspect to feel confidence in his insecure position, the age-old attempt to trap them. That was what he did for Bertie.

The Inspector turned to Ormond, the night guard, who jumped nervously as he was addressed. "You would swear in court that you saw Mr. Scott leave the building before 10.30 p.m.?"

"Yes, sir."

"Did anyone else pass you about that time?"

"A little after the half-hour a crowd of girls came out. I heard one complain of being kept late for a minute. Then, about a quarter to eleven, one girl left by herself. That blonde one who is always losing her pass," he added to Bertie, who said vaguely: "Ah, yes! Miss Patterson, I suppose. A rather scatter-brained young lady."

Inspector Coleman's eyes met mine inquiringly, and I nodded. He got up and, unlocking the door, called out for the ubiquitous Roberts.

"Get that Miss Patterson for me at once."

"I had her waiting for you this afternoon, sir," Roberts reproached, "but you had gone."

"Never mind," replied the Inspector curtly. "I want her here now."

"She'll be on duty," I warned him, "but she should be off for tea presently."

The Inspector hesitated for a moment, glancing at his watch. "She'd better have her meal first," he said in a grudging tone. "You can go too, Miss Byrnes. I'll send for you if I want you."

Bertie got up suddenly. His eyes had lost their absent-minded look. He was probably feeling exactly as Inspector Coleman had intended. I was surprised by his lack of perception and wanted to warn him that he was not out of the fire by a long way. Perhaps it was easy to be observant sitting on the fence as I was.

"If you don't mind, Inspector, I'd like to send Mr. Clarkson back to the trunkroom. There has been no one in authority for some time, which is not at all the thing."

"That'll be O.K. We have finished for the time being. You may go home too, Mr. Scott."

'Crime stands still until we eat,' I thought, rising thankfully from the lounge. I seemed to have been sitting down all day, and yet I felt utterly weary. I was not looking forward to the night's work, as I was sure that everyone would be plying me with questions about the murder. My fears were fully justified. I entered the lunchroom with my paper bag of sandwiches Mrs. Bates had cut that morning in one hand, and was greeted by cries of:

"Here she is now!"

"Hullo, Byrnes. How's the sleuthing going?"

"Where's your policeman boy-friend?"

I wondered how that had got around so quickly. I stood in the doorway eyeing them, and mentally contemplated having tea in the washroom. Then I espied Mac eating her meal in one corner away from the main table where the 3.30-10.30 p.m. staff was gathered. Gloria Patterson was in their midst. The latter was joining in the banter with a feverishness that did not escape me. She looked at me defiantly as I caught her eye.

"Good evening," I said briefly, as I passed the main table to Mac's corner. "May sit with you, Mac?"

She nodded and cleared the table a little. I noticed that her eyes were still heavily rimmed, As I went to the hot-water urn to make tea, there were some indignant remarks made behind me.

"High and mighty, isn't she?"

"She's on a special job. It's too important to discuss with us mere telephonists."

I took no heed of them. Naturally they were all agog to hear the latest news. Then Patterson said spitefully: "She's scared that someone might cut her out with her new boy-friend. Personally, I think that he looks the last gasp. But after all, Maggie is twenty-five, and no one wants to be stuck in this dump for the rest of their lives." This was a bit too much to bear silently. I strolled to their table, tea-pot in hand.

"Thank you, Patterson, for your kindly interest in my matrimonial aspirations," I said coldly. "If you dare to pass such a remark again, I shall be forced—forced, mind you—to indulge in a little blackmail."

Her eyes were frightened, but she said brazenly: "I don't know what you are talking about."

"Don't you?" I queried politely. "I think you understand me very well. By the way, Inspector Coleman wishes to see you as soon as you have finished your tea."

Gloria gave a little affected laugh. "I know that already. Just imagine, girls, he wanted to see me this afternoon to find out if I could help him at all. As you know, I was a little later off than all you were last night."

"Just how late," I remarked, drawing out a chair, "Inspector Coleman will be most intrigued to learn."

"You mind your own business, Byrnes," she flashed angrily. "You always have thought yourself too superior for words."

The other girls looked at each other in uneasy silence. Their good-natured banter, that I would have countered under normal conditions, had developed an undercurrent of animosity. It was beyond their ken. There was nothing more to be said without sounding petty and malicious. The group began to break up quietly. I sat with my back to them, and started to eat lamb and pickle sandwiches.

"Do you know if we can use the restroom, Maggie?" Gordon asked me presently.

"Yes, I think so. The police have gone out to get something to eat. Don't go, Dulcie." I detained her by touching her arm, and she glanced down at me in surprise.

"What's the matter with you, Maggie? You look quite serious!"

"It's a change, is it?" I asked smiling, "Could I have a few words with you? Mac, do you mind moving over a little? Sit down, Gordon, opposite to me." I waited until the others had filed out, Patterson the last.

"We'll have the door quite shut, thank you, Gloria," I called over my shoulder. Mac and Gordon grinned slightly.

"You're psychic, Maggie," said Mac.

"No," I contradicted, exploring some dry-looking fruit-cake, "just experienced. Now then, Dulcie, Mac doesn't know anything about what I'm going to tell you. When she does you can trust her not to say anything. She can be very close-mouthed when she wants to be," I added, glancing at Mac significantly. But her eyes were quite expressionless as they met mine.

"What are you talking about, Maggie?" asked Gordon uneasily.

I looked around the room again, to make certain that we were alone. "The police found a letter of yours in Sarah's room this afternoon," I said, watching closely for her reaction. She stared at me in puzzled inquiry.

"I've never written to Compton in my life," she replied. "I loathed the woman, so why should I send her a letter?"

I leaned across the table to speak more softly. "This was an anonymous letter." She flushed a little.

"And you think that I wrote it," she began in an annoyed voice.

"Hush, not so loud! I am not supposed to be telling you anything about this. Don't you remember a few months ago, when Sarah tried to stop days off, the stink she raised. You told me then that you were thinking of writing an unsigned petition to her to stop it."

"Only thinking," Dulcie said nervously. "I didn't actually write one at all, after what you said."

"I know, I told you that it was a silly thing to do, and that she'd be certain to trace it home to you. But are you sure that you didn't disregard my advice and write an anonymous letter?"

"Of course I didn't," she repeated in an indignant voice.

I did not know whether to believe her or not. I was losing all judgment of sincerity and prevarication.

"Very well." I leaned back and started to peel an orange. "I thought that you'd like to know first, before I told the police. Tell me," I added, changing the subject. "How are the tickets going'!" Dulcie Gordon was one of the ticket secretaries for our charity dance on the following Saturday night.

"They've nearly gone," she replied. "See here, Maggie, you say that the police have this letter. What was in it?"

"If you know nothing about it," I said between sucks at my orange, "then I am afraid that I must not tell you. All very hush-hush, you know."

"Supposing I admit that I have written anonymously at one time or another," Gordon began cautiously, but I waved her aside.

"It's nothing to do with me," I said in a firm voice. "I've given you a warning and there's no more to be said. Have you finished, Mac? Wait for me. We'll go up on the roof for a cigarette."

I got up to push my cafeteria cup and saucer through the grille. There was no one on duty in the kitchen after five, when the cafeteria service finished for the day. In doing so, I thought I heard a slight noise behind the high counter, and stiffened suddenly, my ears alert. I motioned to the others to keep on talking, but there was no repetition of that tiny sound, and I thought I must be imagining things. Why should anyone want to overhear the conversation between three telephonists having their tea? I was becoming hyper-sensitive and making a fool of myself.

Gordon was staring at me in such open-mouthed wonder that I couldn't help grinning. I supposed I must have appeared rather asinine. On the other hand, Mac was calmly clearing the table of crumbs and fruit peel as if I behaved like a pointer dog in the field five times a day. Somehow her attitude encouraged me and whetted my curiosity.

"I'll be back in a minute. Stay here," I murmured, as I slid past them to the door. Once in the corridor, I sped softly along to the cafeteria entrance at the top end. Someone was locking the grille gate noisily. I rounded the corner, and nearly fell into old Bill the liftman. He had been talking to one of the cleaners.

"Hullo," I remarked in astonishment. "I thought you'd be gone long ago, Bill. Just a minute, Mrs. Smith, before you lock up. Can I go in there?"

It was their turn to look surprised. I thought quickly.

"I dropped a teaspoon over the counter," I invented in a hurry.

"I can get it in the morning," she suggested, eyeing me curiously.

"But it belongs to me—sort of family heirloom, you know. Truly, I'll only be a second."

She unlocked the gate in silence, and I crawled under the swing-down counter into the cafeteria kitchen. It was empty. My cup and saucer were still where I had left them, and I dropped on to one knee immediately opposite. But there were only biscuit tins on the inner side of the counter. I moved one or two aside, and a tiny mouse ran out.

"Perhaps you were the culprit," I addressed him. I got to my feet and called softly through the grille to Mac.

"Come over here just where I put my cup. That's right. Now tell me if you can see me." As I got down on the floor again, a small object caught my attention. An insignificant item, almost unworthy of notice to the idle observer, but to me it was highly important.

I heard Mac's amused voice. "Maggie, what in Heaven's name are you playing at? No, I can't see you." But I took no notice of her reply as my hand closed over a small stub of a pencil. I glanced at it briefly, and got up.

"Thanks, old girl," I called, keeping my fist closed. "I'll be with you in one second."

Mrs. Smith's aggrieved voice said from behind me, "Will you be long, Miss? I want to lock up, and get away."

"I am coming now," I answered hastily.

"Did you find it?" she asked.

"What's that?" I asked in a startled voice. "Oh, my teaspoon. No, I didn't. Will you have another look for it in the morning?"

"Very well," she replied in an unbelieving tone. Her eyes wandered curiously down to my clenched hand. Bill must have gone at last. There was no sign of him.

I stood there in the corridor wondering what to do next when Mac came strolling down the passage to meet me.

"Here's your handbag," she said, holding it out.

"Thanks. I suppose Gordon has gone back to the trunkroom."

We climbed up the stairs to the roof. I had been doing exactly the same thing only twenty-four hours ago. It seemed as though a lifetime had passed since we discovered Compton's battered body.

"What's it all about, Maggie?" Mac asked, as we leaned over the rail towards the sunset sky.

"I don't know," I replied unhappily. "I don't know at all. Everything and everyone are out of perspective to me. First you," and she turned her profile to the red sky, "then Gloria, Bertie, Gordon, and now Bill."

"Bill!" Mac exclaimed in amazement. "You mean the liftman. What's he done?"

"Look," I said, opening my hand. She bent over it.

"An indelible pencil. Where did you find it?"

In some surprise, I saw the purple mark on my damp hand, "I wonder!" I cried excitedly. The note that Sarah had received so precipitately in the lift came before my mental vision. I could swear that it had been written in an indelible pencil. That meant my mind leaped on and upwards until Mac's laughing voice called me down to earth.

"Maggie, Maggie, what's the matter with you? Why are you looking so fierce?"

I glanced down at her. "Am I? I don't feel fierce. Only rather sad. Listen, Mac. You know that note Inspector Coleman gave you to read this morning. Would you say that it had been written in an ordinary pencil, or—" and I held out my hand again.

She gazed at the indelible pencil again, and then at me. I could see her dark eyes shining with excitement also.

"Great balls of fire!" she ejaculated, borrowing from Scarlett. "You're right, Maggie. Where did you find it?"

"On the floor behind the cafeteria counter. When I dashed off like a madwoman at tea, I thought that I heard someone there. This," and I held the pencil up, "proves that there must have been someone behind the counter trying to eavesdrop."

"Did you see anyone?" Mac asked eagerly.

"Not inside. That cleaner-woman let me go in before she locked up. But Bill was standing just outside."

"Oh," said Mac.

"Quite," I agreed. "Rather nasty, isn't it? That's the rotten part. I'd hate him to be mixed up in anything like this."

"What's the full story, Maggie? I promise you that I'll be close-mouthed." Her lips twisted a little ironically.

I repeated the facts I had given John Clarkson in the restroom that afternoon concerning the three notes Inspector Coleman had given me to read. Mac interrupted me once. "Those first two letters, Maggie? Were they anonymous too?"

"No," I replied, speaking very slowly and distinctly. "The writer's name was Irene Patterson."

I heard Mac's smothered ejaculation, and went on as she made no further comment. "The similarity between those first two notes and last night's was not the writing, but the fact that practically the same wording was used. I want you to keep that point in mind. To continue, I came back to the Exchange and found Bill on his last trip in the lift. We got talking and I started to ask him a few questions. He remembered without hesitation this girl-friend of Compton's. He was a mechanic at that time. One day he overheard them quarrelling violently about some man. He was able to tell me all this without once scratching his head or saying 'um.' " I paused significantly.

"Are you trying to inform me," Mac demanded, "that Sarah and her girl-friend were both after the one man, and that you think that man was Bill!"

I nodded wretchedly. "It fits in. He talked about Sarah as if—well, as if he had had some sort of an affair with her, and when she got too possessive, he became weary of her and turned to Irene. He is married, you know, with a son and a daughter."

Mac flung her cigarette high into the air. I watched its gleaming descent.

"Silly thing to do," she remarked. "It might start a fire."

"It should be pretty safe," I answered without caring much.

She turned to look at me quizzically. "Are you cogitating on the same thing as I am?" she asked.

"I wouldn't be surprised. Have you ever heard Bill's surname?"

"No, never, have you?"

I shook my head and remarked cautiously: "It could be so. He said that he had a daughter."

Mac's lip curled a little. "I can't see her claiming a parent in a liftman, can you?"

"No, indeed," I agreed, "little snob!"

Mac turned towards the sky again. "Well, it's none of our business," she said in an even voice. She had retired into her shell again after a brief emergence.

"Isn't it? Are you sure, Mac?"

She made no reply. I sighed, "Listen, old girl," I said earnestly. "I'm your friend. Why are you like this? Can't you tell me what your trouble is? Surely I can help in some way."

She gave me a quick cold glance. "Mac," I said miserably, and she laughed, a short and ugly sound.

"Forget it, Maggie. I swear that there's nothing wrong. Let's get back to Bill again. You think he was trying to overhear our conversation at tea, and that he dropped that pencil as he crouched behind the counter?" I nodded. "It sounds a bit melodramatic. What about the cleaner-woman? Wasn't she there, too?"

"She was on her rounds, locking up the building. She wouldn't have seen him. Why was he so long leaving the Exchange if he told me some time previously that he was going home?"

Mac digested this in silence. "You're probably right," she admitted presently. "But what are you going to do about it? Tell Inspector Coleman?"

"I'll have to, I suppose. By the way, he is interviewing young Gloria now. There's a chance he might be learning all this from her. I hope so. Bill is a nice person. I'd hate to have to tell the Inspector what I think. But you remember what he said this morning about telling everything we know."

Mac faced me quickly. I waited for her to speak but she didn't. She only gave that horrid little laugh again. It hurt me to the heart. And in my heart I knew Mac's friendship meant a great deal to me. I spoke lightly trying to disguise that hurt.

"Is it time that we went back to work, or rather that I commenced? I feel like Jekyll and Hyde. Two personalities. Only mine are not quite so sinister; one a detective, and the other a hardworking telephonist."

"Where does Gordon come in?" Mac asked abruptly. We moved off, skirting the lift cabin, where I had overheard Compton the previous night having fun and games.

"Again, I don't know. Did you consider that she was telling the truth when she denied all knowledge of yet another anonymous letter? As far as I can see, this crime has been conducted by correspondence. It's all most confusing."

"I wouldn't care to give an opinion," Mac said slowly, knitting her straight brows. "I haven't had many dealings with Gordon. I should say that she was a straightforward type of girl."

"I thought so of most of my fellow-men, once," I remarked with a sidelong glance. "Now, I am even beginning to doubt my own veracity. To bear that out, our friends in the Force have both more or less called me a liar."

"You're becoming very cynical, Maggie," Mac reproved. "Too much does not suit you."

"That's what my mother would say," I agreed absently. "Which reminds me, I haven't read her letter yet. One came from home this morning, but in the excitement of having Gloria for lunch, I forgot it."

"I wish you wouldn't get away from the point," Mac complained, as we ignored the lift in an unspoken agreement, and went down by the stairs.

"You should talk," I exclaimed. "You mean my little warning to Gordon? She's a silly fool if she's keeping something back. I don't mind her not telling me, but she forgets that this is a very serious affair, and that she's up against trained minds which doubt every word you utter. Damn!" I stopped on the stairs.

"What's the matter now?" asked Mac patiently.

"I haven't got my outfit. A telephonist can't work without a telephone, you know. Didn't I leave it in the lunchroom?"

"I didn't notice it."

"I couldn't have taken it out of my locker after all. That means that I'll have to go back. You needn't wait for me. Tell Clark that I'll only be a minute."

* * * * *

I retraced my steps, leaving Mac at the trunkroom door. 'Silly ass!' I muttered to myself, taking the stairs two at a time. 'I remember now. I was just getting it out when Clark gave me that hearty fright. Then Bertie and the Inspector rolled along. I'll be glad when I settle down to some nice quiet switching, and stop all this rushing about.'

The corridor was now deserted and appeared extra gloomy and silent to my sharpened senses. When I neared the cloakroom door I heard a comforting murmur of voices from the police officers' temporary office, and bars of light shone through the corrugated panel at the top of their door.

'If that blasted restroom door has been locked again,' I thought grimly, 'people would be quite correct in suspecting me.' However it was still standing ajar as we had left it before tea. Beyond giving it a cursory glance I took no further notice as I hunted for my locker key, holding my bag up to the dim light.

Some sixth sense told me something had happened as soon as I put the key in the lock. I hesitated a brief moment before I swung open the door. A sheet of paper, which had been pushed under it, slipped to the floor. Bending to retrieve it, I saw my name printed in block letters. With my telephone held dangling from one hand, I glanced through it thoughtfully, and on impulse walked straight out of the cloakroom to knock at the Inspector's door.

The murmur ceased abruptly, and the ensuing silence was broken by the scraping of a chair. Sergeant Matheson opened the door, the look of surprise on his face changing quickly to one of eagerness.

"The bad penny again," I said coldly. "See what you can make of this."

He stood aside to let me enter. Inspector Coleman raised a frowning face from his papers. On the opposite side of the desk Gloria Patterson sat, her cheeks flushed defiantly. Her eyes looked like those of a trapped animal. I don't mean a caged tiger; more like a sheep which had caught its wool in barbed wire.

"Where did you find this letter?" asked Sergeant Matheson, as I seated myself calmly. I was getting used to this office and its occupants.

"In my locker," I replied, giving Gloria another appraising glance. She appeared as though she had been having a bad time, and I almost felt sorry for her now that she had realized just what an actual *rencontre* with the police meant. They would stand no nonsense, and one couldn't expect them to.

"Do you see, sir?" asked the Sergeant eagerly, "exactly the same type of printing."

"And the same paper," I added. "Tell me, would you say that it had been written in indelible pencil. The light was bad outside."

Inspector Coleman moistened his forefinger and rubbed. "No, it isn't," he replied, turning his keen gaze on me. "Why do you ask?"

"I just wondered," I said airily. That meant that the note had been written and put into my locker during the short time when Mac and I had been on the roof; the author, on discovering the loss of the indelible pencil, had used an ordinary one. However, that did not prove that Bill had written it, because there were Gordon and Patterson to remember. By the former's attitude, I was convinced that she knew something about the little practice of anonymous letters, though it hardly seemed likely that she would go straight from my warning at tea to repeat her performance. On the other hand, she would have had ample opportunity, just as my young friend who was sitting in the same room had.

Inspector Coleman had been searching through his brief-case. He brought to light a grimy slip of paper. He submitted this to the same experiment of rubbing with a wet finger. He looked up and said with a curtness that smacked of chagrin, "An indelible pencil was used on Miss Compton's letter. But how did you guess?"

"It came before my mind's eye some time ago," I had no intention of telling them about my discovery behind the cafeteria counter. I had absolutely nothing to go on in thinking that Bill was the culprit, and to drag him into this affair without proof was unjust and foolish. 'Let the police ferret things out for themselves,' I thought obstinately.

"May I read my correspondence again?" I asked. "I only gave it a brief glance and then came straight to you. Thanks." It was such a typical example of an anonymous letter that I was almost bored. I was warned against prying into affairs which did not concern me, and the note concluded with a dark threat to my general health and well-being. I felt rather flattered by the writer's confidence in my perspicacity. Whoever wrote it did not understand that whatever knowledge I held had been thrust upon my unwilling attention.

"I suppose that you will want to keep it," I said, relinquishing it with a sigh as I thought what an interesting relic it would be to show my grandchildren.

"If you don't mind," said Inspector Coleman gravely. I was amazed at his sudden courtesy.

'Don't tell me that he is starting to respect my powers of deduction,' I thought.

A tap came at the door, and Sergeant Matheson opened it. Part of his work seemed to be the opening and shutting of doors. John Clarkson's anxious face appeared.

"Excuse me, Inspector, but do you know where— Oh, you're here, Maggie. Just when are you going to do some work?" he asked in an exasperated voice.

"They're after me, Clark," I said in a flippant manner. "I've been showing Inspector Coleman my last warning."

"What are you talking about?" he asked almost irritably. "See here, Inspector, if you don't want Miss Byrnes, we are terribly short-staffed tonight. As a matter of fact, I want her to do some monitoring."

"Am I to step into the dead woman's shoes?" I demanded.

"Please be quiet, Miss Byrnes," ordered the Inspector sternly. "Your sense of humour is extremely ill-timed at this moment. I am very sorry, Mr. Clarkson, I'll let Miss Byrnes go as soon as possible. Perhaps if Miss Patterson is of any use, we can dispense with her for the time being."

Clark gave a noncommittal grunt, and held the door wider for Gloria, who made her exit with unflattering haste. We listened to their footsteps receding down the corridor before Inspector Coleman spoke.

"Now, Miss Byrnes," he said in a persuasive way that fitted him as badly as his suit. "bringing this letter straight to us is the first sensible thing that you have done." I eyed him apprehensively, wondering what his game was. "I admit that you have been of great material assistance to us. For an amateur, you show remarkable shrewdness. I am sure," he continued, laying on the blarney with an O.S. in trowels, "that if you could be completely frank with us, you would help us solve the case in no time. Sergeant Matheson tells me that you know the name of at least one anonymous letter-writer amongst your fellow-telephonists. I consider the first step to clearing up this horrible affair is to learn the identity of that person. Now, will you help us?"

'Poor Dulcie,' I thought. 'I can't see you in the role of murderess, but here goes.'

"I told Sergeant Matheson this afternoon," I said distinctly, "that I would not give him the required information until I had, in fairness, consulted with that person concerned, and given her the chance to tell you herself."

"Her!" exclaimed the Inspector. "Then it is one of the telephonists."

I nodded. "However," I continued, "she disclaims all knowledge of the particular letter to which you are referring. As I am inclined to believe her, seconded by another opinion, do you still want to know her name?"

"Whilst admiring your loyalty," observed the Inspector gravely, "I think that it would be wisest."

I took a deep breath. "Dulcie Gordon. She is working from 3.30 p.m. until 10.30 p.m. to-day, if you want her."

"Gordon?" queried Inspector Coleman, frowning.

"Miss Patterson mentioned her name," reminded the Sergeant and his superior officer's brow cleared.

"That's right. Her opinion of Miss Gordon's character was not very high. Sly and deceitful, I think Miss Patterson said."

"Dulcie is not a bit like that," I assured the Inspector. "You never want to take much notice of Gloria Patterson. In any dealings that I have had with Miss Gordon, I should say that she was a very honest type of girl, and extremely conscientious at her work. You can learn a lot about a person's character by working with them, you know."

"Quite true," he agreed. "Tell me, then, your reading of Mr. Scott's."

I glanced down at my hands as I felt myself flushing a little. "My opinion of Mr. Scott," I said slowly, "is wholly at variance with the facts he gave you before tea. He is a splendid boss to work for, and one who knows how to get the best from his staff by his fair dealings with us. However, I must be wrong in my former beliefs."

"Why, Miss Byrnes?"

I looked up straight into those keen eyes. "Because it seems impossible that a man with a private life such as his can be so respected by his employees."

Inspector Coleman shrugged ever so slightly. "You are what is known as straitlaced, Miss Byrnes. I confess I am inclined to agree with you. In furtherance of our duty, we come up against some very sordid details. Although I most certainly do not condone murder, I should say Sarah Compton was a thoroughly bad woman."

"I am not too sure," I disagreed, though not out of my usual perverseness. "At one stage last night, when I was talking to her on the roof—you remember that in my statement—she made me feel almost humble. It was nothing that she said," I assured him hastily, "but her face changed as if she forgot that I was there. It's absurd to describe it so, but she looked—noble; rather like a tragedy queen, but not a scrap histrionic. I'm sorry to be wasting your time like this giving you my impressions. I don't suppose that they are of any use."

"Not at all," he answered politely, but I could see that he was bored stiff. "An accurate insight into the murdered person's character is often a leading clue to discovering the identity of the killer. Will you tell us again, in your own words, the facts of that meeting with the deceased on the roof of the Exchange building?"

I sighed inaudibly. I had gone over and over every detail connected with Compton in my mind, until I was utterly disheartened and weary. But I repeated my story obediently, and the Inspector listened attentively, now and then interrupting to ask me a question.

"The last time you saw the deceased was at about 9.45 p.m.?"

"I didn't see her," I corrected yet again.

"No, that's right," he said hastily, "you heard her; we have the docket that she queried you about, from Mr. Scott. Is that the one?" He handed me a white out-docket. I took it without interest, and returned it to the Inspector after a casual glance.

"That's the one," I confirmed. "On the back, you will see her numerical signature after the *précis* of the inquiry. Some stupid woman rang up to find out why her call hadn't come through. Although I had told her myself, five minutes previously, that the particular person whom she wanted was out, she needed a monitor to impress it on her. You'd be surprised the number of subscribers who doubt a telephonist's word."

"Would I?" he asked, with such a gleam of amusement in his eyes that I could guess his thoughts. "On the back, Miss Byrnes," he continued, turning over the docket, "is a most mysterious code of which neither the Sergeant nor myself can make head or tail. '9.45 p. ppu 10.30 p. ag D376,'" he read out.

"That's just our telephonic way of writing that the particular person is unavailable until 10.30 p.m., and is to be tried again. D376 was Compton's signature," I explained. "We haven't the time nor the space to write it down in full, so some bright person in the Department worked out this code. It's really quite simple, being based on phonetics." I thought that Inspector Coleman looked a shade disappointed, and wondered if he had expected it to be a last message from Sarah Compton.

"Did you go straight home last night, Miss Byrnes?" he asked suddenly, and continuing to study the docket. I was caught unawares, but managed to conjure up a haughty manner on the instant.

"Really, Inspector, that is my own private affair. I don't think that you have any right to ask such a question. Whether you have or not, I most certainly will not answer it."

He shrugged again. "As you will," he replied carelessly, "but it so happens that you went home in a police car, and that we have every right to inquire where it went."

I bit my lip in vexation. "I suppose there was a dictaphone all set up in it to record our conversation," I said sarcastically.

"Quite correct," he declared, grinning in a brazen fashion.

'Heavens!' I thought. 'What did I say in the car last night, and Mac—'

"That's rather low," I said hotly, "considering that we all have alibis."

The Inspector seemed apologetic. "Quite an accident, I assure you. Sergeant Matheson only discovered it this morning, when Mr. Clarkson returned the car to Russell Street."

"He would," I remarked bitterly, meaning the Sergeant. "I thought such things only happened on the films."

The Inspector leaned forward confidentially. "As a matter of fact, it was a wireless patrol car, and your conversation went through to Headquarters on the air. They thought that it might prove useful, so it was recorded. Actually there was no dictaphone."

"I am very relieved to learn the differentiation," I returned, sarcastically again. "Are we all to be arrested?"

"Not just yet," I was assured. "There were one or two interesting points, that perhaps you will enlarge upon for us. Tell me," he continued conversationally, "have you discovered what Miss MacIntyre has on her mind?"

"I don't know what you are talking about," I said flatly, but avoiding those keen eyes.

"Don't play the simpleton, Miss Byrnes. It is not at all in keeping with your previous evidence of acuteness. Come now, I have asked you a question."

"And I refuse to answer it."

The Inspector looked me over speculatively. "One of these days," he observed, "you will carry your sense of loyalty too far. It is obvious even to the meanest intelligence that Miss MacIntyre is hiding something. We intend to find out what it is."

I shook my head. "Not from me, anyway. Last night Miss MacIntyre was tired and distraught, as were we all. We don't stumble on to messy corpses half a dozen times a day in the Exchange. Is it any wonder that we were irritable and suspicious with each other? Miss MacIntyre's demeanour is only a result of this unnatural environment."

"Very well," answered the Inspector, in a disbelieving fashion. "We will pass over last night for the moment. Let's talk of something else. I believe you had a caller this morning."

"You know everything," I said with mock admiration. The party was becoming rough. "As a matter of fact I had two. I suppose my friend Patterson has told you all about it. I hope you found her entertaining."

"Most illuminating," he agreed. "What did she want of you?"

I considered his question carefully, before I parried: "What did she tell you?"

"She gave us some confused and slightly mendacious story, how everyone in the Exchange hated Miss Compton except herself, who was her only friend. She even obligingly supplied the names of several persons, including yourself, who would willingly have murdered your late monitor. She further informed us that she called on you this morning to beg you to confess to your crime, and save unnecessary distress among your fellow telephonists."

"Better than I expected. I thought you'd have fun. Did you get any sense out of her at all?"

"Only that she saw a masked and cloaked figure stealing down the stairs, gun in hand."

"Heaven spare my days!" I ejaculated. "Do you call that sense? Did she tell you that she saw Sarah Compton alive at about 10.37 p.m. last night?"

That made them sit up with a jolt.

"What!" shouted Inspector Coleman, "Quickly, Sergeant, get this down."

As Gloria had been telling calumnious tales about me, I felt that I had sufficiently redeemed my promise to her to speak the truth.

"Miss Patterson paid me a visit this morning to get my advice. She said," and I winced at the memory, "that I was always so sensible. Anyway, she poured forth a tale of woe about being late off, and seeing Compton in the cloakroom, and how she was too scared to tell you in case she would be suspected of having murdered her."

"Quite right," interrupted the Inspector grimly. "We would. Go on."

"That's about all. Except that it sounded rather fishy to me. Patterson was in the cloakroom and as soon as she saw Compton come in, she ducked behind the lockers to avoid her. Sarah had told her that she was to work overtime as she was so late back from relief, and as I know she didn't sign off until 10.35 p.m., I would have thought her conscience was quite clear. But she remained hidden until the coast was clear, when Compton went into the restroom."

"Did she have to unlock the door," Inspector Coleman demanded.

"I was expecting that," I answered resignedly. "I asked exactly the same question, but the fool of a girl couldn't tell me. She was so bent on escaping unseen that she didn't take any notice."

"All this is very interesting. We have succeeded in limiting the time of the murder to a half an hour. Whoever committed the crime certainly planned it to the last possible moment. A very clever person, and one who must know the working of the Exchange very intimately. Any suggestions?"

"None," I replied promptly, crossing my fingers.

"Just a shade too quick, Miss Byrnes. We don't like amateurs in the field. They invariably cause accidents and often get injured themselves. That is a friendly warning."

"Thank you," I said, getting up. "I will bear it in mind. May I go to work now, please?"

Sergeant Matheson rose to open the door.

"Wait one moment," called the Inspector. I turned back from the threshold inquiringly. "I'd like to go along with you. I have never seen the inside of a Telephone Exchange. I daresay Mr. Clarkson will not mind if you show us around."

"You can ask him," I answered, not relishing the idea of becoming a further butt for my facetious fellow telephonists.

As we walked down the corridor, our footsteps echoing dully on the polished linoleum, I buckled on my apparatus in the forlorn hope that I might be given a position to work instead of the job of escorting two policemen around the trunkroom. Clark was talking on the Senior Traffic Officer's telephone as we entered, but he turned around quickly with a frown between his eyes. I approached the desk, and waited until he had finished what he was saying.

"Hurry, Maggie," he said, banging down the receiver and coming round the desk. "Take off that headset and patrol the Sydney boards."

Buzzers were shrilling on the inquiry posts, and a couple of monitors tried vainly to cope with the numerous lights calling for their attention.

"These two gentlemen," I said, unclipping my neckband and dumping the apparatus on the table, "want someone to show them around the trunkroom."

I thought I heard Clark mutter something under his breath as he turned towards them. "I am sorry, Inspector, but I really can't spare any of my staff any longer. Just one minute." He broke off to lift one of the ringing telephones on the desk, calling at the same time to a monitor, "Another half-hour on Sydney, please, Miss Marks. Is that the Sydney traffic officer?" he asked into the mouthpiece, turning his back to us.

I glanced at the two policemen, and shrugged helplessly. "You'd better wander around at your own sweet will," I advised. "I'll be patrolling the floor, so you can ask me anything you want to know. You'll have to excuse me now."

I dashed over to the nearest light that I saw shining on the boards. These were operated by telephonists when they required assistance from higher beings than themselves.

"Yes, what is it?" I asked quickly.

"Is that the new boy-friend, Maggie?" the telephonist asked, closing her key. "Take this down to the Tasmanian board, and tell them that I will release Sydney 10 line right away. I don't admire your taste, sweetheart. He's fearfully plain."

"Shut up," I said coldly. "I'm acting monitor to-night, so I can report you if you don't get on with your work."

"You and who else?" she asked scornfully. I made a mental resolve not to go near that girl again that night: not even if she flashed for assistance a dozen times. The cheeky little devil!

Inspector Coleman had been speaking to Clark, who was looking annoyed and throwing me reproachful glances. I made appealing faces at him, endeavouring to make him understand that it was not my fault, and that I found them as great a nuisance as he did. Presently the Inspector strolled leisurely down the room among all the darting figures to one of the inquiry posts. When I came up to answer a buzzer, he was turning over the inquiry pads on the table top of the position.

"Excuse me," I said, pushing him aside without any ceremony to get to the telephone. "Trunk Inquiry," I announced into the mouthpiece. I felt a touch on my shoulder, and glanced up at the Inspector. He was holding out a sheet from a pad. As I was listening to a long and involved story from an irate subscriber, it was rather difficult to hear what he was asking me.

"Just one moment," I cut in on the subscriber's story. I covered the mouthpiece with one hand. "What did you say, Inspector?" I asked with exasperated calm. I realized that I was in for a night of it, so I considered it as well not to lose my patience at the beginning.

"Is this what was used?" he repeated.

I frowned, trying to get his meaning and remember the details of the inquiry that I had just taken. "The anonymous letters?" I asked quickly. "Yes, that's the paper. I'll be back in a jiffy." I hurried over to the main Sydney board to thumb through the pile of dockets.

"Did you tell them?" someone whispered in my ear. I looked round into Dulcie Gordon's anxious eyes.

"Tell whom what?" I asked, continuing my search. "W M number to Petersham. Has anyone seen it?"

"About the letter," Gordon said softly, marking off a docket.

"Yes," I answered, "but don't worry me now, I'm too busy. Mavis, have you got W M to Petersham?"

A telephonist farther along the boards glanced up. "Tell them to hang up," she said impatiently. "I've been trying to get the caller for the last ten minutes. They've been continually C.B.Y."

"Silly fools!" I remarked. "It's all right, Dulcie. There's nothing to worry about."

"I didn't write it, really, Maggie," she insisted in a low voice.

"Forget it until after work," I said, putting my hand on her shoulder as I passed her to return to the inquiry post.

"Your number is waiting," I told the subscriber. "Will you hang up and we'll connect you right away." I planked the receiver down viciously. "They've been C.B.Y. for I don't know how long," I told the Inspector, who was standing aside looking amused.

"More code?" he inquired.

"It means that the calling subscriber's line is busy," I explained, taking up the receiver again. "Wait until I've cleared this post, and I'll give you an idea where things are. Trunk Inquiry!"

"You girls certainly earn your bread," I heard him remark. I gave him a grateful smile. A word of commendation now and then works wonders with telephonists. Unfortunately they are few and far between. The majority of subscribers suffer under the delusion that our chief occupations are knitting and reading. Indeed, an acquaintance of mine, while commenting once on the number of pullovers that I possessed, suggested in all seriousness that I had ample time to make them at work.

Presently, the traffic became a little easier. I led Inspector Coleman around the room with Sergeant Matheson bringing up the rear, notebook and blunt pencil in hand. I had often acted as a guide at a time when visitors were permitted to look over the Exchange, and it has always been my private opinion that anyone who possesses a telephone should first be initiated into the workings of the whole telephonic system. They would leave the Exchange enlightened and more tolerant if that was the rule. As a matter of fact, Sarah Compton had put forward a similar suggestion a few years previously, but it had been dismissed as being too immense a proposal to be practicable. It was the only matter with which I had been in complete accord with Compton.

Inspector Coleman proved so interested that I asked John Clarkson if I might use the Senior Traffic Officer's buttinsky to let him listen in on a board or two. Clark went through the deep drawers of Bertie's desk in unenthusiastic silence.

"It's not here," he said. "Have a look on top of the booking positions."

"Never mind," I replied, picking up my own telephone set from the table. "They can use this."

"Sorry," I said, returning to my protégés, "but we can't find the one and only buttinsky anywhere." Certain that I would be asked what a buttinsky was, I hastened to explain, while helping Inspector Coleman adjust my telephone to suit his bulk. I always think that it is a ludicrous sight to see a middle-aged male in telephonists' gear; rather like a necklace hung about a hippopotamus. Headsets are built for purely feminine use, or at the very most lads of seventeen or eighteen who are sometimes employed in the Exchange for the dog-watch shifts. It is a strange, but true, fact that the stronger sex invariably makes poor telephonists; perhaps because the work calls for a mind that can deal with several things at once, and that is a feminine trait only.

Quite unintentionally I took Inspector Coleman to listen in on Dulcie Gordon's board. The poor girl became so terribly nervous that I could have kicked myself for making such a mistake. Perversely, the Inspector chose to stay there for quite some time, now and then asking Dulcie a question. I hoped that he did not realize who she was. Presently I persuaded him to leave and to go on to one of the Tasmanian boards, where I explained the working of a M.X. call—"that is one that passes through more than one switching station—for example a call from a country town in Tasmania to a country town in New South Wales."

I was trying to bore them, so I droned on, using technical terms in the hope that they would become tired and leave. But the Inspector, in an annoying fashion, remained interested; especially when I talked in telephonic code. He asked many questions.

Finally I relieved him of my headset and took him to see the delay board and the sortagraph position where Mac was working. We walked down the room, the Inspector sidestepping to avoid a rushing monitor and thereby colliding with her as she did the same.

"Where were you working last night, Miss Byrnes?"

"On Sydney 1 position. Where you were listening in just now. After 10.30 p.m. I moved up a few boards and coupled them together, so as to take all the interstate lines."

The Inspector stopped, and turned around to survey the room. "And Miss MacIntyre? Where was she?"

"On the other side," I said, pointing to the country boards. She closed up her own position at 9.50 p.m. and—went to give a hand," I finished lamely. I had nearly let out about Mac's relief; not that it would matter now that they had Gloria tabbed, but I knew that Mac did not want me to tell them. 'Mine not to reason why etc.,' I quoted inwardly.

"This is the sortagraph," I went on, as we came up to Mac. She barely looked up from her work, and not once did I see her tiny hands falter as she received, dispatched and filed dockets after a brief, casual glance at each. I had never known Mac to make a mistake for all her careless appearance while working. That was her chief charm: being able to get through an extraordinary amount of work without becoming hot and bothered like the majority of telephonists did in times of stress. As I explained the system of the air-pressure pipes bearing the dockets to the sortagraph, and the filing and dispatching, I noticed for the first time that the Inspector did not seem frightfully keen on my monotonous discourse. He ran his hand over the file at the side of the sortagraph absentmindedly.

"Miss MacIntyre," he asked suddenly, "was this where Miss Compton came last night?"

Mac glanced over her shoulder casually, nodded and returned her attention to the board. Inspector Coleman approached her right side. so as to be able to speak in her uncovered ear.

"What was it that she said to you?"

Mac looked him over for a moment. "You have my statement," she replied coolly. "You'll find what she said in that. Anyway, I doubt if Miss Compton spoke to me at all."

The Inspector remained undampened. "It was something like 'that'll fix it,' wasn't it?"

Mac shrugged, and frowned over a docket. "Maggie, take this back to Adelaide, and ask them to complete it. 'Time disconnected' is missing. I don't suppose that silly fool that they've got switching there will know what it is all about if I send it back by the tubes."

'Oh, yeah?' I thought to myself. 'I can take a hint, my love.' I hurried to the interstate boards, keeping one eye on Mac as she turned to speak to Inspector Coleman. He nodded in a satisfied way, and gestured to Sergeant Matheson to take notes. I got held up by a blazing inquiry post, which required my attention until the Inspector came sauntering back with his hands clasped behind him; looking, in my opinion, like the cat that had swallowed the canary. I was feeling more than a little hurt that Mac had dismissed me so perfunctorily, and longed to know what it was that made the Inspector appear so satisfied.

"Will you show me Country Board 14?" he requested. "Miss MacIntyre says that she was working there last night."

Obediently, I led the way across the room, explaining the slightly different operating needed for the toll calls.

"I see," he said, pivoting slowly to survey the distant interstate boards. "Miss MacIntyre was working more or less on a line with you, although with the space of the room between you, while Mr. Clarkson was at the Senior Traffic Officer's table near your board."

"That's correct. When Mr. Clarkson saw that I was so busy, he came to help me until the all-night girls arrived."

"Did Mr. Clarkson use the handset that you were looking for to-night?"

asked the Inspector quickly.

"No, just an ordinary outfit. As a rule, he uses the buttinsky. I suppose that Mr. Scott must have put it away somewhere before he left the Exchange."

"Is that usual?"

"Yes, I think so," I said in some surprise. "Certainly not unusual anyway. The buttinsky is officially Mr. Scott's, so he can do what he likes with it."

"Has he done so before?"

"I can't remember," I answered hesitantly. "Mr. Clarkson may be able to tell you. Why are you so interested in it?"

"You are here to answer questions, not to ask them," he returned coldly. "However, to satisfy your curiosity, I will tell you that we are concerned with all heavy instruments, especially ones that are missing." He turned on his heel and left me.

I felt myself go cold, as I stood in the middle of the room staring after the two police officers. They approached Clark again, and I watched them go through the drawers of the Senior Traffic Officer's desk with him. I had forgotten that the weapon that had killed Compton was still undiscovered. I had no doubt of the significance of the Inspector's words. What a perfect instrument with which to batter anyone to death! Whether they found it in Bertie's locker or not, things would look very black for him. They had only to compare the aspect of the wounds on Sarah's head with a similar buttinsky from the power room to satisfy any doubt that they may have had as to the nature of the weapon. Around me telephonists were going off duty, and I felt vaguely annoyed as I caught their curious glances in my direction. But I stayed where I was, my mind in a whirl of confused facts and speculations, until a hand touched my arm.

John Clarkson's voice said sharply in my ear: "Maggie, what on earth are you day-dreaming about? Get your outfit quickly, and let those 10.30 p.m. girls go."

"Is it time already?" I asked confusedly. The night seemed to have flown. "Clark," I whispered, "they know what was used to kill Sarah." He nodded. His face was pale and grim as it had been last night.

"Get to work, Maggie," he said gently, "and forget it."

I adjusted my telephone, mechanically taking a reef in the strap that held the mouthpiece, and went blindly to the Interstate positions. I listened in a faraway fashion as the telephonists gave me last-minute instructions. They made no comment when I was compelled to ask them to repeat themselves. They seemed to sense that something important had turned up, and left quietly to sign off in the time-book near the door.

Only Dulcie Gordon whispered urgently in my ear: "Maggie, I've got to see you. I'll wait for you in the restroom."

"No," I said. "Not there. Get downstairs to the front door. I'll be out as soon as I can." She nodded, and I began to pick up the lights in the panel.

I worked automatically that night, my fingers fumbling with the keys awkwardly. I tried to remember later if the lines had been busy, but as no reports from irate telephonists and subscribers came to my notice the next day with "please explain" attached. I concluded that the traffic must have been easier than usual. It may have been hours or it may have been minutes before an amused voice penetrated my consciousness, and the telephonist with whom I was booking in Adelaide was cut off. One of the all-night girls had pulled my plug from the board. She handed it to me with a mock bow.

"Don't you want to go home to-night, Maggie?" she inquired laughingly. "You can work my shift if you like."

"What?" I said, startled. I glanced up at the clock. "Oh, am I being relieved? Sorry! I was in a trance. Thanks, Nelson." I slipped from my chair. "I don't know where anything is, so don't ask me."

The all-night telephonist gave me a shrewd look. "You must have been in the wars to-day, Maggie, You're all in."

"I certainly am," I agreed fervently. "Good switching."

"Sleep well," she returned. I went down to the time-book and scrawled my name. Mac stood at my elbow as I was bending over the book, and I dipped the pen into the ink and gave it to her.

"Are you starting your week of all-nights to-morrow?" she asked as we climbed the stairs.

"So far. Bertie said that I was not to change with Patterson. In fact, he said that there were to be no more changes until further notice."

"Why, I wonder," Mac asked, pausing, with a foot on one step.

I shrugged indifferently. "Some new bee in his bonnet. He is the most inconsistent person I know."

"Why, Maggie!" Mac exclaimed in surprise. She knew I regarded Bertie highly.

"He is," I said fiercely, running up the stairs, "and I'd rather not talk about him, please."

She laughed a little at my tone. "Why are you so cross, old girl?"

"I'm sick to death of all the subterfuge going on," I said distinctly. "I don't think you're playing fair with me either, Mac. Why did you want to get rid of me when the Inspector spoke to you?"

"I didn't," she protested. "Really and truly, I didn't."

"Well. what did you tell him that made him look so smug?"

As we turned into the cloakroom, Mac answered in a low voice: "Only that I saw Sarah Compton when I was on relief last night."

I jammed my key into my locker with unnecessary force. "Is that all," I remarked with exasperation. "I thought you wanted to keep it a dark secret."

"I might retaliate," said Mac's calm voice from the other side of the lockers. "Where did you get to to-night? You said that you were only going back for your telephone, and it was after 8.30 p.m. by the time you entered the trunkroom."

"I was talking to Inspector Coleman," I answered shortly, making up my mind to say no more.

Mac came round to my side and gently put a hand on my arm. "Maggie," she said. I continued to rummage in my locker with unnecessary vigour. "We sound like a couple of cats spitting at each other," she remarked whimsically.

I looked down into her fine eyes. They were shadowed still, and so full of sadness that my heart smote me. "Sorry," I apologized gruffly. "I don't know what's got into me to-night. So many things have been happening. Forget it, please."

She hesitated, and then said: "Will you do me a favour, Maggie?"

"Certainly," I replied in amazement. Mac was a most independent person as a rule.

"May I spend the night with you?"

"Why, of course. That's no favour."

"Isn't it?" she queried with a twist of her lips that was no smile. She looked me straight in the eyes again. "Maggie, I—I'm scared stiff." I could feel her trembling, and put out a hand to steady her for a minute.

"Come on, Mac," I said quickly. "Let's get out of here. I promise you that I won't worry you with questions."

"Thanks," she returned, and I fancied that her voice too was not quite steady. Not having seen Mac in such a state of jitters before, I felt all the more concerned. She was not merely shaken as were we all as a direct result of the staggering event that had taken place, namely the murder of a monitor in the restroom of the Telephone Exchange; she was terrified to the very core of her being. Some fearful thing was preying on her mind. Unless that something was removed and removed immediately, I felt afraid that her whole mental balance would be affected.

I forgot my own sensibilities as we went down in the lift, so urgent was my desire to hurry her away from the Exchange and its new and sinister atmosphere.

But I couldn't resist telling her about the missing telephone.

"I think the police have found the weapon that killed Sarah. Or at least that they know what was used. Bertie's buttinsky!"

Mac's dark eyes kindled with fresh horror. She raised both hands to press against her cheeks.

"No, no," she whispered. "How horrible! Poor Sarah."

It was the first regretful remark I had heard uttered since Compton was murdered. For once I forbore any comment that I might have made about Sarah having had it coming to her for a long time in order to spare Mac's feelings.

"Do they think Bertie—" she began in a low voice.

"Yes," I cut in hardly. "He'll have to do a lot of explaining to-morrow. Think well, Mac; do you recall seeing his buttinsky at all yesterday?"

She drew her brows together. "I couldn't be certain. It's the sort of thing one sees lying around, but does not take in. Consciously, I mean. But I am sure that he used it yesterday afternoon. Since when has it been missing?"

"I don't know," I replied, as I slid open the lift doors and got out as quickly as I could. "I remember that Clark used a spare telephone set when he was helping me last night. It must have been missing before that. Don't worry about it now. We'll hear all about it in the morning. Anyway, that's Bertie's pigeon. Let's run, and we'll catch that earlier train."

We set off at a jog-trot down the passage to the Exchange entrance. My unintelligent friend, Ormond, was on duty again, a cup of tea and a doorstep of a sandwich in either hand. We bade him a brief "Good night" and went down the stone steps carefully, as the light was practically nil.

"Maggie," called a voice out of the darkness.

"Oh blast!" I muttered, "I'd forgotten all about you." It was Dulcie Gordon. She had waited for half an hour to see me.

"Yes, what is it?" I asked impatiently. "If you're coming with us, you'll have to run because we're after an earlier train."

Under the shaded corner light, I saw Gordon's face was as pale as paper. I thought quickly. She was only a kid and she too was terrified. She must have wanted to see me particularly to wait all that time.

"Here, Mac," I said, opening my scarlet leather handbag, "take the front door key, and get home to bed. I'll catch a later train."

Mac took the key without comment. I watched her slight figure disappear down the street.

"I'm on all-night to-morrow," I said resignedly, " so this may as well be a dress rehearsal. Can you swallow a milk shake, Gordon?"

She nodded and shrank close to my side as we proceeded down the dark street. Half-way down town I led her to a neat little milk-bar, a regular haunt for telephonists because of its proximity to the railway station.

"Now," I said briskly, having found a secluded corner and ordered two drinks. "What's the worry, Gordon?"

She glanced around the brilliantly-lit room with what I considered unnecessary nervousness.

"Maggie," she whispered, leaning forward over the table between us, "I didn't write that letter."

"So you've told me before," I observed irritably, lighting a cigarette. "Try not to repeat yourself. It wastes time. Or is that all you want to say?"

She shook her head, and made no other answer as the attendant planked two foaming glasses on the table with that scornful air which seems part and parcel of most waitresses. I caught the straw in my mouth and drank eagerly. Gordon watched the froth of her milk-shake blow out in tiny bubbles, as though fascinated by the procedure.

I glanced at my watch, and sighed ostentatiously.

"Maggie," she began, and I wished that she wouldn't call me by name quite so frequently. I was the only one with her, so that too seemed unnecessary.

"Dulcie!" I aped her. She appeared to take no notice, and turned her glass round and round on the table.

"Choke it down," I advised, taking a strong line, "and get on with your story."

CHAPTER V

It was a tragic enough little story, and one that in no way impaired my original animosity towards Sarah Compton. Rather than manufacturing some respect for Compton now that she was dead, I found myself disliking her the more.

A few years previously Dulcie Gordon had been the telephonist at one of our smaller country towns, when Sarah Compton had come into contact with her. The latter was then acting in a temporary capacity as a travelling supervisor—special officers of the Department who moved all over the state for the purpose of checking up on the local switching and handing out up-to-date operational instructions. She took a fancy to Dulcie and suggested her coming to town.

Gordon's people were pleased with the idea. They thought what a charming woman Compton was to take such an interest in their girl. Furthermore, Sarah had promised to take Dulcie under her wing, and to find her a nice home where she could board. Finally Dulcie was persuaded against her will, because she was quite content to stay where she was, to put in an application for employment at Trunks. With a supervisor's influence and recommendation, it didn't take long for her transfer to be effected. After several bucolic farewell parties, Gordon came to the big city, metaphorically holding her benefactress's hand.

It was then that she received a rude shock. But not until Compton had let her one of the rooms in her dismal house, and made her sign a long term lease. It did not take her long to realize what type of woman the charming travelling supervisor was.

"She even used to read my mail," Dulcie said, "saying as an excuse that she had promised my mother that she would be very careful of the company I kept."

"Why didn't you write and tell your people?"

"Oh, I couldn't," she replied pitifully. "You see, they thought that everything was just right for me, and what a lucky girl I was. I didn't want to worry them; especially as the crops had been so bad and they were having a hard struggle."

At last Gordon decided that she could stand it no longer' Matters finally came to a head when Compton discovered that one of the boys at the Exchange had been taking Dulcie out. She got hold of this lad's letters, and magnified the perfectly innocent friendship into a sordid *affaire*, upbraiding Dulcie in a most filthy fashion, and thus spoiling the latter's simple ideas for ever.

"The dirty, dried-up old maid," I muttered to myself.

Compton threatened to write to Gordon's people, and tell them their daughter was behaving no better than a woman on the streets. Poor Dulcie, though not fully grasping her meaning, begged and implored her not to write, promising to give up her nice lad and to be mindful of Sarah's advice in the future.

But that night, while Compton was on duty at the Exchange, she packed her few possessions again and left. She took a room in a house the other side of the city, as far away from Sarah as she could. She was compelled to meet her at the Exchange, but that was unavoidable. She was not in a position to throw in a good job at Trunks. She had been a telephonist ever since she left school and was untrained for anything else but switching.

Compton's attitude puzzled her. She behaved as though nothing had happened. Dulcie was forgetting her nasty innuendoes and starting to enjoy her freedom when letters began to arrive at her new lodgings. Every week Sarah would send in a bill for the rent of her room. Gordon ignored them at first, but at the end of a quarter she became frightened, as a letter from Sarah came threatening to start legal proceedings if she did not pay her rent. Dulcie wrote and told her that she couldn't meet the account, and saw no reason why she should as she had long since left Compton's roof. She received an answer in the next mail in the form of a copy of the lease she had signed together with a short note from Sarah stating that if the account was not paid, she would apply to Gordon's people for remuneration.

"I couldn't let her do that," Dulcie told me. "Dad had been ill, and Mother and my young brother had been trying to run the farm on their own. So I went to see Miss Compton, to beg her to wait until I could save up enough money, She was quite agreeable, and arranged that I pay her so much a week until the lease expired."

"How long has this been going on?" I demanded of the poor girl.

"Nearly two years," she confessed. "You see, I didn't give her the full rental each week. I couldn't, as I had to pay for where I am now."

"You silly, silly child," I said stormily. "Why didn't you tell someone about it. Don't you know that Sarah was only playing a low-down trick on you, and that she had no more right to that rent than I have? She would never have dared to have taken your case to court."

Gordon's eyes filled with tears. "I didn't have anyone to confide in," she answered, her voice trembling a little, "and I thought that if Compton knew, she might start telling people about—about that boy I used to go with."

She should never have left her home town. She was too young and sensitive to be able to break away for herself. As a small-town telephonist, where everyone knew and liked her, she was excellent at her job. But at Trunks thousands of subscribers are handled. You are not regarded as an individual. City work was not for such. She was crying quietly but unrestrainedly. Two years of disappointment, disillusionment and misery were all she had to show for her high hopes to make good in town.

"Cheer up," I said, awkwardly patting her hand. There were times when I wished the maternal instinct was stronger within me. The proper thing would have been to support Dulcie with one arm and let her cry her heart out on my shoulder, at the same time cooing words of sympathy. Her complete relaxation in her grief embarrassed me, and I did not feel like having my frock ruined.

"Don't cry so much," I begged. "There's nothing to worry about. All your troubles seem to have ended now." Gordon raised her face from her handkerchief and stared at me. There was a pause. I saw fear in her eyes as clearly as if the word was written.

"Oh, I see," I said slowly, thinking hard. Here was a motive and an opportunity. If both were presented to the police they would be almost certain to build up a sure case against Dulcie Gordon.

"Tell me," I asked, testing her, "do you know how Sarah was killed?"

She bent her head, dabbing at her eyes again, "Her head was smashed in, wasn't it?"

"Yes, that's correct. But do you know how?" Gordon shook her head, and I looked at her thoughtfully.

"Come along," I said, gathering up my bag and gloves, and putting my hat anyhow on my head. "You take my advice and go straight home to bed. I'll think over what you've told me, and let you know what you'd better do about telling your story to the police to-morrow."

She followed me obediently but made no reply. She appeared to be in a daze. The flood of weeping, followed by the sudden flash of fear in her eyes, had given place to the wide open blank stare of a child. I thought it advisable to escort her to her tram stop. Emotional unrestraint seemed to have fogged her brain and it had ceased to function. When I asked her if she felt all right she only nodded in a faraway fashion.

"Good night," I said as I left her on the safety zone. "Forget everything, and have a good sleep. You'll feel better in the morning." She still didn't reply.

I watched her board a tram before I made my way thoughtfully towards the station. Here was another pretty kettle of fish. As far as I could see Compton must have had a finger in numerous unpleasant-looking pies. There were those known to me who would have been only too glad to have her depart to another world. How many more must still be undiscovered?

The station clock said seven minutes to twelve. I made a sudden spurt for my train that was due to leave in two minutes. The porter was calling through the microphone in definite tones that the train at number nine platform was leaving—stand back, please—as I jumped into a crowded compartment. My fellow travellers eyed me with hostility as I climbed over knees, more often than not standing on white-shod feet. Apologizing profusely, I squeezed myself into a narrow space between a fat woman sucking sweets gustily, and a be-curled child who was sleeping with her mouth open. Luckily my journey was short. I could not have stood the competition between false teeth and toffee for long. If there is a type of person I dislike more than any other, it is the one who eats in public conveyances.

I had made up my mind to put in several hours' sleep before starting to cogitate on the recent discoveries that had come my way. Although having denied at first any interest in the mysteries that seemed to envelop all at the Exchange, I was beginning to be as curious as Mrs. Bates's striped tomcat; only I sincerely hoped that I would not get into as much strife as her feline pet did through inquisitiveness. I was prepared for further brushes with the police, rebuffs from the senior staff and even facetiousness from my fellow telephonists. But I did not anticipate anything like the trouble that was to come my way.

Lewisham Avenue was as dark as a tunnel. I found No. 15 with the practised ease gained through many years of habitation at the same boarding-house, hoping that Mac had left my latchkey in the front door. I did not want to waken her to come down and let me in. But it was not there. I tried the door to see if it had been left unlatched. It was locked. Very remiss of Mac!

'Now what do I do?' I thought to myself after glancing under the mat and in the letterbox, in case Mac had not deemed it wise to leave the key in the front door for anyone to use. I skirted the hydrangea bed, and called up to my window softly. There was no reply. Poor Mac must have been terribly tired.

I tried throwing a handful of gravel in the endeavour to waken her. The tiny stones rattled against glass. "That's odd!" I said aloud. "She must be sleeping with the window closed." I called her name again.

Presently the door on to the top veranda opened, and a voice said sternly: "Who's there? I'll have the police on to you, if you don't go away."

"Hullo, Mrs. Bates," I said, grinning. "Have you come out to play Shakespeare with me? 'Romeo, Romeo, wherefore art thou,' etc."

She peered down over the rail. "Miss Byrne, what are you doing in the garden at this time of night? And mind my hydies, please."

"All right, I'm not touching them. Please, I'm locked out. Hurry up and let in the poor orphan out of the cold, cold snow." Mrs. Bates clicked her tongue several times, before she disappeared. I groped my way back to the front door.

"Where's your key?" she demanded, opening the door as little as possible, though her big frame was draped in a thick, black dressing-gown. I nearly laughed outright when I saw that she was wearing a befrilled nightcap, such as might have been in fashion many decades ago.

"I gave my key to Miss MacIntyre," I explained, as she followed me up the stairs. "She wanted to stay with me to-night."

"I didn't hear her come in," Mrs. Bates declared positively, "and I've heard every hour strike."

"She must have changed her mind," I said carelessly, trying not to feel apprehensive. Mac had seemed so definite in her desire for company, that I was at a loss to explain her sudden alteration of arrangements. I paused in the passage outside my room.

"Sorry, Mrs. Bates, for spoiling your beauty sleep like this."

"I was awake," she said indignantly. "You know that I can't sleep until all my young ladies are safe at home."

"I suppose that I am the last in as usual," I said, opening my door, "so you can go back to your couch with a free mind. Good night."

I stood for a moment inside the door, my fingers on the electric light switch, listening for light breathing. But there was none, and I pressed down the switch. My room was hot and airless. I went to open the window, unhooking the placket of my frock and slipping it over my head at the same time. It was then that I heard light footsteps running madly down the silent road. I leaned over the window-sill, my eyes straining against the night. The gate clicked, and a figure, that I guessed rather than recognized as Mac's, came hurrying up the path.

"Is that you, Maggie?" she called in a hushed tone, gazing up at my silhouette against the lighted bedroom.

"I'll be right there," I said. I hurried down the stairs, unmindful of my deshabille condition. Mac's hot little hands grasped mine as I let her in.

"Wherever have you been?" I asked softly, not wishing to bring Mrs. Bates to the scene demanding explanations again. "I thought you would have been home and asleep by the time I came in." She shook her head ' and together we crept up the stairway. It creaked loudly in the annoying way stairs have when you want to be quiet.

"Can I have a shower, Maggie?" Mac asked, as we gained the privacy of my room. "I feel so sticky."

"Sure. Here's a towel. Make it snappy, will you. I want some sleep. Why are you so late?"

Her voice was muffled as she pulled her dress over her head.

"I came by tram, and it got held up."

"All right," I said patiently. "That'll do until the morning, anyway. I'm too tired to argue. There's a spare toothbrush in that drawer."

"Thanks. What about some pyjamas?"

I got out my best pair of apple-green Chinese silk, and handed them to her in silence.

"Get to bed, Maggie," Mac ordered gently. "You look fit to drop. I'll turn out the light, so that it won't worry you."

I did as I was told, and relaxed with a sigh between the cool sheets. I heard the shower running in the bathroom next door, and tried to rouse myself until Mac came back. For a tram to be held up at that time of night was the thinnest story I'd heard for a long time. But the sound of the streaming water grew fainter and fainter, and soon faded altogether, Presently I saw Dulcie Gordon's hand twisting and turning her glass, It swelled up jerkily until it obscured all other vision and then vanished. A mass of golden hair, which somehow I knew to be Patterson's, appeared and parted like curtains to reveal a pale blood-stained face; Sarah Compton's, jerking her head that way she had on the roof a few hours before her death. And all the time I heard voices yelling unintelligibly but with insane fury. Grotesque faces grew up before me, and threatening hands waved red-dripping buttinskys until I could stand it no longer. I sat up in bed with a jolt. The shower was still running in the next room. I stared around my brilliantly-lit bedroom in amazement.

"That's odd," I said aloud, pushing my hair back with both my hands. "Mac turned the light out before she went to the bathroom. How on earth—?" I stopped and fumbled automatically for my watch. It was half-past nine and the hot morning sun was streaming through the unshaded window. Staring at the tiny hands in a bemused fashion, I realized that I must have slept for nine hours.

"It's my second time on earth," I thought, putting my hands to my head again. It was aching intolerably. Then I remembered with a groan that it was Friday, and that I had an all-night shift to face.

The door opened and Mac came in. She was in my dressing gown and had a towel around her neck.

"Have you been having a shower all this time?" I demanded. She glanced at me in a puzzled manner, and went to the window to draw the blind.

"Thanks," I murmured, lying back against the pillows. "My head is fit to split. What did I do last night to deserve this hangover?"

"Have you any aspirin?" Mac asked, looking about her.

"Top left-hand drawer of the chest of drawers," I directed, closing my eyes and trying to marshal my brain into working lines. I remembered there were several questions I wanted to ask Mac.

"Drink this down, Maggie," said Mac's voice. "Then you'd better try to have some more sleep. You've got the dog-watch to-night."

"Hell!" I groaned. "I'll never do it. Have I got any sick leave owing?"

"Scurvy trick," she answered, starting to dress rapidly. "You'll be all right presently. Didn't you sleep well'?"

I shifted to a sitting position and jammed a pillow against the small of my back.

"Too well!" I exclaimed. "It seemed like five minutes, and during that time Bertie was throwing buttinskys at me in a lively fashion. I guess one of them must have contacted to give me such a head. Have you had breakfast?"

"Yes, thanks," Mac answered, applying lipstick skilfully. "I'll fix everything up with Mrs. Bates as I go."

"Are you leaving already?" She met my eyes in the pink-tinted mirror.

I thought that she couldn't have slept too well herself in spite of her fresh appearance, Mac's eyes are the most tell-tale that I have ever looked into.

"I've got some shopping to do," she declared, looking around for her hat.

"On top of the wardrobe. Before you go, Mac," I continued slowly, "I'd like to know what made you so late last night."

"I've told you," she said, tilting her Breton over her eyes. "The tram got held up."

I watched the back of her head grimly. "That was last night's story. Now give me the true one in the sober light of morning."

"Don't be silly, Maggie," she said coolly. I longed for the energy to get out of bed and shake her. "I'm telling you the truth."

"Mac," I declared firmly, "let's face things clearly. You haven't been straight with me since Wednesday night, and you know it."

She turned around from the mirror slowly. Her eyes were those of a stranger. They looked through me with a hauteur of which I had not thought Mac capable.

"Good heavens, girl," I yelled in exasperation, "don't you think that I'm entitled to some sort of explanation. Last night you came to me trembling with fear, begging to stay the night and now—Mac, if you're tired of me, if my friendship means no more to you, say so. I am so weary of this everlasting hedging. It's driving me mad. I can't understand what you're worrying about. You saw Sarah Compton on Wednesday night going down in the lift-right! Can't you take it in that at least two other people saw her after that? You are as far out of the picture as Clark and I are."

Mac came over to the bed and looked down at me wistfully. "Last night, Maggie," she said in a low voice, "you promised that you would not worry me with questions. Won't you be very much—my friend and keep that promise?" I dropped my eyes from her appealing look and wriggled about.

"I'd like to know what your game is," I grunted. "However, I'll be mum. Sorry for the dramatic outburst."

She went to the door and paused, one hand on the knob. "Shall I tell Mrs. Bates to send up some breakfast?"

"No, don't bother, I rarely have any. I probably won't see you until Saturday now. Are you going to the dance?"

"I'll be on duty for part of the evening, but I'll have a look in after work. Good-bye, Maggie."

"So long," I returned. "Mac!"

She put her head round the door. "Yes?"

"Be careful with whatever you're doing, won't you, old girl?"

I lay back against my pillows and closed my eyes, but not to court sleep. I had no desire to conjure up weird visions again. Mrs. Bates's voice floated up to my room as she saw Mac off the premises. I heard footsteps below my window, and then the creak of the gate.

"She's gone," I said aloud, and wondered why I had spoken so uneasily. "Now," I continued to talk aloud in an absurd fashion, addressing two flies buzzing around on the ceiling, "let's get down to business."

The aspirin seemed to have lived up to all its makers advertised. My brain became keen and alert as I separated and lined up facts into their chronological order. Firstly, there was the central figure of the whole case to be considered—Sarah Compton. Inspector Coleman said a 'thoroughly bad woman.' I cocked my head on one side, considering the phrase. Well, yes, I thought I agreed with him, but somehow the description seemed a little too conclusive. True, she was a blackmailer, an adulteress and a despoiler of youth's innocence—poor Dulcie, for example. Wait a moment, one half of my mind said to the other, we'll deal with Gordon presently. To continue with Compton. She was inquisitive; too inquisitive, that was obvious. An eavesdropper and a backbiter. Surely, there must have been some good in her somewhere! She certainly had the welfare of the Exchange at heart. That devout instinct in any woman was diverted from the usual things in life, such as home, husband and family, to an abstract thing, Central. Perhaps she was murdered for gain. She could have been quite comfortably off, from what I knew of her shady dealings. I promised myself to suggest it to the Inspector, although, no doubt, he had gone into the matter long ago.

The fact remained that Compton was murdered; beaten to death in the Exchange restroom with the buttinsky belonging to the Senior Traffic Officer. That hadn't been definitely proved, but I was working on the supposition that it was true. She was killed between 10.40 p.m. and 11.10 p.m. on Wednesday night, shortly after a clandestine meeting with Bertie, who had owned to intimate relations with her.

Bertie—he had known Sarah Compton for a long time. Perhaps she was putting the screws on him; trying to make him divorce his wife or something similar. Still, he said that he left about 10.30 p.m. and the guard corroborated his statement. Ormond, stupid though he appeared, would not be likely to mistake someone else for the Senior Traffic Officer. Or mightn't he? Supposing Bertie walked out of the Exchange, and then turned round and came in again a few minutes later. Poor Ormond would be so confused at the continual comings and goings, that he would not be able to tell exactly what the Senior Traffic Officer's movements were. A decided possibility! Disregarding that theory, there might be another entrance to the Exchange; one known only to a few.

'I'll have a look-see to-day,' I promised myself again. 'One cannot overlook the fact that Bertie's buttinsky was the weapon used.'

I came to Patterson, and considered her thoughtfully. A fool of a girl or a splendid actress? Without any doubt an unmitigated liar, and Mrs. Bates didn't like her. Still, she's no judge. Compton had had her claws on Gloria in some way, but I didn't see quite how. There were those letters written by someone called Patterson, but that could not possibly be Gloria. I shelved the letters affair into one corner of my mind. Gloria had had something worrying her that Compton had learned about. Hence her desire to keep out of the latter's way. She was the last to see the monitor, except for the murderer, unless she committed the crime herself. But somehow, the idea of Gloria, with her blonde prettiness, stealing the Senior Traffic Officer's buttinsky in a premeditated fashion and bashing Compton's face in, did not seem right. But it was another possibility.

Then there was Bill the liftman. I rather shrank from analyzing his part in the tragedy. He could have stayed back on Wednesday night without the slightest fear of discovery. My opinion of the night-guard was so low, that I considered that there was a strong chance to slip by him without attracting his notice. He would merely think that it was one of the many mechanics who buzzed in and out of the Exchange like flies. There was no reason why Bertie could not have passed as one, if he re-entered the Exchange. A mechanic's bag would be a very useful receptacle for a blood-stained buttinsky. Where could he beg, borrow or steal one? Nothing had come out about a bag being missing. But I was contemplating the liftman's movements. He, too, had known Sarah many years before. Could he be a disappointed lover? Or, better still, as Mac and I had speculated without voicing our thoughts, the husband of Compton's friend, Irene? To further that, if he was Dan Patterson, what relation to him was Gloria? Was she the daughter that he owned to having, or was the same name just a matter of coincidence? Working on the supposition that Irene was his wife, it would be quite probable that he knew the strength of the quarrel she had had with Sarah. The fact that he had overheard the quarrel seemed a bit too plausible. I didn't like the way he could remember things that happened years before quite so clearly.

'I wish that I'd never started this,' I thought miserably. Then there was Bill eavesdropping at tea last night, and the indelible pencil that I had found. How easy it would have been for him to manipulate the lift from the cabin on the roof so that it stopped while he threw down his letter to Sarah. In spite of all these cogitations, I could not believe Bill had anything to do with Sarah's death. He was too decent. I had always respected and liked him. Surely he would not let me down as Bertie and Mac had.

Thinking about the letters brought me to Dulcie Gordon, the latest applicant for the role of the killer. She had protested, perhaps too vehemently—Shakespeare, tagged my mind—against having written to Sarah at all. Yet last night she told me that she wrote to her, making an appointment so as to talk over the matter of the rent. Had that slipped her mind, or didn't she want it known that she had had any correspondence with Compton? If Gordon had lied there, why had she lied again about writing that seemingly harmless anonymous letter? Perhaps there was more in that last letter than met the untutored eye. Inspector Coleman had praised my perspicacity when I concluded that he had chosen those three letters from Compton's pile for some good reason. Hitherto, I had deemed only the two written by Irene Patterson of any importance. Now I wondered if the Inspector thought so, in spite of Sergeant Matheson's declaration to the contrary. Why waste time with a foolish threat that some infantile brain had concocted? With someone who would be a very unworthy candidate for the position of a cunning, coldblooded killer. It was thus they had described Sarah's assassin to be. Were they giving the murderer a build-up that was not at all accurate? Perhaps it had been Inspector Coleman's invention to scare Mac and me into telling all we knew.

Whether Gordon had been the author of that last letter or not, I would not have cared to say. The only facts I went on when I accused her were the recency of the note and the connection between the memorandum Compton was about to send into the heads regarding Sunday work, and the one mentioned in the letter. Overshadowed by the more major events of Wednesday night, it seemed a very flimsy excuse for inventing an anonymous letter. Continuing with Gordon's case, I recalled the definite look of fear that came into her eyes the previous night, when I comforted her with the reflection that now Sarah was dead all her own troubles were ended. I started to nibble my forefinger thoughtfully. Somehow, that quick shadow across her face was not quite in keeping with the Inspector's conception of the killer.

"We must not," I declared to the buzzing flies, who had become my confidants, "disregard the fact that Gordon had both the motive and the opportunity."

It would be a simple task to steal Bertie's buttinsky without anyone observing the deed. He left it lying around, and it was a thing no one would miss too soon. It would just be presumed that someone else was using it, and would return it by and by. As to hiding it until the right minute for use—"Aha," I said slowly, and my mind went quickly back to the afternoon of the crime. Four girls were playing cards in the restroom when I entered-they were all on the 10.30 p.m. rota. We had chaffed Patterson a bit about her large wardrobe, and Dulcie Gordon had mentioned about Observation on the restroom telephone; also, that her locker had been rifled. Could it be possible that she had said that to disguise the fact that she had Bertie's buttinsky hidden therein.

'By Jove, she's deep,' I thought. 'That is, if my deductions are correct.'

I did not feel in the least frightened by the idea of having a friend of mine a murderess. Rather, I was full of admiration at that moment for the skilful planning and daring needed to carry out such a crime. Therein I made a very grave mistake, it was not until I found myself where I am now that I realized what an appalling thought had been mine. I felt so smug and pleased with myself and the plausible conclusion that I had come to, that I overlooked the warnings issued by Inspector Coleman and his shy Sergeant concerning the type of person we were up against.

"I won't tell the police yet," I said aloud, almost buoyantly. "I'll wait for definite proof. I wonder what Mac will say."

At the sound of her name the satisfied smile faded from my face. 'Oh well.' I shrugged. 'I can't see how this will hurt her at all. Maybe Mac is doing the same as me—playing amateur detective. That might account for her fit of temperament.' I hoped that she wouldn't be sore with me for making the great discovery first. As I was in the middle of a pleasant day-dream, where the Chief Commissioner of Police was presenting me with a Royal Humane medal or whatever would be its equivalent in the world of crime, the front door bell rang far away. One half of my mind listened ca-sually to Mrs. Bates's lumbering steps down the hall, while the other was busy rehearsing a modest, declamatory speech of thanks. Voices sounded, coming up the stairs. I brushed away the Commissioner's congratulatory hand and leaped out of bed.

"Charlotte!" I yelled, dragging on the dressing-gown that Mac had left lying over a chair for Mrs. Bates's sake.

"Hullo, darling," said my mother, opening the door gingerly. "Aren't you up yet?"

"No. I was fearfully late last night, and I've got the dogwatch to-day. What are you doing in town? Come and sit down." I closed the door in Mrs. Bates's face and heard an indignant sniff.

"Didn't I write and tell you?" asked my mother, looking around her vaguely as she peeled off her gloves. "I am sure I did."

"As a matter of fact," I admitted, "a letter came yesterday, but I didn't have time to read it. So many things have been happening."

"So I heard," she returned calmly. She was surveying me critically from every angle. "Darling, you're getting terribly thin. I'm sure you're smoking too much."

"Correct," I grinned. "That and work keep my figure. You rarely see a fat telephonist. Do you remember Sarah Compton when she came to Keramgatta on a supervising trip?"

Charlotte began to strip my bed and turn the mattress. My mother was that type of woman who could never sit still when there was work to do. Even if it was someone else's work.

"The woman with the nose?" she queried.

"What was the matter with her nose?"

"It preeked. Didn't you ever notice?"

I shook my head. "Sorry, but I've never even heard of the word. But I can guess your meaning. You know she's been murdered?"

Charlotte had started to make my bed, so I went to the opposite side to assist.

"So I read in the papers. Your father was in a great state when he saw your photograph."

"I didn't give it to them," I protested, folding back the sheet. "If I had had any say in the matter, I certainly wouldn't have let them print that one. Did you observe the Byrnes profile?"

My mother laughed a little. "It jutted. Tell me," she asked abruptly in her customary manner, "how's your friend, Gilda?"

"Gerda," I corrected. "You're thinking of *Rigoletto*. What about her?"

"She actually found the body, didn't she?"

I grimaced. "What an abominable word! Yes, she was the first that ever burst, etc. But I was close on her heels. Did you know I fainted?"

Charlotte looked round horror-stricken. "Darling! Dear me, you've not done that since you were twelve."

I nodded. We spread the disguising day-cover over the bed. "Running to school," I confirmed. "I told the Sergeant. Do you recall meeting a policeman up our way called Matheson?"

Was that his name?" asked my mother doubtfully. "A shy boy with freckles? He found some shorthorn cattle in one of our own paddocks, after your father had reported them stolen."

"How very embarrassing for them both. I don't vouch for the freckles, but he certainly seems bashful. He's assisting on the case." I was hunting about for my soap and bath powder, and heard Charlotte say "Oh," in a certain tone behind me.

I laughed. "No, Charlotte."

"Darling, I didn't say a thing," she protested mildly.

"But you were thinking," I accused her. "How are the boys? They haven't written to me for an age."

"They're both fit. Tony thought he'd save postage and send a letter by me. Are you going to have a bath?"

"A shower. I won't be long. Read the daily news, and let me know the latest about the Exchange murder."

My mother glanced at me shrewdly. "I should have thought that you knew more than the papers."

"Maybe," I answered briefly over my shoulder.

I came back from the bathroom feeling fresh and cool to find my mother tidying up my room.

"Sit down and relax," I begged. "You give me the fidgets. You haven't told me yet why you're in town."

"I thought I'd like a hat," she replied, continuing to dust the wardrobe. "Only a garden hat. One of those straw things you used to be able to get in a nothing over two-and-six pence store."

" Don't tell me that you've travelled over two hundred miles just to get a garden hat!" I said in astonishment, "Come on, own up."

She began to fiddle with the ornaments as Mac had done the previous day. I almost expected to hear the pin-tray crash again. "I suppose that l came to see how you were."

"That's better," I grinned, "but what for?"

My mother went off at a tangent. "How's work? Are you still as busy as ever?"

"Pretty hectic," I agreed, waiting patiently.

"Do you still see that John Clarkson you wrote about?"

"Now and then," I answered carelessly, knowing that the point had now been reached. "We play golf together as often as duty allows. As a matter of fact, I am to have a game with him on Sunday, but I'll cut it now that you're down."

"Don't do that. Is he a good player?"

"Very. Come along with us. I'd like you to meet him."

Charlotte looked dubious. "Won't Mr. Clarkson mind?"

I laughed. "I don't think so. You'd better get to know him sometime."

An expression of resignation came into her face. "I thought so," she announced. "Goodness knows what your father will say."

"I don't think it will matter," I said lightly.

"A warning, Maggie?" asked my mother gravely.

I laughed again and put an arm through hers. "Most uncalled for," I confessed, "and quite unnecessary."

"Well, I hope he's nice," she remarked inadequately, going to the wardrobe. "What dress do you want? It's very hot out."

"It should change soon," I said, I glanced out the window trying to read the sky. "Give me the navy horror I wore yesterday, and I'll take a coat. But we are not going out yet, are we? Don't forget that I'm not on duty until eleven to-night!"

"We'll have lunch here," promised my mother. "Can Mrs. Bates squeeze me in somewhere for the weekend?"

"I think so. Are you only staying until Monday? That won't give you much time to find that hat."

"What hat? Oh, you mean my garden one. Perhaps you could keep a watch out for one, Maggie, and send it home to me. I'm not in any violent hurry for it."

"Charlotte," I said, taking her by the shoulders and shaking her gently, "you're an old fraud."

"Why, darling?" she asked with a surprised look.

"You know what I mean," I said, opening the door. "Come down to the lounge. It's cooler."

* * * * *

We chatted companionably for some time about home. I read Tony's letter while Mrs. Bates fixed up a room near mine and Charlotte unpacked. The Exchange and everything connected with it went out of my mind until half-way through lunch. I got up suddenly from the sweet course.

"Where are you going, Maggie?" Charlotte asked. "Come back and finish your pudding."

"I'll only be a second, I want to make a 'phone call." I closed the door on her mild protestation, and made for the telephone. it took a little time to trace my number. I found what I wanted by making a few inquiries with the Personnel Branch of the Telephone Department. "Is Miss Gordon there?" I asked, as a male voice answered.

"Who is speaking, please?"

"Miss Byrnes," I replied haughtily. What business was it of his? I glanced down at the receiver, puzzled at the sound of muffled conversation, as the man at the other end put a hand over the mouthpiece. Presently the hand was removed. I heard someone say: "I'll speak to her." A voice asked me crisply: "Miss Byrnes? This is Sergeant Matheson."

I knew that something had happened as soon as he spoke. A fearful excitement shook me. "I wanted to speak to Dulcie Gordon," I said hesitantly. "What are you doing at her boardinghouse?" The police had got on to her tracks quicker than I had expected. Poor Gordon! Poor little kid!

"I've got some bad news for you," the Sergeant's voice said gravely. I gripped the receiver hard. I thought I knew what was coming. "Miss Gordon was found dead early this morning."

I could neither speak nor move. The shock was almost overwhelming. Somewhere in the distance, through the drumming in my ears, I could hear the Sergeant's voice saying urgently: "Miss Byrnes. Are you there, Miss Byrnes?"

"Yes, I'm still here," I replied, leaning against the wall to support my weak legs. "It's just the shock. When you say dead, what—"

"She was found gassed."

"That means suicide, doesn't it? Did she leave a note?"

"None has been found," he replied, and a dreadful tremor passed through my body.

"The Inspector," I whispered. "Does he think-is it another murder?"

"We don't know yet. Can I trust you to keep this quiet?"

"You may," I replied, reviving a little. "I suppose that I'd better own up to the fact that I was probably the last person to see Gordon alive; that is, if you disregard tram conductors and the like."

His exclamation nearly deafened my eardrum. "Don't speak so loud," I ordered acidly. "Well?"

"We can't talk over the 'phone. Someone might be listening in. Where are you now?"

"At my boarding-house," I informed him, overlooking the slur aimed at the telephonic escutcheon, "in the middle of lunch."

"I'll be right over," Sergeant Matheson said. "Don't go out, will you?" But he hung up before I had time to reply.

I didn't go back to the dining-room at once, but stood against the wall staring stupidly at the 'phone in my hand. "Poor Dulcie!" I repeated to myself. "She must have got the wind up properly last night when she left me, and felt that she couldn't face it."

But perhaps it was murder, though it seemed a difficult way to get rid of anyone by gassing them. There would sure to be marks of a struggle. No one in their right senses would put their head into a gas oven without making some protest if they were being forced to. Gradually the sick feeling left me. I walked slowly back to the dining-room.

"Hullo," I said to myself, in a disinterested way, "Mrs. Bates is trying to convert Charlotte."

My mother was saying in her gentle way: "That's all very well, Mrs. Bates, but one can't possibly speak the truth always. Dear me, you wouldn't have a friend in the world. Maggie, dear, what's the matter with you? You're as white as a sheet."

"Come and have your tea in the lounge," I ordered. "Will you please excuse us, Mrs. Bates?"

"But Maggie, what about your sweet?" I glanced at the caramel custard without enthusiasm.

"No more, thanks. Very nice though, Mrs. Bates," I added hurriedly, as she presented an offended back towards us and poured out two cups of tea. I carried them carefully up the hall. My hands were shaking. I closed the lounge room door and wandered restlessly over to the window. Charlotte waited in silence.

"Dulcie Gordon has committed suicide," I blurted out without turning my head. I couldn't trust myself not to give way if I met my mother's eyes.

"Did you put sugar in mine?" asked my mother, stirring her tea. "Who's Dulcie Gordon, dear?"

"One of the girls," I replied, pulling the curtain aside to watch the gate. "She may have been murdered. The police wouldn't commit themselves, but I don't know. You see, I was speaking to her last night."

"It's all rather dreadful," my mother said quietly. I talked about our conversation in the milk bar the previous night, and my own speculations that morning, until Sergeant Matheson arrived. I couldn't stop chattering. Charlotte's matter-of-fact attitude calmed me down greatly.

"You've lost your freckles," Charlotte remarked as I introduced the Sergeant. He reddened uncomfortably, and laughed.

"Don't be personal, Charlotte," I rebuked her. "Well, Sergeant?"

"Well, Miss Byrnes?"

I made a gesture of impatience. "Was it murder or suicide? I don't think you need go," I added to my mother, as I saw her making a half-hearted attempt to leave the room.

"We are inclined to consider that it was suicide," answered the Sergeant with habitual caution. "There is no evidence of death from any other cause than gas, and no marks of a struggle. There is always the possibility of the unfortunate person having been stunned first, and then the mouth placed over a gas jet in order to give the impression of suicide. The only strange feature of this case is the lack of any farewell note, explaining the reason for taking life."

"Did you look underneath everything?" my mother chipped in. "Men never seem to."

"We made a very thorough search," he assured her, smiling.

"Perhaps Gordon thought there were already enough letters in this business, and that she would not add to the confusion," I remarked flippantly.

The Sergeant gave me a direct look. "You don't seem very upset by your friend's death."

"Did you want another fainting act? I could have obliged you before, but now I am feeling more interested than sick. Where are your questions?

Don't tell me that you came just for the social visit!"

"No, indeed," he answered, searching his inner pockets.

"I knew it," I said in a resigned voice. He glanced at me, puzzled. "You haven't sharpened your pencil yet."

Sergeant Matheson laughed again. He became serious. It was amazing how young he could appear and then how awe-inspiring when he adopted his official manner. I never knew where I was with him.

"What time did you leave Miss Gordon last night?"

"At about ten minutes to twelve," I replied promptly. "We parted at the Commercial Insurance corner. I managed to catch the seven minutes to twelve train."

"Was she alone?" he asked, writing carefully in his book.

"Yes. I had just bought her a milk shake at Peter's Bar. She had been pouring forth her soul to me. It's amazing the number of secrets that I've come across since last Wednesday."

"It is a pity that you don't divulge them to the right quarters," Sergeant Matheson said sternly. I smiled at him, not rising to his bait.

"I am quite willing to tell you what we talked about," I informed him kindly. "Don't be afraid to ask. In fact, if this tragedy had not occurred and brought you hurrying to my side, so to speak, I would have sought out your superior officer to lay certain facts before him. They might have enabled him to make an arrest. Savvy?"

"Certainly. There is a decided possibility that by taking her own life so suddenly Miss Gordon stands a self-confessed murderess."

I felt unreasonably annoyed that he had followed my somewhat obvious theory so closely on his own.

"Did you know that our late lamented monitor was more or less blackmailing the poor kid?" I demanded.

"We had a fair idea," he confessed in a meek voice. "That mail that we went through yesterday at Miss Compton's house was sent on to Russell Street for further inspection. There were several copies of letters written by Miss Compton to Miss Gordon. We also came across some of Miss Gordon's own, written by some lad she knew rather well."

"You can get rid of those," I said firmly. "You're not going to drag that poor child's love affair into the limelight if I can help it. She may have murdered Sarah Compton, but I, for one, don't hold it against her. That woman deserved everything she got and more."

"Maggie, darling," protested my mother. "Don't be so vindictive. Don't forget that Miss Compton is dead."

"What does that matter?" I retorted. "Furthermore, Compton seems to be making just as much nuisance of herself dead, as she did when she was alive. If she hadn't tried to mess up Gordon's life, she wouldn't have been murdered. If she wasn't dead, that poor child wouldn't have done away with herself."

Sergeant Matheson said calmly: "You seem very certain that Miss Gordon killed Miss Compton."

"I am," I returned with emphasis. "Though a very humble amateur in the game of detection, I would say that the first thing one should look for when hunting a murderer is motive. Dulcie had a motive. A very good one, I consider. She also had the opportunity. You may go to that awful idiot, Ormond, and ask him who went in and out of the Exchange during a specified time, but I am willing to bet you a hundred to one, in pennies," I added cautiously, "that anyone could pass him without being observed. It's impossible to remember everyone, accurately."

"And yet," the Sergeant put in dryly, "he remembers Mr. Scott and Miss Patterson."

"Two!" I replied scornfully. "Bertie is well known, and Gloria was already well-impressed on his mind by a previous *rencontre*. Take Gordon, now. She was a nondescript-looking girl. I doubt if I, who have worked with her for years, could tell you even the colour of her eyes. She was the type that you don't notice. She moved quietly, and she talked quietly. I suggest that you go back to her room, and have another thorough search for a farewell letter. Suicides always leave them, I'm told; especially women. It would be quite easy to stay behind after the other 10.30 girls had left. They would not mark her absence. She could hide in the lunchroom opposite until Sarah came along to the cloakroom. Even the fact that Patterson was hanging around would not matter, as she left as quickly as she could. Then Gordon—" I stopped, as Sergeant Matheson spoke.

"Wait a moment. What weapon did she use?"

"Is that a rhetorical question?" I demanded, "or don't you know? Last night, the Senior Traffic Officer's buttinsky—a mechanic's telephone, Mother, very heavy—was discovered to be missing. Unless Mr. Scott has shown its whereabouts this morning, a better weapon for bashing anyone's head in could not he used."

"There is no trace of it," answered Sergeant Matheson shortly. "Mr. Scott professes himself completely in the dark as to its absence. He remembers it last on Wednesday morning, but could not say when he first missed it."

"I knew it," I declared in triumph. "It's the sort of accoutrement to the Exchange that you don't notice, and certainly don't miss. You just presume that the other fellow is using it. It would be quite simple for Gordon to lift it on her way to tea and put it in her locker. When I came into the restroom before having my own tea, several of the girls were playing cards. Incidentally, Charlotte, I took a hand and made two over with four trumps. Dulcie was one of them, and she mentioned, just casually of course, that some of the lockers including her own had been disturbed. What an admirable way to cover herself, if Bertie's buttinsky had by some extraordinary stroke of bad luck been found before she could use it on Compton. None of the other girls corroborated her statement nor did they contradict it, naturally thinking that the lockers belonged to other telephonists."

"Have you any suggestions as to where Mr. Scott's telephone is now?" asked the Sergeant smoothly.

"None. Charlotte, where would you have put it if you had murdered Compton?"

"What a horrible thought, Maggie! What is a buttinsky like in appearance?"

"About a foot long, with a length of flex that could be easily removed. The dial and mouthpiece are at one end, and the earphone at the other."

"Quite a difficult thing to hide," remarked my mother. "I should throw it away."

"Yes, but where? Don't forget that it would probably be rather messy after the use to which it had been put."

"I would just throw it anywhere if that was the case," she answered firmly. "I'd be only too glad to get rid of it."

I turned to Sergeant Matheson. "There you are! We'd just throw it away. When and where, I can't tell you."

"From a window," added my mother, inspired.

"From the roof," I shouted in excitement. "There's a small dump-yard on the east side of the building; it would only mean a matter of dropping the buttinsky over the side, and it would be certain to land amongst the rubbish. What about it, Sergeant?"

He looked as excited as I felt. "Miss Byrnes, you should be in the Force," he declared emphatically.

"I thought of it first," Charlotte protested. I patted her on the back in a congratulatory fashion.

Sergeant Matheson closed his book with a snap, and got up. "If we find the weapon it looks pretty well as if the case is broken; even in spite of the missing letter."

"How did she do it?" I asked, growing grave.

"A gas-ring in her room. No one noticed the smell for a long time as she lived in a small back room, right away from the other boarders."

"The poor little girl," said my mother sadly. "Have you advised her people?"

The Sergeant nodded, preparing to leave. "A telegram was sent. You have nothing more to tell me, Miss Byrnes?"

"Nothing," I repeated, "though as far as I can see, you already knew what I was going to say. Wait a moment. There is something."

He turned back.

"She said quite definitely that she did not write that anonymous letter about the memorandum that we found amongst Compton's pile. I think," I continued slowly, "that I am inclined to believe her now."

"Thank you," he answered, making a note. "We missed that out on questioning Miss Gordon last night, so we have to rely on your evidence. Good-bye, Mrs. Byrnes."

"I'll see you out," I declared, ignoring his protest. Mrs. Bates was polishing the brass hat stand in the hall. It was an ancient piece of furniture and seldom used, but she kept it gleaming like gold. As a rule it was attacked first thing in the morning. I guessed its second polishing was just an excuse for Mrs. Bates to be within call of the lounge room. I grinned at her cheerfully as I shut the door after Sergeant Matheson.

"Who was that?" she demanded, without beating about the bush.

"The police," I said tragically, clasping my hands together in a dramatic fashion. "They have discovered all. Dear Mrs. Bates, in your mercy, will you still house a criminal?"

She stared at me round-eyed. "If they arrest you," she declared with a wheeze, "I'll give them a piece of my mind."

"It's just what they require," I answered, kicking open the lounge room door viciously. "Are you ready, Charlotte? Let's take a constitutional."

"Not too far, darling. It's so very hot."

"We won't be in for dinner," I told my landlady, as we went up the stairs to my room.

"We'll go over to the Gardens," I suggested. "It should be cool there. Then what about a meal in town and a show before I go on duty?"

"Won't you be too tired, Maggie?"

"I can sleep to-morrow," I answered, shrugging. "By the way, we've got a hop on at the Exchange to-morrow night. Would you care to come? I am going to honour it with my presence for a couple of hours."

"I'd love to," replied my mother promptly.

"I'll have to get a leave-pass for you. Actually the dance is only for the Exchange employees, but I think I'll be able to wangle it."

We took a tram round to the Domain, and walked through the Gardens until we found a cool place to sit and browse. The lake looked hot and muddy. A few white swans wilted to and fro. In the background, the towers and spires of the city rose up in a misty haze.

"Were you suspected of murder?" asked my mother presently. She seemed quite placid about the idea.

"I don't think so," I replied, tilting my hat over my eyes against the glare. "You see, the police had the crime timed for between 10.40 p.m. and 11.10 p.m., when Mac, Clark and I were working flat out in the trunkroom. Having such a good alibi naturally they were wary of us, but I think that they will be satisfied now that Gordon has made her fade-out. It's very odd that she left no letter."

"Perhaps someone took it."

"A brain-wave!" I said approvingly. "But I don't see why; unless, of course, Dulcie was going to spill the beans about someone else. But who was to know that she was going to gas herself last night? I would be the only one who had any idea of what state of mind she was in, and it certainly didn't strike me last night that she might commit suicide. If she didn't kill Sarah, I can't understand why she did it. After all, Compton had very little with which to blackmail her; just an innocent boy and girl friendship, and a threat to tell Dulcie's people about the money that she owed. I told her last night Sarah didn't have a leg to stand on."

My mother made no comment and I was glad. Gordon's suicide had shaken me more than I had admitted. It was rather grim wondering if I had said the wrong thing the previous night and precipitated the affair. I shouldn't have let the poor child go home by herself. But even if it had occurred to me, which it didn't, what could I have done? I already had Mac sharing my bed. I couldn't go bringing half the trunkroom home to sleep with me.

"Maggie, do look at those sweet little ducks!"

A half-dozen or so came streaming under the bridge in the wake of their matronly-looking mother.

"She looks like you," I remarked, jolted out of my reverie.

"Darling, how rude! What show would you like to see?"

I told her what was on in the city. We argued amiably for a while about the relative enjoyment of a good show amidst uncomfortable surroundings and a feeble film at one of our most up-to-date theatres.

"I bet we make it a newsreel in the end," I said, glancing at my wrist watch. "Charlotte, I want to go up to the Exchange for a few minutes. Can you amuse yourself in town? You can start a search for your garden hat," I added mischievously.

"Very well, dear," she answered, ignoring my hand to help her rise. "I'm not that old. Did you leave something at the Exchange and want to collect it?"

"Preeker!" I replied, grinning. "I want to make sure about something.

If I find what I am looking for, I'll tell you. I'll meet you outside the Town Hall about six o'clock, and we'll find some nice place for dinner."

We strolled on leisurely through the Gardens, and came out at one end of the riding-track alongside the river; pausing to watch the horses and to comment on their riders. Presently, we caught a river ferry back to town, where I left Charlotte to roam about the shops. I continued along to catch a bus to the Exchange. It must have been some sort of charity day as stalls, displaying home-made jams and pickles, lined the streets. The city was crowded, especially around the circus, where grotesque dolls were being raffled. These appeal days are great fun if you have plenty of time in which to wander about, but when you are hurrying to work they are only a source of irritation as you get caught up in the throng.

The bus made a slow trip through town, steering a careful course between the traffic and the crowds that spread on to the road every few yards. Having once got a particular idea into my head, l wanted action. It was irritating to be held up thus, and made me feel fidgety.

Sergeant Matheson came out of the Exchange door while I was hunting for my pass in a handbag that I had sworn to clear out every day. He looked pleased to see me, and drew me away from the guard's hearing.

"You were right, Miss Byrnes," he said excitedly. "It was in the dump-yard at the side of the building."

"What was?" I asked, turning over letters in the endeavour to find that piece of blue cardboard. "I seem to have mislaid my pass. Will you vouch for me at the door?"

"The buttinsky! Don't you remember telling me this afternoon to look in that dump-yard?"

"Did you actually find it?" I asked in astonishment. "Well, well! What a fluke on my part!"

"Don't spoil it," replied the Sergeant, grinning. "The chief thinks that you're nothing short of a marvel. In fact, you've been so clever throughout that he is beginning to suspect that you must have known more about the murder than you told us."

"You told me that yesterday," l pointed out. "You may inform him, with my compliments, that I stumbled on this business by the merest chance. The sooner I see the last of you both, the happier I'll be."

"Well, we're pushing off now. Inspector Coleman is just clearing up a few matters inside. Are you really glad that it's all over?"

"Very," I replied firmly, and held out my hand. "I like a quiet life. Good-bye."

The Sergeant looked down at my hand with a serious expression on his face. "Won't you come to that basketball match with me?"

"No, thank you very much."

"What about tea one day at that place we were yesterday?"

I shook my head. "Certainly not, You behaved like a cad."

"Somewhere else then," he pleaded. My heart melted. His expression was far from official at that moment.

"Give me a ring in a few weeks' time," I suggested, "and I'll think it over. Tell me, was the buttinsky all—er—you know?"

"No. It was rusty but not from blood. She must have run a tap on it in an attempt to remove the stains. It's been a foul business."

"Poor Dulcie," I said sadly. "She was just a frightened kid. But I'm glad that it's turned out like this. At least it was short. Now come and tell that guard person that I can go in."

We shook hands again in a friendly fashion on the steps, the Sergeant promising to call me in a week's time.

'I doubt if he will remember,' I told myself. 'Not that I care much, but he's a nice lad.'

I walked quickly along the corridor to the front stairs near the lift well, feeling as if my quest was rather futile now that the case was solved. But that old nagging something in my brain urged me to satisfy my curiosity. Things seemed at loose ends in my mind. I wanted to tie up all those ends neatly and then forget about the whole distasteful business. Although the actual murder had been solved, there were still several matters uncompleted; for example, the anonymous letters and the strange behaviour of Bill the liftman.

'He must have written them,' I told myself, descending the stairs to the basement.

I had long since put down Mac's hand in the affair to the same as mine; namely, an inquisitive disposition and a desire to have a shot at amateur detecting. How stupid and foolish I was not to realize the accuracy of inspector Coleman's words when he talked about amateurs in the field causing accidents.

One or two mechanics passed me on the stairs. They glanced at me curiously. It was no place for a telephonist as the men had a locker-room in the basement. A passage ran down one side of the building. On my left were different rooms used for storing odd pieces of apparatus and filed dockets. Besides being lighted by electricity, there were a few skylights let into the pavement above. I could hear the muffled tread of people in the street outside. I turned a corner of the passage and nearly yelled in excitement. Even in the dim light I could see the definite outlines of a door behind stacks of empty wooden boxes piled high in front of it. On a cursory examination it looked as if it hadn't been used for years, but at least

I had found what I was looking for. A second entrance to the Exchange!

'What a pity!' I said softly. 'If Dulcie hadn't more or less confessed to the crime, I would have been able to break Bertie's alibi.' The boxes were only light, three-ply affairs, which could be moved in and out of position before anyone would notice a disturbance. As for the key to the door, Bertie would certainly know where that was; if he didn't already have it in his possession.

'When Sergeant Matheson rings me next week,' I promised myself, 'I'll tell him about it; just as a point of interest. I wonder how many people know of this exit.' I started to retrace my steps, intending to go round by the right-of-way and have a look at the door from the outside.

One of the doors, now on my right, opened suddenly, and a girl crashed straight into me. I caught her by the arms as she stumbled, turning her face up to the light. It was Mac.

"Hullo," I said uneasily, mindful of the coldness between us. "Don't tell me that you've been making the big discovery too!"

She looked very pale, and was panting a little. I noticed a smudge of dirt on one cheekbone, and glanced down instinctively to her hands. They were filthy.

"What do you mean?" Mac asked quickly. Her eyes were raking my face.

"The hidden door," I answered, pointing down the passage. I thought I heard her breath quickly indrawn in a sigh.

"Oh, that!" she said, following my finger. "It's been locked for years. Haven't you ever seen it before?"

"Nor heard of it. I fancy that there are not too many people in the Exchange who have."

"I have to come down here after dockets," Mac explained carelessly.

"Indeed! Perhaps you can tell me if those boxes have been disturbed lately."

Mac walked on ahead hurriedly. "I haven't been down here for some time now. Anyway, I doubt whether I would have noticed."

"Precisely," I nodded, satisfied. We climbed the stairs in silence.

"What have you been crawling around in the dirt for?" I asked curiously.

"Looking for some dockets. What are you doing here at this hour? I thought you were on all night."

"So I am. I was snooping. I say, isn't it foul about Dulcie?"

"Awful," Mac agreed in a precise little voice. I frowned. Somehow, for the first time since I had known her, Mac had sounded insincere.

"The mater is in town," I informed her. Her face brightened.

"When did she come down? Give her my love."

"Only this morning. Don't you remember that I told you that I had forgotten to read her letter in all the excitement. It was rather a surprise when she arrived. She wanted to—buy a garden hat," I finished hurriedly.

"Buy a garden hat?" Mac echoed, and then laughed gaily. "How like her. She's a darling! Will I see her at all?"

"She might be coming to-morrow night, if I can manage to cadge a leave-pass from Bertie. How is he to-day, by the way?"

Mac shrugged a little. "As moody as ever. I think the suicide rattled him."

"You can't blame him. It is rather grim. I'd better go up and see him at once. Is Clark on duty yet?"

"He changed over to the all night with Bancroft," answered Mac cooly. "Didn't you know?" I felt elated and tried not to show it. I turned away to press the lift bell.

"He didn't tell me," I said lightly. "He'll be a good boss to have for the dog-watch. I'll be able to catch up on a few hours sleep."

The lift came down to the ground floor. I bade Bill "good day" as we entered. He answered my greeting quietly. As we ascended I made another search in my handbag.

"I can't find my pass anywhere," I explained to Mac, as she watched my fumblings casually. "Wait a bit, this looks like it." I separated a little red engagement book and a letter to retrieve it. The pass had been caught between them. As I moved it to a more conspicuous place, my eyes fell on a small stub of a pencil. I brought it out thoughtfully, and tapped Bill on the shoulder on impulse.

"I think you dropped this," I suggested, watching him closely.

He looked down at my hand, and then straight up into my eyes. "It doesn't look like one of mine," he said, bringing the lift to a standstill. "Indelible, isn't it?"

"That's right. Are you sure that it doesn't belong to you?"

Bill opened the doors, and Mac stepped out. "Quite," he answered curtly. I did not press him further, and put the pencil back into my bag. After all, it did not matter much, now.

Mac had gone through the glass doors to the trunkroom without a backward glance. I could see her straight little figure walking down the room to the sortagraph as I waited by the Senior Traffic Officer's table for Bertie. He was over at the Sydney boards. When he saw me the frown deepened between his eyes. He came hurrying back to his desk.

"Where have you been?" he demanded. "You should have been on an hour ago."

I stared at him uncomprehendingly for a minute. "But I am on all night, Mr. Scott." He slapped papers about on his desk. I moved aside out of range.

" You changed with Miss Patterson," he barked.

"No, I did not," I contradicted. "I wanted to, but you wouldn't let me. Didn't she turn up to-day?"

"She's not here. She's not on the sick-sheet, and your change is in the book."

"I know nothing about it, and I certainly didn't sign the change."

Bertie gave me a sharp glance under his bushy brows. He pulled out the book, and flipped over the pages. "You see?" I pointed out gently. He stared at the page.

"Well, where is Miss Patterson?" he demanded. Some of the edge had gone out of his bark.

"I couldn't tell you. I suppose she'll turn up to work all night."

He banged the book back, and started to open and shut drawers fiercely. "It's disgraceful!" he remarked vehemently. "Too many mistakes like this are occurring. There's to be no more changing until further notice, do you hear?"

'They could hear you out in the street,' I thought acidly, not game to tell him that he had given the same order two days ago, and hence the mix-up. I had come up to see him to beg a favour. I put on what I hoped was a winning smile, and asked prettily: "Mr. Scott, my mother is in town for the week-end. Could it be possible for her to come to the dance?"

"The dance," he repeated blankly. "What dance?"

"The charity social to-morrow night," I replied patiently. The telephones were ringing on his desk. I hoped he would give me the leave-pass before he got off the track again.

"That'll be all right," he grunted. "I'll write out permission, and leave it here on my table. You can pick it up to-night."

"Thanks, awfully," I said gratefully. "If Miss Patterson comes in to-night, what will we do?"

"You'd both better work all night, I suppose," he replied irritably, picking up a receiver. "Don't worry me now."

I had got what I wanted, so I left without a word. It was obvious that he was in a foul mood, perhaps because of the knowledge he knew I held about him; not that he had any need to worry. I had no wish to spread his story around the Exchange. Bertie was a good man to work for, and as such he would remain to me. After all, his private affairs were none of my business. I would never be able to treat him with that respect and admiration, as had been my wont. I longed to tell him about my discovery in the basement in order to observe his reaction. As I had thought with the pencil that Bill had dropped, what did it matter now? Compton and her murderess were both dead. The mystery of the anonymous letters and other troubles that she had left in her wake would remain. But there was no need to stir up the murky depths that Sarah's death had left to lie stagnant. They might evaporate in time.

I found Charlotte crossing from one corner to another with the traffic lights, and laughed.

"I couldn't remember which one you said," she excused herself. "People must have thought I was mad, but I didn't want to miss you. Did you get what you wanted?"

"Yes, thanks. What about the garden hat?"

"I forgot to look for it," she confessed. I guided her up town to a little continental café where the fish course is always superb. My mother insisted on "something to bring the colour to your cheeks," so we shared a half-bottle of Sauterne. I certainly felt better after dinner, and lighting a cigarette over coffee, began to tell her of Bertie's misdoings. She made a little moue of distaste, but let me go on uninterrupted until I concluded with the discovery of the door in the basement.

"All very interesting, Maggie, but to where does it lead you?"

"To the right-of-way on the west side of the building," I answered literally. "Although the door was bolted and barricaded, it would have been just too easy if anyone had really wanted to use it. Furthermore, in spite of Mac's assurance that most people knew of its existence, I didn't. And I've been at the Exchange for a good many years now."

"But everything's finished," protested my mother. "The case has been solved. Why are you worrying about out-of-the-way doors?"

"I don't know," I replied slowly. "There are a few matters that I'd like explained. But I suppose you are right. Everything's finished—including my coffee. Shall we go?"

We had decided on the good film at the second-rate theatre. But I did not see much of it. My brain was going around and around; turning over first this fact and then that. I should have felt satisfied. I kept repeating to myself: "Everything is finished, everything is finished," but my mind was restless and alert as though still awaiting a climax. Dulcie's suicide did not seem like the end of the story to me. Instead it seemed bizarre, extraordinary; even an anticlimax.

"It is because there was no letter found," I told myself, wondering what the simpering blonde on the screen had to do with the picture. She reminded me of Gloria, and that made my brain tick over again.

What part had she played in the murder? Was she too the innocent victim of our late unlamented monitor? And Bill! He knew something about that pencil I had offered him, I could swear. His manner was just a shade too off-hand and casual. I stirred restlessly, and Charlotte sh-h-d me to be quiet.

To hell with the Exchange and everyone it contained! Let them keep their guilty secrets! It was none of my business, thank Heaven. I tried to wipe all those nagging little thoughts from my mind and to concentrate on the screen.

"Very clever, don't you think?" my mother asked, as we came out.

"Excellent," I agreed mendaciously. I walked on to the road to compare the Town Hall time with my own watch. "I'll have to fly, Charlotte. It's ten to eleven. Will you be all right going home? Catch the No. 16 tram."

"I hate you going to work at this hour," Charlotte remarked plaintively. "It's not natural. Be very careful going up that dark street."

"I'll take the bus," I promised. "It'll drop me right outside the door. See you in the morning. Sleep well."

CHAPTER VI

I darted through the after-theatre crowd, thinking of them enviously. They would all be going home to bed, while I had to keep awake to serve them. The ungrateful cattle!

A telephonist's lot is a hard one, especially the all-nighter. I had started to yawn already. It is very difficult at the beginning to switch your working hours around to night-time. Once the first couple of nights are over, you become more or less accustomed to it. I always hated the first night of the dog-watch; you were relieved in the morning by fresh, clear-eyed girls, while you yourself were looking and feeling like death warmed up, Thank goodness, the all-night shift only occurred once every three months.

I caught the bus, and fell inevitably into the company of a couple of other all-nighters. They had brought books and knitting to while away the more tedious hours when traffic would be infrequent. I cursed my lack of foresight in not arming myself with similar weapons to keep me from further jumbled speculations about Bertie Scott and Bill.

"Have you seen Patterson?" I asked them, as we got ready for work in the dormitory on the seventh floor. It was a long room with curtained cubicles that more than adequately supplied accommodation for all-night operators. The following day it would be cleared and decorated for our charity social. I intended to help during the afternoon.

"Patterson? Patterson?" repeated one girl in mock concentration. "Who's she?"

"The girl with 'it,' " put in another.

"Oomph," I corrected. "Don't be out of date."

"Were you talking about me, Maggie?" asked an icy voice behind me. I swung round, adjusting the neckband of my outfit. Gloria stood in the doorway, a picture of dignified disdain.

"Well, well," I said brightly. "Look who's blown in. Yes, sweetheart, I was talking about you. And you can just take that nasty expression from your face. As a sneer, it is very feeble. What do you mean by putting a change in the book without telling me?"

She shrugged lightly, slipping the silver fox stole from her shoulders. "You said that I owed you a pay-back, and Bertie signed it."

"Well, next time, please let me know. As we are going to be overstaffed to-night, I intend to get in as much sleep as I can. I am just as glad that you made the mistake. But don't think that I am thanking you," I added hastily.

"You're a cat, Byrnes," Patterson burst out, losing her nonchalance. "One of these days, I'll get even with you."

"Try it," I advised. "You've already made one attempt and failed. Your first endeavour in telling lies about me to the police didn't get you very far."

"Getting an opinion of yourself after the notice they took of you, aren't you?" she sneered, this time more successfully. "No wonder Gerda is getting fed up." I stiffened suddenly. As she observed me wince, Patterson pressed home her attack. "I suppose that you know that your policeman is married, and has a couple of children."

"How interesting!" I said coldly, trying to bring the subject away from Mac. "And just where did you get this information which you have told me so thoughtfully?"

"That's my business," she drawled.

"Stop squabbling, you two," interrupted one of the others. "It's well after eleven, so hurry up."

So Mac was getting fed up with me! How did Gloria know that we had quarrelled—no, not exactly quarrelled. A shadow had grown up between us; a wall that had begun from withheld confidences and half-truths and had grown into indifference. It did not sound like Mac to go talking about our dissensions, especially to Gloria of all people. I pondered over it, puzzled and uncomprehending.

Mr. Bancroft was on duty as traffic officer. We were sternly rebuked for being late. He was a tall man, painfully thin, and suffered from diabetes, though I doubted whether that was the excuse for his continual tea-drinking. Every half-hour or so he would slip out of the trunkroom and brew a pot of tea. Almost everyone who worked in the Exchange developed some pet peculiarity. That was why I found my colleagues not uninteresting. We might be regarded like so many cogs in the wheel, but we retained some individuality above our work.

The late telephonists were all a trifle terse. The usual custom was to relieve a few minutes early; even if one was kept working until the stroke of eleven, which was the exact time that the late telephonists' duty ends, one felt hardly done by.

I took over the country boards, far from the rest of the staff. As an interstate telephonist, I thought the slight change in operating might make up for the lack of other amusement. I regretted my decision immediately. I knew that once I got by myself the old doubts would start running around in my brain again, and I would have no peace unless some hard switching demanded my full attention. That would be unlikely to happen after an hour or two when the lines became slack, and if the traffic officer on duty was a decent fellow we could go off for some sleep, or knit and read.

Clark came in a few minutes before the half-hour. He talked for a while with Mr. Bancroft to learn the state of the traffic, and if any of the lines were out of order. Presently, he passed me on his way to dismantle the delay-board. The room grew quieter as the power fell to half-pressure, and calls became more and more infrequent. The chatter of the girls the other side of the room echoed hollowly. I half-listened, casually drawing faces on the back of a docket for want of something better to do. When their voices fell to a murmur I realized that I was the subject of the conversation. It didn't worry me much. After all, my position during the last few days must have been the subject of a lot of discussion.

Suddenly Patterson's voice arose, shrilly, "Personally, I think that she was to blame for poor Dulcie's suicide."

There was no doubt as to her meaning. A dead silence fell. I stared for a moment at the absurd faces that I had sketched, and then swung round in my chair filled with an indescribable mixture of emotions. Anger, there certainly was. Who would be able to keep calm in the face of such an accusation? But there was also a dread, cold feeling of horror. Could it be that Patterson's word spoken with malicious intent held some degree of accuracy? Had I killed Dulcie? Had I forced her to commit the terrible crime of taking her own life by my untimely intervention in her affairs? It had occurred to me before, but not quite like that. I had been blaming myself for leaving something unsaid; a few comforting words that might have coaxed Gordon out of her despair. Had my clumsy advice only deepened her sense of hopelessness? In those few minutes as I stared across the room to where Patterson faced me defiantly, I went through an age of torturing fear and self-condemnation. I could not utter a word to defend myself, but continued to gaze horror-stricken at my tormentor.

John Clarkson came striding briskly down the room. "Now then, you girls, what are those lights doing in the panel? Get going." He must have heard Patterson. No one in the room could have missed her raised voice. He continued on his way towards me. I watched his approach miserably, my eyes altering their focus as he came nearer. He turned my chair around gently so that I faced my position again. I felt the firm pressure of his hand on my shoulder before he walked round to the back of the boards, and leaned over the low top opposite me. I looked at him beseechingly for a minute in silence. I was forced to whisper as my throat felt parched and tight.

"Did you hear what she said? Clark, I—" He stopped me, putting a finger to his lips.

"Take no notice," he replied gently. "She was only trying to bait you." But the way he spoke made me say urgently: "Is she right? Is that what everyone is saying, but she was the only one game enough to speak straight out? Am I the cause of Dulcie—that poor child-?"

"Hush, Maggie, pull yourself together, or you'll go to pieces properly. Dulcie took the best way out if she killed Sarah."

"If!" I repeated almost hysterically. "Supposing she didn't kill Sarah? Then I am to blame for her death as surely as if I killed her myself."

"Don't talk rot," Clark said sternly. "Look! There's a light waiting for you. Get on with your work and stop thinking idiotic thoughts."

I fumbled blindly for the key, and dialled out a number for Leongatha. Clark stayed where he was, glancing now and then over my head at the other telephonists. I was glad that he was so near. I needed assurance and plenty of it at that moment.

"Margaret," he spoke my name in a low, kind voice. "Gordon did kill Sarah Compton. The police are satisfied. They must be, as they've packed up and left. Won't you forget the whole horrible business for ever?"

"Never," I replied vehemently. "I can never forget what Patterson said. Oh, I don't hold it against her, as she only spoke with the idea to get a rise. But it would be just the same if my best friend, or even you, made such an accusation. I'm not going mad, Clark, so don't worry. I am beginning to think clearly for the first time, and there is one fact in my mind that stands out. It may be ridiculous, and it may have been proved that I am wrong, but of this I am certain. Dulcie Gordon did not murder Compton. She was incapable of such a deed, and I know it. Granted, she had both the opportunity and the motive, which I, in what I thought was my clever way, pointed out to the police. But I will never believe her guilty. That is, not until some letter is found from her definitely stating that she murdered Sarah.

Clark's eyes narrowed a little, and I thought he looked concerned. "Leave it, Maggie," he advised. "You're only a kid yourself. Be satisfied with the police decision. It's the best in the long run, and will spare you needless self-reproach."

I felt a surge of despair go through me, but I looked up at him almost triumphantly. "You see," I said. "You don't think that Dulcie did it either."

"I didn't say so," he answered sharply. I shook my head in an unbelieving fashion. I had seen the doubt in his eyes for a moment, and it had convinced me utterly that he, too, believed Dulcie had had nothing to do with Sarah's murder. I completed a couple of calls mechanically, as Clark went to answer a ringing phone on the Senior Traffic Officer's table. My brain as for ever searching for a lead that would enable me to take a satisfactory case to the police. If only I could find some small clue that might get them to revise their decision. But there seemed to be no loophole whatsoever. Sarah's real killer must have been rubbing his hands with glee at this lucky turn-up. I sighed despondently reaching for a pile of dockets marked A.G.

I flipped through them disinterestedly. What was the use of trying them again, and dragging people out of bed at this unearthly hour. As I started to re-mark them for 8 a.m. the following day, a name caught my eye. My attention froze on to it immediately. It was an almost absurd coincidence. I stared at it stupidly. But there it was in black and white, or rather yellow because an in-docket recorded the call from Bertuna to a city number, personal to Mr. C. Gordon. I turned it over quickly, and discovered that it had been a particular person unavailable all night—to be tried again urgently.

I shot a glance at the clock. It was nearly 1 a.m., but that did not deter me. I dialled the first country town that switched for Bertuna.

"A line to Merriup," I demanded and waited patiently. Presently a sleepy voice came on to declare the station.

"Melbourne speaking," I said, flashing my monitor's light to bring John Clarkson back. "A line to Bertuna, please."

"They're closed, Melbourne," answered Merriup with some indignation. "It's after twelve."

"I can tell the time, thank you," I remarked crisply. "Open them up."

"It'll be an opening fee," declared the voice doubtfully.

"Open them," I repeated. "I'll take the responsibility." I heard a few clatters as Merriup put down her hand-set, and rang on the Bertuna line. Presently her aggrieved voice remarked: "They're not answering, Melbourne."

"Ring them again," I ordered stubbornly. "And keep on ringing until you get them. I'll stay on the line."

"Getting through, Mel?" asked the main switching station.

"Yes, thanks; leave me on until I ring back on the line, will you? Are you calling them, Merriup?"

"Yes," snapped the voice, "and don't you tell me how to switch. I've been at it for twenty-five years."

"You should be due for your pension any time now," I suggested, and received a nasty threat to report my rudeness.

"What is it, Maggie?" asked a voice in my right ear. It was Clark. I pointed to the yellow docket in silence. He picked it up and whistled long and low.

"It might be interesting," I said. "Will you get a hand-set?"

His eyes danced for a minute, but his face was quite grave. "It's against the rules, both moral and the Department's, but I'll risk it."

"I won't split. Yes, Merriup, Melbourne waiting. Oh, is that Bertuna? Sorry if we woke you. I want 7D please, a party line."

"There'll be an opening fee on this," Bertuna threatened me.

"I know, I have already been warned. You'll get your miserable eighteen pence. Tell me, who is the subscriber at 7D?"

There was silence as Bertuna pondered for a while. After all, it was rather difficult to summon all your faculties to work out whose number it was at a moment's notice; especially at that early hour of the morning. "Charlie Gordon's place," she said at last. It didn't surprise me. I had guessed as much. The Bertuna telephonist waxed conversational as she called on the party-line. I could hear the ring-two long and a short.

"His daughter did herself in early this morning," she informed me. I nodded to myself wearily. As if I wouldn't be likely to know! "She worked at Trunks," the voice went on. "Did you ever come across her?"

"On occasions," I replied, listening intently for an answer from 7D.

"They're very cut up about it round here. She was such a nice girl. I couldn't believe my ears when they told me." I heard a click, but it was only Clark plugging in on my board. He grinned at me as if I was a fellow-conspirator, and drew up the adjacent chair.

"To whom are you talking?" he whispered, covering his mouthpiece with one hand. Bertuna was still flowing on about her impressions and emotions at the news of Gordon's suicide.

"Bertuna," I replied helplessly. "We're a gossipy clan. Yes, I'm here."

"You're through, Melbourne."

"Thanks, Is that Bertuna 7D?" I asked as a subdued female answered. "You booked a call earlier to Mr. Gordon in Melbourne."

"Have you found him?" asked the voice eagerly. "Hullo, Charlie. Are you there, Dad?"

"Just a minute, I only wanted to know if you'd like me to try your call again."

"Oh, please," said the voice on what I thought was a sob.

"Hold the line, please," I ordered, dialling out the number of a residential hotel down town.

I knew the telephonist on duty rather well, but did not tarry to yarn with her as was our wont; rather, I attempted to disguise my voice, but to no avail.

"He's in room 304, Maggie," she told me. "Have you got a cold?" Clark shook silently beside me. I gave him an indignant glance.

"Just a touch of laryngitis," I replied airily. "Where's this bloke been all night, anyway?"

"On the razzle, I bet. I know these farmers when they come to town." But Dulcie's father sounded far from gay as he answered his telephone.

"Mr. C. Gordon?" I queried. "Bertuna calling," I closed his key. "Are you there, Mrs. Gordon? Your number is waiting. Go ahead, please." I closed both keys, but opened the observing line, and leaned back in my chair.

"Now!" I breathed to Clark. There was dead silence on the line. I re-opened the keys, puzzled, wondering if the monitoring line was out of order. Like so many subscribers, the Gordons were sitting facing each other and not uttering a word.

"You're connected," I said patiently. "Please start your conversation."

"Hullo, Charlie," said Mrs. Gordon in a faltering voice. His deep one answered gravely: "Is that you, Mother?"

"I've been trying to get you all night, but they said you were out. Where have you been?"

"I was up at Russell Street most of the time. Then I went for a walk. It's no use, my dear. They're convinced that she killed Miss Compton."

I heard Mrs. Gordon sob a little, and could visualize the tears flowing unchecked down her cheeks. "She couldn't have done it. Not our little Dulcie! She was such a good, quiet girl." I nodded to Clark in an 'I told you so' fashion. He frowned and rested his arms on the board, listening intently.

"Charlie," went on Mrs. Gordon hesitantly. "I've got a letter here-from Dulcie. It arrived in the night's mail." I nearly jumped out of my chair in excitement. What fools we had been not to guess! Of course Dulcie would not leave a farewell note in her rooms for all the world to read. She would send it to her people-post it last night before- It took all my control to stop from going on the line to demand what she had written. I heard Charlie Gordon's troubled voice ordering his wife to read it. Mrs. Gordon did so, interspersed with pauses when I could hear her weeping pitifully. It was a pathetic little note, that filled me with fresh dread, particularly when my own name was mentioned.

"I have told one of the girls, Margaret Byrnes. You have heard me speak of her. She's one of the nicest girls at Central, and I know she would not tell the police. But they are bound to find out sooner or later, and I can't face it. Forgive me, darling Mummy, but I am so miserable. They say that it is just like going to sleep, but I don't care much, It is better than being hanged." The letter ended there. There was no fierce contradiction to being guilty of murder. Dulcie Gordon had gone out of this world as quietly, and with as little fuss, as she had lived.

Were the police right after all, as Dulcie had not denied killing Sarah? 'She's guilty. She's not guilty,' sang my brain over and over until I felt that I was going mad. Why couldn't she have said one thing or the other, and not left me in this horrible suspense of doubt? Had I been the means of causing her to commit that unpunishable crime, or did she anticipate the hangman and prevent the law from completing a conviction?

The Gordons talked on, but I took very little notice of their conversation. Indeed, I felt rather mean eavesdropping on their secret sorrows. Presently they speculated whether it would be better to hand Dulcie's letter over to the police at once or to destroy it, and keep some particle of their daughter's name unsullied. However, Charlie Gordon was adamant, and insisted that the police should learn of its existence. After all, as he told his wife and as I had considered earlier, they were already convinced of Dulcie's guilt. The fact that she had neither admitted nor denied having killed Compton might help them to change their decision, and work from the angle that she was innocent of any implication in the murder. The probable cause of her taking her own life was not the knowledge of actual guilt, but the fact that circumstantial evidence pointed her way. She knew that no jury on this earth could acquit her.

As the conversation had started on a repetitive course, I considered that it was high time that they finished useless speculations, and had some respite from the sadness that their conversation was causing each other. A glance at the clock showed that they had been connected for nearly a quarter of an hour.

"Three minutes have expired," I informed them with largesse. "Are you extending?"

"No, thank you," said Mr. Gordon hurriedly. "Good-bye, Mary, I'll be home to-morrow night. Try to be brave, my dear."

"Finish up, please," I said without emotion, marking off the docket and signing my name.

"That's that," I remarked calmly to Clark, pulling my earpiece on to my temple and rubbing a sore ear. "It leaves us precisely where we were before. To put it in a nutshell—did she, or didn't she?"

"I wouldn't like to give an opinion," Clark answered slowly. "It seems impossible that such a nondescript girl would have the brain to work out such a cunning plan and yet—"

"And yet," I continued, "it couldn't have been such a marvellous idea. Look how she ended up! Committed murder on Wednesday, and killed herself on Friday. It's too brief to be wholesome. No, there's more in this business than meets the eye," I added reflectively.

"What do you mean?"

"I don't quite know," I confessed. "But I think that I will keep an open mind as to Dulcie's guilt for a while."

"Listen to me, Maggie," Clark said sternly. "The police are not fools. They are trained, clever men. It's their job to discover the truth. If they are satisfied to leave things as they are, I am too."

"And I," I declared in a low voice, "am a telephonist. My job is switching, at which I think that I am fairly capable."

"Correct, you conceited woman," he said with a half-smile. "Stay in your own sphere, Maggie. Don't go prying into things that don't concern you."

"Like Sarah Compton?" I interpolated gently. A sudden look of fear flashed through his eyes before he replied gravely, placing one hand on mine.

"Precisely, my dear. If our idea is correct and the killer is still at large, there is all the more reason why you should stay out of the picture."

"I believe that you're concerned about my fate," I remarked watching him surreptitiously. His hand tightened.

"Don't, Maggie," he said in a low voice, as he arose from his chair. "You know that I—" and he stopped.

"I know—?" I prompted.

"No matter," Clark replied curtly, starting to clear the boards of dockets and odd pencils. Presently he came back to inquire lightly: "Why do you always call me that?"

After a moment of puzzlement, I parried: "Why do you call me Maggie?"

He laughed. "*Touché!* Nicknames are the devil! Would you like some relief after the gruelling work you have put in?"

"I don't think so. Not for a while, anyway. Will you do me a favour?"

"Anything," he answered promptly, with mock gallantry.

"Send Gloria Patterson over here to switch, I want to have a talk with her."

Clark raised an admonitory finger, "Now, Miss Byrnes!"

"Nothing about murders," I assured him hastily. "I want to ask her about something purely private."

Under the pretext of collecting some dockets that I had pushed to the floor, I watched Clark approach Gloria. She started suddenly as he touched her shoulder and spoke a few words. An artificial smile spread over her face, and one hand pulled at the curls near her ears. 'That girl would ogle anything in pants,' I thought disgustedly, sighting a docket half-hidden under the boards. I was compelled to go the full length of my telephone flex like a dog on a leash before I could retrieve it. Patterson's voice sounded slightly patronizing behind me as I got down on my hands and knees.

"What on earth are you doing, Maggie?"

"Playing hunt the thimble," I retorted, rising to my feet and feeling red in the face and untidy from the exertion. Gloria was looking so impossibly well-groomed and smug that I longed to slap her.

"Clark sent me over to help you," she continued, taking a chair beside mine.

"Good of you, Gloria," I remarked gravely, wondering if the girl ever saw through anything that anyone said to her. She inclined her head graciously as she turned over dockets, disturbing my neat pile.

"Are these to be tried?" she asked.

"Don't be silly," I said irritably, "It's going on for two."

"Is it?" she asked in surprise, looking around for a clock, "I've been talking to that American I told you about, I haven't noticed the time, In fact, I was terribly glad when Clark told me to move, I simply couldn't get rid of the man."

"What is it you've got that I haven't?" I asked, interested.

"Really, Maggie!" Gloria said, looking almost unbearably pleased. "Perhaps if you were a little more conciliatory," she suggested, "you'd not lack boy-friends. You're quite attractive, you know."

"Thank you," I said dryly.

"But you don't make enough of yourself," she insisted. "Wearing your hair straight back from your face like that makes you look hard. Then you're so blunt and matter-of-fact. Men don't like that."

"I must take a course of lessons from you," I suggested. My sarcasm went over her head as usual. "This Yank—was he the one you met at the 'Australia' on Wednesday night?" I thought that if I had said the night of the murder, Gloria's dim insight might have penetrated my little game. Putting it as I had, there was a chance she wouldn't connect my questions with anything else but a desire to learn more of the art of beguiling man. So far, so good. She had started a long dissertation on where she had met her American, what he looked like, and how much money he had. The saga included descriptions of numerous other conquests, matched by a different dress each time. I listened patiently, waiting for an opportunity to lead her carefully back to what I at least considered was the point.

"I suppose," I remarked, putting out a feeler, "that he was the cause of you being late back from your tea-time?"

"Absolutely. He kept talking about what a sensation I'd be in the States, until I thought he'd never stop. I'm positive," she added, pulling at the curls again and giving me a sidelong glance, "that he was leading up to a proposal. I think I'd rather like to live in America."

"I'm sure you'd be a riot. But tell me, as you came up in the lift did you see anyone at all?"

Gloria appeared not to be listening, so intent was she on the rosy dream that I had abetted.

"I don't remember," she answered abstractedly.

"Your rota was going down by the stairs to the trunkroom," I prompted. "They saw you."

"Did they?" she asked, surprised. "Why, yes, I believe some of them did pass me."

"And you went on straight to the cloakroom to get your outfit?" I asked cautiously, hoping that she was not becoming suspicious.

"I had to take off my orchid as well," Gloria explained. "That beast, Compton—"

"Quite so," I interrupted. "Did you see anyone else hanging around the corridor?"

"Only one of—" She stopped abruptly, eyeing me. "I saw no one," she snapped. "Isn't there any work to do here? Clark said that you were practically in a bag."

"It's about time we started testing the lines," I said with haste. In the endeavour to make her forget her suspicions and come back to her movements later on, we callously roused drowsy telephonists all over the state to get them to ring back on their lines to see if we got their signal. It was tedious work, and one that brought a large amount of abuse on our heads. I knew that Gloria would not have the gumption to realize that the testing was quite unnecessary at that hour. By the time we had finished her shallow brain had forgotten my pertinent questions.

"What about relief'?" I suggested on a brain-wave. "You can go first.

It won't matter if you're late back. Sarah Compton is not here," I laughed heartily.

"How can you be so callous, Maggie!" Patterson replied, opening her eyes wide. "Poor Sarah. I'm sure she didn't mean to be so snappy with me that night. We were great friends as a rule, you know."

'Oh, yeah?' I thought. Sarah didn't have a friend in the world, and certainly not in the Exchange; barring Bertie perhaps, after his amazing story. Even then it seemed a hit-and-miss affair.

"I suppose you wanted to ring up your Yankee friend that night?" I suggested, "And you couldn't get into the restroom to use the telephone."

"I had to go all the way over to the public box in the other building," she answered indignantly. "You really think that Sarah would have understood."

"Too bad! She made you work overtime just for that. You're sure that the restroom door was locked?"

"I tried it several times, and so did Gerda. I told you that."

'Well, that's settled,' I thought. The door must have been bolted some time between 7 p.m. and when the reliefs started. But the fact that it was locked worried me. It seemed so very unnecessary. It wasn't as if Sarah had been murdered already, and the killer wanted to delay the discovery. She had been very much alive at that time; sitting on the roof playing 'peepo's' with me. No, there must have been someone or something in that room that had to remain unseen until the right time. A very large object, or more probably a human being, that required a whole room in which to stay hidden. It might have been the murderer who locked himself in the restroom, but how was Compton able to walk straight in later on? It was either unlocked then, or else Sarah had a key.

I shook my head again, puzzled. Putting myself in the role of a murderer, I could not see myself staying two or three hours cooped up in a room waiting for my victim to approach. It was definitely unreasonable. No murderer, however cold-blooded he or she might be, could remain quietly in one place for all that length of time. It did not fit in at all well with my conception of the killer. It was a fast crime. One that was planned and executed by a swift-moving brain; a brain totally dissimilar to poor Dulcie's.

'Unless,' I thought wearily, bent on looking at the situation from every angle, 'she was so subtle that her quiet demeanour was just the work of a skilled actress.'

But I couldn't see the same girl who had fallen headlong into a trap laid by Compton being so clever.

'Anyway,' I told myself. 'Dulcie is out of this altogether. I am working from the angle that she is innocent.' The only fact of any benefit that I had gleaned from my careful questioning of Gloria, if one could call it a fact, was that she had seen someone in the vicinity of the cloakroom on the night of the murder.

'Only one of—' and there she had stopped. I repeated the words two or three times audibly in the endeavour to finish the sentence, but gave up in despair.

'I'll wait until she comes back, and then see if I can get some more out of her,' I promised myself.

The door at the end of the country boards opened suddenly, and Gloria came in on a bound. Her face was as white as paper. Tears of stark terror were rushing down her cheeks. She looked like a child who had awoken from a nightmare.

'Now what?' I thought, not without some interest. I watched her cover the shortest distance between two points in record time; the farther point being Clark. She clung to him like the proverbial ivy. I could not hear the exact gist of her stumbling words, but it was obvious that she had received a tremendous fright. Clark removed her clutching hands firmly, and led her back towards me, his brows raised in comical despair. I grinned at him sympathetically, guessing that Gloria's experience was not as overwhelming as she had made it appear.

"Ghosts!" Clark whispered in mock awe. "I have to lay a ghost."

I glanced down the boards, and as all seemed quiet, asked if I might tag along. "I wouldn't be out of it for worlds. Laying ghosts is one of my favourite pastimes. Where are they, Gloria?"

"We don't want you," she snapped, her spirits evidently reviving.

"Gloria, how can you! Clark isn't an adequate enough protection for you, are you, Clark?"

"You can come and look after me. Now, Miss Patterson, where is the phantom?"

"It isn't a laughing matter," Gloria said earnestly, leading the way up the stairs. "I tell you I saw Sarah Compton in the restroom."

"What!" I exclaimed, running ahead.

"Maggie, come back," she shrieked. I heard Clark laugh.

The corridor was as black as pitch at that hour. The eighth floor was seldom used by all-night telephonists. Only one shaded light hung at the top end of the passage near the lift. I began to regret my impetuous dash. I slid my hand along the wall until the cloakroom door-knob came under my fingers, and fumbled for the light on the inside. As I pressed it, a slamming noise came from the inner room. I jumped like a frightened rabbit. But the voices coming up the stairs encouraged me to walk boldly to the restroom door, which stood open. The noise sounded again, and I peered cautiously into the room. A huge white object billowed out to meet me. I fell back, readily understanding Gloria's terror.

"Are you there, Maggie?" asked Clark, coming round the lockers with Gloria shrinking behind him.

"Is this your ghost?" I asked her scornfully, switching on the light and indicating the long dust-blind which eddied to and fro in the night wind. Clark swore gently as Gloria peered gingerly over my shoulder. He took himself off in disgust.

"I thought it was Sarah's ghost," she remarked naively, "and it's only the blind."

"Only the blind," I echoed thoughtfully. "Either you have a very guilty conscience, or else you wanted to attract notice, Gloria. Now which is it? Come and sit down, my pet, and tell me all about it. Yes, sit there." I pushed her into the arm-chair at the foot of which Mac and I had found Sarah Compton's sprawling body. There could not have been a better position in which to place her. I had made up my mind to attack her directly.

"Do you realize," I went on brightly, seating myself near the door. "that you must be in the same chair as Compton was before she was killed? The police say that she was seated when she received the first blow. Now, isn't that interesting?" Her eyes were dilating. Her hands closed convulsively on the arms of her chair as the blind flapped again. John said later that I used poor Gloria badly, but as I pointed out to him, I had to start on my inquiries somewhere and what I discovered was of great value to clearing up the mystery.

"Now, Gloria," I began. "Will you tell me whom you saw on Wednesday after you came back from the 'Australia' ?"

Her tongue passed over her lips before she replied stubbornly: "I saw no one. Just who do you think you are, Byrnes? Have the police given you the authority to go round asking questions? I am going back to the trunkroom."

"Oh, no, you're not," I said, standing up and moving across the doorway. "Not if I have to hold you here by force. I am very strong, you know. Sit down."

She sank back, trying to assume a nonchalant attitude by crossing her exquisitely shod feet.

"There is also another matter that will hold you here by moral force. I suppose you realize I could sue you for making slanderous statements about me; first of all, to the police themselves, and they would be very excellent witnesses, my child; and secondly, your very uncalled for remark to-night. If you wish to blame anyone for this discomfort you may blame yourself. You are the direct cause of me making these inquiries. As you probably gather by now, I am most dissatisfied with the decision the police have come to about Sarah's death. I may have agreed with them, had you not passed that remark. It started me thinking. Do you follow?"

Gloria nodded. Her wide blue eyes were like those of a bird fascinated by a snake, which simile though apt, I considered as very derogatory to myself. I had made up my mind to be without mercy until I had got what I wanted.

"On Wednesday night," I began my questions, "after you had put your precious orchid away and did the less important thing of getting your telephone on, did you go straight to the trunkroom?"

"Yes," she answered after a slight hesitation. I sighed.

"No good, Gloria. If you want to make a success of lying, you must answer quickly. Not too fast, of course. I have it from your rota that you took a considerable time to rejoin them. What held you up?"

"I won't tell you," she said promptly, drawing out a cigarette case.

"It does give confidence," I agreed, helping myself to her case without invitation. "But I am forced to remind you of my little threat unless you answer my question. I would get such good damages, Gloria. Suppose I ask you again. What made you late?"

"I was talking," Gloria replied sulkily. She knew she was cornered. Her only way of escape was either bluff or skilful lying. I was on the alert for both.

"To your unknown friend? Was that all? Are you sure that you did not go up to the roof, and better still to the lift cabin?" Gloria looked disdainful as she shook her head.

"All right. Perhaps this might stir you up. What does the name Irene Patterson convey to you?" I certainly dropped a bombshell of some sort. I had expected defiance or sullenness to this question, but not the sudden paling of her skin and then the hot blood that flowed under it in swift succession.

"Evidently something," I remarked. "Well?"

Her tongue passed over her lips, and I had to strain my ears to catch her low reply: "That was my mother's name."

"Was?" I inquired awkwardly. "Do you mean that she's dead?" Gloria bent her head as she nodded. I felt an odd mixture of disappointment and excitement. So Irene was Gloria's mother after all.

"Have you a father?" I asked her quickly.

"Yes. Yes, of course. Why do you ask?" she stammered.

I felt a new exultation as I observed her embarrassment. "What does he do?"

"What business is it of yours?" Gloria asked furiously. "If you really must know, my parents separated many years ago. I live with my aunt. I haven't seen my father for years."

"But you'd know him if you saw him, wouldn't you?"

"I suppose so," she replied uncertainly.

"You don't happen to know our liftman's name, do you?" I asked, having decided on a *volte-face*. Again I saw the blood pound under her fair skin.

"No, I do not," she answered shortly. "Nor am I interested."

"But I am," I said, pressing the attack, "keenly interested. Perhaps if I suggest that the person you saw in the corridor was the liftman, Bill, it might help jog your memory."

Gloria got up from her chair to wander about restlessly and also to hide her tell-tale fair skin from my never-flagging scrutiny. She did not dare make a dash for it through the door. I must have her more under my thumb than I knew.

"Well?" I inquired, almost loath to do so. "Was it Bill?"

She turned around and looked at me in a peculiar manner. I was unable to analyse that look. "Yes. It was Bill."

I covered my eyes with one hand. This was almost as bad as proving Dulcie Gordon had killed Compton, a choice of two evils. I felt a strong desire to tell Gloria to forget all I had asked her. I wanted to go and hide myself far away and forget the whole business. I glanced up and caught that odd expression in her eyes again. I remembered her indirect accusation in the trunkroom uttered only a little time ago, and my will grew firm. If I wanted any peace for the rest of my life, I had to rid myself of the responsibility of Dulcie's death, no matter who was the scapegoat.

"Sit down, Gloria. You're as bad as Bertie for fidgeting. We come now to another matter which concerns me very much. On what grounds did you make that remark that Mac was getting fed up?"

"I don't blame her," Gloria said viciously. "You're becoming as interfering as—"

"I know," I interrupted. "Our late monitor. Already two people have pointed that out to me. I am getting just a little tired of the comparison. You haven't answered my question."

"She told me," Gloria replied with a malicious spark in her eyes.

"I don't believe you," I exclaimed, sitting up swiftly. Mac, Mac, was that what our friendship had come to? As Gloria shrugged, I asked: "When did she tell you?"

"We had lunch together in town."

"You had lunch together," I repeated in amazement. "Don't tell me

Mac made an appointment to meet you!"

"Why not?" she asked, stung. "I am just as much a friend of hers as you are."

"It's the first I've heard of it," I answered, giving up. "Go on. What else did Mac say?"

"She rang me up this morning. She wanted to see me, so I suggested we meet at the 'Blue Wren.'"

"I knew it. Who paid for the lunch?"

"Gerda did. She insisted so you needn't look like that. As a matter of fact, I didn't have any change," Gloria paused, evidently expecting some comment. I merely nodded for her to continue.

"Well, that's all," she said lamely. "Gerda just wanted to hear about what I did on Wednesday night. She said that she might be able to help me."

"And did she?"

"No, not exactly. But she was kind and more understanding than you were. She told me to stop worrying, and to forget all about the murder. You've no idea what I've been through. I've always been sensitive, and then Sarah going like she did!"

"Going where?" I demanded, busy with my own thoughts.

"Stop trying to be funny," she snapped. "You know quite well what I mean."

"And you stop trying to make out that you and Sarah were bosom friends," I retaliated. "It doesn't go down with anyone, and only puts you in a very bad light. You'll find that advice quite as good as Mac's."

"It's easy to see that you're jealous," Gloria sneered, as she rose to her feet. "I'm going back to the trunkroom, and don't you try to stop me."

"I don't want to now. You may go with my blessing. Tell Mr. Clarkson that I'm going to have a sleep for an hour, will you?"

"Give your own messages," she snapped, flouncing out of the room.

* * * * *

I lay full length on the lounge and pulled a cushion behind my head, not to relax waiting for sleep to overcome my senses, but to reflect on what I had learned from Gloria. That damned blind started to flap in the rising wind. I hauled myself up to go and shut the window, which overlooked the dump-yard where Bertie's buttinsky had been found.

This building up a case against a person or persons unknown to vindicate Dulcie Gordon was harder than I had expected. I sighed despondently. As soon as I jumped on to one interesting point, all the other questionable happenings left my mind. It was difficult trying to blend them all together. One fact would jerk up in my mind, and make the others fade into insignificance.

"I'll start all over again, and run through the main figures as I did this morning," I said aloud, finding a companionable flying beetle to talk to, instead of the fly I had confided in before. "Though I don't know how long I am going to stand your stupid buzzing," I warned it. I decided to turn off the restroom light to stop the irritating noise. The subdued glow from the cloakroom drew its attention, and I lay down on the lounge once more. I often wondered later why I wasn't nervous lying there alone in the dark room where Compton's bloody body had been found. I suppose it was because I did not realize then what a danger I was to the killer's safety. If I had, I would promptly have taken myself as far from the Exchange as possible. But there were too many disconnected pieces of information running around in my mind to give me time to think of myself. All I wanted to do was to put them together and make one whole picture, so that I could go to Inspector Coleman in the morning and beg them to reopen the case.

Mac's piquant face came before my mental vision so vividly that I wondered for a moment if I had fallen asleep, and was dreaming. There seemed no reason why I should think of her suddenly. I tried to analyse the disturbed feeling that her name gave me. What was it that Gloria had said lightly, but with malicious intent? That I was jealous? Perhaps she was right in that assertion; not because of Mac's abrupt appreciation of Gloria, but the fear that she would get in before me with her own amateur inquiries. I felt a sense of possession in regard to the whole affair, that was as foolish as it was absurd. After all, Mac had been in on practically every happening since Wednesday night. She had every right to pursue her own line of detecting. The kindly attention, which Mac had shown Gloria when she had taken her to lunch that day, was not due to a sudden liking for Gloria's company, but a means by which she might tactfully discover what Gloria was so obviously hiding. I wondered if she had found out why our blonde friend was so anxious to avoid meeting Sarah on Wednesday night.

Mac must have got what she wanted, because of the way in which she told Gloria to forget all about the nasty business. I resolved to see Mac the next day, and lay my cards on the table so that we could work together. Perhaps in that way we might resume the old footing of frank camaraderie and break down the barrier which, in all justice, had been most of Mac's making.

Then there was John Clarkson to remember. It was obvious that he was as dissatisfied with the police decision as I. Certainly he seemed reluctant to commit himself further. That was all very well for him, but he didn't have the awful dread of wondering if he were responsible for the suicide of poor Dulcie. I knew my Exchange and fellow-telephonists too well not to realize that, although the majority would recognize Gloria's accusation as a product of her nasty temperament, the rumour would swell and enlarge into an ominous size. It would take some drastic move to destroy the rumour. As far as I could see, that move had to be made on my part, and as quickly as possible. It was a choice between my own peace of mind and leaving things as they stood, or trying to construct a case against someone else. Perhaps I was selfish in choosing the latter course, but I knew now that nothing I could have done would have altered the turn of events.

I closed my eyes as my head started to ache from intense concentration. It was dark and still in the restroom. Only the distant thud-thud from the power-room kept me conscious of my surroundings. I jerked my head up from my chest to which it had fallen, and let it rest against the side of the couch. I must have fallen asleep, but I did not realize it at the time. I certainly did not hear anyone switch off the cloakroom light and come creeping into the restroom. But my muscles were still tense and unrelaxed when I heard the telephone across the room click as the receiver was lifted. The dial was spun round softly.

I stared wide-eyed in the darkness searching for the door to the cloakroom, not daring to move. My breath came quickly and my heart pounded against my ribs. I was so silent that I could hear the faint burr-burr of the 'phone ringing. It stopped as a voice crackled metallically for a few seconds, and then the click was repeated as the receiver went back into place. Whoever had dialled out on the restroom telephone in the pitch-black darkness had not uttered a word. The caller had merely listened to the person at the other end of the line, and then glided out as quietly as before.

I longed for the courage to call out but dared not. I waited for minutes to pass before I was game enough to put one foot to the floor. My heart still thumped sickeningly, and I counted up seconds to three minutes.

'I'll get up then,' I told myself firmly. 'I'll walk straight over to the door and switch on the light.' But I was coward enough to allow another sixty seconds to pass before I slid carefully from the couch and felt around the wall, ready to make a dash if the need arose. The room flooded with light under my hand. I blinked rapidly, trying to change my focus. The pedestal telephone stood in its corner quietly, and I tried to visualize a hand spinning the dial around softly. As I stared at it in fascination. my heart began to slow down to its normal tempo. My panting breath had left me parched. Taking one last look around the room, I switched off the light again and walked rather unsteadily through the cloakroom to the lunchroom opposite to get a drink of water.

I forced myself to drink slowly between deep breaths, and felt much better after doing so. As I was draining the glass, an idea occurred to me. I put down the tumbler quickly, and dashed out of the lunchroom and along the corridor to the lift. It was waiting for me at the eighth floor. I paused for a brief moment then shrugging hopefully, I locked myself in and pressed the button for the first floor. As the lift started on its descent with a jerk, I clung on to Bill's empty chair, staking my faith in the law of averages. I had come through another harrowing experience in the restroom unharmed, so surely my solitary journey in the lift would be unmarked by any further disturbances. Four, three, two, and as the lift came gently to rest, I pulled at the doors hurriedly and jumped on to the solid concrete of the first floor.

The landing was the replica of the other floors; the stairs curving away to the left and a glass door on the right. There, the power could be heard more clearly, and as I opened the door the occasional click of dial feelers in the automatic boxes came to my ears. The long room was lined with grey-painted apparatus, and was as close as an oven. Someone was whistling cheerily at the far end. I made my way down the room, calm once more within the sound of that unconcerned whistle. In one corner, I found the all-night mechanic plaiting multi-coloured wires that billowed from the insides of the structure. He looked up from his work, startled, and the whistle died away in a long breath.

"I thought you were a ghost," he said, grinning, "but I see now that you're an angel. Have you come to keep me company in the long hours before dawn?"

"I was always taught that angels were beautiful spirits," I retorted.

He shook his curly head. He was only a youngster of twenty or thereabouts. I had got to know him slightly when he had mended my telephone.

"You're wrong, lady. Anyone in skirts looks pretty good to me when I'm stuck amongst all this stuff." He waved his hand indicating the apparatus, and arose from his squatting position, pulling his mechanic's dustcoat into place. The whirr of a dial feeler reminded me of the need for haste.

"I want you to show me where a certain telephone is," I said hurriedly. "It's frightfully important, so just lead me to it, and don't ask questions. I'll explain in a minute."

"What's the number?" he asked, looking surprised.

"M—" I stopped short. Heavens! I had forgotten it in the stress of the moment. "The telephonists' 'phone up on the eighth floor."

"This way," he answered briefly, leading me down a narrow passage between the rows of boxes. "Here you are!" The mechanic tapped one just above his head.

"Thanks. Is it possible to trace a number that has just been dialled out on it?"

"How long ago?" he demanded. I felt grateful for his quick appreciation of my strange request.

"It must be about a quarter of an hour, but I shouldn't think the 'phone would have been used again."

"Hold everything," he ordered. He ran back down the passage calling over his shoulder. "Keep your eye on that box. If anyone starts to dial, pull out the pip with the red cord connecting it."

I watched gingerly, always having had a dislike of tampering with things about which I knew nothing; especially wires with power running through them. A small light glowed above the box suddenly. I yelled: "Quick! I think someone is going to dial." The mechanic appeared at a run, holding a buttinsky in his hand. "Pull the red out," he commanded, and as I obeyed him the glow vanished. Unfolding the flex that was wound around the handle of his instrument, he opened the box and placed the fork-shaped tip on a wire.

"Sorry, we're testing on here," he spoke into the mouthpiece.

"Who is it?" I whispered.

"It's a woman's voice," he returned softly, closing the mouthpiece with his hand, "and she's going mad at me for using the line."

"Let me listen," I said urgently. He handed over the buttinsky without any comment. I knew the voice immediately. There could be only one person in the Exchange who made such a business of pronouncing her vowels.

"Tell her to wait a moment. It won't take you long to trace the last call, will it?"

He shook his curly head again, and repeated my message to Gloria. Presently he started fiddling at the bottom of the box, peering through the wires, and now and then pushing the fork on to a line.

"You're in luck," he commented. "It looks like a city west number. Go round the other side and see if any light flashes."

I ran around quickly and took up a position against the wall, my eyes raking the tall structure.

"No light," I called to my mechanic friend. He grunted something inaudible.

"Try now," he said, and I saw a light flash two or three times towards the left, far above my head.

"Hold it," I yelled, almost dancing with excitement. It continued to flash as I counted the boxes carefully to its position. "I've got it. It's the seventeenth on the second row from the top. You're a marvellous man," I added, as the mechanic joined me, buttinsky still in his hand.

"Thanks, lady," he grinned. "I don't know what you're getting at, but at a word like that from you, I'm willing to blow up the whole place."

"Sometimes I'd rather like to do it myself. Can I come up with you?"

"Sure," he replied, mounting the steep steps that led to an iron landing, from which the mechanics attended to the higher places of the apparatus. "Be careful in those heels. It's pretty slippery."

"I will," I promised, following him cautiously. It reminded me of a gangway of a ship, and I wondered if the correct thing was to descend backwards.

The mechanic walked along the landing carelessly, counting each box with a tap of his hand. "This'll be it," he said, opening the door and reading the plate fixed to the back. "M9173. Would you like me to call them?" He glanced at the clock in a dubious way.

"It's only quite early," I remarked airily, "but I'll take the blame if there's a rumpus."

"There'd better not be," he returned, grinning mischievously, "or we'll get the sack. You shouldn't be here at all. There's probably a long paragraph in the security regulations forbidding the entrance of pretty females into the apparatus rooms."

"Well, that wipes me out," I said serenely. "Here, give me that buttinsky, and I'll put on an act. I promise you there won't be any row." I took the instrument and slid my hand down the flex to the metal fork. "What do I do with this thing?"

The mechanic guided it to rest on a wire. "Mind your ear," he warned just in time. The automatic ring reverberated through the earpiece. It rang for a long time. I was almost calling it a day, when the 'phone was un-hooked at the other end and a man's voice said: "Well?"

Thinking that I had better not attempt my laryngitis disguise again, I adopted a high-pitched tone like Gloria's.

"Oh, doctor! Will you come at once? I feel so dreadful ringing you at this hour, but I really can't stand it any longer. Do you think that I should go to hospital?"

"Who is speaking, please?" asked the voice levelly.

I hesitated a fraction of a second, thinking quickly. "Mrs. Thompson," I answered in a plaintive voice. "Mrs. William Thompson. Doctor, do you think I should go?"

"You can go to hell!" said the voice crisply, and the receiver was slammed down in my ear. I pulled out the fork and let my mechanic friend shut the door. He was grinning like an ape as he led the way back to the stairs, re-wrapping the flex.

"My, my! I would never have guessed it of you. You do keep your secret well."

"Don't be so indelicate," I rebuked him. "I had to say something. Does one climb down these steps sailor-wise?"

"You'd better let me help you," he replied in mock anxiety. "Hang on to my arm."

"Will you shut up?" I begged.

"What about your girl friend who was waiting to use the 'phone?"

"Oh, blast!" I exclaimed. "I'd forgotten all about her, and I wanted to listen in to what she was saying too. I suppose she's made her call by now."

He looked at me oddly. "Are you sure you're feeling all right?"

"Quite, thank you," I answered in surprise. He did not appear to be acting the fool now.

"I was just wondering," he remarked casually. "I'm not accustomed to strange women rushing in and interrupting my work to get me to butt in on lines so that they can listen in."

"I'm sorry," I apologized, "but it's really terribly hard to explain. In fact, I don't think I'd better yet. But I promise you that you won't get into a row if this little adventure is found out. If anyone says anything, just refer them to me."

"That'll be grand," he said blankly. "Just refer them to you. They'll know whom I mean, of course."

"They will," I agreed sweetly, "if you say that the name is Margaret Byrnes, and that I am an interstate trunk telephonist."

"Gosh!" he stammered suddenly. "You're the girl who found that monitor's body."

"One of them. You'll keep my visit under your hat, won't you? By the way, what's your name?"

"Dan Mitchell. Are you doing a spot of detecting? I thought they knew who committed the murder." He walked with me to the door and swung it open.

"Thanks, Dan," I said, passing through. "Just for your information only, and I know that I can trust you, I'm trying to break the police decision. I know it sounds an awful cheek. But I worked with that girl who was supposed to have killed Compton, and I can't believe that she's guilty."

Dan Mitchell's boyish face was flushed with excitement. I heard him repeat: "Gosh!" as I let the door close quietly behind me.

I walked up the stairs automatically; not because of any fear of taking the lift again. I wanted time in which to think. The first thing I wanted to find out was the name of the subscriber the mysterious caller in the restroom had rung, and that was going to be a difficult job. Mentally, I ran through the list of telephonists with whom I was acquainted on the Information desk, and who might be able to trace it for me without wanting to ask too many questions. We trunk telephonists over in the new building were rather isolated from the "Infa." girls, and consequently it was unusual for the two sections to become friendly. But I once had a session of relieving at the position, and recalled one girl who had been helpful in showing me the ropes.

Information was a thankless job, and one that received more abuse than any other position in the whole of the Exchange. Subscribers ran to the "Infa." girls under the slightest pretext, and it was amazing the good results they received for some of their outlandish inquiries. It was also the place where complaints were lodged. It was no wonder that the higher percentage of nervous breakdowns was always found amongst the telephonists working at the Information desk.

'I'll call the all-nighter from the boards as soon as I get back, and see if she can do anything for me,' I promised myself. Once having discovered the subscriber's name and occupation, I would have something to work on. It seemed odd to say the least that someone should be ready to answer his telephone at a city number, where the greater majority of subscribers' numbers were offices and not even hotels or flats. I hoped that the man had presumed my call was just an error of dialling, and had not started to get suspicious.

I half-closed my eyes in the endeavour to recall the restroom episode more clearly. I remembered my head jerking forward before I let it fall back against the cushion. The cloakroom light was still on then. I did not know for how long I had slept, but it couldn't have been more than half an hour. In that time the light in the cloakroom had been extinguished, and the unknown caller had crept into the restroom, oblivious that it was already occupied by a weary all-night telephonist. The prowler evidently dared not use the light for fear of attracting attention, though it seemed more likely from the unhesitating way in which the dial was turned that the number was familiar, and that a light was unnecessary.

'Whoever it was,' I reflected thoughtfully, 'must be a telephonist. Firstly, there would be no one else on the eighth floor, and secondly, only a telephonist could use a dial accurately without looking at it. Furthermore, that same person must be up to something fishy.' The whole episode was too quietly performed for it to be a legitimate or casual call; especially at that hour. Another sinister aspect was the fact that, although the man I had called in the apparatus room had spoken, the caller had not uttered a word; just dialled, listened, and hung up the receiver all in the space of a few seconds.

I climbed the last few stairs to the sixth floor, and rounded the landing just as the lift was moving down. I heard two or three male voices talking inside it, and tried to catch a glimpse of the occupants through the long narrow glass windows set in the outer doors. I turned away and saw John Clarkson standing by a window in the trunkroom with his hands in his pockets. He was staring out into the dark sky. I watched him absently for a while, the long hours of the first dogwatch telling on my tired body. His straight profile was lifted slightly, and although his eyes remained blank the lips above that square chin of his moved continually as though he was repeating something over and over. Presently, as though aware of my scrutiny, he turned his head. I smiled weakly, feeling a little foolish. It came as a surprise that there was no answering flicker in his eyes. Instead he drew his hands from his pockets and strode over to the door, his brows drawn together in a heavy frown.

"Where on earth have you been?" he demanded angrily, but not without an underlying tone of anxiety. I motioned to him to close the door and to join me on the landing.

"I've been having adventures," I replied coaxingly, trying to banish the annoyed look from his face. It was not often that I saw him thus. "Who went down in the lift just now?"

"Only Bertie with a couple of the Heads of the Department," he replied in a hard voice. "They paid a surprise visit to see if everything was under control." I ignored the heavy sarcasm in his voice, as that sense of excitement that was becoming so familiar shook me from head to foot.

"That's marvellous!" I cried. "But quickly—how long has Bertie been in the Exchange?"

"Are you mad, Maggie?" Clark asked in exasperation. "Don't you realize what this means? The Heads come in unexpectedly hoping to catch someone falling down on the job, and some of my staff is missing. I can tell you I looked pretty silly. I couldn't even say where you'd got to."

"I'm sorry," I answered with real contrition. "I'll explain to Bertie when I see him; not that it's so frightfully important against what I have discovered."

Clark looked at me searchingly. "What have you found out, Maggie? I thought I told you to let well alone."

"I was seriously considering your advice, but not now. I'm in this business until the end."

"Well, make sure that it doesn't mean your end," Clark said, relaxing a little. "Where have you been all this time?"

"Asleep," I replied airily. "In fact, I'm not too sure if I haven't been dreaming. Is the girl Patterson in the trunkroom?"

"She is now," he answered irritably. "She's another one who was missing when Bertie arrived."

"Is that so?" I remarked with interest. "Where had she been?"

"Asleep too, so she informed me. You girls beat everything. There will be a nice long report for me to-morrow with 'please explain' on it. It's all very well you saying that you'll take the blame, but the Officer in Charge is the one who receives most abuse on an occasion like this."

"It's the first dog-watch we have worked for a while," I said soothingly, "and all-nights take some getting used to. Were Gloria and I the only ones missing when the Heads walked in? Incidentally, how like them to come in without any warning. To-morrow night I'll ring Bertie's number, and drag him out of bed just to punish him."

"They arrived soon after you two women went ghost hunting. By the way, did you succeed in banishing the phantom?"

"For a while. It reappeared later when I was having a sleep in the restroom."

Clark looked at me admiringly. "You've certainly got iron nerves to be able to fall asleep peacefully in that room."

"Never again," I assured him firmly. I went on to tell him about the mysterious prowler and my subsequent inquiries in the first-floor apparatus room.

"Do you think we'll be able to trace the name of that man?"

"Your doctor pal?" Clark asked, grinning as Dan Mitchell had at the ruse I had used to disguise the nature of the call. "I should say that it would be a long and tedious job; in fact, well-nigh impossible. My advice is as before. Leave well alone. So will you kindly come in and do some work, and forget all this nonsense?"

"I want to see justice done," I said gravely, following him.

"So do I. But I fail to see how calling unfortunate subscribers at three in the morning is going to help. The best thing you can do is to go and see that flatfoot friend of yours and turn on the glamour. He might be able to start the ball rolling again." This struck me as a good idea, but I didn't tell Clark that Sergeant Matheson had seemed rather keen to see me again.

"Where do you want me to work?"

"You can let those interstate girls have a break. If you are looking round for your outfit, it's over where you left it on the country boards."

"Thanks. I'm in a bit of a daze, Clark," I added softly.

"Well?" he asked, half turned to the Senior Traffic Officer's table.

"I'm terribly sorry if I made you anxious." There was a slight pause.

"You nearly had me demented," he said gruffly. I went lightly down the room to collect my telephone.

The girl on the first Adelaide position was supporting a heavy head in her hands as I plugged in on the board.

"Go and sleep in the right place," I advised, leaning over her shoulder to pick up a light in the panel. "Just a minute, Ad."

"I've been calling you for five minutes," declared a peevish voice.

"Well, another few seconds won't make any difference," I replied testily. "Get out—quickly, Miller, before she lays an egg."

Adelaide ordered three or four calls in quick succession. I glanced at the clock in surprise. "What's wrong with you over there? Don't your subscribers go to bed?"

"I'm sure I don't know," she answered on a yawn. I glanced down at the calling number on the in-docket under my fingers. Even interstate numbers became familiar after a while. The calls originated from the South Australian Police Headquarters.

"Looks interesting!" I remarked, dialling out. "Have they caught spring-heeled Jack?"

"I'm here to switch, not to listen in on calls," Adelaide replied primly. "Anyway they want the calls on the secrecy line." I re-switched their position, feeling thwarted.

"O.K. They're waiting. I'll meet you on three."

"You look as if you're making up for lost time," John Clarkson said in my right ear. "What's happened in Adelaide to cause this rush?"

"Police calls," I answered briefly.

"We'll have a delay if she keeps on going like this," Clark observed with raised brows. "An unheard-of occurrence at this hour! Is that a call on the secrecy?"

I went in on the observing line and heard a distorted jangling of voices. There was absolutely no chance of overhearing anything on secrecy. "It looks like a big-noise confab to me."

"I suppose so," Clark replied, without interest. "Watch them, Maggie. The Adelaide lines have been a bit dicky."

"Like a mother," I promised, and he grinned. He made as if to say something but evidently thought better of it. He turned back to the Senior Traffic Officer's table without comment.

The remaining hours of the dog-watch dragged on, but not without further disturbances. As I went to switch near Gloria Patterson, she remarked snappishly: "If you start any more funny business, I'll report you to Mr. Scott."

"What funny business?" I asked innocently.

She hunched one shoulder. "You know very well; asking me stupid questions, and then locking me in the dormitory."

"I locked you in the dormitory," I repeated, surprised.

"Don't keep repeating my words," Gloria answered crossly. "I'm going to put down what you did, if I get a report to-morrow."

"Do as you please, of course. But just as a matter of interest, I have been nowhere near the dormitory since I came on at eleven."

"That's what you say," she replied viciously.

"This accusing me of locking doors seems to be becoming a habit. How did you get out?"

"Clark was looking for both of us. Mr. Scott had come in, and we should have been in the trunkroom. He was furious when you didn't turn up."

"So I gathered. However all is now forgiven and forgotten. There is just one point that I want to query; that is, if it doesn't come under the heading of funny business. How come you were locked in the dormitory and yet you were making a call from the restroom at the same time?" I watched her profile keenly.

"That was after—" she began quickly and then stopped, turning her head away from me. "I haven't used the restroom 'phone all night."

"You borrowed that bit from me," I accused her. "It's no use telling me lies, my sweet. I'm one of those people who know all. Yes, like your late bosom friend, I agree. You were quite definitely making a call when I was down in the apparatus room on the first floor."

"You mean that you listened in?" she asked angrily.

"No, I didn't. To be quite honest, I meant to. But something more interesting than a practical lesson on how to tame man, which I suppose your call was about, turned up. You went out of my head completely. Isn't that strange?" Gloria made no comment. She busied herself needlessly with some re-booked dockets.

"Leave them alone," I ordered. "You'll mess up my system. Tell me, Gloria, keeping in mind my little threat of blackmail, did you turn out the cloakroom light about half an hour after our chat in the restroom and re-enter to dial a number in the dark?"

She turned her head. "I've told you I was locked in the dormitory," she replied stubbornly, "and I won't answer another question, so hold your tongue."

"You will," I said cheerfully, getting up to lower the back of my chair, "and they won't only come from me. It's quite on the cards that the case of the murdered monitor is going to be reopened to-morrow." I moved quickly. The flex of my outfit tugged at its plug as I caught her before she slid to the floor.

"Gloria," I said urgently, stripping off her telephone and throwing it on to the boards with a clatter.

John Clarkson came up at a run. "What's up now?" he asked in a resigned voice. "Has she really fainted? Or is it another act?"

"Don't be so callous," I rebuked him. "I'll help you to carry her to the dormitory if you like."

Clark slid an arm under Gloria's shoulders, and hoisted her none too gently. "I think I can manage."

As Gloria's head fell back over his arm, and golden hair streamed all over Clark's dark sleeve, the other telephonists watched the operation with interest. A faint or two is all in the day's work to us. But the sight of John Clarkson carrying a wilting blonde down the room was worthy of the movies. l must have appeared rather superfluous bringing up the rear. I wasn't going to leave Clark alone with a swooning vamp like Gloria, who would make as much as she could out of the situation.

Clark placed her carefully on one of the beds in the dormitory and stood aside, panting a little. "I had no idea she'd be so heavy. Shall I get water or something?"

"No need," I replied, bending over her. "I think she's coming round."

Gloria's eyelids were flickering. She murmured softly, opening her eyes: "Where—where am I?"

I giggled as Clark said with a wealth of expression in his tone: "I knew it!"

"Don't spoil it," I reproached him. "You fainted in the trunkroom, Gloria. Mr. Clarkson carried you up here. How do you feel?"

Inevitably, she put one limp hand to her forehead. "Terrible! Could I have a drink of water?" She gave me an appealing look which I ignored. Clark went to the other end of the room to the wash-basin.

"It's odd the way you went out to it, Gloria," I observed, completely callous. "I remember that I had just told you that—"

"I heard what you said," she interrupted snappishly. "And if you think that made me faint, you're quite wrong. As a matter of fact, I haven't been feeling too well all night."

Clark came back with a glass in his hand. "You'd better stay here for a while. Will you be all right by yourself, or would you like Miss Byrnes to keep you company?"

"No," Gloria snapped again. Clark shrugged.

"Come along then, Maggie. You may take your time, Miss Patterson."

"Don't you let her lock me in again," Gloria shrieked after us.

"What is she talking about?" Clark asked, closing the door quietly. "I don't know what possessed me to change with Bancroft. It's been a hell of a night!"

I nodded sympathetically. "It has indeed. Still, this sort of thing can't go on indefinitely. The rest of the week will be nice and quiet."

"I don't know," he answered gloomily, keeping step as we went back to the trunkroom.

"Don't tell me you're developing an instinct!" I laughed mockingly. "I thought that belonged to the female sex only."

Clark stopped, and caught me roughly by the shoulders. I was standing a step above him and our eyes were on the same level.

"It's you," he said in a hard voice. "You worry me to death wondering what you're up to, and what's going on in that keen brain of yours. It is, you know, Maggie. You are a very intelligent person. That is what makes you so attractive. I'm frightened you might come to some harm through your very acuteness."

His words thrilled me, almost unbearably. They were so very unexpected. I felt tongue-tied. "Don't worry about me," I stammered. "Please!"

Clark released me abruptly. We went on. "Margaret," he said.

"Yes, John," I asked softly. He threw out his hands in a helpless gesture. "Just—be careful."

"Don't worry," I repeated, trying not to sound forlorn. "There's an old woman up home who is always telling me that I was born to be hanged, not murdered."

"That's not funny," he said in a tight voice.

"No, I suppose not," I answered reflectively, "though the angle from which you are thinking did not occur to me when I spoke. Many a true word, etc. Doesn't that sound trite?"

Clark laughed shortly. We stopped outside the trunkroom door. "Maggie, you're impossible! Are we playing golf on Sunday?"

"I'd like to if my mother can come too. She's in town." He glanced at me quizzically, and I felt myself reddening. "She'll probably clean us both up," I went on hurriedly. "You'll enjoy a game with her."

"I'm sure I will. Morning or afternoon?"

"Say late afternoon. It'll be light enough. Don't forget that we both have to work all night tomorrow."

"I'm not forgetting," Clark said with a mock groan. "I wonder if Bancroft would like to switch back to his original shift."

"Don't do that," I said, without thinking. "I mean—it's a foul enough shift without having an old maid of a traffic officer on duty."

"I won't change," he promised, laughing gently. I felt absurdly elated as we entered the trunkroom.

The last few hours before the early morning calls were always the most tedious of the all-night shift. There was never very much work to do. I kept my eyes idly on a patch of sky waiting for the stars to fade one by one. The blackness paled to grey and the clouds gathered towards the east, awaiting the sun. It was going to be another hot day, and the light breeze that fluttered the dockets anchored on the boards by odd pencils held the promise of developing into that scorching dusty north wind that most people loathe. Almost imperceptibly the grey light deepened into lemon and then a rich saffron, while the clouds became pink-tipped as the sun neared the horizon. Gradually long beams shot up from behind the distant mountains, which seemed themselves ablaze with light. The dazzling mid-summer sun edged up inch by inch until the trunkroom was aglow with golden light, and I was forced to remove my eyes.

Presently the 6 a.m. staff came in, yawning and complaining of the early hour. A couple of charwomen started to sweep and dust. Patterson had not returned. I was wondering whether she had gone home neglecting to sign off, when in she walked as fresh as if she was just about to begin work.

"Do you feel better?" I asked, as she paused behind my chair.

"Much," she nodded, "May I sit next to you?"

"Certainly," I assented in some surprise. "Here are a couple of 6.30 a.m. calls. If we split them up, maybe we won't get in a bag."

Gloria gave that high artificial laugh that always made me grate my teeth. "Fancy being able to be witty at this hour," she remarked in a gracious manner. I stared at her in amazement, not unmixed with suspicion. She turned over the dockets, saying casually: "It was frightfully silly of me to faint like that. I felt such a fool. Has anyone said anything about it to you?"

"I don't think so," I replied slowly, wondering at what she was driving. "The final stages of the dog-watch are never chatty ones, you know."

"Don't tell anyone, will you?" she asked, turning on a dazzling smile that filled me with further suspicion.

"Why not?"

She shrugged lightly.

"I just don't want anyone to know what a fool I was," she said, examining her trim, naked leg. "Don't you think I'm getting browner, Maggie?"

"Rather," I agreed drily. "Never break away from the point so abruptly, Gloria. It merely attracts attention to what you are trying to disguise. The correct meaning of your sudden benevolence is that you are afraid that I will start telling people the reason why you fainted. Don't bother to contradict," I went on hurriedly, as she opened her mouth to speak. "I know my assumption is correct, and you know that I know. But what I don't understand, and you'll observe that I am laying my cards on the table, is why you got so frightened. From what I know of your charming character, and without wishing to offend you mortally, I should say that you wouldn't have had the guts to bash in the head of your so-called bosom friend. You're in this business somewhere, Gloria," I went on, shaking my head, "but I'm damned if I know where."

"I don't know what you're talking about," she replied, looking everywhere but at me.

"I knew you'd say that," I sighed. "Your vocabulary, my pet, is very limited. I think that it would be better for you to say nothing rather than make that inane remark. It's so obviously an untruth, and one that only whets my appetite to discover more of your part in our late monitor's schemes. You had better put on those calls before you destroy them completely."

"Do them yourself," Gloria snapped, tossing over the dockets she had been twisting and turning. "And if you aren't more careful, Byrnes, you'll get what has been coming to you for a long time."

"Do you know," I remarked gently, smoothing out the crumpled dockets, "that strikes a chord in my memory. Now, of what does it remind me?" I paused to book a call with Sydney. When the connection was completed, I turned back to Patterson. She was watching me fearfully. "I remember. The day after Sarah's murder I found an anonymous letter pushed into my locker with almost the identical phrasing as your little threat just now."

Gloria's skin underwent that curious change I had previously noted. "I don't write anonymous letters," she muttered.

"No?" I queried politely. "Perhaps you might be interested to know that I consider the identity of the writer one of the most important things to discover if I want to break the police decision and exonerate Dulcie Gordon."

I saw her finger-tips whiten under their polish as she pressed her hands against the board.

"We must have another little talk later on," I suggested conversationally. "Just now, breakfast and bed are my one ambition. I think Mr. Clarkson is approaching to tell us that we may go."

CHAPTER VII

John read through the untidy sheets up to this point when he came to see me one day. They do allow visitors occasionally in this dreadful place. I asked him for assistance in describing that fateful Saturday when the charity dance was held at the Exchange. I was a little undecided how to begin. His advice was the same as when he started me off on this manuscript. It was quite simple. As a record of my part in the affairs of the Exchange during that week, it must contain certain details of what I had thought was my ordinary life.

"But I can't tell people that I had bacon and eggs for breakfast," I objected. "It's too mundane."

He laughed, and suggested that perhaps that could be quite well omitted without misleading anyone, but to continue with the first items connecting with the terrible event that was to occur later.

"I'd better say at what time I awoke," I remarked, sighing despondently, "though that seems rather futile, too."

I arrived home that morning feeling very weary and grubby, with just enough time to snatch a shower and change into a cool dirndl before breakfast. I took one depressing look in the mirror, and then strolled along to my mother's room.

"Are you up, Charlotte?" I called, tapping her door gently with my fingertips.

"Come in," she answered. I pushed it open. "Darling, you do look dreadful!"

"Don't rub it in," I replied irritably. "I've been up all night, you know. Are you coming down to breakfast?"

"Why don't you go straight to bed," she coaxed. "I'll bring you up a tray."

I shook my head so violently that I was compelled to retie the narrow white ribbon I wore to keep my hair from my face.

"I'd fall asleep before I ate anything. What will you do with yourself to-day?"

"I've got an engagement for this afternoon," she replied placidly. "I'm going to watch a basketball match."

"What!" I yelled, unable to believe my ears.

"A basketball match, dear," Charlotte repeated distinctly. "That nice boy who used to have freckles is taking me."

"You mean Sergeant Matheson? I'll have you know that you're cutting me out. He asked me first."

"So he said," agreed my mother, "but he told me that you didn't seem keen to go. The poor boy was quite disappointed. I felt so sorry for him that I said I'd never seen a basketball match, and if he didn't mind, would he take me?"

"When did all this take place?" I asked.

"He rang you up last night. Mrs. Bates told him you were on all-night shift, so he asked to speak to me. By the way, Maggie, Mrs. Bates was giving me such peculiar looks when I was on the 'phone.

"She was probably worrying about the Sergeant's intentions," I explained. "She hates men."

"How odd of her! I must get your father to meet her. I'm ready. Shall we go down?"

We strolled down arm in arm. In the lower hail I paused and said half-laughingly, half-earnestly: "There's more in this than meets the eye. Are you really going to see that absurd game for the fun of it? Or are you trying your hand at the same game as your daughter?"

Charlotte never gave much away. "I thought it might be interesting if I could have a little chat with that nice boy," she remarked, opening the dining-room door. "I used to know his mother many years ago."

"Then the conversation will be purely personal? All right, we'll let it go at that. Perhaps if Sergeant Matheson hasn't anything better to do, he might drop in later this evening. Will you ask him for me?"

"Certainly," my mother replied with surprise. We seated ourselves at a small table near a window. "But I thought you didn't like him."

"He's all right," I said carelessly, unfolding my table-napkin. "I should imagine that he makes a very nice husband and father. I gleaned that bit of news last night, so you can take that innocent look from your face and keep it for Sunday. I've arranged a game for you."

"Have you, Maggie?" she asked, selecting an orange to squeeze into a tumbler. "That'll be enjoyable. Is Mr. Clarkson a terribly good player?"

"Moderate. You may be able to beat him; especially as he might be nervous."

My mother sipped her orange juice. "Why should he be nervous?" I grinned at her even though I felt a slow blush creeping into my face. "Darling, how dense of me!" she said apologetically, changing the subject in a hurry. "Tell me, what are you going to eat?"

The dining-room was almost empty of my fellow-boarders. Being Saturday, many took the opportunity to sleep on and skipped breakfast. I nodded briefly to one or two who entered, not being in a sociable mood, and escaped as soon as I could to my room. Charlotte came in to draw the curtains, and to make the room as dark as possible by anchoring the blinds with pillows to prevent them from blowing inwards. Trying to get a sound sleep by daylight was one of the major problems of the all-night telephonist, but I was so tired that I would probably have fallen asleep with a searchlight blazing into my face.

"Stick up my 'Don't disturb' notice on the door," I murmured, turning over, "and remember you're a lady when you're watching that riotous match."

"I will," my mother promised to both requests, closing the door carefully behind her.

I fell at once into that hot, restless slumber that brings no refreshment. My brain kept turning out grotesque dreams that seemed almost real, so vivid were they. It was the same sort of troubled sleep I had had the previous night. Familiar faces and places, distorted but still recognizable, grew up in my overexcited brain. Voices and noises were as clamorous as before. Presently I heard one voice speak quite clearly: "You'll enter only over my dead body." I shook myself into semi-consciousness. There was a short, metallic laugh and the sound of footsteps, then the banging of a door. I heard all three as separate impressions. I tried to rouse myself completely, but the effort was too great and I sank into a deeper sleep.

It was the flapping of the curtains that awoke me finally. I turned over on my back in exasperation and watched the room fill with light and then darken with each motion. Suddenly I sat up, my body tense, searching in the recesses of my mind for some thought that was nagging at my memory. It was only the middle of the afternoon, but more sleep was impossible when I remembered the brief laugh that I had thought was part of my dreams. I slipped back into my dirndl quickly and made for the stairs, going down two at a time. Mrs. Bates was peeling potatoes in the kitchen, her voice uplifted in some dreary song.

"Stop that row," I ordered, entering in a rush, "How can you expect me to sleep?"

She dropped a potato and stared at me in offended dignity. "That was a hymn of hope."

I grinned. "Sorry, but it sounded like nothing on earth. Tell me, has anyone been to see me this afternoon?"

Mrs. Bates nodded virtuously. "I wouldn't let her disturb you. I knew you were worn out and wanted to sleep."

"You didn't seem to realize it just now. Was it Miss MacIntyre by any chance?"

"She came about two," Mrs. Bates said, resuming her potato peeling, "but I wouldn't let her go in. I stood at your door and said 'You'll enter only over my dead body.' When she saw I meant what I said she left." Mrs. Bates looked around at me, waiting for commendation.

"I wish you'd woken me," I said, troubled. "Was Miss MacIntyre anxious to see me?"

"I couldn't say I'm sure. She wouldn't leave any message with me."

I smiled and let it pass without comment.

"Did she say if she was coming back?" I asked, but Mrs. Bates shook her head. "Thanks very much for not disturbing me," I said mechanically and went out of the kitchen.

I mounted the stairs slowly, lost in thought. Mac had wanted to see me. It must have been something important, otherwise she wouldn't have risked breaking in on my sleep. Telephonists respected each other's hours of rest, especially when they were on the all-night shift. She was probably going to make an effort to lower that barrier that had come between us, and I had missed the opportunity. I felt restless and uneasy, and walked round my room tidying up in an unseeing fashion. I wished that my mother hadn't been out. She was a grand person to talk to, and Mac might have come straight with her.

On impulse, I went to my wardrobe and found a pair of sandals to slip on my bare feet. I settled a rough straw hat anyhow on my head, and snatched up my handbag.

Mrs. Bates poked her head into the hall at the sound of my running footsteps, her eyes round with curiosity. "Will you be in to dinner, Miss Byrnes?" she asked.

"Yes, I'm only going out for a moment."

I cut down the right-of-way where John Clarkson had driven me home that awful night of Sarah Compton's murder. The wind billowed the full skirt of my dress, and made me clutch my hat as I rounded the corner of the street where Mac lodged.

As was the custom of all boarding-houses, the front door was ajar. I passed in without bothering to ring. Mac used an outside bungalow as a bedroom. I went down the hail and through a side door to reach it. It was a fibrous-plaster building, shaped something like a tent with a sloping roof and fly-wired all the way round just below the ceiling. I knocked gently, calling her name. There was no answer. A slovenly woman came round the side of the house, wiping her red hands on her apron.

"Is Miss MacIntyre in?" I asked.

"I'm sure I don't know. Isn't she in her room?"

"I've knocked, but there is no reply. Do you know where she is?"

The woman thought for a minute. "Have you looked in the front room?"

I presumed that she meant the lounge, so I hurriedly retraced my steps. Boarding houses in the Park area were all much the same. I had no difficulty in finding my way around. There was always a long hall dividing the rooms on either side, which led past the steep stairs to the first floor down to the kitchen premises and back yard. The first room on the left was usually given over to a living-room. But Mac was not there either. It was unoccupied, except for a middle-aged man reading the newspaper and listening to the radio.

I went back to the bungalow, thinking that I would wait there for a while. It was too early for her to have left for work. I knew that she wasn't on duty until 7 p.m. that evening. The slovenly woman seemed to have disappeared. I tried Mac's door and found it was unlocked. That meant that she must have been coming back presently. No one leaves their bedroom door unlocked in a boarding-house; especially an easily accessible place like a bungalow.

"That's funny," I said aloud, standing very still with one hand on the door knob. The room was a riot of confusion. Drawers were hanging open and their contents billowed forth untidily. Even the bed had been stripped, with the bedclothes dumped on the floor and the mattress folded double one end of the bed. I looked down at the knob in my hand, and then at the keyhole on the outside. The woodwork around it had been scratched and torn. My heart missed a beat as I realized the significance of that untidy room.

It wasn't like Mac to leave her bedroom in such a mess. She was always so neat and orderly. Therefore, there was only one explanation. Someone had forced her door, and had ransacked the room in a desperate search. But who it was and what they were looking for, I could not even hazard a guess. As I surveyed the scene grimly, I told myself that Mac would probably have been able to answer both those questions had she been at my side that moment. What was more, the search must have been conducted not long before my appearance on the scene. The person who had made the room into such a rubbish dump must have been very urgent indeed to risk a daylight raid. The possibility of burglary drifted into my mind. I dismissed it immediately as I saw a tiny gold-bar brooch of Mac's pinned to the lace runner on the dressing-table. No burglar would be fool enough to overlook that.

I pulled the mattress back and sat down to think. Should I go and tell the landlady of the establishment that one of her guests' rooms had been ransacked? Or should I wait until I saw Mac, so that she would be able to decide what was to be done? There was one conclusion that I came to: Mac could not be returning for some time. Otherwise, such a thorough search would not have been risked. As I sat there on Mac's bed brooding on what was the best way to get in touch with her, I suddenly remembered the most likely place where she would be.

'I'll tidy up a bit,' I told myself. 'She might get a fright when she sees her room like this. It's giving me the jumps just looking at it, and I don't have to sleep here to-night. It's horrid knowing that someone has been going through your possessions.'

I re-made the bed and closed drawers. The floor was littered with papers. I bent down to gather them up. Suddenly I stiffened and rose to a standing position slowly, holding one scrap in my hand. It was a piece from a notepaper set that I had given Mac the previous Christmas. I remembered the trouble that I had had in obtaining that particular shade and quality of paper. She had evidently been writing a letter, and had torn it up after making some mistake. The name "John" leaped to my eyes, and I stared at it wonderingly. There could be only one John where Mac and I were concerned. I forgot all the nice manners my mother had taught me as I knelt quickly and gathered together the rest of the papers that had been spilled from the overturned wastepaper basket. I dumped the heap on the bed and went through them, feeling puzzled. They were all the same type of paper, but I finally came to one that fitted into the torn slip that I held in my hand. It didn't convey much. Mac had only written a few words in her neat hand and then tossed it aside. It started off "Dear John, I don't know how to—" and there it stopped.

Filled with an overwhelming curiosity, I tried fitting other pieces of the heap together and discovered that they all began with the same address, and continued with a similar, unfinished sentence that conveyed nothing.

'What on earth was she trying to write,' I thought irritably, 'that it takes her sheets of paper to compose?'

A door slammed in the main house. I started guiltily. 'I'm pretty low,' I thought in disgust, piling the scraps into the wastepaper basket and standing it in its corner. I gave the room a final look over before I closed the door carefully after me, and went round the side of the house to a back gate. It opened on to a lane that would take me to the tram route.

* * * * *

There was an atmosphere of gay expectancy at the Exchange, which was wholly at variance with the groups of quietly gossiping telephonists of the past few days. Girls in working kit were calling brightly over the banisters to others who were dressed for the street. As far as I could understand the principal topic of conversation was what everyone was going to wear that night to the charity social in the new building. I was filled with a sudden sense of bitterness. Although I was on the ticket committee, the only pleasure I would get from it would be an hour or so before I went on all-night duty at 11 p.m.

'There's one good thing about it, anyway,' I told myself, as I proceeded to the seventh floor. 'It has made people forget the unpleasant events of the past few days.' I wondered if I was doing a very foolish thing in trying to stir up more trouble.

The dormitory echoed hollowly with the sound of laughing voices and the occasional thud of a hammer. I opened the door and saw half a dozen girls decorating the room with long streamers and pieces of asparagus fern. It had been cleared of furniture and the floor gleamed with polish. At the far end on a small dais, where the three-piece dance band would play that night, I recognized the curly head of the mechanic, Dan Mitchell. He was wiring a group of multi-coloured lights, cunningly hidden amid a mass of greenery. I was greeted with derisive remarks as to the way I had timed my entry when all the work was practically finished.

"I was on all night," I protested indignantly. "Anyway, the room looks so beautiful that I doubt whether I could have done much to improve it."

"What's all this about Gloria Patterson fainting in Clark's arms last night. I wish it had been me. Weren't you jealous, Maggie?"

"Not in the least. Fainting is never enjoyable."

"Why did she faint?" asked another curiously. I thought for a minute. But it was not from wanting to comply with Gloria's wishes that I replied: "The heat, I suppose. It was red-hot in the trunkroom all night."

My interrogator spoke coyly: "A little bird told me it was something you said that made the fair Gloria collapse."

"Really! And did the same little bird tell you what it was I said?"

"No," she replied with regret. "I suppose it's no use asking you?"

"No," I said curtly. "Has anyone seen Gerda MacIntyre this afternoon?"

They looked at each other. "Mac?" queried one. "She came in for a while. The bell from the centre light is her contribution. It makes the room, don't you think, Maggie?"

"It looks fine. When did she go?"

"I don't know. Did anyone see Mac leave?"

They shook their heads. "She must have been gone for some time."

"Thanks," I said, and strolled down the room to the dais. "Those lights will be pretty, Dan."

He glanced down to see who had spoken and then grinned. "Hullo, lady, you don't look quite so angelic by daylight."

"Sorry you're disappointed," I retorted. "Has anything been said about last night's adventure?"

"Nothing." He climbed down the stepladder and dropped a coil of wire and hammer to the floor. "Anything new on the horizon?"

I glanced over my shoulder, but the others were busy clearing up odd fragments of fern. "Our Senior Traffic Officer, Mr. Scott, came in last night when I was in the power-room."

Dan whistled, and raised his brows comically.

"Not a word," I whispered warningly. His eyes danced with excitement.

"Are you coming to the social?" I asked, raising my voice for the benefit of the others.

"Sure," he replied clearly, giving me a knowing look. "Will you keep a dance for me?"

"If you like, but I'll only be there for a short time. I'm on duty again to-night."

"I'll be seeing you," he promised. I walked back to the girls. "Haven't you finished yet? The roof won't stand many more decorations."

"Get the ladder someone. Maggie, you're the tallest. Jump up and twist that red one to match the other side."

"I will, if someone holds on to the ladder," I agreed cautiously. "Isn't that someone knocking at the door?"

The girl Martin hurried over to it, throwing instructions over her shoulder. "Not too much now, Maggie."

"Where's this ladder?" I asked. "Thanks, Dan. You might hang on to the base while I climb. I always did loathe heights."

I unpinned the streamer and started to twist it, holding on with one hand. "Is that enough, Martin?" She drew her head into the room and shut the door. "That'll be right, Maggie. Just pin it firmly and then you can get down."

"Thank you," I said gratefully, descending the ladder. "Who was that at the door?"

"Only one of the cleaners wanting to know if we were ready for her to sweep up. Stay where you are a minute, Maggie, until I look around. There may be some others that want fixing."

I needed no second bidding to remain stationary half-way down the ladder. I was frozen to the spot, with one foot in the air and my hands gripping the sides. The words which the girl Martin had spoken all unwittingly re-echoed in my brain.

"What's the matter, Maggie?" she asked sharply. "You'd better get down at once if you're feeling dizzy."

I looked down at her wonderingly. "Who did you say was at the door just now?"

"One of the cleaners. Get down this minute. If you go fainting up there, I won't catch you when you fall."

"You're a hard-hearted woman," I remarked, placing one foot firmly on the floor. "Dan can go up next time. He's used to climbing around the apparatus. I'm going home."

Dan Mitchell followed me to the door. "Why did you behave so queerly just now?" he asked softly, as he held open the door.

"I am not quite sure. It was something that Martin said. I thought that

I had heard it before, and connected it with something important. But when I asked her to repeat it, the parallel went out of my head."

"It might be silly," he said hopefully, "but I noticed that the second time she said 'one of the cleaners,' she left out 'only.'"

I stared at him for a moment, puzzled. "Only one of the— You're right!" I declared excitedly. "Only one—Listen, Dan, this may be frightfully important, so if those girls want to know what's up, don't let on that you know."

"Neither I do," he answered, grinning. "You're much too deep for me."

"I'll try to explain it all to you to-night," I promised. "I've got too many facts jumbled up in my mind at this moment. If I don't go somewhere and have a quiet think, my brain will burst."

"Well, be careful. I don't like a kid like you trying to do everything on your own."

"Don't sound so pompous," I retorted. "You're only a child yourself."

"I'm nearly twenty-one," he said in a dignified tone.

"You look about seventeen," I grinned. "See you to-night." I left him quickly, still smiling to myself at the offended expression on his face, and proceeded to walk down the stairs. Half-way I paused, and then retraced my steps as far as the trunkroom.

As it was late afternoon the boards were sparsely staffed, with a monitor in charge. Practically the only traffic that went on during Saturday afternoon were race calls, when tipsters and starting-price bookmakers swung the telephonists into sudden activity immediately before and after each race. The monitor was rather a good sport and she greeted me cheerily.

"Come to help, Maggie? These damn race calls will be the death of me. We've already had a row with one bookie."

"That's too bad," I said ironically. "Was the call five seconds too late?"

She grimaced. "Something like that. What do you want here? Aren't you in this dump often enough without paying a social visit?"

"Too often. I was wondering if anyone had seen Mac. She was helping in the dormitory a while back."

The monitor frowned. "She did pop in for a minute, to see one of the girls. Jean Mills, I think. Go and ask."

"Thanks, I will. Are you going to the dance to-night?"

"Rather! The room looks good, doesn't it?"

"Marvellous. Where's Mills? Oh, I see her. I gather that I have your permission to speak to one of your telephonists?"

"Go right ahead," she said generously.

I strolled over to the country boards, and had to wait as the telephonist cross-switched several stations on to the one caller. I heard a metallic voice give the last result before Mills closed her key.

"Flat out?" I asked sympathetically. She unscrewed the mouthpiece of her outfit and shook it free of moisture. The ebonite was sweating from her breath.

"These fixed calls," Mills remarked with disgust. "One minute you're all nice and relaxed dreaming of the frock you're going to wear to-night, and the next you're doing three girls' work."

"Rotten," I agreed. "I believe that Mac came in this afternoon to see you. Do you know where she has gone?"

"Home, I suppose. Did you want her?"

"Not particularly," I replied carelessly. "But what did she want of you?"

"Just a yarn. I was on the 10.30 p.m. staff the fateful night, you know. In fact I just missed the fun."

"You're not on Patterson's rota, are you?"

"No, but I had changed that night. Mac was interested in my impressions of that evening. She said that she was going round all the girls who worked that night."

"Really," I said, playing idly with the keys on the adjacent board. "What's got into Mac?"

"She's thinking of compiling her memoirs," Mills laughed. "Don't fiddle, Maggie. You've already flashed the monitor's light twice, and I'm damned if I want Miss Lord over here again."

"She's a friend of mine," I said with a grin.

"Oh gosh, is she? Go away, Maggie. These calls are to come off. I don't like senior telephonists watching me work."

"You're quite a good switcher if you keep your head," I said kindly, getting up. She put out her tongue at me as she readjusted her mouthpiece. So Mac was writing an autobiography! That was interesting! What a rotten actress she was. I was sure I could have thought up a better one than that, and yet Mills seemed to have found her excuse plausible enough. How was she to question Mac's activities; not having known her for as long as I, and only being an outside figure in the recent drama. Mac was up to the same game as myself; of that I was convinced. I felt a sudden thrill as I thought of what we might be able to accomplish between us in helping to clear Dulcie Gordon. It was a nuisance that Mrs. Bates had interfered that afternoon. We could have got together to discuss ways and means, and resumed our old friendly footing. I hated the break that had occurred between us. Mac had been my friend for too many years to terminate our companionship so abruptly without leaving a nasty wound.

'I'll give her a ring when I get home,' I said to myself, 'and find out what's to do. I wonder if she'll notice about her room?'

The west end of the city was practically deserted, but as I passed the Block, people started to swarm out of the group of picture theatres on the eastern hill. They were too far away to worry me so I kept on walking, thinking hard as I went. As I had told Dan Mitchell, facts were jumbled up in my head. The best thing I could do would be to retire to some quiet spot and take a pencil and paper to the problems.

I strolled leisurely out of town across the bridge, unmindful of my sandalled feet until it was too late to take a tram as I was nearing my objective. I found a secluded seat on the bank of the lake and sat down to concentrate. The sinking sun blazed full in my face, and I narrowed my eyes against the glare to watch the tacking yachts. To and fro they skimmed in line across the narrow stretch of water handled for the most part by male enthusiasts clad in trunks. I followed them idly for some time, wondering what there was in sailing that makes people so keen. I had been once, and had spent the whole time trying to keep dry and dodging the jib.

My mind darted from one thing to another and finally settled on my latest speculation, to which one of the decorators of the dormitory had all unknowingly given me the clue. It opened up tremendous possibilities. I kicked myself mentally for not having thought of it before. I stayed there brooding, now and then making some note in my little engagement book. Presently I became conscious of the sun nearing the horizon, and the tight, dry feeling of my skin warned me that I was in for a dose of sunburn. It was a stupid thing to sit full in the blaze, but I had been so wrapped up in my thoughts that I had not heeded. A quick glance at my hand-mirror corroborated my belief. Comforting myself with the reflection that I might be able to tone down the colour of my skin to at least magenta with powder. I slipped my book back into my handbag and got up.

However, it must have been worse than I knew. As I entered my mother's room and found her dressing for dinner, she let out a small shriek: "Maggie, your skin!"

"You're always passing some remark about my face," I reproached her, walking over to the bureau mirror to scan it more closely. "It's not so bad," I said hopefully.

"Where have you been to get so burnt?" she asked, picking up a pot of cold cream and turning my head around to her with one hand.

"In the sun. I went down to the lake for a walk. How did the basketball go?"

Charlotte frowned as she dabbed cream on the tip of my nose. "Most uninteresting, darling," she confessed, "but your friend, the Sergeant, seemed to be wildly excited at times. Hold your head up."

I did so obediently. "Haven't you put enough on? Dinner will be ready soon, and I'm not dressed. I take it that your long skirt is not for Mrs. Bates's sake?"

"Will I look odd?" she asked, lifting the black lace a trifle. "I had to change when I came in, so I thought that I may as well get ready for to-night. What time do we get to the Exchange?"

"Any time," I shrugged. "It all depends on when Sergeant Matheson calls. I hope you remembered to ask him."

"I think so," answered my mother vaguely. "Anyway, he's in the lounge-room now. You can see him at dinner."

"I didn't tell you to ask him to dinner," I said, feeling cross. "I only wanted to see him professionally. You're making it a social turn."

Charlotte wound up her watch carefully before putting it on. "I'm sorry, darling, but I had to do something to repay him for the outing. I think the poor boy wanted to stay. Do you dislike him that much?"

"No," I shouted, "but he's a married man. What would the Old Man say if he knew that you were running around with policemen?"

A dimple appeared in one cheek as she replied: "I don't think he'd mind just this once. Can I come and watch you dress?"

"No. Go and entertain your boy friend. I won't be long."

"But, Maggie," she protested. "I've been talking to him all day. He doesn't think that poor child killed that horrid woman either."

I turned back quickly. Charlotte had the habit of wrapping up gems of information in thick layers of superfluous remarks.

"Doesn't he? Charlotte! You're marvellous. How did you persuade him?"

"I told him that you were convinced that the police were wrong," she said flatly.

"He must think I'm a cocky person," I interrupted. "Go on."

"Why should he?" demanded my mother on the instant. I smiled at her lovingly. "I told him everything you told me, that's all. But he seemed to lose interest in the basketball all at once, for which I was very grateful. Such a limited game, darling. Not enough room to run about. He started asking me a whole lot of questions. That was when I remembered to ask him to call."

"I'll go and get dressed at once. I want a nice, long talk with Sergeant Matheson. Does Mrs. Bates know that we have a guest for dinner?"

"Two guests," she corrected. I turned back from the door in surprise.

"Who? Oh, I see, you mean yourself."

"Indeed, I don't," said my mother placidly. "Your little friend is coming—"

"Do you mean Mac?" I demanded. "When did you see her'?"

"She was waiting in the lounge for you when I got home. As I didn't know where you'd got to, I told her that she would be certain to catch you at dinner time."

"That's wonderful!" I said heartily. "Mac wanted to see me this afternoon, but Mrs. Bates wouldn't let her waken me. She thought she was doing the decent thing, of course, but it meant that I've been chasing Mac all this afternoon, even to the extent of going into town to the Exchange. We'll form a big four after we've eaten and get down to business. We ought to be able to do something between the lot of us."

"She said she was on duty at seven," my mother interrupted warningly. "It won't give her much time to be in on the discussion."

"Time enough. Gosh, but I'm glad Mac has come around. We'd had a bit of a row. Things haven't been quite the same between us the last few days."

I just had time to slip into a long dress of flowered cotton before Mrs. Bates's one maid walked up and down the hail playing tunes on the gong. I walked slowly down the narrow stairs, happy in the knowledge that I was looking my best. Sergeant Matheson, who was standing with his back to me at the foot of the stairs and talking to my mother, swung round quickly. There is nothing like a staircase for making a good entry.

"Very nice, darling," said Charlotte approvingly. "Don't you think so, Sergeant?" He reddened a little, but the admiration was blatant in his eyes. I felt a glow of satisfaction.

"Hullo," I said coolly, joining them. "Who won the match?"

"Varsity," he replied, staring at a point over my head in an irritating fashion. Was he as shy with his wife, or didn't she like him admiring other women? "They deserved to win. They were the better team."

"Were they, Charlotte?" I asked teasingly.

"What, darling? Oh, yes, indeed. It was most thrilling. You must take Maggie next time, Sergeant."

"I'm pretty booked up for the next few weekends," I said hurriedly, throwing my mother a baleful glance. "Hasn't Mac arrived?"

"We were waiting for her. Does she live far away?"

"Just round the corner. I'll give her a ring and see if she's left. You two go in to dinner and start."

I knew Mac's telephone number so well that the dial practically spun itself. In spite of our proximity, we were forever ringing each other up under the slightest pretext. As I waited to be switched through to Mac's room, I recalled an occasion when she had told me a joke on duty one night. The full strength of it didn't strike me until many hours later, when I sat up in bed and laughed until I was sick. I crept down the stairs and gave Mac a ring to tell her that I had seen it. My reminiscences were cut short as a familiar voice spoke in my ear.

"It's Maggie," I said heartily, trying to disguise a feeling of embarrassment and thus making it worse. "Dinner's waiting. How long will you be?"

There was a short silence. Then Mac's voice said in a strained fashion: "I can't come, Maggie. I'm sorry."

"Why on earth not?" I asked with rising impatience. "You're behaving in the most extraordinary fashion. At first you're frightfully anxious to see me, and now you won't walk one block when I'm waiting for you."

"I'm sorry, Maggie," she repeated in a low voice, "but I don't feel well."

I felt justifiably incensed and tried to swallow my annoyance. "It's all right," I replied gruffly. "Will you be at the dance to-night? Perhaps we can have a talk then."

"I'll probably see you then. Good-bye."

"Good-bye," I echoed, replacing the receiver and staring at it as though it might be able to explain the mystery of Mac's sudden change of front. I shrugged my shoulders helplessly. She was really the most exasperating person I had ever known; although I had to admit that her vagaries were of a recent vintage.

"Will she be long?" asked my mother.

"She's not coming," I said shortly. "Yes, soup, please, Betty. She is feeling sick. She may see me to-night."

Sergeant Matheson cut his bread into neat cubes. "Miss MacIntyre is still behaving in a peculiar fashion then?" he asked casually. I shot him a quick, speculative look. If he was convinced of Dulcie Gordon's innocence, and, although not wishing to detract from Charlotte's persuasive powers, the thought must have been there before she told him my side of the story, just how much was he dining with us officially and how much socially? I gave the matter a little thought under cover of seasoning my broth.

"Miss MacIntyre's behaviour," I said distinctly, emulating his style with a slice of bread and dropping the blocks into the liquid, "has been for the last few days, from last Wednesday evening to be accurate, questionable to say the least. But suppose we enjoy Mrs. Bates's excellent cooking before we take other people's characters away."

I dropped my table-napkin to the ground. As we both bent to retrieve it, I whispered: "They're an inquisitive lot here. You never know who may be listening." He nodded understandingly. "Thank you, Sergeant," I said aloud. I caught a slight smile on my mother's face as she wrestled with corned beef and salad.

'There's no doubt about you,' I thought admiringly. 'You're up to every dodge around the place, though one wouldn't think it.' Charlotte always seemed so vague and helpless. The only factor which betrayed my mother's astuteness was the wily way she handled a number seven near the green.

We chatted for a while on a superficial plane. Sergeant Matheson tried to explain the rudiments of his sport with the aid of the cutlery until the sweet course arrived, which necessitated the removal of the dessert spoons from acting as goal posts.

"She was telling the truth," said my mother softly, as we carried our coffee cups up to my room for privacy's sake. Mrs. Bates came hurrying out of the kitchen juggling a couple of plates in either hand. Her brows rose in a scandalized fashion as she observed Sergeant Matheson bringing up the rear.

My room was hot from the all-day sun. I stood between the window and the door, stirring my coffee and trying to persuade myself that there was a cool draught.

"Yes, she certainly was," remarked my mother absently. She seated herself in my one armchair, while the Sergeant propped his shoulders against the wall.

"Who was what?" I asked, searching in a drawer for cigarettes.

"Your little dark friend. She looks as though she is on the verge of a nervous breakdown."

"Mac is always rather pale," I said uneasily.

"Not only that, but her eyes were enormous, and I noticed her jump at the slightest sound. I thought she was going to faint when she saw Sergeant Matheson."

I looked up quickly over a lighted match. "Did Mac see him before or after you told her to come to dinner?"

"After, I think," Charlotte said doubtfully. "Why do you ask?"

"That," I said, flicking the first ash from my cigarette, "is probably the reason why she backed out."

"Why, Miss Byrnes?"

I turned to him slowly. "Miss MacIntyre has been trying to see me all day, and yet on the weak excuse of not feeling so good, she missed her best opportunity. It's obvious that you're the snag."

The Sergeant looked amused. "I realize that, but why should I be in the way?"

"I couldn't say," I replied, taking my cup to the bedside table and sitting down. "The only reason I can think of is that she had something of importance to confide in me, and that she didn't know how much you were dining with us officially. I will make no secret of the fact, since it was also apparent to Inspector Coleman, that she has had something worrying her ever since Compton was murdered."

Sergeant Matheson nodded in agreement. "Yes, we know that. Supposing, Miss Byrnes, that she was going to pass on to you certain information that would help you to build up a case against someone, say, for example, Miss MacIntyre herself, what would you do? Would you submit the knowledge to the right quarters?"

I thought for a moment before answering, regretting again my quixotic desire to clear the name of a dead girl. First Bertie had shown me his clay feet, and now there was the possibility of Mac doing the same. I wondered if my loyalty to her would weaken, or perhaps grow so stubborn that whatever she had done, or was about to do, would remain forever a secret between us.

"You're taking a long time to answer the Sergeant's question," reproved my mother.

"Sorry," I replied quickly. "Supposing yet again, that we wait until such time as Miss MacIntyre gives me her confidence."

Sergeant Matheson shook his head. "That's no good. I'd rather have your promise now."

"You will certainly not get that," I said haughtily. "My friends mean more to me than a desire to help you to honour and glory."

He flushed, but replied steadily: "It's not only that. Like every other amateur, not only in the field of crime, you are liable to underestimate the professional; in this case, the real murderer of Sarah Compton. Yes, I think you are right and so does Inspector Coleman. But faced with the facts we had, what other decision could we come to? Furthermore, the father of your unfortunate fellow-telephonist has presented us with a letter that rather clinches the matter. It was written by Miss Gordon and posted just before she took her own life."

"I suppose," interrupted my mother, "that it was definitely suicide?"

"I'm afraid so, Mrs. Byrnes," he said seriously. "There was absolutely no indication at all of foul play. Believe me, we were on the look-out for it."

"But why? Why?" I exclaimed despairingly. "I keep thinking over and over that if Dulcie didn't kill Sarah, what was the point of her taking her own life?"

"You are in a better position to answer that than I am," he returned. I felt a familiar wave of dread swamp me as I braced myself for his next words. Was he going to blame me for what Dulcie did too?

"You knew the type of girl that Miss Gordon was: young, inexperienced and very impressionable, the best victim for an unscrupulous woman, who could play upon her minor peccadilloes until the poor girl thought herself a hardened criminal. Then there was the matter of a letter that we found amongst Miss Compton's correspondence. It contained a threat to do something desperate unless she stopped asking for money."

I looked up from my clenched hands. The dread had changed to relief. "I didn't know about that," I said in bewilderment. "Why didn't you tell me before?"

His brows rose in surprise. "I just presumed that Miss Gordon herself had spoken of it."

"Maggie, what are you looking so pleased about?" Charlotte asked. "It doesn't seem quite nice."

"Nice!" I exclaimed. "It's marvellous. Don't you two realize that I have been going through hell since Dulcie killed herself, blaming myself for forcing her hand. But now I know that I wasn't to blame. It wasn't anything that I said that made her commit suicide, but the fact that she had once threatened violence to Compton. She was afraid that if the police got hold of that letter it would mean a conviction." I lay back on the bed in sudden exhaustion.

"Why, Maggie darling!" said my mother, rising and coming over to me quickly. "Did you really think—? My pet, don't cry."

"I'm not," I shouted into the counterpane. "It's just that—that I feel so relieved." I sat up and shook Charlotte off. "I'm all right now. Sorry I was a fool, Sergeant."

"You weren't a fool," he said gently, "but I wish that I'd known. You must have felt rotten about the business." I grinned at him weakly and blew my nose. "And now," he continued slowly, "that the blame has been shifted from your shoulders, what are you going to do?"

I met his eyes straightly, and asked in a quiet voice: "What do you want me to do?"

He came over to where I sat with Charlotte's arm through mine and put his hands on my shoulders. At that moment he did not seem to be the shy, uneasy policeman at whom I had scoffed. His face was stern and his eyes cold as he asked me very gravely: "Does that mean that you are ready to help me all you can?"

I nodded, and his hands dropped. He strode over to the window, drawing back the curtain to stare into the street. "I'm glad," Sergeant Matheson said simply.

"I don't like it," Charlotte said, breaking a short silence. "What can Maggie do that the police can't?"

He did not turn his head. A smile flickered on his mouth. "She is already in possession of a good deal more information than we are."

"Didn't you tell the police everything?" asked my mother in a shocked voice.

"Certainly," I replied airily, and received a severe look from the Sergeant. "All right," I said hastily. "I'll come clean. Let me get up, Charlotte."

I rummaged in my handbag for the little red-covered diary in which I had jotted down some notes by the lake, and handed it to Sergeant Matheson.

"What is this?" he asked, without opening it.

"Turn to last Wednesday. I have made a few notes. Perhaps if you read them it will be easier than asking me questions. You'll find everything that I know under the different dates of the last few days."

"Very neat, Maggie," approved my mother. "You're just like your father. Read them aloud, please, Sergeant."

"Wednesday the 13th February," Sergeant Matheson began, "hours of duty—4 p.m. to 11 p.m. Bertie in an uncertain mood again." He looked up inquiringly.

"Mr. Scott," I explained, "for no reason at all wouldn't permit me to swop shifts with Gloria Patterson. He had been acting oddly for some days. Go on."

"'Constant observation on restroom 'phone.' Is that unusual, Miss Byrnes?"

"Most. Why should the telephonists' private line be observed?"

"I must check that up," the Sergeant said, making a note in his own book. "Mr. Scott will be able to tell me."

"Will he?" I queried, sotto voce. "Read out the next bit."

"'Found door ajar, but only one of the cleaners in the cloakroom.'"

"Don't ask any questions yet," I ordered. "I'll explain later."

Sergeant Matheson read on in silence. Presently he raised his head and stared in front of him, frowning. "Can you remember the size of the paper Miss Compton was reading on the roof?" he asked, keeping one finger on the page.

I concentrated hard, shutting my eyes in the endeavour to visualize a scene that had taken place four days ago. "It wasn't as large as an inquiry slip. I think that it might have been about three inches by four, but that is only a guess."

"More like an ordinary docket," suggested my mother. I swung round quickly.

"Quite possibly," I said. "In fact, it must have been. There are only three types of stationery used in the Exchange: a long foolscap which Bertie uses for reports, and the inquiry and booking pads. If it was anything connected with the trunkroom, the paper that Compton was behaving so oddly about was a docket. Isn't my mother a wonderful woman, Sergeant?"

"I can see from where your own astuteness comes," he answered gravely, though his eyes twinkled.

"This is becoming interesting," I said excitedly. "I wonder what was on that docket?"

"A booked call, probably," said my mother, intent on following up her own brilliant suggestion.

"I suppose you're right. But it is not the custom to take dockets out of the trunkroom; in fact, it's forbidden. Too many have been mislaid that way. Compton always stuck by the rules very rigidly. It wouldn't be like her to take a docket away from the boards, certainly not a booked call."

"What's this next note, Miss Byrnes?" Sergeant Matheson held out the diary, pointing with one finger in a puzzled fashion.

"Where? Oh, that! When you took my statement do you remember I told you there was something in the back of my head that I couldn't put my finger on? I wrote that down just in case it came to me later."

"And has it?" he asked.

I shook my head despondently. "I'm afraid not. All I can remember is that it is something odd or rather out of the way that I must have heard or seen."

"It's a pity," said the Sergeant. "That knowledge might make all the difference."

"I don't think so. It's probably something quite trivial."

"It is often the most trivial fact," he said seriously, "that is the criminal's one mistake. I advise you to keep on concentrating."

"I will," I promised.

He asked me to explain what I meant by the note 'The murder: I expected it.'

"Another shot in the dark, I'm afraid. I don't pretend to be psychic, but all that night I was waiting for something to happen. It was beastly hot, of course, so perhaps that helped the general atmosphere of tension. Absurd?"

"Not at all," Charlotte put in. "Don't forget your grandmother MacPherson. She was fey."

"I daresay," I said, "but Sergeant Matheson wants facts, not figments of the imagination. Am I not right, Sergeant?"

As he bent his head over the diary, one corner of his mouth quirked upwards. "The only explanation I have to offer for your expectancy is that you probably knew the murder was going to take place."

Charlotte let out a horrified gasp, but I laughed gleefully. "What about my alibi?"

"You're pretty safe," he admitted, "providing that you are not an accomplice after the fact."

"How dreadful that sounds," remarked my mother, with a sigh of relief as she realized that we were only joking. "To whom is Maggie an accomplice, please, Sergeant?"

"Anyone. Let us say Miss MacIntyre, for instance."

"You read that in my notes," I declared defiantly. "Now you know about Mac, what are you going to do?"

"Unfortunately there is nothing I can do; beyond questioning her as to the reason why she didn't tell us at once that she saw Miss Compton about 10 p.m. going down in the lift. I can't understand why she withheld the knowledge, especially as it was well-known that Miss Compton was not killed before 10.40 p.m. and had been seen by two other people after Miss MacIntyre."

"I don't understand it either," I said, troubled.

"I wish that I hadn't frightened her away," Sergeant Matheson said with a sigh. "Had I felt that I had you on the right side of the law, I would have been willing to depart discreetly and leave her in your capable hands."

"How do you know that I've joined the hounds for good?" I asked out of mischief.

He held up my little book. "If you haven't, you would not have given me this diary." Sergeant Matheson was a difficult person to tease. It was not because of any lack of humour on his part. He was so quietly reasonable that he made one's remarks seem superfluous.

"You're right," I admitted, feeling flat. "I am in this to the end now. At first I didn't care one way or the other, enjoying the adventure of it. But when Dulcie—died, and I heard—someone more or less accuse me of being responsible for her death, I made up my mind either to clear myself by proving that she really did kill Compton, or else find out the identity of the real murderer."

"And now," said Sergeant Matheson quietly, "that you realize that you were not the cause of Miss Gordon's suicide, you still want to continue. Why, I wonder?"

"I dunno," I said, shrugging. "Probably for the fun of it again."

"I don't think so, Miss Byrnes," he said, coming to stand beside me. "I think that you are like most decent-living people. You know that Miss Gordon did not murder the monitor, and you want to see fair play done. There is a sense of justice deep inborn in you that demands that you do your share to help the police whatever the cost. I admire you greatly for it," Sergeant Matheson held out his hand.

I felt myself blushing awkwardly. "Thank you, Sergeant," I replied shyly, and we shook hands on an unspoken bargain.

"You're with the law now, my girl," I told myself. "You can't back out." I caught Charlotte smiling gently to herself, and said hurriedly: "Go on with the notes."

"The notes? Yes, of course. Where were we?" The Sergeant frowned at the open page. "Miss MacIntyre is certainly an enigma. Have you any explanation to offer for her behaviour?"

"Only one," I answered, "and I hope that it is correct. In fact it seems to be the only explanation. Last Wednesday night Mac, not having been as sensitive to the atmosphere as I, received a tremendous shock when she saw Sarah lying dead on the restroom floor. After all she saw her first, while I had time to more or less prepare myself."

"And yet," suggested the Sergeant, "you were the one who fainted, not Miss MacIntyre."

"That doesn't count," I went on hurriedly. "Fainting is a matter of glands. Anyway, Mac told me later that she was violently ill. To get back to my theory. It sounds a bit like cheek, but I think that Mac is jealous of me; for two reasons. One is quite personal and wouldn't interest the Sergeant in the least." He flicked through the pages of the diary, his face expressionless. "The other is the notice that the police took of me. Mac wasn't the only one by any means. I might add that I have had to stand up to a considerable amount of baiting. Mac, seeing the fun that I was getting out of the situation that was excluding her for practically the first time, made up her mind to start on her own and beat me to the punch, so to speak. I don't think for one moment that she ever entertained the conviction that poor little Dulcie murdered Compton. In that she scored over me, when I thought that I was being terribly clever. I only discovered to-day that she has been going through those telephonists who worked late on Wednesday night, questioning them. Whatever line she is working on must be somewhere near the truth."

"Why do you say that?" asked Sergeant Matheson.

"Her room was searched to-day," I said grimly. I had the doubtful pleasure of seeing his eyes become filled with anxiety. "I went round to her boarding-house this afternoon after Mrs. Bates had told me that Mac had wanted to see me. But she had evidently gone straight from here into town."

"It might have been a burglar," suggested my mother hopefully.

I shook my head. "Although the room was in a terrible mess, I don't think that anything was taken. Incidentally, Sergeant, I'm afraid that I did the wrong thing. I tidied up a bit. I didn't want Mac to get a fright when she returned. Does it matter?"

"I suppose not," he replied, writing again in his own book. "There would have been very little that the local police could have done, providing Miss MacIntyre called them in, which somehow I don't think she would."

"Mac's playing a dangerous game," I remarked with a sigh. "I almost wish that I had left her room in the state it was. It might have made her realize what she is up against. Why doesn't she go straight to Inspector Coleman and tell him everything she knows?"

I met the Sergeant's eyes accidentally. They were twinkling merrily. "That is exactly the same sentiment as I have been trying to drum into you for days," he observed.

I had the grace to blush. "I was a fool," I admitted. "Wait until I see Mac. I'll persuade her. I think it is most likely that she wanted to tell me her side of the story this afternoon, don't you?"

"I sincerely hope so," he replied gravely, "and when she does, don't forget your promise, will you?"

"I've learned my lesson," I answered reassuringly. "Not that I intend to have any further dealings with the police as soon as this affair is cleared up."

"You are very optimistic," the Sergeant observed, smiling.

"Certainly," I replied stoutly. "As soon as we know what Mac has discovered, we'll break the case. Then you'll get promotion, and everything will be marvellous all round. No more mysteries and suspicions."

"I didn't mean that," he murmured, making another note with his inevitable blunt pencil.

"I am sure that I have a better one than that," said my mother, searching in her handbag. "Here, Sergeant."

"No, thank you, Mrs. Byrnes. I'm rather attached to this pencil. It was the same one I used on my first murder case."

"It looks like it," I remarked tartly. "However, talking about pencils brings my wandering attention back to the matter in hand. Suppose you read on, Sergeant."

"I have been, Miss Byrnes. With your leave, I'll copy one or two points for my own benefit."

"Go right ahead. What has taken your interest?"

"Only that you say that Miss Patterson knew more about the murder than was printed in the Press."

"That is correct. She was able to tell me where Compton was found dead when she came to see me here the following morning. I jumped on to it. She got scared immediately."

"Did she tell you how she knew?"

I shrugged. "Some rigmarole which I didn't swallow about one of the girls ringing her from the Exchange. Bear it in mind until you reach a bit further on, and I bet you'll sit up with a jerk. What comes next?"

"'The anonymous letters!'"

"This is where I'll take over again," I said. "I hope I'm not boring you."

"On the contrary. What have you to say about the anonymous letters?"

My bedroom was growing steadily darker. I leaned over to switch on the bedside light. Somehow the subdued glow did not give such an impression of heat as the ceiling lamps. The light fell on to the Sergeant's hands as he sat near the window, but his head and shoulders remained in a shadow. Outside the north wind had dropped to a hot sigh every now and then, while crickets screeched in Mrs. Bates's garden. I lighted another cigarette and half lay on the bed, leaning back on one elbow with my legs crossed.

"Inspector Coleman gave me three letters to read," I began. "The first two were written by Irene Patterson. At once I was struck by the name being the same as that of a telephonist who already seemed to be connected with the crime. There was also the similarity between those two early letters and the one that Compton received in the lift. The conclusion that we all came to was that Irene Patterson was somehow connected with the last anonymous note that Compton was to receive. Could it be that she was an employee of the Telephone Department? The writer of that note most certainly was. Working on the theory that Irene Patterson might be an employee, we ask ourselves what relation is she to the telephonist, Gloria Patterson? Is she her mother, which would seem the most likely? Or is she no relation at all? At this point, I am forced much against my inclination to inform you that Gloria has told me that her mother is dead, and her father deserted her many years ago. So that sort of wipes that out, doesn't it? But don't be downcast, as I have another little theory to come to." I looked at the tip of my cigarette in silence for a few minutes, fighting an inward battle. Presently an impatient sigh from my mother penetrated my consciousness. "Go on with Thursday's notes," I said curtly to Sergeant Matheson.

As he bent his head, I guessed that he had been gazing at me through the shadows. "'Tea with S.M.'" he continued.

"You can skip that," I interrupted, smiling.

He nodded gravely. "'Discovered B. knew of S.C. years ago!' Who is B., Miss Byrnes?"

"The liftman," I said shortly, "and a gentleman in the truest sense of the word. This is where I strongly regret ever having set eyes on you, Sergeant. But I don't go back on a promise, so I think that it is only fair to give you some facts and ideas about Bill."

"Maggie is one of those persons who are almost tediously loyal," said Charlotte, aside to the Sergeant.

"An excellent trait," he agreed, "but unfortunately, in a case like this, there must be nothing that cannot be unfolded and looked at from all angles. Go on, please, Miss Byrnes, I am getting interested."

"At last?" I queried, my reluctance making me sarcastic. I retold the story of Bill overhearing the quarrel between Sarah Compton and Irene Patterson, and the theory Mac and I had evolved silently between us that he was Gloria's father, Dan Patterson.

"I was very surprised to learn that he was married and had two children, a boy and," I paused for a moment, "a girl." The Sergeant made no comment, so I continued. "Not long afterwards it occurred to me that although we had seen our liftman day after day for many years, not once had I heard his surname. I asked Mac, but she, too, was in ignorance. In fact, I doubt if a dozen persons in the Department would be able to say what it was. He is Bill to all and sundry. Was the daughter he had owned to switching side by side with us? In fact, Gloria? Working on that assumption and knowing what a ghastly little snob she can be, we realized that her obvious disinclination to come into contact with Compton was due to the fact that the latter knew of the relationship. Perhaps Compton was becoming nasty about it, though I fail to see what difference having a liftman as a father would make to the normal person. But Gloria is not normal. She lives in a rosy mist of fabrication. If the identity of her father got around the Exchange, the fact would be too real and prosaic for her to continue her romancings. Perhaps she was afraid of being laughed at. Believe me, Gloria would hate that. She has little or no sense of humour. My theory is that she appealed to Bill to stop Sarah and that he tried to do so through the medium of an anonymous letter. That is, the one thrown down into the lift on Wednesday night.

"Now we come to the matter of yet another anonymous letter. This time it was sent to me, and I took it to the police at once. It was a most unoriginal note. The only interesting thing about it was that it was written in an ordinary pencil, not an indelible one. You remember me asking you that, Sergeant?"

"As a matter of fact, we wondered what you had in mind," he confessed. "Even Inspector Coleman hadn't observed that the first letter was in indelible writing."

"This is what I was getting at. That note must have been written and put in my locker between the time I found that pencil during tea on Thursday, and when I came down from the roof to collect my headset prior to going on duty. I discovered Bill eavesdropping on my conversation with Dulcie Gordon about the practice of writing unsigned letters. He knew I was becoming curious and wanted to stop me before I learned too much Having lost his indelible pencil crawling under the kitchen counter to hear what I was saying he had to use an ordinary one. I showed it to Bill yesterday, but he disclaimed all ownership, his manner abrupt and totally different from usual. I let the matter drop as I considered then that it was pretty conclusive that Dulcie Gordon was guilty. Either she had written the anonymous letters or else they had nothing whatsoever to do with the case. Whichever way suited me as I was fast losing interest until, as I have said, I overheard something," I paused to press out my cigarette.

My mother remarked with the air of one making a great discovery: "Darling, I have never known you to speak at such length before."

I laughed. "Sorry if I've been holding forth too much. Shall I shut up, Sergeant? Those notes of mine should be fairly explicit. "

"No, please go on, Miss Byrnes. I find your impressions most interesting."

"All right. Tell me when you're getting bored. Where was I?"

"Eavesdropping," said Charlotte.

"Indeed I wasn't," I protested indignantly. "The remark was made for my ears but the speaker, one Gloria Patterson, lacked the guts to accuse me face to face. Perhaps you can guess what it was."

"What a nasty, spiteful girl!" said my mother sharply.

"I see that you've caught on," I observed, shrugging. "Yes, she gave out the opinion that I had forced Dulcie Gordon to her death. If I had known then of the threatening letter that Dulcie had sent to Compton, I wouldn't have worried, I would have put the remark down to sheer spite. It is just as well that I didn't know, otherwise this little meeting wouldn't be taking place."

"I don't think that you would have stayed satisfied with our decision," Sergeant Matheson said.

"Perhaps not," I agreed. "If you don't mind me saying so, it was a wobbly sort of solution. There seemed to be a lot of gaps; those letters, Bertie, and—Mac. It would have been better if those had been cleared up too. On the other hand, I doubt if my entry in this case will make much difference. You too were not satisfied, and I know of another."

"Who is that, Miss Byrnes?"

"Mr. Clarkson," I replied, busying myself with a hand mirror and comb. "Though he didn't admit it in so many words."

"How on earth—" began the Sergeant.

"Maggie just knows," interrupted my mother. "Haven't you ever heard of a woman's instinct, Sergeant?"

"I have," he replied grimly.

"Don't deride it," I warned him, wondering if his wife possessed one. "I am working purely on intuition."

"Gloria!" said my mother patiently. I glanced at her in surprise.

"Oh, I see," I said, light dawning. "It's your fault anyway—sidetracking. But we'll leave Gloria for the moment as I have a little piece to work in about her and I want to achieve a dramatic effect. What else have I got down under Thursday?"

"'Night guard sees Bertie enter Exchange about 10 p.m.'"

I turned to my mother, grinning. "Forget your sensibilities, Charlotte. Your daughter is about to deal with some sordid facts."

"I don't like it, Maggie," she said plaintively.

"I'll be quick," I promised, turning back to Sergeant Matheson. "We had it most reluctantly from Mr. Scott's own lips that Sarah Compton was his mistress, and that she had phoned him earlier on Wednesday night to meet her in the observation room on the third floor. Ormond, our stolid guard, who vouchsafed the opinion that Bertie entered the building about 10 p.m. and left before the half-hour, let drop, most accidentally I am sure, an important point. At 10 p.m. Bertie creeps into the building with his hat over his eyes, trying to make himself inconspicuous, but when he leaves at 10.25 p.m. his demeanour does not arouse any comment from our observant friend, Mr. Ormond. In other words, he enters surreptitiously, but leaves in such a manner that Ormond cannot fail to recognize him. In fact, I'm willing to bet that he didn't know Bertie at 10 p.m., but presumed that it was he when he saw him leave half an hour later. Do you follow what I mean?"

"Very subtle," remarked the Sergeant, nodding. "What are you leading to?"

"I hold the theory that if Bertie entered the Exchange once without being spotted, but let the night guard get a good look at him as he left, he could re-enter unobserved. He made his exit so blatantly that Ormond would hardly expect to see him again. If a hunched-up figure entered the building flashing a pass some minutes later, I am willing to bet you yet again that it was Bertie, and that Ormond presumed that he was just another mechanic coming on duty."

There was a pause. I looked over at the Sergeant's shadowy outline. "Well?" I asked.

He stirred restlessly. "Quite possible, but—"

"I'm ready for you," I interrupted. "You think that my theory is rotten. That's all right by me, but just you listen to this one. While working on the idea yesterday, I was struck by a brainwave that sent me down to the basement to explore. There, more than half-hidden by boxes, I came across a door leading into the lane on the west side of the building."

I saw the Sergeant sit up with a jerk. "How many people know of it?" he asked swiftly.

"I'm afraid I couldn't say. It came as a great surprise to me, if that is anything to go by. But Mac knew of it. She had been rummaging around the storeroom for a docket when I met her. I am of the opinion that very few people know of it, and that those few would only be the Heads."

"The Heads? Is Mr. Scott one?"

"Sure," I replied, noting his sudden excitement. "He comes under that category. Would you like me to stop while you have a think?"

"No," he said like a cross child. I leaned back, smiling in the darkness. Even on duty the Sergeant was not without a chink in his armour.

"Now we've found a secret entrance for Bertie," I continued, "though I am still attached to my first theory, we will get down to the subject of motives, opportunities, and last but by no means least, the weapon. If there had been any doubt as to whether the murder was an inside job or not, I think the buttinsky that bashed Compton's head in settled the question. It was a premeditated crime, with the weapon chosen well in advance. Only one conversant with Exchange ways would be able to select such an instrument to kill somebody. You could rely on a buttinsky to do the job thoroughly. No murderer could have chosen a more suitable weapon."

I felt my mother shiver a little in spite of the heat. "Don't, Maggie," she said in a quiet voice.

"Sorry, Mother," I answered contritely.

"It certainly looks bad," nodded the Sergeant. "Mr. Scott owned that the buttinsky was his. We presumed at the time that Miss Gordon had stolen it for her own use."

"Bertie couldn't say when he first missed it?" I asked hopefully. He shook his head. "He's appallingly absentminded. I must introduce him to you to-night, Charlotte. It should be rather good value to bring you two together."

Sergeant Matheson was continuing his own line of thought. "There is certainly a motive in Mr. Scott's case."

"We all know what it is," I said hastily. "Don't bring up the subject again. Mother doesn't like it, do you, darling?"

"I am sure your father would have done the same in Mr. Scott's position," Charlotte declared vaguely.

"Mrs. Byrnes!" I exclaimed in a scandalized voice.

"What's wrong, dear? What have I said?"

"Only that father would have—er—a friend," I said solemnly.

"I didn't mean that. I am sure he wouldn't think of such a thing."

"Well, what did you mean?" I demanded.

"If someone was trying to break up his domestic life, I am sure that your father would take steps to remove that person," she explained, not very lucidly.

"That's almost as bad," I pointed out. "You're making the Old Man out a potential murderer. Let's drop the subject, Charlotte, before you become more involved. Keep it for Bertie to-night."

"I will," she promised. I laughed, not taking her seriously. I thought that I knew my mother, but therein I made yet another mistake.

"Miss Byrnes," Sergeant Matheson addressed me so abruptly that I jumped. "Could anyone have taken that buttinsky from Mr. Scott's desk?"

"Anyone," I replied promptly.

"Miss Patterson could have taken it then?"

"She could. But I can't see Gloria wielding it with such a terrible effect as it was used. I don't hold much brief for Gloria, and although she knows quite a bit about what has been going on during the last few days, she is no murderess. But her part may have been to provide the instrument," I suggested.

"H'm," said the Sergeant thoughtfully, and I waited for him to speak. Presently he looked towards me. I thought he was smiling.

"Where's your bombshell?" he asked. "I thought you said you were leading up to a climax."

"I was waiting for my cue," I replied with a mock bow. "There is yet another figure to be introduced on the stage of this drama. So far, that person has remained discreetly in the background, probably for reasons best known to-herself. To be strictly honest, the same person only came to my notice this afternoon. But on thinking back, I am astounded at my lack of perspicacity, as she has been somewhere on the stage during each scene."

"Her!" exclaimed the Sergeant. "One of the telephonists?"

"Let me tell my own story," I begged. "Yesterday, as you know, I was on the all-night shift. By a lucky chance, Gloria Patterson was also on duty. It gave me the opportunity to ask her some leading questions."

I sat up from my reclining position, and bent forward so as to be able to see the Sergeant's face. It did not seem natural to be addressing one's remarks to a dark object presumed to be one's audience.

"At that time," I continued with a sigh, "my mind was in a sad muddle. I don't know whether it was the heat or the readjustment to different hours, but I thought it advisable to go right back to the beginning and ask Gloria her movements on Wednesday evening. It had to be done very tactfully, because I knew that she would be on the alert. However,

I learned that although the girls on her rota saw her arrive on the eighth floor as they were going down the stairs to the trunkroom, she did not appear there until some time later. When I faced her with the question as to whether she had seen anyone in that time she shut up like an oyster, but not before she let slip a few unguarded words. Those words were 'only one of—' and there, as I have just told you, she stopped."

Sergeant Matheson leaned forward, his hands clasped between his knees. The light fell on both our faces.

"I repeated that phrase over and over again," I went on, "but I could not complete it until this afternoon. Gloria had become suspicious, so I sent her out on relief in the hope that her wariness would evaporate if I let her alone for a while. Presently she came dashing back in what can only be termed as a 'state.' She had been in the restroom and had seen Sarah Compton's ghost. I offered to go and allay her fears. Needless to say, they were quite unfounded. But they only went to manifest further that the murder was on her mind."

Sergeant Matheson had taken out his notebook once more and was transcribing my words. I continued: "Rather meanly, I admit, I caught her on the hop and made her stay in the restroom while I asked a few more questions. I won't say how I compelled her, as it may shock the Sergeant. I finally got it out of her that the person to whom she had been talking that Wednesday night was Bill the liftman. That clinched the matter as far as I was concerned. Had I not overheard a chance remark this afternoon, I was going to present you with a cast-iron case against our liftman."

Sergeant Matheson's face was stern as he looked across the narrow space between us. "It can only be hoped that the liftman can present an alibi for the time between 10.40 p.m. and 11.10 p.m. on Wednesday night. Otherwise things will look very black for him."

I did not interrupt him. I wanted to see what he thought of Bill's position first.

"Let us suppose that he is the Daniel Patterson we are looking for: the man who married Irene, and the father of Gloria. Suppose that Miss Compton had already found a way to repay the injury his wife had done her, and that he in his turn set out to revenge that injury. What was there to stop him from stealing the buttinsky from Mr. Scott's desk? I daresay that he has entered the trunkroom many times?" I nodded, and watched him thoughtfully.

"You yourself have provided a way by which he could enter the Exchange building without having to use the front door. But perhaps that was unnecessary as he might not have left the building at all, but hidden himself either in the restroom itself or the lift cabin on the roof.

Then there are those letters. Who would be more conversant with Irene Patterson's style than her own husband? Who would have been better able to be on the lookout for the right time to send that note down into the lift to Miss Compton? He could have arranged the open emergency hole before he went off duty with just that view in mind. No, Miss Byrnes, I fail to see any alteration to the facts that you have given me."

I uncrossed my legs, and leaned back again to stare dreamily at the shifting shadows on the ceiling. "Only one of—" I murmured softly. "How those words worried me until this afternoon." I turned my head and smiled gently at the Sergeant.

"Well?" he asked crisply. I saw him looking annoyed under my teasing.

"This afternoon," I said, transferring my attention once more to the ceiling, "like the Latin tag about a dog, I returned to the Exchange. Charlotte, I hope you don't follow my simile. It is rather vulgar. I went into town with the object of finding Mac. My search took me to the dormitory on the seventh floor, which was being prepared for to-night's show. I missed Mac, who had been in earlier, but the decorators demanded my services because of my height. I was forced to mount a rickety ladder to alter some streamers. While I was in this precarious position a knock came at the door. One of the girls answered it. When she came back presently to direct my faltering hands, I asked her quite casually who it was."

I rolled over on to one side and propped my chin in my hand. "What do you think she replied?" I asked idiotically, bent on achieving a dramatic effect: "'Only one of the cleaners.'"

There was a dead silence. Charlotte was frankly gaping. I waited for my words to sink in. I thought Sergeant Matheson looked a shade disappointed, and hurried to enlarge upon the new theory.

"Let us go back to Wednesday again," I suggested, starting to enjoy myself. "You remember that I told you how Gloria Patterson left us playing cards and I noticed the restroom door ajar. There was no sign of her when I looked out into the cloakroom, but there was someone else, and it was—"

"Only one of the cleaners," my mother chimed in triumphantly. "Go on, Maggie, quickly."

"It's funny," I mentioned pensively, "that although there are a tribe of middle-aged charwomen around the building, you never seem to notice them. I suppose that they are like the case of the missing buttinsky, insignificant but important. Gloria comes back from her cocktail at the 'Australia,' and with whom does she pause to chat? You know the answers, so I won't repeat myself in a tedious fashion. But there is one more instance where the same phrase fits in. It occurred that night I had tea with Mac and Dulcie Gordon. I dash off searching for the eavesdropper and there I see Bill the liftman, quite overlooking the fact that with him is one of the cleaners locking up the cafeteria."

"Was it the same woman each time?" demanded the Sergeant.

"I don't know about Gloria's friend. It was the other times."

"Do you know her name?" asked the Sergeant with his pencil poised.

"Smith or Jones," I replied after a moment's thought. "Something typically insignificant. Smith, I think."

"That's a familiar name," remarked my mother absently.

She looked up in surprise as Sergeant Matheson and I laughed together.

"We'll go into the matter," Sergeant Matheson promised me, "but I rather fancy the liftman. However, as I said before, every possibility must be explored. Is there anything else, Miss Byrnes?"

"Yes," I replied. "You're forgetting Bertie. My money is on him at the moment, and I can give you a good reason why. I told you that I had Gloria in the restroom last night. After she departed in rather an annoyed way, I settled down on the couch for a bit of sleep. It was cool and comfortable there, and the fact that my late antagonist would probably be occupying the dormitory did not urge me to leave. I rather think that I fell asleep. Anyway, I turned off the light to that object, leaving just the one globe in the cloakroom burning."

"Maggie, dear!" protested my mother.

"I know, Charlotte," I replied, "and never again. I thought that my last moment had come. And was I in a blue funk! I awoke with a jerk to find myself in complete darkness, but not alone. Someone had stolen into the room without realizing that I was there, and was making a call on the telephonists' phone. Now, here is what struck me as odd. Although I could hear someone talking the other end, the unknown caller made not one remark, and presently hung up the receiver and crept out again."

"You have no idea who it was?" asked the Sergeant.

"It may have been Gloria again, but I'm not sure. I waited where I was. In fact, I don't think that I could have moved, I was so terrified. After a few minutes, I got out of that room as quickly as I could. Believe me, you won't see me going into it alone again. Then another brainwave struck me. I didn't know the caller, but at least I could have a shot at discovering the number that was dialled. I rushed down to one of the apparatus rooms on the first floor; incidentally, Sergeant, forgetting my qualms about using the lift. There I found a mechanic who proved most helpful."

"Did you find out the number?"

"It is in my book, M something or other. From the initial letter I can tell you that the subscriber is somewhere in the west part of town. A friend of mine on the Information desk is trying to trace it, but I'm afraid that it'll be a long job." I looked speculatively at the Sergeant, who seemed to be brooding deeply.

"I hope that you're not thinking of ringing the number yourself," I ventured.

He laughed shortly. "I was," he admitted. "Whoever answers may be able to give us a line to work on."

"I don't think so," I murmured.

He glanced up sharply. "You've tried already?"

I nodded. "A man answered. He told me in no uncertain terms where to go. I certainly picked on a bad time. But I believe that 3 a.m. is not an unusual hour for babies to demand entry into this sorry world."

"Maggie, darling!" said my mother distressfully.

"What on earth are you talking about?" asked Sergeant Matheson in bewilderment.

"Charlotte knows," I said, grinning. "Trust a woman to catch on quickly. I thought that it would be less suspicious if I pretended that I was calling a doctor. I think it was swallowed. I didn't learn much, except that the unknown subscriber was a man. I wouldn't go using the same trick if I were you. He may become suspicious."

"After that episode we'd better wait for your friend's result. Will she take long?"

"Not if she's lucky. It means wading through a list of automatic numbers in the City West group. It may be at the top. On the other hand, it may be at the bottom. They don't run in numerical order, you know."

Sergeant Matheson glanced through his own notebook. "Anyway, I've got plenty to work on for the time being. I'll just compare these notes I've made with yours, Miss Byrnes. I gather that you've finished all you wish to say."

"At long last," I agreed. "Do you mind tossing me over an orange from the chest of drawers. My throat is dry after all the talking I've done. They're just behind you. Do you want us to shut up while you work!"

The Sergeant had placed the two notebooks side by side on my bedside table. "No, you may keep talking. I hope that I'm not keeping you."

"Not at all," declared my mother politely. "There is no particular time that you wanted to arrive at the dance, is there, Maggie?"

"We'd better go soon if I'm to get any dances before I go on duty. Would you care to come with us, Sergeant? I will be able to get you in without a pass. You will be able to see everyone who seems to be concerned in this affair unofficially, so to speak."

"Thank you," he replied with alacrity. "I'm very anxious to talk to Miss MacIntyre as soon as possible. I don't like the idea of an amateur running about loose with information that should have been lodged in the right quarters long ago."

I glanced at him uneasily. "You don't think—" I began hesitantly. He looked at me straightly without a word. "Come on, Charlotte," I said quickly, "Let's get going at once."

CHAPTER VIII

We were all very quiet during that drive into the city, and I gripped my mother's hand in a way that I had not done for years. She returned the clasp, although her face, when I looked into it, seemed as placid as usual. The traffic lights on the city side of the bridge held up the taxi that Sergeant Matheson had ordered so munificently. I was in a fever of impatience. I had only one idea fixed in my mind, and that was to find Mac.

'Nothing can happen to her at the dance, surely,' I told myself. 'Why, everyone will be there. All the Heads of the Department and the Engineering Branch. There's nothing to worry about.'

The Heads! I had told Sergeant Matheson that Bertie was one of them.

My mother remarked casually: "It's astounding how long those lights take to turn green when you're in a hurry," and I knew that she, too, was eager to reach our destination.

The car swung around west away from the traffic in the heart of town. Presently it mounted the hill steadily to the Exchange building. Cars of all descriptions were lined up in the parking area outside. There were even a couple of mechanics' motorcycles standing cheek by jowl beside the Superintendent of Telephones' limousine. As the wind rose and fell, I could hear the faint thud of a percussion instrument and a drift or two of dance music.

"We will make a spectacular entry," I said lightly, following my mother out of the car. "We seem to be the last. Have you got that pass I gave you, Charlotte?"

"I think so," she replied, letting her long skirt fall as she opened her handbag. "Yes, here it is."

"Come along, my children," I said briskly. "I believe that it is our friend, Mr. Ormond, at the door. Do you want a word with him, Sergeant?"

"I'd better tell him who I am. I'll follow you in a minute." "He'll probably ask him about Bertie on Wednesday night," I whispered to my mother, guiding her along the dim passage to the lift. "What did you think of my theory?"

"About Mr. Scott departing and then coming back? Quite good, dear, but not likely if he knew about that door in the basement."

We paused outside the lift, and I pressed the button. The sound of the music was stronger now that we were in the new building. The dance was in full swing only seven floors above our heads. The rhythm of the three-piece band that we had hired made me tap one foot, and forget momentarily my original urgency to see Mac. The atmosphere of the Exchange seemed charged with gaiety and utterly devoid of the tension of the past few days. It would be rather absurd to go rushing up to Mac and dragging her aside for serious conversation. The lift settled at the ground floor. It was empty.

"Is that the place?" asked Charlotte, pointing above her head.

"It is," I replied, running my finger carefully down the row of buttons. When the lift had started on its way, I turned to her, saying: "Let's forget everything, and have a good time for a while. I'm heartily sick of deducing and theorising. I mean to enjoy myself for the next hour or so. How do you like the band?"

"They sound quite good," she replied cautiously. "Am I expected to dance?"

"Rather. They'll line up as soon as they see you. But I want you to meet Bertie first."

A shutter fell. I glanced at the indicator quickly. "That'll be Sergeant Matheson. Shall we go back for him?" I jammed the emergency stop without waiting for her reply. The lift came to a standstill.

"Damn! I hope I haven't messed up the works. No, we're all right. She's on the move." I looked over my shoulder at Charlotte. "Did I give you a fright?" She did not seem to hear me.

"Mother," I called softly.

She started. "What, darling? I was thinking."

"What about?" I asked her.

"Nothing, really, Maggie. are you sure that nice boy is married?" she asked hopefully.

I grinned unashamedly at her transparency. "I think so. Gloria Patterson told me, and she usually knows these things. A careful reconnaissance of whether a man is married and how much money he has is Gloria's first move in the game."

"Such a pity," Charlotte said regretfully. I frowned at her warningly as I opened the doors for Sergeant Matheson.

"Hullo," I greeted him. "Did you fix things up?"

He nodded. "I thought you said that you were not going to travel in this lift again even with a policeman," he said grinning.

I laughed back at him. The music must have had the same effect on him as it had on me. His ordinary-looking face was alight with expectancy.

"Don't bring the subject up," I begged. "Let's enjoy ourselves for a change. I hope you realize that to-night's affair is going to cost you half a crown, not to mention odd sixpences for raffles, with which you'll be pestered."

"I'll charge it to Russell Street," he returned blithely. "If you notice any change in your next year's assessment, you'll know who to blame. That's a jolly band you've got here," he added, opening the doors at the seventh floor.

"We were just passing the same remark. Do you dance?"

"A little," he replied modestly. "May I—"

"Sure. Wait here until I run and put this case away. I had to bring a change of clothes. I can't go home to-morrow morning in this rigout. Do you want to powder your nose, Charlotte?"

"If you think that it's necessary, dear. Where do we go?"

"Follow me. You stay near the door, Sergeant. We'll only be a minute."

"What a crowd of people!" said my mother, as I cleaved a passage to a small room the other end of the corridor. It bore the title of Ladies' Cloaks. Several voices greeted me gaily. The spirit of carnival was in the air. It was expressed by the lighthearted chatter around us, the beat of the slow foxtrot that the band was playing, and the flimsy frocks of the girls, which whirled and mingled against the dark background of their partners. Nobody seemed to be remembering those grim happenings that had taken place only three days previously, and I made a mental resolve to forget them too. After all, having delivered whatever knowledge I held into the Sergeant's hands, I was no longer responsible.

The cloakroom was like an oven, and crowded with telephonists repairing their make-up. As I have mentioned before, news spreads quickly in the Exchange. I was chaffed immediately.

"I see that you've brought your policeman boy-friend, Maggie. What will Clark say?"

"Shut up," I replied without heat. "This is my mother. Charlotte, these are a few of the poorer class of telephonists. You know, the ones who give you wrong numbers."

There was an indignant outcry. I retired to a corner and got busy with a comb and hand-mirror. Charlotte chatted with one or two for a few minutes before we rejoined Sergeant Matheson. He was still standing where we had left him, but John Clarkson was there too. I was struck by the insignificant figure the former cut beside Clark. I wondered if it was only the rhythm of the dance that made my heart beat faster as I approached them. Clark looked around, smiling.

"Mother," I said, taking her elbow. "May I introduce Mr. Clarkson, one of our traffic officers. Sorry we're so late. How's everything going?"

"Fine," Clark replied, shaking Charlotte's hand. "I believe that you're giving me a stroke a hole to-morrow, Mrs. Byrnes."

Charlotte eyed him cautiously. "I don't think I will now. You look as though you can play."

"He's pretty feeble," I told her.

Clark laughed. "A dance, Maggie?"

"Sorry," I answered regretfully. "I've promised Sergeant Matheson. But will you do something for me? Find Bertie and introduce him to my mother. She is anxious to meet him."

"I didn't say so," Charlotte protested.

"Yes, you are," I insisted, going into the danceroom with Sergeant Matheson.

He danced remarkably well for a policeman. He laughed when I told him so, and asked if there was any reason why he should not.

"None at all," I replied, following an intricate corner turn which I was sure that he made solely for my benefit. "I have always suffered under the delusion that one of the qualifications for the Force was flat feet."

"You forget that I worked in the country for some years," he reminded me. "If you can't dance there, you're a social outcast."

I felt as if he had won that round and made no further comment. Curious glances were directed towards us as Sergeant Matheson swung me down the centre of the room. I began to regret my last-minute invitation.

'I'll never hear the end of this,' I told myself. 'It didn't matter so much asking him, but I should have known better than to have a dance with him.'

The Sergeant's voice broke in on my thoughts. "You look like royalty," he remarked, smiling.

"That's very nice of you. But why?"

"You seem to have done nothing but bow and wave since we arrived. Do you know everyone here?"

"Practically," I nodded, looking round his arm. "I haven't seen Mac anywhere. I wonder if she is off duty yet?"

"Probably she's changing," he suggested, as the music stopped. "Thank you, Miss Byrnes. I enjoyed that very much." He led me down the room to where my mother was sitting and talking to Bertie. The Senior Traffic Officer rose abruptly as he saw me approach.

"Good evening, Mr. Scott," said the Sergeant pleasantly. "It looks like a successful night."

Bertie eyed him with transparent hostility, and muttering some excuse left us.

"He's scared of you," I said softly to Sergeant Matheson. He followed the Senior Traffic Officer's figure with his eyes as Bertie passed from group to group and finally went to sit with a faded-looking woman the other end of the room.

"That must be his wife," I remarked, directing surreptitious glances towards the Scotts. I saw Bertie offer his arm, and the pair of them went out of the room.

"What did you think of him, Charlotte?" I asked.

"Very nice, dear. Is he always so fidgety? He made me tired to look at him."

"He's a nervy person," I answered, turning round in answer to a touch on my bare arm. "Oh, hullo! What do you want?"

"The next dance, please," Dan Mitchell replied firmly. "Where have you been all night?"

"We've only just arrived. Mother, this is Dan Mitchell."

"How do you do?" she asked gravely. I motioned to Sergeant Matheson to come nearer. "This is my friendly mechanic," I said significantly, as the two men shook hands. The boy's eyes gleamed as I spoke the Sergeant's name.

"I'm glad you're here, sir."

"Not so loud," I warned him. "Mother, did you see Mac at all?"

"Only for a minute. She was going to the cloakroom to change."

"You're a good detective," I informed the Sergeant. "No, I am sorry, Dan, but I think that this is Mr. Clarkson's dance. Go and find someone else."

The boy's face fell. "But I thought you said—" he began. "The next one," I promised, looking around the room. "Go and ask that girl in blue over there. She's a good dancer, and such a nice person."

Dan went off grumbling a little. I seated myself one side of my mother.

"I promised to tell him a few facts to-night," I explained to the Sergeant across Charlotte. "Do you think that I should now?"

"He's the one who helped you to trace that call, isn't he? I suppose that it's only fair to give him some of the dope. Is he a trustworthy lad?"

"I think so. What would you say, Charlotte?"

"Such a nice fresh look about him," she commented. "What did you say his name was again?"

"Dan Mitchell. Didn't I introduce him distinctly enough?"

"No, it's not that," she answered slowly. "I wanted to make certain of his name. You said Dan, didn't you?" I nodded impatiently. "That's not a very common name, is it, Maggie?"

I had been looking towards the door watching the dancers come in. "It appears as though I have been left flat," I remarked lightly. "What did you say, Charlotte?"

"It doesn't matter," she replied. I was surprised to see Sergeant Matheson was staring at her thoughtfully.

"Thank you, Mrs. Byrnes," he said. "It might be worth going into."

"Probably a coincidence," Charlotte said apologetically.

I glanced from one to the other. "What on earth are you two talking about?" I asked, puzzled. "Here's Clark at last. Hullo! Did you want this dance with me? If not, I'm a wallflower."

"I'll spare you that humiliation," he replied, holding out one hand. As I slid into his arms, he bent his head to whisper: "What's bitten your friend of the Force?"

"Why?" I asked, craning my neck. Sergeant Matheson was staring across the room. Presently I saw him say a word or two to Charlotte and get up. He wended his way around the edge of the dancers until he came to stand before a blonde girl, sparsely clad in gold satin.

"Gloria!" I said violently.

Clark glanced down at me quickly. "What's the matter, my sweet?"

"Take me down to the band end of the room," I ordered. "Sergeant Matheson is starting to dance with Patterson. I want to hear what they are saying."

"You can't do that, Maggie," Clark protested.

"Oh, can't I? If that girl is going to start telling lies about me again, I'll slap her face."

"You're jealous," he said, with amusement.

"Indeed I'm not," I said indignantly, looking straight up into his face. His eyes held mine for a moment searchingly. Then he gave a short laugh and whirled me round as the Sergeant had done.

"Stop, Clark," I begged, laughing. "I've got to work soon, and I won't have any breath left with which to talk."

"Poor Maggie," he said, easing into a slow waltz. "It's a damn shame we're on duty. I tell you what I'll do. I'll get one of the boys to transmit the music to the trunkroom. We won't feel completely deprived of the party."

"With Bertie and the others here!" I exclaimed. "We wouldn't have a chance."

"I can get them to put it on a line," Clark explained. "How would that be? At least we could listen in."

"Can it be done?" I asked doubtfully.

"Of course. You wait here and I'll dash downstairs. I won't be long."

"I'll go and sit with Charlotte," I called after him. He nodded before disappearing into the crowd.

"Bored, darling?" I asked my mother.

"Not at all. I have just finished a dance with such a nice man. Poor fellow! He only had one arm, but it didn't seem to embarrass him a bit."

"That would be Bill," I remarked, holding a hairpin between my teeth as I adjusted the bow I had been wearing.

"I thought it might be," she nodded calmly. "Who is that beautiful girl Sergeant Matheson is dancing with?"

"Gloria Patterson. I thought you said that she was nasty and spiteful."

"She looks as if she could be," commented my mother. "Such a pity with that face and figure. Where are you going, Maggie?"

"I thought that I'd have a hunt for Mac now. Clark has gone downstairs to fix something up for me, but I'll be back before he returns. Will you be all right for a while?" Even as I spoke, Mr. Stornham from the Engineers' Branch came up to ask her for a dance.

'I suppose that some of these old codgers aren't game to ask the younger girls,' I thought. 'Charlotte is being rushed. Good for her, anyway.'

I watched her for a while, and waved cheerily from the doorway before making my way along the passage to the cloakroom. As I opened the door the noise that issued forth was like the monkey cage at the zoo.

"Is Gerda MacIntyre there?" I yelled above the din. The abrupt silence that fell was almost ludicrous. But Mac was not there. The chattering and giggling started again as I withdrew. The corridor was almost empty, and I returned to the danceroom to rake the dancers for Mac. There was still no sign of Clark, and the waltz the band was playing was nearing an end. My mother's partner was bowing her to her seat. I saw, with some amusement, Sergeant Matheson remove himself gently from Gloria's clinging hands. He must have had two dances in succession with her, and I wondered what he had discovered to be brave enough to do that. As I stood there in the doorway, girls rushed by me to the cloakroom to attend to that ever-important and all-absorbing matter, one's make-up. I caught one or two by the hand, but none of them had seen Mac for some time. The only information that I gleaned was that she had been in street clothes when she came off duty, and the suggestion that she was probably somewhere changing.

"Did you look in the cloakroom?" I was asked. "She left a case there earlier. It had her evening dress in it." That reminded me of my own bag. I retraced my steps.

"Hullo, Maggie," the girl Hemingway said. "Is my hair right at the back?"

"Marvellous! Do you mind moving over while I pull my case out?"

"I believe you're staying the night here," she remarked, sitting on the edge of a table.

"By compulsion, and not of my own desire," I replied, getting down on my knees. "Of all the nights that there should be a dance, I would be on the dog-watch. Hullo, what's this?"

"What's which?" Hemingway asked inanely. It was amazing how a simple dance went to some people's heads.

"That is Gerda's case you've got," she informed me. "Now we know who has the taking ways around here. What do you think you're doing?"

On impulse I had snapped open the lid. The first thing that met my eyes was a pair of tiny gold sandals. I sat back on my heels, frowning.

"That's funny," observed Hemingway. "Mac can't have changed after all. I thought she finished at 9.30 p.m."

"Haven't you seen her since?" I asked swiftly.

"I haven't," she replied, "but I believe that she looked into the dance-room for a moment. I wonder—"

"Don't," I said shortly, closing the case and shoving it back into place. I got up slowly. "Don't say anything about this, Mavis, will you? Not until I tell you."

"All right," she agreed in surprise. "What are you looking so serious about, Maggie?"

"I'll tell you later," I said over my shoulder.

I hurried down the corridor, encountering severe looks as I bumped from one person to another in my desire for speed, and into the dance-room. There I was compelled to go slowly. The floor was packed. Gradually I worked round to where my mother was sitting, my eyes ever searching the shifting couples.

"Hullo, darling," she called, patting the seat beside her. "Will you be able to wait for supper? They are calling the supper-dance next."

"Charlotte, where's Sergeant Matheson?" I demanded, ignoring her question.

She looked at me sharply. "I haven't seen him for some time. Maggie, has anything—"

"Never mind," I cut in. "Did Clark come back?"

"No, not yet. Maggie, where are you going?" she asked, half rising.

"Stay here," I commanded her abruptly.

'I knew it,' I repeated over and over, running as quickly as my long skirt would allow me down the corridor to the stairs. I took them two at a time, pulling my dress up to my knees. How quiet the sixth floor seemed after the row taking place only one floor above me. No more than half a dozen girls were on duty in the trunkroom. There was a monitor in charge. She looked up sternly at my whirlwind entry.

"I thought that Mr. Scott gave instructions that no one was to come into the trunkroom if they were not on duty."

"Never mind," I said peremptorily, my anxiety gaining the upper hand over my manners. Her mouth fell open in amazement at such insubordination. "When did you last see Miss MacIntyre?"

The monitor still stared at me stupidly. Out of one corner of my eye I could see the telephonist on Sydney one position watching the scene curiously. I repeated my question sharply. The tone of my voice galvanized the monitor into action.

"She went off duty at 9.30 p.m. Just what do you mean by this behaviour? I'll report you to Mr. Scott."

"I give you my permission to do what you like later, but please answer my questions now. Do you know if Miss MacIntyre was going to the dance on the floor above?"

"I couldn't say," said the monitor crossly. I turned to the room at large.

"Girls," I said clearly. "Do you know if Gerda MacIntyre was going to the dance to-night?"

They looked at their monitor doubtfully. The girl on the Sydney position nodded. "She'd put her evening clothes in the cloakroom."

"I know that," I said impatiently, "but she hadn't changed her mind at the last minute about going?"

"No, because she told me quite definitely that she intended making Bertie—that is, Mr. Scott—dance with her."

I smiled involuntarily. That sounded like the old Mac.

"Thanks," I said, turning back to the monitor. "Sorry to have troubled you, Miss Howden."

She swallowed hard. "You'll hear more of this," she promised in an ominous tone.

"I suppose I shall," I agreed pleasantly. "By the way, did Mr. Clarkson come in here during the past half-hour?"

"He was here a few minutes ago. What a shame you just missed him!" There was a nasty meaning in her voice. I merely shrugged and left without making any comment. What was the use of wasting important time on a dolt like Howden.

I stood there on the sixth-floor landing, chewing absently at one finger while I thought. But my brain seemed as heavy as lead and refused to budge. Above, the sound of the Master of Ceremonies' voice calling for supper partners came to my ears. It penetrated my consciousness and made me start up quickly. I almost laughed with sheer relief. What a fool I was! Supper! That was it. I remembered now. When this social was being organized, the committee had been divided into different sections, each one with a special job to look after. I was appointed to the decorating, while Mac had been given the supper arrangements. Small wonder that she hadn't changed if she was cutting up greasy sandwiches. I walked lightly up the stairs. I knew where I would be able to find Mac: where she had probably been that afternoon, and I hadn't realized how near she was. How we'd laugh together over the way in which I had burst in on Howden, more or less telling her to shut up.

It had been arranged that the cafeteria on the eighth floor would be given over to supper. I continued up the last flight of stairs, whistling the tune that the band was playing below and wondering if Clark would be annoyed to find me gone. I hesitated on the last step at this thought. It wasn't very kind leaving him flat, especially as he was doing me a favour. I shrugged, and turned the corner to the lift landing. The grille door of the cafeteria was open opposite. I could see a woman in a white overall bending down to the oven. I sniffed the odour of sausage rolls as I stepped over the bar into the counter space.

"Hullo," I said, full of party spirit. "Nice way to be spending your time at a dance!"

The woman swung around startled, an oven cloth in her hand. I raised my brows in surprise. "I didn't know cooking was in your line, Mrs. Smith," I remarked. She stared at me in silence.

"Don't mind about me," I went on testily, becoming restless under that opaque gaze. "Get going with what you want to do."

"Supper is not ready yet," she said.

I was annoyed at the impertinent way in which she spoke. "I haven't come up here to eat. Not yet, anyway. Has anyone been helping you?"

"One or two," she replied grudgingly, placing sandwiches on the thick Departmental china. "They were more in the way than anything."

"A small dark-haired girl hasn't been here, has she?" I suggested. "She was in ordinary clothes."

Once more I bore the full brunt of her uncanny eyes. "She was here. You mean Miss MacIntyre, don't you?"

I nodded. "I'll go into the lunchroom and have a word with her. That is, if I'm not in the way."

"She's not there," said the woman shortly, turning her back to me. "She only came in for a minute."

"How long ago?" I asked. "About 10 p.m.?"

"I couldn't say. If you don't mind, I have to put these sandwiches on the tables."

"Go right ahead," I watched her push the plates through the grille on the opposite counter. "Leave them there," I called across the kitchen. "I'll slip round to the lunchroom and fix them up for you."

She gave a grunt, which I took as a sound of appreciation.

'This is Mac's work,' I thought peevishly. 'I did my bit by standing on that damn ladder this afternoon.'

It was odd that I should have thought of it just then. Perhaps I should say that it was a coincidence. The one or two dances that I had had in the festive atmosphere on the floor below had completely removed all remembrance of the notes that I had given to Sergeant Matheson earlier. There I was, face to face with my new figure in the case, and it hadn't even occurred to me to ask her any leading questions.

'I haven't any time now,' I thought. I heard the first part of the supper-dance finish, and the clapping of the pausing dancers. I decided to leave it until later. Perhaps, after supper, I could sneak a few minutes from the trunkroom, and come back to the kitchen to help Mrs. Smith clear up. That would put her into a good mood. It was amazing what you could learn from people while you worked side by side; especially washing dishes, when you would talk about anything to relieve the monotony. I walked down the corridor, thinking out the best plan of attack. A direct approach or maybe the tactful method I had used with Gloria? I was going to enjoy my encounter with Mrs. Smith. She was my own pet discovery. I stopped short outside the telephonists' cloakroom.

The door was closed, but a faint bar of light was on the floor at my feet. I turned the handle quickly, and put my head in, calling: "Hullo! Are you there, Mac?" There was no reply. I switched off the light and reclosed the door.

I don't own to psychic powers, in spite of what my mother told Sergeant Matheson about Grandmother MacPherson, but I could have sworn that some inner voice told me to act, and act quickly as all was not well. I threw open the cloakroom door, and ran my hand down the row of lights, switching them on one by one until every nook and cranny of that room was ablaze with light. Without a second's hesitation, I hurried around the lockers to the inner door of the restroom. It was half-open. When I tried to push it to the limit, a heavy object blocked its advance. My face and hands became wet all at once, and my heart pounded at a suffocating speed, but still I did not pause. I slipped through the narrow opening, my fingers feeling for the switch. The light shone down full on that second terrible scene. I turned my face to the wall, resting my forehead against the cool plaster, and fighting for self-control.

How long I stayed there, I couldn't say. But I do know that not a single sound passed my lips. I was beyond screaming, and that faraway voice bade me not to make a scene. Gradually I turned around, my teeth biting into the back of one hand as I tried to absorb the realization of what had happened. Horror shook me from head to foot as I knelt down beside that quiet figure. Such a small, helpless, huddled bundle, lying face down with one arm, clad in a short lemon-coloured sleeve, bent across her back. I mouthed Mac's name but still no sound came. I put out one finger to touch the curled hand. It was slightly warm, but stiff to feel. The pencil that was held between the first and third fingers did not move.

The sound of clapping penetrated my consciousness, and made me start up quickly. Any minute now, the dancers would be trooping up the stairs and along the corridor past the cloakroom door. I didn't touch Mac again. There was nothing I could do. I longed to look into her face, but knew that I must not move her. Leaving the door ajar as I had found it, but with the light still on, I ran through the cloakroom, and pulling the key from the inner side, locked the door behind me. I had some confused remembrance of Mrs. Smith's complaining voice addressing me, but I took no notice. I fled down the stairs, nearly tripping in my long skirt, the key to the cloakroom held tightly in my fist.

The third encore of the supper-dance had begun. I realized that I could only have been away a few minutes. It seemed an age had passed. The music swelled as I ran down the last steps, and laughter, gay and unconcerned, came to my astounded ears, Here there was light and gaiety, while only one floor above—I shook my head violently, and nearly collided with a couple coming out of the danceroom. They called to me good naturedly, but still I took no notice. John Clarkson's tall head appeared in the middle of the room. I brushed aside the dancers as I made for him.

He was demonstrating an intricate step to a blonde girl, dressed in gold satin, when I pushed her roughly aside and put his arm around my waist.

"Well, really!" I heard Gloria exclaim angrily. Clark looked down at me in astonishment.

"Dance with me," I ordered quietly. He guided me down the room mechanically, my fist, still firmly holding the key, a ball in his hand. I felt his fingers gently prising mine open, and spoke urgently. "Something terrible has happened. No, let go my fingers, Clark. Mac has been killed."

I heard the quick intake of his breath, and a tremor passed through his body. His face was white, but the line about his lips was even more so. His eyes, that stared down into mine, must have mirrored the horror that still held me in its grip.

"Keep dancing," I insisted, as I felt his steps faltering, "until we work out something. There's such a crowd here. We don't want a scene."

I heard him breathe "Gerda" over and over. Presently he asked abruptly: "What have you got in your hand?"

"The cloakroom key." I saw a fresh gleam of horror in his eyes.

"Not——" he began in a low tone.

"The restroom," I replied. "I didn't want to touch the door in case of fingerprints, so I locked the outer one."

Clark nodded approvingly. "Good work!"

"Clark!" I said and my voice quivered. "What will we do? Bertie?"

"No. Sergeant Matheson is here. I'll tell him right away."

I had forgotten all about him. Clark stopped near the dais where the band was playing, and bent down to my ear. "Tell them to keep going," he ordered, "while I find the Sergeant. Make any excuse you can to keep this mob from going up to the eighth floor."

I nodded and tried to steady my knees, as I approached the pianist. "Supper has been delayed," I called up to him. "Will you give another encore?"

He nodded in time to his music, and I turned aside to follow Clark's dark head with my eyes as he wended his way round the edge of the crowd. A hand caught my arm roughly, dragging me into a corner. Gloria Patterson faced me, her eyes ablaze and her perfect skin slightly mottled.

"How dare you humiliate me so!" She was choked with rage. I watched her in a dazed fashion, wondering what she was driving at. "I could kill you," she breathed in a venomous voice. But still I stared at her, bemused. I felt so tired all of a sudden, and now Gloria was worrying me about some trivial business. What else mattered except that Mac lay dead above my head.

"Go away," I begged her wearily. "Tell me about it to-morrow."

"I'll get even with you, Byrnes, if it's the last thing I do. I could kill you," she repeated on a rising note.

I looked about me nervously. "Oh, hush!" I said. "Don't say that. You don't know who might be listening."

She stared at me in amazement. "What's the matter with you?" she demanded. "You look queer. What has happened?"

"What has happened?" I repeated. I heard myself laugh, even though I hadn't meant to. It needed a stupendous effort on my part to pull myself together and avoid the threatening hysteria.

'Quiet,' I told myself. 'You must be quiet and think.' But how could I, when all I could see before my eyes was the pathetic figure on the rest-room floor. The years rolled back as I closed my eyes, leaning against the dais, and though the music was loud in my ears, I could still hear the ping of the ball off the tee, and Mac's joyous laugh sounding hollow in the open air, and see her small hands moving across the switching keys, and remember all the fun that we had had together . . .

The music slowed to an end, and I jerked myself into the present hideous nightmare. I had a job to do. I must keep all these people from going upstairs and finding Mac. I must not allow a panic to begin. But even as I hurried forward, someone pulled me gently aside, and I felt a strong arm around my shoulders.

"The key, Miss Byrnes. Give it to me," said Sergeant Matheson. Although his voice was kind, the note of authority in it made me unclose my fist. He took it out of my hand and left me standing there, staring at the red mark it had made on my palm.

The music stopped, and the pianist played the final chords, indicating the definite end of the number. I made as if to go forward, but stopped suddenly as I saw John Clarkson standing on the edge of the dais near the microphone. The dancers crowded up towards the platform, and I edged as near as I could. As I looked up into Clark's face I saw that he was smiling, a ghastly imitation of his usual grin, and wondered what he was about to do. He held up one hand for silence, the other gripping the stem of the microphone until the knuckles showed white.

"Ladies and gentlemen," he began, speaking quietly yet distinctly. "Owing to an—unforeseen occurrence, supper has been delayed." There was a slight stir amongst the crowd, and one or two called out at him in a mock-annoyed fashion. Clark raised his hand again. "I know, I know," he said. "You're hungry. So am I, but I have been commissioned by the organizers of this dance to amuse you for a few minutes, so let's see what I can do on an empty stomach."

The crowd laughed gaily. I stood very still, watching him tensely. How long was this hideous parody to go on?

'Tell them,' my brain shrieked. 'Tell them what has happened in the restroom above their silly, empty heads. That will stop their laughter and their inane remarks.'

"I have a little game for you all to play," Clark continued, and a groan went up. "I want you to get as near as you can to the partners you danced with to-night. Come on now, boys. Find that girl you were kissing on the roof a few minutes ago."

There was a scramble as the crowd broke and formed into groups, giggling and throwing silly remarks at each other. Someone protested that he had not been dancing. I think that it was Miles Dunn, one of the Heads from the Department. Clark bent down to call over the noise: "Get near the people you were talking to, then."

The chattering abated, and they looked towards the dais, awaiting instructions.

"Just a minute," Clark said. "I'm in on this, too." He looked round the crowd, until his eyes met mine. For a second he held my gaze, and I saw one finger brush his lips.

"Come on, Maggie," he called. "You were with me a while back, and Gloria. Where's Gloria Patterson?"

"I'm here, Clark," she said, coming forward.

"Right you are! You two girls come nearer to the microphone. I could swear that there were some others. Step forward, the girls I honoured to-night," and one or two joined us at the foot of the dais, bringing with them other swains. Clark grinned down on us cheerfully. He was throwing everything that he had into this absurd game, and only I knew the effort that it must be taking.

"Are we all ready?" he asked, and an assenting murmur went up. "Now this is the game. Don't delude yourselves that I have made it up on the spur of the moment. I have a name for it. It is called 'Alibis'."

I guessed then what he was up to. I stole a glance behind me to see how the crowd was taking it. Some looked surprised, while others seemed frankly puzzled.

Clark continued: "I am giving you boys and girls a chance to check up on each other. For instance, you, George," he turned towards the left, "will be able to discover if Joan has been behaving herself to-night, and not been flirting with anyone else. Let us hope that Mrs. Scott will be able to give an account of her actions without raising the suspicions of our Senior Traffic Officer. Where are you, Mr. Scott, by the way?"

"Right here," he replied. Everyone turned their heads to the doorway where Bertie stood beside his wife. I thought that he looked slightly annoyed; small wonder in the face of Clark's audacious remark.

"Now, good people," John Clarkson continued. "The instructions are as follows. You are to question each other as to your respective movements. Those who can prove that they have been on this floor of the Exchange building all night, please step aside. The others, who stole a few minutes on the roof or elsewhere, give their reasons why. I, myself, will conduct my inquiry with these charming ladies, who are at my feet; literally, not metaphorically, of course."

A buzz of talk broke out. As Clark leaped lightly down from the dais, the greater portion of the crowd stood aside.

"Where's Sergeant Matheson, Clark?" asked Gloria plaintively. "I had two dances with him."

"Just one moment," he returned, and raised his voice over our heads. "It appears as if the sheep have separated themselves from the wolves. Will the sheep please proceed to the supper-room on the eighth floor, and start eating."

An indignant murmur arose from the small group left standing on the floor as the "sheep" filed out, jostling one another.

"Don't worry," Clark went on. "There's an—interesting outcome to this game, that they'll miss more than you will your supper. Get going, folks."

As the last wave of the crowd swamped through the door, I saw Bertie still standing with his wife. His eyes had never left Clark's face since that first remark.

"I can't see Sergeant Matheson anywhere," Gloria declared.

"Perhaps he's one of the sheep," suggested Mavis Hemingway. Gloria shook her head. "He's telling fibs if he's gone with the others," she asserted, "because I saw him going downstairs a while back."

"Never mind about him," Clark said. "We'll concentrate on you first, Gloria. Can you tell us your movements to-night, without making me jealous?"

"Oh, Clark!" Gloria exclaimed, in what I can only describe as a simpering voice. How canny Clark was! Such a remark put Gloria into a good mood, when she would be neither suspicious nor apprehensive, and would reply with truth.

" Well, go on," he said, and I could detect an underlying anxiety in his voice, "What time did you arrive?"

"It was about 9 p.m.," Gloria replied. "I was held up in town by a friend of mine. In fact I thought that I would be the last to arrive," and she cast a malevolent glance in my direction. I smiled slightly; we must have spoilt her entrance.

"Let me see," Gloria went on. "With whom did I dance first? There were so many—oh, it was you, Jim, wasn't it?" she added, turning to Mavis Hemingway's partner. He nodded without enthusiasm. It was obvious that Gloria's glamour meant nothing to him.

She went on to name a couple of other lads, trying to express by direct innuendo how much in demand she had been all the evening. "I finally escaped," she said, with an artificial laugh, "and ran upstairs."

"What time was that?" asked Clark in a bantering tone. "Were you with anyone?"

"It was about 9.30 p.m. I told the boys I was skipping that dance, as I wanted to—" She paused, and remained with her mouth open slightly, gazing from Clark to me.

"Go on," he said encouragingly.

"I wanted to see if the supper arrangements were all right," she finished slowly.

I stared at her profile. "That's funny," I remarked. "I thought that you were one of the ticket secretaries."

"Why is it funny?" Gloria snapped, turning towards me. "There is no reason why I should be interested in only one thing. I may have been able to help."

'Oh, yeah?' I thought. 'As if you'd do more than your share in anything.'

"Did you see anyone?" asked Clark quickly. "Didn't any of the boys follow you upstairs?"

Gloria smiled at him meltingly. Silently I congratulated Clark on his tact. "I would have told them off properly, if they had. I didn't see anyone around on the eighth floor, only one—" Again she stopped, and I saw her face whiten a little.

"Only one of the cleaners," I finished for her. She didn't turn towards me this time, though I continued to gaze at her half-averted head.

"I had a dance with you about 10.30 p.m.," said Clark teasingly. "So there is a whole hour for you to account for. Are you sure you were unaccompanied?"

"I was only away for a few minutes. Then I came back here and danced. Sergeant Matheson insisted on having two running. I thought you'd brought him along, Maggie," she finished in a patronizing voice.

"He only wanted to see you," I told her gravely. "I was the means to the end." I felt Clark's foot touch mine, as Gloria swallowed this with a self-satisfied expression on her face. It made me nearly laugh outright. Mavis was less controlled than I, and was compelled to turn a giggle into a cough. Gloria appeared to take no notice.

"Then there was that one with you," she said to Clark, her eyes darkening, "which I was enjoying very much until Maggie came along. Did you think that it was an Excuse-me, darling?" she asked me very sweetly.

"I have to get partners somehow, Gloria dear," I answered confidentially, and to my amazement I believe that she actually swallowed that too.

"I am sure Clark would have danced with you some time during the evening, wouldn't you, Clark?" Her tone conveyed that perhaps out of the kindness of his heart, he would have spared me one.

"Well," Clark said heartily. "That's fixed you up. Between 9.30 p.m. and 10 p.m. you were somewhere on the eighth floor, but you refuse to say with whom."

"I wasn't with anyone," Gloria declared, becoming a little annoyed.

Clark raised one finger. "Now, now," he said idiotically. "You can't expect us to believe that; not a pretty girl like you!" But Gloria did not react to the treatment as she had done before. I shook my head at Clark. With a slight shrug, he turned to Mavis Hemingway.

"And what have you been up to?" he asked brightly.

Mavis looked at her partner, and they smiled self-consciously at each other. Light broke on Clark, but I was frankly puzzled at the idiotic expression on their faces.

"Not really!" he exclaimed, holding out his hand to Jim. "Do the boys in the power-room know about this yet? Or are we the first?"

"Are you just engaged, Mavis?" drawled Gloria. "My best wishes. But fancy being proposed to in a place where you both work! How extraordinary!"

I shook hands warmly with Jim. He was a nice lad, and a promising engineer. "All the best, Mavis. Don't make us wait too long, will you?"

"I gather that you were in some quiet secluded spot," said Clark, grinning naturally for the first time. "If it isn't too indiscreet—"

"On the roof," Jim replied bashfully. "We took the lift up."

"That rules you two out," remarked Clark absently, I nudged him warningly as Gloria looked up. She made as if to speak, but I got in first, saying with a forced laugh: "I think it's your turn, Clark. Stand quietly, while we fire questions at you."

"I got here about 8.30 p.m.," he began, "but I was in the trunkroom for about half-an-hour before I came upstairs to the dance; some time before your party arrived, Maggie. I had a dance with Joyce Mettiam—where is she, by the way?"

"A sheep," I told him, "She's gone to supper."

"Has she? Then you arrived. I thought that I'd give you a break, but you were booked with Sergeant Matheson. I sighed with relief, until you insisted on having the next. So I danced with Mavis here; I know now why you trembled in my arms, Mavis. At the time I thought it was for love of me."

"I am so sorry to disappoint you," she returned with a mock curtsey.

"Not at all, but Jim's a lucky fellow. After that dance, my fair interrogators, Maggie grabbed me—"

"You're a brute," I interrupted heatedly. I could see that Gloria was taking all his nonsense at its face value. Heaven knew what stories she would spread around the trunkroom at the first available opportunity.

"During the course of the gyration, which, with any other but Maggie, would have been a dance, she ordered me to put up a line in the trunkroom to amplify the music downstairs, in order to while away the tedium of working."

"I didn't," I protested. "It was your idea."

"So, obediently," Clark went on, ignoring the interruption, "I betook myself down to the power-room, and spent the next half-hour or so running from the first floor to the sixth and back here to the seventh making noises like a sheep to ensure perfect transmission in order to please Miss Byrnes."

"My grateful thanks," I said dryly.

"I'm glad to hear them," Clark retorted, "for when I returned to reclaim the rest of my dance, Mavis, Gloria and Jim, the bird had flown. In simpler parlance, Maggie had disappeared."

"Low trick," commented Mavis, smiling at me. "Where did you get to, my girl, and with whom?"

I started to become worried, and looked at Clark for guidance. He was sailing close to the wind. Did he want me to tell where I had been or not? He nodded slightly.

"Be careful what you say, Maggie," he said gaily. I caught the significance behind his words.

"I had to get rid of him, somehow," I began, imitating Clark's light tone as I turned towards the others, "or else my toes would have been squashed to pulp."

"It's funny," Gloria interrupted, though not actually addressing me, "how some people can never learn to dance."

"There you are, Clark," I said triumphantly.

"I didn't mean Clark," Gloria snapped at me. I looked at her in such a bewildered way that she became embarrassed, and dropped her eyes.

"Having got rid of him," I continued, "and not seeing anyone rush me to complete the dance with them, I took the opportunity to move around to greet a few of my friends. Did I say 'Hullo' to you, Gloria?" I asked innocently, but she merely gazed past me disdainfully. This time I dropped my eyes. Not from any desire to avoid her glance, but rather to stop myself from staring at Clark when I remembered the horror which would be revived for both of us presently. With a strong effort, I kept my voice on a light pitch. My lips felt strained with the artificial smile I wore.

"I wandered along to the stairs, and up to the trunkroom to give the girls on duty a cheerio."

Mavis looked troubled suddenly, and I felt my heart skip a beat. What had she learned?

"I wouldn't go telling anyone about that, Maggie," she said hesitantly. "About being on the sixth floor, I mean. Bertie has forbidden anyone but those on duty to use the trunkroom floor."

"I am going on duty myself soon," I replied. "But thanks for the tip, Mavis. Where was I?"

"In the trunkroom," said Clark promptly. "By the way, how is it that we didn't clash there?"

"You probably saw me first," I retorted. "Miss Howden informed me that I had just missed you."

"That woman always reminds me of Sarah Compton," put in Mavis absently. I glanced fearfully at Clark. She saw the swift look that passed between us, and put an arm through mine. "Sorry, old girl, I'd forgotten that you—"

"Forget it," I cut in gruffly, and took a further grip of myself. Gloria was very quiet, and I wondered if she was scenting something in the wind. Surely it was obvious to everyone. But the gay chattering and laughter still went on around me as I paused.

"It was about 10.20 or thereabouts when I went upstairs to the cafeteria. I thought that I might find-Mac there " I stared down at my entwined fingers, and unlocking them, leaned my weight against the dais half-turned away from the others.

Clark spoke very gently from behind me. "Did you see anyone on the eighth floor?"

"Mrs. Smith," I answered jerkily. "That's—all."

"You came back to the dance-room without encountering anyone?"

"Yes," I replied, and my voice seemed to rasp in my ears.

"Is that all, Maggie?" Clark asked very quietly.

Slowly, I turned towards the room, and it seemed to my throbbing brain that a sea of faces watched me, waiting for my reply. I tried to pick out the emotions expressed on those nearest to me, to gauge my words, but my eyes had lost their focus. It was almost as if I had suddenly been struck blind.

The crowd seemed to sway to and fro, and I put my hands to my head in a desperate endeavour to control my outraged nerves. As I stared at those people in front of me, I suddenly realized that their movement had not been a result of my disordered senses, but that they were making way for someone to pass. A combination of relief and apprehension threatened to overwhelm me as I saw the huge figure of a man coming straight towards the dais. It was Inspector Coleman from Russell Street Police Headquarters. Though his eyes were scrutinizing me keenly, his first words were addressed to John Clarkson.

"You've done a good job," he said approvingly. "On behalf of the Department, I want to thank you for the service you have rendered."

I watched the ghastly smile fade from Clark's lips and his face become white and set, and wondered how he had deceived people by his hearty manner in the first place. It had been so obvious to me that I couldn't understand why others had not called out their alarm. Inspector Coleman turned to me, and I shifted my gaze dumbly.

"You're all in," he said curtly. "Go and sit down somewhere."

I passed my tongue over my lips. "Work!" I exclaimed disjointedly. "I should be on duty."

"Go and sit down," he repeated, and his voice was kind. "I'll arrange to have you relieved for tonight. You're in no fit state to work."

I felt an arm go around me gently to lead me away, and looked dazedly into my mother's face.

"I'd forgotten you, too," I said confusedly, thinking of the way in which I had run to John Clarkson with my terrible news, instead of to Sergeant Matheson who was the more suitable person. Inspector Coleman's voice called after us, "I'd like her to stay in the room, if possible, Mrs. Byrnes."

Charlotte nodded, making for a small alcove formed by one side of the dais and two walls. I was away from staring people there, but I could see the Inspector's back as he stood on the platform, and hear his words, I gripped my mother's hand hard, as he began in his cold, distinct voice.

"Ladies and gentlemen, I think that you have by now realized that something very serious has happened. I don't intend to mince words. I will give it to you straight. A second murder has taken place." He paused to let his words sink in.

"Why hasn't someone screamed or fainted?" I asked Charlotte, puzzled. "Don't they realize what has happened?"

"Hush," she replied, pressing my hand.

I watched that big figure as the Inspector went on to introduce himself. "I understand," he said, "that all you people here in this room have, at some time during the course of the evening, had occasion to be on other floors of the building. I want all those who can prove that at no time tonight have they been on the eighth floor to step aside."

"He's dividing the wolves into packs," I remarked softly to Charlotte, feeling calmer. The crowd shifted and shuffled themselves. I was surprised to see how few were left standing in the centre of the room.

"You people who have moved aside, please realize that you will be questioned individually. If any one of you wants to change his mind about his decision, please do so at once."

They looked up at him in silence, but they caught the underlying warning in the Inspector's voice. One or two seemed scared as he continued to look down on them piercingly. Suddenly a lad stepped forward, aided and abetted by a nudge from a junior telephonist at his side.

"Do you mean those who were actually on the eighth floor," he asked hesitantly, "or do you count those who used the eighth floor landing as well?"

"I don't follow you," said the Inspector curtly. "Will you try and make your meaning clearer?"

The boy reddened and shifted his feet. "I mean," he spoke up bravely enough, "that quite a few of us went up to the roof during the evening. Some went by the lift. Others walked up the stairs."

"I see what you mean," said Inspector Coleman, nodding. "No, I only want those who actually were on the floor, not those who passed on their way to the roof."

A small sigh went up from the group in the centre of the room, and a few more stepped aside.

"There are not many left," I remarked, peering across my mother. The awful feeling of numbness was passing and I was beginning to take an interest in the proceedings. But I didn't dare let my mind wander to Mac, trying to visualize the terrible affair impersonally. In that way I would be of more use to the police. Charlotte must have sensed my reviving spirits and removed her arm from my waist. She still held my hand. I counted up the people in the isolated group in the middle of the room. They were directly under the gay paper bell that—

'One, two,' I began swiftly and silently, heading away from that absurd ornament which was so dangerous to my peace of mind. "That's a coincidence," I said to Charlotte. "There are eight people who visited the eighth floor."

"Very remarkable," she agreed placidly. "Do you think that Inspector Coleman will be long? I'd like to put you to bed."

"I'm all right now," I declared stoutly. "We'd better wait until he gives us leave. After all, he can't keep us here all night. Where's Sergeant Matheson, I wonder?"

As soon as the words were out of my mouth, I regretted them. I knew at once where he would most likely be. Charlotte gazed at me anxiously.

"You know who it was?" I asked in a shaking voice and she nodded.

"I saw Sergeant Matheson coming out of the cloakroom," she replied. "I was one of the first batch to go to supper. He called me aside and told me."

"That horrible game of Clark's!" I exclaimed wearily. "Didn't you suspect something then?"

"I thought it was odd," Charlotte answered, "or perhaps I should say that I considered it bad taste; being so close to the other —"

"I understand what you mean," I interrupted. "But he did it for a purpose."

"I realize that now. It was very clever of him."

"Yes, wasn't it?" I agreed, "Inspector Coleman was very pleased. It has narrowed his job down considerably."

I watched the Inspector as he moved amongst the people on the floor, his big frame towering over all except Clark.

"He's taking down statements," I said with my superior knowledge of the working of the police. A thought suddenly occurred to me. "I needn't worry about Dulcie any more. This second—business proves that she had nothing to do with Compton's death."

"Poor, foolish child," said my mother sadly. There was a depth of feeling in her voice. "She knew something, but wasn't brave enough to tell the police. I wonder why?"

"Are you talking about Dulcie?" I asked, puzzled.

Charlotte turned round to look into my eyes gravely, but without saying a word.

"Mac?" I queried, my voice quivering again.

She inclined her head slowly. "Margaret," said my mother suddenly. She only used my full name when she was in deadly earnest. "I want you to promise me that if you know anything that you have hitherto not mentioned, to go straight to the Inspector and tell him. Do you understand? I am commanding you, and although you are over-age I am still your mother."

I continued to look straight into her eyes. "I swear by everything that I hold precious that whatever knowledge I am conscious of, the Sergeant learned this evening." We stared at each other in silence until Charlotte caught me by the hand again.

"My dear," she cried softly. "I'm so afraid."

"Afraid! You!" I said, smiling, "What are you scared about?"

"That something might happen to you as it has to your little dark friend. Be very careful, Maggie."

"Sure," I answered, trying to sound cheerful. "I value my own skin more than you, you know."

"I doubt it," she said dryly. "You're as headstrong as your father. By the way, I don't know what the darling will say when he learns about to-night."

"I hate to think," I remarked. "Thank heaven, to-morrow is Sunday, and there'll be no screaming headlines in the papers. Otherwise he'd be down on the first train to drag us home."

"I'll ring him in the morning," Charlotte declared, looking up as a shadow fell across us.

"How are you feeling, Miss Byrnes?" asked Sergeant Matheson.

"Fine, thanks," I answered carelessly, his solicitous gaze irritating me a little. "I think that I'll be right for work now. If Inspector Coleman doesn't want me, I'll go."

"You're not going to switch to-night, Maggie," said my mother firmly. "I forbid it."

"You're behaving like the heavy parent to-night. I know what you want to do to me. Put me to bed with a couple of aspirins. Is that your suggestion too, Sergeant?" I asked slyly.

"No," he replied promptly. I felt as if the wind had been taken out of my sails. "If you're really feeling better, Inspector Coleman would like to see you for a few minutes." He looked doubtfully at Charlotte.

"You go home and take the aspirins yourself," I advised her, getting up carefully. My legs seemed fairly safe, but I marked time once or twice to test them.

"Yes, do, Mrs. Byrnes," the Sergeant said, as my mother showed signs of protestation. "I'll bring your daughter home. You needn't worry about her."

"All right," she agreed reluctantly. "But no work, Maggie."

"I promise," I said. "Where is Mr. Clarkson?"

"He's gone to the trunkroom. Inspector Coleman told him about you."

"I hope that it won't make him short-staffed, dropping out suddenly like this," I said, worried. "He's in no fit state to work himself."

I hesitated, wondering if I should mention that Clark had been very friendly with Mac, and that the shock of her death must have been terrible. I saw the Sergeant looking at me curiously, and held my tongue.

"Good night, Charlotte," I said, bending to kiss her. "Be careful going home, and don't worry about me. Don't forget that I've got the promise of a police escort."

* * * * *

I waited while she collected her coat and bag, and then put her into the lift with several others. Their quiet demeanour was not in keeping with the gay frocks. One lad wore a forgotten paper cap on the back of his head. The effect was grotesque in the face of the shocking end to the revels.

"Where is Inspector Coleman?" I asked. Sergeant Matheson waited until the lift indicator showed that it had stopped at the ground floor, and then pressed the button.

"Where are we going?" I asked fearfully.

"The Inspector is in that little room we used before," he answered. With his head thrown back, he followed the progress of the lift by the indicator lights. I made no comment, steeling myself for the ordeal of passing the cloakroom door. Sergeant Matheson must have sensed my inward agitation, and said awkwardly, holding out one hand: "I'm terribly sorry about all this. It should never have happened. I blame myself."

He seemed so upset, that I took his hand warmly.

"Don't," I replied in a husky voice. "It's as much my fault as yours. I didn't take the position seriously enough. I thought that she—Mac was jealous, and that was the reason why she was so secretive. You see, she and Mr. Clarkson used to be—" I threw out my hands helplessly, not looking at him.

"I understand," said the Sergeant slowly. But I wondered if he did, as he added: "Poor chap!"

We walked side by side down the corridor of the eighth floor. I asked him jerkily, pointing to the closed door of the cloakroom: "Have they—I'd like to see—Mac for the last time. Do you think it could be arranged?"

He put one hand under my elbow. "Better not," he advised gently. "She was lying face down when you found her, wasn't she?"

I nodded, and the horrible realization dawned on me why I must not see Mac. Sergeant Matheson paused for a minute outside that little disused office.

"Look here!" he said seriously. "If you're really not fit enough, the Inspector will wait until tomorrow. Would you like to go home right away?"

'Home!' What a sweet sound it had, even though it meant to me in town a rigidly-run boardinghouse. How wonderful it would be to sink into bed, and relax and sleep until my strained nerves and body regained their freshness, and I would be able to look at Mac's death in such a way that would not make me quiver all over at the very mention of her name.

'Time!' I thought suddenly. 'Time is important. Who was it said that to me centuries ago?'

"Well?" said the Sergeant with anxiety. I raised my head. As I did so, two uniformed ambulance-men came out of the cloakroom bearing a stretcher, I received a quick impression of something white before Sergeant Matheson grabbed me by the shoulders.

"Look at me," he ordered roughly, and I obeyed. I heard the men's footsteps go heavily along the corridor, and stop outside the lift. Then the gates clicked and the whirr of the automatic came to my ears as they descended with their ghastly burden. I gazed and gazed into the policeman's face until I knew each contour and feature by heart.

"I'm ready," I said huskily. "Shall we go in?"

Inspector Coleman glanced up for a brief moment at our entry, and then resumed his writing.

"Take a seat," he said casually, as if I had come to apply for a driver's licence during ordinary office hours, instead of presenting myself to be questioned about a murder at nearly midnight. However, his prosaic attitude did much to calm my inward turmoil caused by the scene that I had just witnessed. It was with real gratitude that I heard him suggest to his subordinate to find some coffee and sandwiches for me.

"Get Roberts to fix it up," he said.

"Is he here again, too?" I asked stupidly. It was as if they had never left, so familiar was the sight of the sprawled papers on the desk before me, and the ever-alert gleam in the Inspector's eyes. My mind flew back to that other time when I had sat before the two men. Mac had been with me, cool and detached. It had been hot then, just as it was now, but the sun had been blazing through the drawn blinds and the flies had been troublesome. Now the windows were dark, and moths and flying beetles battered themselves in vain against the panes.

Inspector Coleman did not say a word until Roberts, solemn-faced as ever, came in with a tin tray from the cafeteria. On it were two cups, a jug of coffee and a plate of tired-looking sandwiches. I looked inquiringly at Sergeant Matheson. The Inspector still wrote on, despite the interruption of Roberts, whose movements were not as quiet as his tongue.

"Not for me, thank you, Miss Byrnes," he said in his deep voice, without raising his head. "But you help yourself, Matheson."

"Thank you, sir. I could do with it."

I poured out, watching my shaking hand with interest. It was funny what your nerves did to you. The Sergeant got up as I handed him his cup, and took two sandwiches at once. The coffee was stale, and had evidently been re-heated, but I felt better after I had drunk it. I had only to use one hand to hold my second cup, and felt vaguely triumphant.

"A cigarette, Miss Byrnes?" asked the Inspector.

"Thank you," I said gratefully.

"I haven't got any. But perhaps Sergeant Matheson can oblige." The Sergeant arose hurriedly, setting his cup on the tray with a clatter.

"Thanks," I said. "I hope that you're keeping an account of how many of yours I've taken. I'll pay them back one day." I had nearly finished my cigarette before the Inspector spoke. I was starting to become slightly irritated. Did he, or did he not want to see me?

He leaned back in his chair, which creaked protestingly, and surveyed me critically.

"You're looking better," he observed. I recognized his forethought in letting me have a breathing space in which to pull myself together.

"Now, Miss Byrnes!" he began and I put my brain into concentration order. "I want you to tell me in your own words just how you came to find your friend, Miss MacIntyre. I realize that this is going to be very painful

236

for you, but you are a sensible girl and must know that the sooner we get it over the better."

"I can stand it," I answered in a tight voice, "if it will lead to finding out who killed Mac."

"It will, I promise you," he said grimly. "This time there will be no forced decision if I can help it. Please begin."

I pressed out my cigarette, prodding it with a dead match while I thought.

"Two days ago," I began, "in this room, you issued a warning to the effect that those who kept any useful information from the police were placing themselves in a very dangerous position. At that time, I must confess I did not take your warning seriously, thinking how clever I was in withholding facts from you. I might still have been doing so, if something had not happened. Sergeant Matheson can tell you about that later." I looked at him for a moment, and he nodded.

"Had I known that you were speaking from the depths of your experience, I would not have hesitated one minute. I realize now, through bitter experience"—here I paused remembering what experience it was—"how very foolish I was. This evening I asked Sergeant Matheson to call, in order to put before him certain facts that entirely disagreed with the decision that you published about the murder of the monitor, Sarah Compton. Amongst other things, I told him that Miss MacIntyre's behaviour, which you had also observed as mysterious, had not altered since Dulcie Gordon was convicted posthumously of Compton's murder. I laid it down to the fact that she was jealous of me, and the notice that you had paid to my deductions. I thought that she was setting herself up as the opposition, so to speak, and was endeavouring to find out the truth before me. I also mentioned to Sergeant Matheson that during this afternoon Miss MacIntyre called to see me while I was asleep, and the reason I gave was that she intended to enter into a partnership with me, so that we could work together."

The Inspector stirred irritably, and I glanced up meekly. "When I learned that she wanted to see me," I went on, "I went round to her boarding-house. She was out, but her room was in terrible disorder. At first I thought that it must have been the work of a burglar, but no burglar leaves jewellery untouched. There was a brooch of Mac's pinned into her dressing-table runner. The only conclusion, therefore, is that her room had been ransacked by someone to whom money or its equivalent had no value; someone who wanted to satisfy himself or herself that Mac was not on the right trail, or, what is more probable, to destroy any evidence that she might have had in her possession. It is quite likely that Mac made notes as I did, and perhaps the killer learned of their existence."

Inspector Coleman looked at me sharply. "What have you done with your own?" he demanded.

"I have them here, sir," said the Sergeant, drawing out my little red diary, and putting it on the table in front of his superior. The Inspector picked it up idly, but made no attempt to read the notes. Evidently he was satisfied, now that they were out of my hands.

"I was very eager to see Miss MacIntyre," I went on, "especially after finding her room in the state it was, so I came into the Exchange, hoping to find her assisting at the decorating of the danceroom. I learned that she had been in, but had left some time previously. I had a look in the trunk-room. One of the girls on duty, who worked late on Wednesday night, told me that Mac had asked her about her movements on that night. It appears that she had been questioning all the 10.30 p.m. girls, and the excuse that she gave was that she wanted to include the story of Compton's death in her memoirs. That did not seem plausible to me, and further enhanced my conviction that Mac was up to the same game as myself."

I paused for a moment to give the Inspector an opportunity to ask questions. He nodded for me to continue.

"When I got home," I said slowly, "my mother told me that Mac had called again and, finding me out, promised to come back later to dinner. When she did not arrive, I phoned to see if she was coming, but she put me off with the excuse that she was feeling ill, but would probably see me later at the dance. After dinner, I gave Sergeant Matheson the notes I had made that afternoon, and told him exactly everything I knew. Mac completely left my mind until the Sergeant expressed anxiety about her. I became uneasy. But when we arrived at the dance the atmosphere was so normal and cheerful that gradually I lost my fears. I thought nothing could possibly happen to her with such a crowd of people in the Exchange building."

Inspector Coleman said in an exasperated way: "It is usually the ideal place in which to commit murder. The more people around the better. It takes time to account for everyone's movements, and that gives the killer ample opportunity to cover his tracks. I'm surprised at you, Sergeant."

Sergeant Matheson remained calm under the rebuke. "I'm sorry, sir. I'm afraid that I shared Miss Byrnes's idea that Miss MacIntyre would be all right if she kept with the crowd. There were other matters that I wanted to attend to first."

"Mac had an odd temperament," I tried to explain. "Hitherto at every move I had to force her confidence; she shut up like an oyster. I thought that it would be better if she came to me, instead of rushing to find her and asking what it was she wanted to see me about. She could be very obstinate when she liked. If she had seen Sergeant Matheson, I doubt very much whether she would still have wanted to confide in me. His presence at dinner to-night was the cause of her suddenly becoming indisposed."

Inspector Coleman moved the papers about on his desk restlessly, "It is obvious that Miss MacIntyre knew something important," he remarked, "and yet she was afraid to tell us until the last minute."

"What do you mean?" I asked eagerly.

"The receiver of the telephone in the restroom was off its hook, and although certain circumstances existed, we thought it was worth while investigating. The credit goes to Sergeant Matheson for the idea."

"To Miss Byrnes, rather, sir," he interpolated quickly, and turned to me. "I remembered the way you told me you traced a call, so I found that young mechanic friend of yours. He caught on to what I wanted immediately. The first three numbers, including the Exchange alphabetical number of Russell Street Police Station, had been dialled."

"Miss MacIntyre must have been calling us," carried on the Inspector, "when the killer struck."

I shuddered at the frightful scene that his words conjured up. I could see Mac spinning the dial in desperate haste, while from behind crept her assassin. Did she know what was going to happen? Did her heart leap with a suffocating terror, as she turned around to look into the murderer's eyes and read her fate? Did she utter a last helpless cry, before she fell to the floor in that pitiful heap? I knew that I was mad to start thinking along those lines, but a part of my mind had caught on to a phrase that the Inspector had used.

"You said the receiver was off its hook," I began hesitantly, steeling myself. I had half-realized the significance his words had held.

He looked at me kindly. "I think that you can deduce what I meant when I spoke about certain circumstances."

"Please explain," I begged in a low voice. "I'd rather hear it from you correctly, not from rumours around the Exchange; or even be left to imagine."

Inspector Coleman paused as if to gauge my control. Presently he spoke, and his voice was hard. "The telephone, in what is known as the telephonists' restroom, is a pedestal type. The flex had been tugged from its socket in the wall, near the table on which it stood, by some tremendous force. The killer picked up the telephone by its stem and struck Miss MacIntyre down with it."

I closed my eyes and felt myself swaying slightly in my chair. Someone—I supposed that it was the Sergeant, since he was the nearer—thrust my head down to my knees. I stayed there obediently under a firm hand on the nape of my neck.

"I'm all right now," I said presently. "Sorry to give way like that. It doesn't help any."

"Take your time," said the Inspector.

"No," I said fiercely. "Get going with your questions, I'll stay here all night if it will help you to find who killed her. My poor Mac," I added brokenly. "Do you think that she called out?"

"Most unlikely," he replied swiftly. "The first blow from the heavy base of the telephone would kill her immediately. Don't worry yourself into thinking of her last agonies. She probably knew nothing about it."

"But she must have known what was coming," I insisted. "It was her face that was struck, wasn't it? I realize that, because when I saw the back of her head, there was no mark visible. Therefore she must have seen the murderer coming towards her with the intention to kill in his eyes."

"Stop thinking about it," ordered the Inspector sternly. "If you keep on like that, you'll be no good to me. Just treat it as you did before, and answer my questions."

"I'm sorry," I said again. "What do you want to know?"

"Did you see Miss MacIntyre at all to-night?"

"No. But I know of several persons who did. My mother was one. Mac spoke to her for a moment when she came off duty. She said that she was going to change into evening dress."

"She was found in ordinary clothes."

"I know. When I went to find her later, I saw the case containing her frock in the cloakroom near the danceroom. It gave me a fright until I thought that there was a possibility of Mac helping upstairs with the supper. That was how I came to go up to the eighth floor."

"What time was that?" asked the Inspector.

"About 10.30 p.m.," I replied, after giving the matter some thought. "Supper was timed for a quarter to eleven. The supper-dance had begun as I walked up the stairs, so it may have been a few minutes after the half-hour."

Inspector Coleman stopped me with one raised hand. "I want you to take this down, Sergeant."

"Very well, sir." He brought out a sheaf of papers from his inner pocket, and turned them over to select his notebook.

"Go on, Miss Byrnes. Try to remember every detail."

I knew what I was about to tell him would be a severe strain on my nerves, and gripped the sides of my chair, uncrossing my legs.

"I had a look in the cafeteria kitchen, first. Mrs. Smith, one of the cleaner-women, had come in to do whatever cooking was necessary. She told me that Mac had been in, but there was no sign of her in the supper-room. I concluded that she must have gone down again by the back stairs, which was probably the reason why I had missed her. I didn't worry unduly, and offered to set the tables, As you know, the cafeteria and kitchen is one room, though they are separated by a counter with an iron grille reaching down from the roof. The only way to get from the kitchen to the lunchroom is by the corridor." I paused again, re-living that awful feeling of apprehension as I saw the light glowing from the telephonists' cloakroom.

"I don't know what made me go in, but somehow that light didn't look right. There was a special cloakroom fixed up on the seventh floor for the dance. Why should anyone have gone into the telephonists' cloakroom up here? There was no one in the room, but I saw that the restroom door was half-open. The situation was so horribly reminiscent of last Wednesday night that I ran across and tried to push it open. But it wouldn't move," I continued, my mouth becoming dry once more. "I think that I knew then what had happened. I switched on the restroom light. You know what I found." I bent my head down to my knees again as my own words drummed in my ears. Presently I looked up. The two men were watching me gravely.

"Be brave," said the Inspector. "I want you to give me a description of what you saw. Don't think that I am being callous, but the first impression may be important."

"But I locked the door after me. No one could have got in and—and disturbed anything."

"Please do as I say, Miss Byrnes," he commanded.

I stared at him, words of defiance running through my mind. 'You're cruel, cruel! Don't you realize that she was my friend? I won't describe to you a scene that I am trying hard to forget. Will I ever forget once I put into words the memory of her lying there? She looked so small. Little Mac, who was so gay and companionable. Now she's dead, and you want me to gloat over the nature of her death. I can't.'

I knew I was being foolish. He wouldn't have asked me to do anything so painful without an object in mind. He knew what he was about. He was the law, and I had promised to help. I heard my own voice speaking, almost dispassionately.

"She was lying face down, her body along the door as though she had been trying to escape. One arm was stretched above her head, while the other lay across the small of her back. It was such a peculiar position that I bent clown to look at it. I thought maybe it was broken. As I did so, I noticed a pencil caught between her fingers. Was it still there when—?" I paused, and the Inspector pointed to the table.

"May I pick it up?" I asked, worrying vaguely about fingerprints.

Inspector Coleman passed it to me, and I took it gingerly, It was almost new, and of the type that Bertie gave out periodically to the staff.

"Mac couldn't have been writing anything," I observed thoughtfully, feeling the lead with my forefinger. "It's too sharp."

"Perhaps she was stopped just in time," replied Inspector Coleman. "Does the pencil convey anything to you?"

I told him that Bertie had a drawer full of them.

"That's not much help," he remarked, shrugging, "but it's odd that Miss MacIntyre should be holding it. There doesn't seem to be any reason for it, especially as there was nothing found to write on when the room was searched. The murderer would hardly have taken away an unused piece of paper."

"Unless," I said quickly, "Mac was about to add to some notes that she had already made. The murderer would want to destroy them."

The Inspector frowned. "Do you actually know of the existence of such notes, or are you presuming?"

"I'm only presuming," I confessed. "But I am sure my idea is correct. Mac was making inquiries. Right! So was I. Apart from the fact that I had had the advantage of observing the police methods, I found that it was impossible to assemble circumstances and information into one reasonable whole without writing them down. In my brain they were just a jumbled assortment, but when I put them down on paper they seemed to take shape. Mac was a much more orderly person than I, both mentally and physically. If I made notes on the case, she would have also."

"Quite conclusive," agreed the Inspector, smiling a little. "And you think that is what the person who searched her room was after?"

"I don't see why not," I replied, feeling ruffled at the patronizing way in which he had accepted my theory.

"You're probably right," he said hastily. "But to get back to to-night, how long did you stay in that room?"

"It could only have been a few minutes," I answered, and an involuntary shiver passed through my body. "I knew that there was nothing that could be done for her. There was so much blood coming from the head," I explained, amazed at the detached way in which I spoke. "I don't think I touched anything. I left the restroom door like it was on purpose, but locked the outer one leading from the cloakroom into the corridor."

Inspector Coleman had picked up the pencil, and was running it absently through his fingers. "This woman in the kitchen," he remarked. "You didn't tell her what had happened?"

"No. She must have guessed that something was wrong. I remember she called out to me as I passed the top door of the cafeteria. But I was too intent on getting down to the danceroom to take in what she said. What has she told you?"

"I'll tell you by and by," he said. "Go on with your own statement."

"That's all," I said lamely.

"You told Sergeant Matheson that another murder had been committed?" he asked, and I frowned a little.

"No, Mr. Clarkson must have told him. I was a little distraught at the time," I remarked dryly. "When I reached the seventh floor I didn't know quite what I was doing. The first person I saw was Mr. Clarkson, so I dashed over and told him."

"What did he say?"

"I don't remember," I replied tartly. What did one say on learning that a second brutal murder had taken place a floor away; especially when the victim was a girl to whom you were very attached? "The supper-dance was almost finished and I knew that the last thing the police would want would be hordes of people on the eighth floor, trampling on clues."

"Thank you, Miss Byrnes," said the Inspector.

I glanced at him suspiciously as he had cast his eyes down to the papers in front of him. "Don't thank me," I replied carelessly. "It was Mr. Clarkson's suggestion that I go and keep the band playing as long as I could while he searched for Sergeant Matheson. Where were you by the way?"

"Keep to the point," said Inspector Coleman sharply. I felt even more suspicious as the Sergeant reddened a little.

'Petting with some girl, I suppose,' I thought scornfully. 'I only asked you to the dance so that you could see people with their masks off, as it were.' I turned my shoulder towards him, hoping that he noticed the snub.

"Presently he came to me for the cloakroom key."

"You hadn't given it to Mr. Clarkson?" asked the Inspector.

"I don't think that he had any doubt as to whether I was telling the truth," I replied with heat, "so there was no need for him to go investigating as well. Our main idea was to tell the police immediately."

"Mr. Clarkson has a quick brain," said the Inspector approvingly. "I can't thank him enough for what he did."

I felt a glow of pride, and made a mental note to tell Clark what the Inspector had said. Perhaps it would be some comfort to know that he had acted in Mac's best interests. It suddenly occurred to me that now she was dead, I no longer had any worries concerning the friendship between Clark and myself. I banished the thought immediately, feeling horrified and disgusted.

The Inspector picked out one sheet of paper and scanned it closely. "Owing to Mr. Clarkson's good work," he remarked, "we were able to obtain brief statements from the persons who were on the eighth floor during the course of the evening."

"What about Mrs. Smith? Did you get one from her?"

"Not yet. She had left the building before we had any opportunity to question her."

"She must have known that something serious had happened," I insisted. "I wonder why she went?"

Inspector Coleman laughed shortly. "We are an unpopular breed," he observed. "However, the lady can't stay out of our reach for ever. Her evidence may be very helpful as she was in the best position possible to see those who came and went."

"Only the front stairs," I objected. "Anyone could come up the back way and get into the cloakroom unobserved from the kitchen, or even the lunchroom. Don't forget that Mrs. Smith was busy preparing supper, and might not have looked up when she heard footsteps. I know that she did not turn round from the oven until I addressed her."

The Inspector's laugh was an expression of genuine mirth that time. "You're ready to throw the spanner in at every turn," he observed. "Perhaps it is just as well. Constructive criticism never harmed anyone."

"I have got a nerve," I confessed, "telling you how to run the case. But you see, I am deeply concerned with the outcome."

"I know," he returned gently, "and I promise you faithfully that we will do everything to revenge your friend's death. But you must continue to give us assistance."

"I?" I said in surprise. "I've told you everything that I know. What more can I do?"

The Inspector leaned over the table. His eyes looked steadily into mine. "You can do a great deal," he declared slowly and distinctly. "Keep your eyes and ears open; not only for the sake of the police, but for your own as well."

I felt my eyes widen as I continued to stare fascinated into his. His words left me in no doubt as to his meaning, and I stayed very still. Gradually the tenseness went out of my muscles, to be replaced by long, slow shudders that I sought in vain to control.

"Those statements," I said, clenching my teeth to keep my voice from trembling too. "May I see them?"

He must have thought me a fool, letting myself go suddenly like that. But if he had noticed the shuddering, he made no comment. He turned his attention to his desk. "Not to-night. I want to go home to bed."

Was he being tactful, or didn't he want me to see them at all? I rather favoured the former idea, and felt a sudden warmth towards him. He wasn't such a bad old stick, which was more than I could say for his subordinate.

"Will it be all right for me to take Miss Byrnes home, sir? I promised her mother."

"Quite," answered the Inspector promptly. "You'll hear from me later, Miss Byrnes."

I arose with difficulty, praying that Sergeant Matheson would be able to get a taxi at this late hour. I could not see my legs standing the strain of much walking. My body was like a sack of potatoes. It was impossible to organize my muscles into co-operation with my brain, which was not too clear either. I have but a confused recollection of the drive home. It was as if my spirit was far removed from my body, and it stood afar off surveying the automaton curiously. I remember Sergeant Matheson's hand cupping my elbow to help me into a patrol car outside the Exchange entrance, and asked whether the wireless had been switched off. He laughed. I wondered why, feeling annoyed in a dazed fashion. I think Sergeant Matheson drove the car. I crouched in the back seat, watching the light come and go as we shot past the street lamps. He may have spoken once or twice, but I have no recollection of what he said and how I replied. I half-sat and half-lay against the leather upholstery, my head wedged in one corner, and counted the number of times the car filled with light. There were such a lot of things that I wanted to think about, but my mind seemed a complete blank. Only Inspector Coleman's words ran through my brain. 'Keep your eyes and ears open, not only for the sake of the police, but for your own as well.' He was asking me to help him, and yet he issued a grave warning as to the danger in which I stood if I did so. I felt rather indignant. I had told them everything that I could remember. Why not leave me alone in peace, and do the dirty work themselves?

I wondered vaguely where Mac was. As we passed over the bridge, I remembered that the morgue was somewhere near the bank of the river. It was odd the jokes that people made about the place and the way the telephone number was Central 13. I shivered at the remembrance of the macabre humour. They had probably taken Mac there, and put her on a cold marble table. Perhaps a doctor was already bending over the horrible remains of Mac's piquant face, poking and prying to discover the nature of her death. It was just another body to him, a little messy to work on, but it was his job.

'She must have been a pretty little thing. Fine eyes, from what one can tell now. Pass me that instrument over there, will you?'

My brain went on with its horrible imaginings. Presently I saw my mother's face instead of Mac's and tried to tell her to keep her eyes and ears open. The effort was too great. 'I'll tell her first thing in the morning. Where's a pencil to write it down. I've got a memory like a sieve.'

Someone was pulling my dress over my head. Suddenly I felt small and very young. I was sick, and my mother was putting me to bed. But what was wrong with me? Had I caught the 'flu again?

A glass was put to my lips, and I knew that I had to drink. Lemon juice and aspirin, I supposed, though it didn't taste much like it. Bed was good, but I mustn't doze off. I must keep my eyes and ears open, or maybe I'll have my face smashed in like Mac.

"Mother," I shrieked, "help me to stay awake!" There was no reply, but a cool hand held mine, and I felt safe.

'Mother won't let him kill me,' I thought, satisfied, sinking into the blackness.

CHAPTER IX

Mrs. Bates had got rid of the horrible oak suite at last. What a relief it was to see plain painted deal, instead of those knots and streaks that were an undeceiving imitation of the genuine article. I felt satisfied that my nagging had not been in vain until my eyes lighted on the window. What a beastly cheek the woman had! She had taken down my curtains, and put up some coarse white net in their place. Where were my sheepskin rugs? And the pink-tinted mirror that Mac had given me?

I sat up in bed, ready to leap out looking for a brawl. A pain shot up the back of my neck. I felt my tongue cautiously with my teeth. A hangover?

'Tut, tut, Maggie, my girl! I'll lie quietly for a while with my eyes shut, and try to sort things out. The room is nice and cool. The wind must have changed.'

It was marvellous not to wake up to the blind flapping and the sun streaming in hotly. I screwed up my eyelids.

'That's odd! If the wind has changed, it would be blowing from the south. That means that the door would have to be propped open; otherwise it would slam. This can't be my room in Mrs. Bates's boarding-house, and yet it looks familiar. I can't be at home either. The wood-cut Tony made usually hangs opposite my bed. He'd have the horrors if he saw what was in its place.'

'Curiouser and curiouser,' I quoted aloud. 'Here I am in a strange bed in a strange room, nursing a sore head and a thick tongue that are both very reminiscent of what I have been told of the "morning after" feeling. What did I drink last night to warrant a hangover? Just in passing, what happened last night? This is absurd, ridiculous! Have I gone crackers, or am I suffering from—what is it called that is so popular with novelists and playwrights? Amnesia, that's it. Well, I haven't forgotten the English language anyway.'

A figure walked cautiously past my open door.

"Hey!" I yelled. "Come back."

"Are you awake, Miss Byrnes?" asked Mrs. Bates, fitting neatly in the doorway with only a few inches to spare on all sides.

"No, I'm talking in my sleep," I retorted testily. "I'm very glad to see you, however; a thing I never thought I'd be. Your solid presence before me proves that I am still in your boardinghouse. What do you mean by throwing me out of my own room?"

"It was Mrs. Byrnes's idea," she replied without any outward indignation. No matter how you spoke to my landlady, she still preserved her equanimity.

"My mother?" I said, puzzled. "Is she in town?"

Mrs. Bates looked at me fearfully. "I'm not mad," I assured her irritably. "I just can't seem to think above this head of mine. Where is she?"

"In your room. She slept there last night after we put you to bed in here."

I had a terrible thought. "Don't tell me I disgraced your house by coming home tight?" I asked, scandalized. She folded her lips together without any comment. "I'd better go and find my mother," I said uneasily. This was a dreadful state of affairs.

Charlotte was staring out of the window when I entered on the echo of my knock.

'It can't have changed after all,' I thought stupidly, feeling a breath of hot air.

"Hullo, darling," she said, turning around and surveying me anxiously. "Do you feel better?"

I was too ashamed to meet her eyes. "Yes, thanks," I answered in a gruff voice, and stood before her like a child waiting for punishment. She made no rebuke until I could stand the silence no longer. "How did I come to be drunk last night?" I burst out.

"Maggie, dear, what a dreadful thing to suggest," said my mother placidly.

I looked up, bewildered. "What's the matter with me then? I feel like death warmed up this morning. I suppose that it is morning, isn't it?"

She glanced at her wrist. "About two in the afternoon," she replied.

"Go and have a shower. You'll feel better, and then I'll get you something to eat."

"I'd be sick," I said frankly.

"No, you wouldn't. Go and do as I say before you start asking questions."

"Just one," I begged, and hesitated. "Am I all right? I mean—my brain hasn't gone or anything equally ghastly, has it?"

Charlotte came quickly, and put her arms about me. "Maggie, you didn't think—" she began. "Oh, darling, I am so sorry. It's probably the sleeping tablets I gave you that are making you feel odd."

"How many did you force down my throat? I bet I didn't take them willingly."

"Two," she answered, standing back.

I clapped one hand to my forehead. "It's a wonder I'm not dead. Where's that shower? It might clear the old brain a bit."

I let the cold water run hard on my body and over my aching temples, and presently came back towelling my head vigorously.

"Why the change of rooms?" I asked, my voice muffled.

"I thought the sun would waken you in the morning. I wanted you to sleep as long as you could."

"Thanks, Charlotte," I said, going over to the chest of drawers. "You always were considerate." I started to hunt for fresh clothes, and presently looked up into the mirror to see if my face was as bad as it felt.

"This pink tint is very flattering," I observed to my mother. "Mac gave—" I stopped short, meeting her eyes over my head. They were full of sympathy, and quite suddenly I remembered. I didn't say a word, but put up my hand to touch the clear glass gently. My fingers left a mark, and I stared at it while my mind flew back to the events of the night before. I saw my own eyes darken with horror, as step by step I approached the climax, and my jaw harden resolutely as I recalled the interview with Inspector Coleman.

"Maggie," said my mother in a frightened voice. She was standing directly behind me, and her reflection was now hidden. I turned round slowly.

"It's all right, Charlotte," I said quietly. "I remember now. What, tears? Darling!" I exclaimed, putting my arms about her comfortingly in my turn. It was very rarely that my placid, easygoing mother ever had recourse to tears. She pulled at the handkerchief in her sleeve, and blew her nose hard.

"You sound like an elephant," I observed lightly.

"Maggie, come home. I am so worried about you."

"Worried about me?" I repeated, misunderstanding the cause on purpose. "I'm quite all right now. It takes more than two pills to kill me off."

"Don't," said Charlotte huskily, making me feel a brute. "Come home before anything else happens at that horrible place."

"No, Charlotte," I said gently, but firmly. "If it had been anyone else than Mac, I would have considered it. But I can't go now. I must stay in town until—"

"Until something happens to you like it did to her," she burst out.

"Nonsense," I said bracingly, trying to smother the sick, uneasy feeling her words invoked. 'If anyone else tells me that my life is in danger,' I thought, 'I'll get Inspector Coleman to lock me in a cell until the murderer has been found. I am sure he could find a nice quiet niche for me out at Pentridge.'

"Listen to me, Charlotte," I said in a reasonable voice. "Nothing is going to happen to your only daughter. I've told you before that I value my skin too highly to run any risks. Moreover, I'm out of the picture now. Once I publish it abroad that the police have all the information I ever held, there will be no point in killing me off. Now, cheer up, and get me that food you promised."

"You're very like your father, Maggie," sighed my mother, going to the door obediently. "How long will you take to get dressed?"

"I'll be in the dining-room within five minutes."

As I came down the stairs to the lower hall, clad in a dirndl and sandals, the telephone rang.

"I'll take it!" I yelled towards the kitchen, and walked leisurely up the hall.

"Is Miss Byrnes in, please?" asked a male voice.

"She is," I replied, pulling the hair away from my ear. "How are you, Clark?"

"Is that you, Maggie. How are you?"

"I asked you first. I'm fine."

"So am I." There was a pause. What liars we both were!

"No, I'm rotten," declared Clark emphatically.

"I'm pretty low, too," I admitted. "How did you get on last night?"

"Grim," was the succinct answer. "I'm glad that you dropped out. You'd never have stood the staff I had. How I longed to wring each respective neck! They chattered all night like magpies."

"How ghastly!" It was better to keep the conversation on a light plane. You could control yourself more easily. Once I let go again, it would be the end of me. I would shriek and shriek until I collapsed into an oblivion of insanity.

Clark said in a strained voice: "I'll call for you in about half an hour. We can't talk properly on the phone."

"Come as soon as you can," I begged.

"What about your mother?" he asked quickly. "Is she still taking me on?"

"What do you mean?" I asked, puzzled. "You're not coming to pick me up for golf?"

"Why not? You made the date."

"I couldn't go now," I declared faintly.

His voice was stern over the wires. "Listen to me, Maggie. You're going to play this afternoon, and I mean it. I don't care about your mother, but you are coming. You'll be a screaming lunatic soon, if you don't have some sort of relaxation."

'That's a coincidence,' I thought grimly.

"Now go and get ready like a good girl. I'll be there as soon as I can rake up a car from somewhere." Clark hung up without a word of farewell. He was right, of course. I must get out and forget things for a while. Maybe I'd be able to think more clearly after the fresh air and exercise.

The dining-room door opened.

"Come along, Maggie," said my mother briskly. "Your lunch is ready." Charlotte seemed to have regained her composure so completely that I wondered if the weeping woman of a few minutes ago could possibly have been she. The small table near the window, where Sergeant Matheson had sat with us at dinner the previous night, held a plate of freshly-cut tomato sandwiches and a pot of black coffee.

"Do you think that this will be enough on which to play eighteen holes?" I asked, watching carefully for her reaction. But my mother's expression did not alter one atom.

"With some fruit, it should be quite adequate," she replied, sitting down beside me. "I think I'll have some coffee, too."

As she poured out, a thought suddenly occurred to me. "Charlotte," I commanded solemnly. "Show me your feet."

"Why, darling?" she asked, turning sideways in her chair. I looked down, and then at the tailored linen dress that she wore.

"Where are your clubs?" I asked slyly.

"In the hall," she answered. "By the way, will you be using your putter? Mine seems to be missing. I remember your father was practising long shots on the front lawn a few days ago. He probably forgot to put it back in my bag. Why are you looking at me like that, Maggie?"

"By any chance," I asked carefully, "did you use the telephone to-day?"

"Several times. I rang your father."

"What did he say?" I asked, instantly diverted. "No, never mind. Wait until I've finished with what I was going to say." She glanced at me inquiringly. "I don't suppose," I went on, "that one of the calls you made was to a Windsor number?"

"I might have," she replied cautiously. "Why do you ask?"

I took another sandwich, satisfied that I was the victim of a conspiracy. "Clark just rang to make certain if the game was still on. He'll be round shortly."

"That'll be nice, dear," was the only comment she made. I felt a little nonplussed.

"What did the Old Man say?" I asked presently.

"Don't call your father that," she protested. "He got a bit het up when I broke the news, but he was pretty right by the time we rang off. He told me to bring you home."

"Now, Charlotte," I began argumentatively.

"I told him that the police probably wouldn't let you leave town," she finished in a mild tone.

"How did he reply to that?"

"He grunted, but I think that he understood. However, I received strict instructions to return tomorrow. Bertha forgot to put salt in the porridge this morning."

"What a calamity!" I said, grinning. "Do you want to go home?"

"Not much," she confessed. "I told your father that I hadn't found my garden hat yet. He gave way when I promised to return as soon as I found one."

"You'd better try looking for it in shoe stores," I advised, folding my table-napkin and rising from the table. "At least until the case is solved."

Charlotte got up too, and we walked arm in arm to the door.

"Do you think that they'll ever find out?" she asked despairingly. "I can't make head nor tail of the business."

"Of course they will," I replied, though I shared her apprehensions. It would be ghastly if the case dragged on for months, perhaps even years, like the Albury pyjama-girl mystery. I sighed despondently.

"I'll run upstairs and get those putters," I said. "You wait in the hall."

I came down, clad in a grey linen skirt and checked shirt with my golf bag slung across my shoulder. Clark had arrived and was practising mashie shots with a matchbox as a ball.

"Mind the light," I called from half-way down the stairs. He came forward with the iron against his shoulder. I was shocked at his appearance.

"Did you have any sleep at all?" I asked severely.

"Not much," he replied. "You look fresh enough."

"I'm better now. Charlotte gave me a sleeping draught when I got home, unbeknown to me. The net result was a splitting head and a tongue like cotton-wool."

"A game will do us all good. Are you ready?"

We travelled towards the south-eastern suburbs where the sandbelt lay, and where most of the best courses ran side by side.

"I thought it might have changed," I remarked, letting down the window as I sat in the front seat with Clark, "but it is still as hot as ever. Are we going to Riverlea?"

He nodded, turning the wheel with one hand. "I booked for 4 p.m., but I don't think that it was necessary. Most people will be playing in the clubhouse over beer."

I glanced over my shoulder. "It won't be too hot for you, Charlotte?"

"No, dear," she replied, following the flying landscape on her right. "I like summer golf. It makes my ball go farther."

"That's what she says," I remarked confidentially to Clark. "I've seen my mother drive a hundred and fifty yards along a marshy fairway in the middle of winter."

"I am going to ask for two strokes," Clark said solemnly.

We drove on in silence for a while, until he asked abruptly: "Are you working to-night?"

I had been humming a little tune, but his words pulled me up with a jerk.

"I suppose I will. There's no reason why I shouldn't. What about you?"

"There is no need for a traffic officer to-night, my pet. Bertie is coming in."

"What's the idea? He's never worked on all-night before."

Clark shrugged, lifting his hands from the wheel. "Search me. However, it lets me off. I won't question his actions."

"I'm glad, for your sake," I admitted. "You'd better get my mother to give you a couple of those pills. Are there any left, Charlotte?"

"I loathe forced sleep," said Clark emphatically.

"Never mind! You do as I say for a change. We'll collect them on the way home."

"Just as you wish," he replied in a meek voice, and I touched the rough sleeve of his coat for a second.

The course, as Clark had foreseen, held but few players, while the lounge of the clubhouse was crowded with rubber-soled feet. I ran a ball down the empty race idiotically, and went to tee up.

"I'll show you the way, Charlotte," I called, my club held between my bent knees as I pulled on a grey felt hat. "Red flags out—white flags in."

Our first drives landed us about the same distance, although my ball lay slightly in the rough. I took out an iron, calling to the others cheerfully: "Watch me hit the pin!"

I saw Clark take my mother's bag before I swung. As I followed my lifting ball, shading my eyes with one hand, I remembered how Mac had always sliced on this first hole, whereas I usually pulled. It had been quite a joke between us.

"Just off the green," said Clark's voice behind me. "Your mother is on, but I think that I have hit through."

"Bad luck," I said tightly, striding along in step.

Charlotte had holed out in three when we reached the green. As I flung down my bag, kicking it aside to give me room for a stance. Clark crossed to the other side, and disappeared into a bunker. The chip shot was a failure, and it took me two putts to achieve the hole. I straightened after picking the balls out of the tin, and caught Clark looking at me queerly.

"Five, Maggie?" asked my mother, marking her card as she walked ahead.

"Six," I corrected, fumbling over my shoulder for my club. "Your honour."

We watched her drive off in silence. I half-closed my eyes, visualizing a slimmer, smaller figure following the stroke through gracefully. What a farce the whole idea was! Nobody wanted to play, excepting perhaps Charlotte, and then she was probably only doing it for my sake. I might have known that the very feel of a club in my left hand would bring back agonizing memories of Mac.

'We were fools to think that it would do us good,' I told myself bitterly. I nodded briefly to Clark to drive off before me.

He made no comment, but for once I didn't care. How fickle we humans are! Those dead become infinitely more precious than those alive, yet while our friends are on earth we quarrel with and criticize them unmercifully. What a difference there would have been if I had been more patient, more understanding with Mac!

'It looks as though I may be responsible for another death,' I thought dully, as I placed my ball on the tee and stood back to survey the fairway mechanically. Now I must go through the rest of my life reproaching myself that my loyalty to Mac was not so strong after all.

I knew as soon as I reached the top of my swing that something was wrong, but I did not reckon on mis-hitting. In earlier days. such a catastrophe would have aroused my mirth. but I merely stared gloomily at the ball now.

"Maggie, darling," said Charlotte in a shocked voice. "Your left shoulder!"

I grunted. A shadow fell across my stance. "Take it easily," said Clark.

I looked up to see his face white and set. Was he talking about the game or had he some other thought in mind? His face was expressionless in a way that would convey nothing to the ordinary observer. But I had seen that look before, and knew that his mind was surging with conflicting emotions.

Charlotte coughed significantly, rousing me out of my daze. I drove off unseeingly.

"What a fluke!" said Clark, pushing me gently onward. "Stop admiring it, Maggie, and get a move on." His voice held that would-be hearty quality that only increased my gloom. This was going to be terrible, and we'd only played one hole. Only Charlotte remained unconcerned, and kept her mind on the game. One would have thought that Clark and I had guilty consciences, the way we stroked that round. Perhaps we had, in so far that each of us was reproaching ourselves for the lack of concern we had shown Mac in the last few days before her death.

The sun had sunk below the horizon when we walked slowly up the path to the clubhouse. Clark had offered to take my mother's bag, but she had refused independently, and strode along ahead of us adding up the scores. She was the only one of the trio who was not hot, weary and thoroughly unhappy.

"Don't bother with mine," I called out irritably. "It's well over the hundred."

"I hope that you're deducting eighteen from my score, Mrs. Byrnes, though I doubt that it will make any difference to the final issue."

"Don't, Clark," I said wearily. "Don't try to pretend."

He slid my bag off my shoulder. "I must," he answered in a quiet voice. "Otherwise I'll go mad. What a fool I was!"

"We both were," I corrected. "If only I'd realized. But Mac was more than half to blame. She wouldn't have told, no matter what persuasion I used."

"She was just as stubborn with me. Wait until I lay my hands on the fiend who killed her. There won't be much left of him to hang."

I shivered at the grim note in his voice, not envying anyone who chose Clark as an opponent.

"I never thought that I'd be glad to finish a round of golf," I declared, turning back to survey that part of the course which lay amongst the trees in the valley. Even under the strong February sun, the fairways were still unburnt, while the greens were circles of a more vivid colour. The rising evening wind fluttered the triangular flags on the pins, and, brushing aside the branches of the evergreens, fanned my face. I put up one hand.

"I'll he the colour of mahogany soon. This is my second dose of sunburn within two days."

Charlotte called from the steps of the clubhouse, motioning that she would go in and not wait for us.

"How did you happen to get burnt yesterday?" Clark asked absently. "You should have been asleep."

"So I was until—" I stopped short, and he eyed me speculatively. "There are such a lot of things that you don't know about," I went on, "that I was taking for granted that you do."

"What has happened?" he asked swiftly.

"Nothing concrete," I replied, sitting on the bottom step of the clubhouse and lifting my head to the vivid sky. "It's a funny thing," I mentioned idly, my eyes sweeping a line from the zenith to where the sun had left its final mark, "that if any artist mixed his paints to match exactly this scene of sky and trees, and painted it accurately in every detail, the result would only be appreciated in such terms as 'pretty' and 'dainty'."

Clark made a gesture of impatience. "Are you heading me off, Maggie?"

"Not at all. I was trying to remember how I began."

He came to sit beside me, looking puzzled.

"I made a list," I explained, "in my diary. Sergeant Matheson has it now. I'll get it back from him if I can, so that you can read my notes."

"Can't you remember what you wrote?"

"Not without a wash and a drink," I answered meaningly. "Pull me up, Clark, and we'll find Charlotte. She'll be wondering what's happened to us."

He rose stiffly, and held out his strong lean hands. I put mine into them, and was surprised to find them so hot.

"You're not getting a chill?" I asked anxiously.

He stared at me in silence, still holding my hands. With a swift movement he put his head down to mine, and I heard his voice muffled in my hair. "Maggie, I'm tired! So damned tired!"

Very gently I slid my hands to his shoulders, and we stood together in silence. Presently a burst of noise came from the veranda above. The door into the lounge had been opened to emit someone. Clark must have noticed it too, and straightened himself quickly.

"Sorry," he said. "What about that drink?"

It must have been an effort to pull himself together after that sudden collapse, but as we went up the steps he held his head high. The straightness of his back made me wonder if the few minutes I had spent so close to him in his weakness had not been a dream. Twice in the same day people to whom I looked for strength and encouragement had come to me for comfort. First of all my placid mother, who usually remained undisturbed in the biggest crisis, had clung weeping and imploring me to go home. And now Clark, the debonair hero of the junior staff at Central, had manifested that his resistance to emotion was not as strong as I had previously believed. I don't think I was disappointed. After all, it would be very tiring to live with anyone who had an unquenchable vitality. But Clark had always been, as it were, on top of the troubles of the past few days. Then I remembered that this had been our first time alone since Mac's death, and I felt a sudden pang of jealousy. Was she the one that he really loved after all? Or was his feeling for her now like mine—sad that I hadn't shown proof of my devotion during the last hours before she died?

Charlotte came round the corner of the veranda. "Oh, there you are! I've ordered drinks to be brought out here. The lounge is packed."

"I must have a wash," I said. "What about you, Clark?"

He held out his hands for Charlotte to inspect. She bent over them critically.

"They'll do," she declared. "You'll find us around the side, Maggie, and don't be long."

But I dallied on purpose, taking a long time over my face and hair, to give them an opportunity to get to know each other. So far the only chances had been in a crowded danceroom and on the links, where the topic of their conversation, that is myself, had been with them. I knew that Charlotte would want to make a genealogical research, and such a task could not be accomplished without time. I experimented with a hair-do à la Gloria, only to become convinced that my usual method was better. I'd rather look hard, as Gloria described me, than the poor imitation of a girl I disliked. Certain that Charlotte should have reached the great-grandparents at least, I took a circuitous route through the lounge to the side veranda.

The lounge was full of smartly-dressed women with impossible vowels, and their appendages. The latter were, for the most part, inclined to Falstaffian figures, and to them golf was a means of diminishing their poundage. Not that to-day's playing would do much to accomplish that. Rather to the contrary; that is, if most of them had spent their time on the nineteenth, as they appeared to have done. White-coated waiters sped to and fro, handling trays of chinking glasses with amazing dexterity. I nodded briefly to one or two golfers, with whom Clark and I had had a foursome one crowded day. I was just refusing an invitation to join them in a drink, when a crash sounded near the far wall. There was a sudden lull in the conversation, as heads turned quickly to survey the scene.

One of the waiters, no more than a lad of sixteen, was nervously dabbing at the erstwhile immaculate slacks of one of the armchair golfers. He was a middle-aged man, fair, but with that high complexion that deepens to a purple when its owner becomes incensed. I watched the transition interestedly, feeling very sorry for the hapless youth, and grimaced at a woman whom I knew slightly and whose accent was genuine. She shrugged hopelessly in answer, as some deep-throated swearing was heard from the purple-faced man. I considered it high time to retire and made for the main swing doors. Unfortunately, at the same moment the angry man, his trousers stained with beer, was also departing, followed by the protesting waiter.

"Excuse me," I said coolly, as we both placed a hand on the doors. He muttered something under his breath, but stood back, the lad behind him saying in an apologetic voice: "Sir, will I go and—"

"You can go to hell," declared the man roundly. I walked out ahead of him, just as Clark came down the veranda.

"Hullo," he said. "You've been an age, and you don't seem to look any different."

"At least my hands are clean," I retorted. "Who is that man who came out behind me? He's just crossing the gravel to the car park now."

Clark glanced over his shoulder casually. "Atkinson. The bad-tempered swine!"

"I quite agree with you. You should have heard the language when young Tom upset some beer over his slacks. I came to find my mother immediately," I finished virtuously.

"For her sake or yours?" he grinned, and then became serious.

"How are you feeling now?"

"Pretty right, as long as I don't start to think. The brain is a treacherous thing when you try to co-operate it with your emotions. You start wondering if you're not a murderer yourself."

He made no comment, as we rounded the corner to find Charlotte lying in a long chair sipping dry ginger ale. Mentally I kicked myself for being so tactless. Clark probably blamed himself for not having forced Mac's confidence, and thereby—but there was no use speculating. The fact remained that Mac was dead, and it was up to us to keep in a calm state of mind in order to help hunt her murderer.

'When it is all cleared up,' I promised myself, 'you can begin lamenting. You can show your regard better by not becoming rattled.'

But it was hard to sit at my mother's feet and look up at her head against the gay cushions and not visualize Mac's pale, piquant face, when you remembered that once she had lounged her slight figure in the same chair and crossed slim brown ankles one over the other, as even now my mother had.

Charlotte was looking a little disturbed. I wondered if a great-uncle of Clark's had been a bushranger, or whether St. Vitus's dance ran through his family. However she smiled at us both placidly, and started a lecture on putting until I cut her short.

"I think the game is lousy after my effort to-day."

"That was because your mind wasn't on it," said Charlotte wisely. "To play the game properly, you must be concerned with two things only. One is the ball, and the other is yourself."

Clark stirred in his chair, re-crossing his long legs. He had offered no contribution to the conversation, and I guessed the cause of his impatience.

"That's enough about golf," I said. "Let's get down to business."

"And I was trying to keep your minds away from the Exchange!" exclaimed my mother plaintively.

"Not possible," I replied grimly. "Now you know why I took an average of four putts a hole."

Clark bent forward, resting his forearms on his knees, his eyes alight with interest. "Go ahead, Maggie, but don't make it too loud. You never know who may be listening."

I cocked my head on one side. "Your bad-tempered friend, maybe?"

He frowned, and took out his cigarette case. "Atkinson? He's no friend of mine."

"Who is he?" I asked, taking a cigarette from his proffered case.

"Something in the city. A broker, I believe, but I'm not certain. What about you, Mrs. Byrnes?"

"I don't smoke, but do you mind removing this glass to a safer place than the arm of my chair?"

Clark got up. I watched his movements frowningly. "Do you know whereabouts in the city?" I asked.

"Atkinson? Queen Street, I suppose. That is where brokers are as a rule. Why are you so interested in him?"

"Queen Street," I repeated with growing excitement. "That means that he'd be in the City West Exchange, wouldn't it?"

"Providing that he is at the top end, he would," Clark admitted, watching me curiously. "What's got into you, Maggie? What has Atkinson to do with us?"

I bent towards him, so that he would be able to hear me. "You remember on Friday night," I whispered, "how I was missing from the trunkroom when Bertie paid us his surprise visit? I had fallen asleep in the restroom, and was awakened by the sound of someone calling out on the phone. What with dialling a number in the dark and then not saying a word, I got suspicious, to say the least. I dashed down to young Dan Mitchell in the power-room, and he traced the call for me. I rang the number. I won't tell you what ruse I used to cover myself, as I have already shocked Charlotte once, but a man answered."

"Do you mean that his voice was similar to Atkinson's?"

"It may be," I replied. "I haven't thought about that. No, wait, I'm quite serious. It wasn't so much the likeness between the voices, but the fact that they both used the identical phrase."

"But you've never spoken to Atkinson," objected Clark.

"As a matter of fact I have, not that my words were important, but I have got that way that I feel compelled to correct every delusion. It's from working with the police, I suppose."

"Stop chattering, Maggie," said my mother, "and tell us what the identical phrase was."

"'You can go to hell,'" I replied promptly. I laughed aloud at the shocked expression on Charlotte's face, before she gathered that I was not addressing her.

"But everyone passes remarks like that," Clark objected again, when the grin faded from his face.

"So Charlotte thought. But it's a strange coincidence, don't you agree? For several reasons. Both men exhibited a remarkable lack of restraint where their patience was concerned. Then you tell me that Atkinson's telephone would be a City West number."

"No, I didn't," corrected Clark. "I only suggested that his office would be in Queen Street."

I looked at him reproachfully. "Don't spoil my theory. Lastly, the words themselves." I stamped out my cigarette, half-smoked, in my excitement. "I want to ask your opinion, Charlotte," I said, turning to where I could see her face as a white blur in the gathering dusk. "If you wanted to consign someone, in words, to the hottest place in existence, what would you say?"

"Nothing," she replied firmly. "I was brought up by a strict mother."

I smiled at her. "Whereas I was not, I suppose? But seriously, Charlotte, what would you say? Your answer may be important."

"Well, if you must, Maggie," she sighed. "Wait a minute while I concentrate on someone with whom I don't agree too well. Let me see, who is there?"

"No one," I declared emphatically. "Hurry up and say it. Don't worry about achieving an atmosphere."

"Go to hell!" said Charlotte with surprising force.

"Good work! Now you, Clark."

He shook his head. "This sounds idiotic to me."

"I have a reason," I coaxed. "Please."

"Go to hell," he said expressionlessly, and I clapped my hands together in triumph.

"There you are! It's just as I thought. Charlotte," I declared pompously, "you have a remarkable daughter."

"Yes, darling, but what are you driving at?"

I laughed with pure enjoyment. "You are about to listen to an example of exquisite reasoning. Let us suppose that the man I rang from the power-room and Mr. Atkinson are two different persons. Just as you two are. In expressing indignation at being called in the early hours of the morning, he used a phrase of five words. When I asked you both to repeat the gist of his remark, only three were necessary. You. Clark. declared that it was the sort of phrase anyone would use. I agree with you. But what I am trying to point out is that the majority of people would use only the three words, and therefore coupled with the probable fact that Mr. Atkinson's telephone is connected to City West, I say that Mr. Atkinson and the man I rang are the one and same person."

I sat back as they meditated on my deduction. Presently, Clark tossed his cigarette end over the side to fall in sparks amid the heavy scented petunias.

"Perhaps you're right," he admitted slowly. "What are you going to do about it?"

"There is only one thing to do. Tell the police."

"They already know about the caller in the restroom?" he asked quickly. I nodded. "Have you any idea who it might be?"

I addressed the roof casually, lying back against my mother's knee. "It was odd that the Heads should choose to come in that particular night. Who else was there besides Bertie?"

"Miles Dunn and Rattray from the Engineers' Department. But why should one of them want to use the restroom, when they have all the telephones they want at their disposal?"

"I haven't the faintest idea," I said candidly, "but I daresay the police will cook up something. They have a never-ending source of ideas."

"I don't like it, Maggie. Supposing that Atkinson is not the right man. There'll be a terrible row, and he's a bad type to cross. I've heard one or two stories about his dealings in the city."

"A broker covers many different types of business, doesn't he?" I asked thoughtfully. "I wonder what shady game he is up to now?"

Clark shook his head in a puzzled fashion. "I don't know what connection he can have with anyone in the Exchange, let alone with the murders. What else have you discovered, Maggie?"

"Well, that's all about him," I replied reluctantly, and went on to tell him about Gloria and the anonymous letters, which finally brought me to Bill.

"I don't believe it," said Clark emphatically. "He's one of the whitest men in the building."

I looked at him unhappily. "I hate the idea as much as you do, but you can't get away from the facts."

"What about this cleaner woman? She was actually on the eighth floor when Gerda was—when the murder was committed."

"The police know about her too. She skipped out before the inquiries started, but I suppose that they have traced her by now. I'd rather like to have a word with her myself. You know, Clark, there's something about that woman that has always struck me as familiar, even before Compton was killed, but I just can't seem to put my finger on it."

"Probably the similarity to the rest of her trade. The charing staff all look alike to me."

I made no comment, striving after an elusive memory.

"What about Gerda?" said Clark jerkily. "Are you sure that she did not give you some hint? I mean about what she had discovered?"

"Not a syllable! As a matter of fact, the last time I saw her was down in the basement on Friday evening."

"What on earth were you doing down there?"

I looked at him in amazement. "Haven't I told you about that? I went to find out if there was another door into the Exchange. Did you know of the existence of a door opening from the basement into that lane at the west side of the building? No, neither did I. But Mac did. I met her as she was coming out of the storeroom. I wanted to discover if the murderer could have entered from the outside, instead of sharing everyone's opinion that it was an inside job. The door was half-hidden by boxes. Only someone who was looking for it would observe it."

I saw Clark grinning through the deepening shadows. "I bet the police didn't like that little find. It widens the stage rather, whereas they'd much prefer to think that it is an inside job still."

"Exactly. What was to prevent someone like our friend with the stained trousers from doing the deed?"

"He'd have to know the Exchange routine rather well," Clark objected. "Don't forget the murders were brilliant pieces of timing."

"But with someone directing him from the inside," I insisted, "it would be quite possible."

"And who would that be?"

"I dunno," I replied, "unless it was Gloria. She knows a lot more than I could coerce from her."

Clark laughed gently. "I gather from that, that you have tried hard enough. I suppose your third degree was the cause of her fainting on Friday night?"

"No, indeed! I was merely chatting along agreeably when that happened. I remember that I had just mentioned something about the case being reopened when down she flopped."

"She makes a rotten accomplice," remarked Clark, frowning. "That is, if she is one."

"I'm certain that she is something in this affair, anyway. Did you observe the way she hesitated with her alibi in that horrible game you invented?"

Clark's face set into hard lines. "I found it just as ghastly as you did," he said, quietly.

"I know," I replied, stretching out one hand impulsively. "You were wonderful. It helped the police and-Mac a great deal. They were very appreciative, Clark."

He looked down at my hand resting on his coat sleeve. "Maggie," he began hesitantly. "Would you mind—I mean, would it be too grim, if you told me just how you found her?"

I withdrew my hand, and said quietly: "Not at all. We had come to the dance, Charlotte, the Sergeant and myself, primarily to find Mac to force her to tell us what she knew. You see, her room had been searched that afternoon and Sergeant Matheson was worried."

"Her room?" Clark demanded. "What do you mean, searched? Was it a burglar?"

I shook my head. "Nothing of any value was taken, I think—in fact, I'm certain that it was the murderer, who was hunting for some evidence that Mac had. Supposing she had made out a case on paper, as is quite likely. The murderer must destroy that, as well as her."

"Go on," said Clark roughly.

I didn't spare him any of the details. I knew that he'd be able to forget them later with greater ease, just as I had, if I described them accurately and without restraint. It was not knowing that hurt more.

"The pencil she was holding has the police puzzled. The point was unblunted, so Mac couldn't have been writing anything. The only suggestion that I could offer was that the killer failed to find any documents in her room, but came on her suddenly just as she was about to add to her notes. But I don't like it. It's too much of a coincidence that she should be caught just in the nick of time."

Clark lit another cigarette, and I could see his hands trembling ever so slightly.

I said without emotion: "The police say that Mac never knew what happened. The first blow from the pedestal 'phone would have killed her."

His voice was hard and bitter as he replied: "They always say that."

"If she did call out," I went on, "Mrs. Smith would have heard her. Surely she would have gone to investigate?"

"Not if she knew what was going to happen," was the quick suggestion. "After what you have told me, I consider that her position wants to be carefully looked into."

I wrinkled my nose. "There's something fishy about her," I remarked. "The fact that she voluntarily took over the supper cooking when she is nominally a cleaner is odd, to say the least. It looks as though she wanted to be on the spot last night."

Silence fell. I noticed that the chatter from the lounge had diminished to a murmur.

"It must be getting late," I said, rising. "Charlotte, have you gone to sleep? You've been very quiet."

"No, darling, I've been thinking."

"With your eyes shut? Come on, before we are chucked out of here."

*   *   *   *   *

Clark was very quiet as we drove home through the hot dusk. Now and then I stole a sidelong glance, wondering what he was thinking. It was only when an approaching car flooded our faces with light that I saw the intense weariness in his face. It was deeply lined, and his eyes were dull and half-closed.

"Would you like me to drive?" I suggested, as he took a right-hand corner in a wide semicircle. Charlotte gasped as the car narrowly missed a cyclist. Clark shook his head without speaking. Words were evidently beyond him until we drew up outside Mrs. Bates's boarding-house.

I hesitated before getting out. "Will you come in and have some tea with us?"

His voice was hoarse with fatigue. "No, thank you, Maggie. I want to go straight to bed. What about those tablets you promised me?"

Charlotte heaved herself out of the back seat. "I'll run in and get them," she said tactfully.

I glanced at Clark in surprise. "You hardly seem to need a sleeping draught now, but you're welcome to have them."

Clark gripped the wheel with his hands, and spoke in a low, fierce voice. "That's the trouble. I'm dead tired, but I can't seem to relax. When I've got nothing to occupy my mind, I start thinking." He slid his hands off the wheel, and clasped mine hard. "Maggie, if I don't get Gerda out of my head, I'll go mad. Mad, do you hear?"

At the sound of Mac's name, my body went cold. My hands were lifeless under his grip. Was she to become a shadow between us for the rest of my life?

'You're not fair to me,' I cried silently and resentfully. 'If it was Mac you wanted, why didn't you say so in the first place?'

Then I observed his strained eyes again, and was filled with shame and pity. "Hush! Try not to think about her. You'll be better after you've had some sleep."

He removed his hands abruptly, and stared unseeingly through the windscreen. Neither of us said a word. I wondered how long Charlotte would be. There was no need for her to be so tactful, if Clark's mind was filled with memories of Mac.

His voice sounded strangely calm through the darkness of the car. "I wonder if it is possible that Gerda left some message. Some hint of what she was about, that only those who knew her would be able to appreciate."

"I doubt it," I replied grimly. "I think that the murderer would have seen to anything like that."

Clark shook his head with an impatient movement. "There must be something," he declared. "If Gerda knew she was playing a dangerous game, she would have insured herself somehow against any possibility of—of—" His voice trailed away, but I knew what it was he shrank from putting into words. "Can't you think of anything that she did or said that could give us a lead?" he asked helplessly.

"I told you the last time that I saw Mac alive was on Friday evening; after that, I only heard her voice on the 'phone, and spoke to people who actually saw her just before her death. My mother was one of them."

"What did she say to her?"

I shrugged. "I haven't asked Charlotte any details, but I don't think that there was anything important mentioned. Mac merely said that she was going to change. She had a case in the cloakroom nearby. Then Mavis Hemingway told me practically the same thing."

Clark said slowly: "She must have changed her mind at the last minute, and gone upstairs to the restroom. I wonder why?"

"To ring Russell Street," I replied absently, and felt Clark jump in the seat. "How do you know? Quickly, Maggie, answer me."

I hesitated. "They checked up on the line. Although the telephone had been used to—to kill Mac, they thought that there might be a possibility of her having made a call. The first three numbers of Police Headquarters had been dialled."

"But Sergeant Matheson was actually in the building. Why didn't she go to him?"

"Mac couldn't have seen him. After all, one doesn't look for a policeman at a dance, and I didn't ask him until the last minute. No one knew that he would be present."

Clark gave a soft groan. "Evidently Gerda was calling Russell Street just as the killer entered the restroom. He must have torn the 'phone from her hand, and struck her with it again and again until she died."

I bowed my head without a word. Clark's description of what had happened brought a vivid picture before my eyes. Once again, I saw that slim, twisted figure lying at my feet, and the blood that splayed out from the dark head. I saw Mac's arm rounded across her back, and the curled fingers holding a pencil.

'Mac certainly died with her boots on,' I thought grimly. 'Anyone would be able to tell her profession, holding a pencil between her fingers like that.' Only a telephonist was capable of doing intricate finger work, and not letting a pencil get in the way. It was almost as though Mac was just about to complete a docket with the time disconnected and her signature.

Suddenly my mouth went dry, and a flicker of hope shot through my brain. A pencil! A docket! Did it hold any significance? Was Mac in her last agony trying to convey a message that only a telephonist would understand? Did she remember me in her last desperate thoughts, and hope that I would notice that pencil and construe an explanation. The blood drummed in my ears.

"Clark!" I said sharply. "It's a clue. Mac knew that I'd notice it. She was trying to tell me something."

Clark gripped my arm. "What did she say? I thought you said that she was already dead."

His fingers bit into my bare arm, but I barely felt them. "She *was* dead. It's that pencil I mean. Before it seemed all wrong that she should be holding one, but now I know. Who do you see holding pencils in that peculiar fashion, between two fingers?"

"Go on, quickly," he commanded, shaking my arm.

"Telephonists switch with one. You get that way that you don't notice it, and it doesn't impede your work. Your pencil is as much part of your apparatus as the mouthpiece is. I'll swear that Mac was trying to say something. She was trying to convey that she had written down something on a certain type of paper that that pencil is used for. A docket!"

I felt Clark's body go tense beside me, and heard his hard breathing. "If that is correct, Maggie," he said very slowly, "we've got that inhuman brute."

I was filled with a wild exultation. How wonderful, how magnificent it would be to hand Mac's killer over to justice; to waken one morning in the early light and know that not far away someone was being hanged by the neck as a revenge for killing Mac. Compton I disregarded completely. I had no interest in avenging her death. But my little Mac, so gay, so alive! Whoever snuffed the flame of her vitality must die an ignominious death, and I would shout and clap my hands with awful glee when I heard the prison bell tolling.

Clark's voice roused me from my frenzied thoughts. "Where would she have hidden it? In her locker? Her handbag?"

My own voice sounded quiet and reasonable in my ears. "No. If the murderer went to the trouble of ransacking her room, he would have made certain about those two places."

"But a docket," Clark insisted. "The killer would be looking for a notebook or a plain sheet of paper. Probably that is why Gerda used a docket. It would be less likely to attract attention."

I thought for a minute. What Clark had said was quite true. Moreover, if the killer was a telephone employee and accustomed to the stationery, the docket would probably have been passed over.

"I'm going straight in to the Exchange. What number was Gerda's locker?"

"You're doing nothing of the kind," I declared firmly. "If you're going straight to anywhere, it is to bed. I'll have a hunt through her locker to-night."

"What if someone catches you?" asked Clark, weakening visibly. His fatigue must have been great indeed to make him give in so quickly.

"I won't be caught," I said confidently. In fact, I felt so sure of myself that had anyone told me what was going to happen that night, I would have laughed in their faces.

Charlotte arrived at this point with her box of pills, and strict instructions how to take them. Clark thanked her gravely. He seemed to have recovered some of his spirits since my inspiration about the pencil. It was a frail hope, but evidently he placed a great deal of dependence on the outcome of a search of Mac's locker. Charlotte and I stood at the gate to watch him drive off, after giving his solemn promise to swallow at least two of the sleeping tablets.

"They will nearly kill you," I told him blithely. "But at least I can guarantee you some sleep. I'll ring you first thing in the morning about that other business."

"What other business?" asked Charlotte, when we were seated in the privacy of my room some time later. Mrs. Bates, after grumbling meaningly about the unpunctuality to meals of some people, had finally served a cold meal in the empty dining-room. I had avoided my mother's eyes, as I knew that she was waiting for me to ask her what she thought of Clark. Somehow I didn't want to hear her opinion, and put my lack of interest down to the fact that Mac's affair must come first.

I told her about the message that I had read in the pencil Mac had held in her dead fingers, and that I was going to search her locker that night.

Her eyes flickered once or twice, before she asked placidly: "Can't you ring Sergeant Matheson and tell him first?"

"That man!" I exclaimed scornfully. "He'd take hours going into the whys and wherefores. In the meantime the murderer might have woken up to the idea, and stolen a march on me." I stripped off my shirt, preparatory to getting into a dressing-gown in order to stretch out for a while before going into town.

Charlotte said dryly: "As long as the murderer doesn't happen to search the locker at the same time as you, I suppose it's a good idea."

I paused, one arm thrust through the loose sleeve of my gown. "Just let him," I said darkly, tying the wide sash and climbing on to my bed.

"Can't you wait until to-morrow?" Charlotte pleaded, but I closed my eyes, determined not to be frightened out of my resolve.

A couple of hours' rest did much to restore my ever-flagging vitality, although I did not actually go to sleep, I dared not, and kept my mind working on all the different incidences of the past few days. Presently, I came to speculate on the sudden entry into the picture of Mr. Atkinson, broker and golfer. Was it, as Clark had declared, too much of a coincidence that I should identify that mysterious voice with a man in the lounge of the Riverlea club-house? It was certainly remarkable that the man who answered me that night in the power-room should be a member of a club whose numbers were not over-large. On the other hand, entry to Riverlea was very much sought after. Why shouldn't Mr. Atkinson be the successful one out of thousands who were all angling for admittance?

'I'll tell Sergeant Matheson,' I thought inwardly. 'It should be a job after his own heart.'

But if Mr. Atkinson was by profession a broker, who and why would anyone be ringing him in such a secretive fashion from the Exchange? Why, too, did he do all the talking, while the unknown dialler stayed silent?

I had to stop these interesting, and so far unanswerable, questions in order to dress for work. I chose a dark-coloured frock in case I wanted to appear inconspicuous any time during the night. My heart was beating hard more from excitement than anything else. I had put Cliarlotte's grim warning out of my head. She was reading in bed, as I went to bid her good night on my way down the hall.

"Turn off the light," I commanded from the doorway, "and don't lie awake, waiting for your daughter's corpse to be brought home."

"I don't like it at all, Maggie," she answered, shaking her head. "You'll be very careful?"

I told her gravely that I had not the least ambition to be murdered, and was rewarded with a watery smile.

There is only one thing worse than working all-night, and that is working the Sunday dogwatch. The city was almost deserted, and as quiet as a graveyard. Public conveyances were infrequent. I found myself on the same bus as the other all-night telephonists.

By that time I was getting used to curious and awed glances, but when Bertie Scott stepped into the bus just as it was about to move off, and seated himself next to me, those girls positively goggled.

I greeted him coldly, and not without apprehension. It was rather unnerving to share a seat with someone who you thought might be a double murderer. Bertie said "Good evening," and left his mouth open as if he were about to say more. Then he shut it abruptly, coughed, and stared at his own fidgeting feet as though they did not belong to him. Rather pointedly I fixed my gaze out the window; in fact, if I had had to watch Bertie fidgeting much longer, I would have screamed. He coughed again, and bent nearer.

"I met your mother last night, Miss Byrnes," he confided softly.

"Did you?" I asked, edging away from his pince-nez.

"I was very happy to make her acquaintance," he went on, holding on to the handle of the seat in front of him, as the bus swung round the corner and started to climb up to the Exchange. I murmured unintelligibly, unable to think of any suitable comment to make.

As the bus stopped and the other girls got out, he burst out suddenly: "I think your mother is a most remarkable woman. Will you tell her so from me?"

He rose to his feet. I slipped out of the seat without replying. What on earth had Charlotte been up to? Was Bertie looking for a successor to Compton already?

"I'll send her home to-morrow," I told myself with alarm, "garden hat or no garden hat. Before she gets into any serious mischief."

I caught up with the others as they waited for the lift, and one of them said awkwardly: "Sorry about Mac, Maggie, It was a terrible shock to us all, but it must be worse for you."

I thanked her briefly, not wishing to open a way for any questions. I think that they saw my reluctance. No one queried me that night, except on matters of switching.

It was after midnight when the relieving started, and I saw to it that I would be the last. I wanted a clear coast before I began rifling Mac's locker. Presently the last girl came back. Slipping from my chair, I strolled casually up the room, despite the fact that my heart was beating hard. Once out the door, I stripped off my headset and dashed up the stairs to the eighth floor. It was, as I expected, dimly lit. My running feet echoed uncannily. It was almost as if someone was approaching in the opposite direction. I paused outside the cloakroom, trying to still my breathing in order to catch the slightest sound. The floor was very quiet, but for the wail of the rising wind seeping through the ventilators.

I fumbled my way to my own locker without turning on the lights, and felt for the small torch I kept there for use after working late shifts. The battery was getting weak, and flickered several times as I stole round to where Mac's locker was at the bottom of the rack. I didn't dare to glance in the direction of the restroom. There was no difficulty in opening the locker, as my own key, in common with many others, fitted the lock perfectly. I stood the torch upright on the floor so that its failing beam shot up the side of the lockers, and rummaged carefully amongst Mac's belongings.

There was her telephone with the faint perfume Mac always used still clinging to it, and an old cardigan that she kept handy in case the weather changed. Numerous pencils, rubbers and pieces of paper lay on the floor of the locker. I inspected each sheet carefully, but there was nothing to be construed as a secret message. I sat back on my heels, filled with a bitter disappointment. What a reward for our high hopes!

As I started to rise slowly from my cramped position, the stealthy move of a footstep came to my ears. I froze to the spot. I remember thinking to myself how Charlotte could say: "I told you so," as I stood there, paralysed with fear. Suddenly, as I was loosening my throat to scream, every light in the cloakroom flashed on. The footsteps, no longer stealthy, came around the corner of the lockers. I kicked Mac's door shut, just as Bertie Scott came into sight. He stopped short and stared at me, his pince-nez glittering in what seemed to me a fiendish fashion. I gazed back, fascinated. Were these the eyes that Mac had looked into?

Suddenly Bertie advanced. Step by step I backed, my hands feeling behind me. There was no way of escape. The lockers and the wall hemmed me in on three sides, and Bertie was in front. I remembered how empty the eighth floor had looked when I came up. No one would hear my desperate screams. As abruptly as he had moved, Bertie paused. He bent down on one knee like an animal about to spring. His eyes never left my face, as his hand felt for the locker that I had just opened. I began to think that the final show-down had come when a strange thing happened. It was really an anti-climax. There I was, ready to die, and Bertie merely locked Mac's door, held out my key in silence and stood aside.

I crept by him fearfully and, snatching my key, fled out of the cloak-room and down the corridor. There was no need for the girl Jameson to tell me that I was as white as a sheet when I seated myself, panting and trembling in every limb, at the Adelaide board. Who wouldn't be after such an experience?

It was some minutes later when Bertie came into the trunkroom. I heard the creak of the door opening, and then his fussy, short-stepped walk which paused at the Senior Traffic Officer's table. I did not dare look around as he came down the room to where I sat, turning over dockets nervously. His voice sounded over my head.

"Go down to the Tasmanian boards, Miss Jameson, please." My neighbour pulled out her plug and departed.

"Is there any traffic waiting, Miss Byrnes?" he asked, his voice raised slightly, obviously to let the room know what he was saying.

I swallowed hard. "Not much," I managed to croak. "There are a few calls to A.G." I felt his hand come down firmly on my shoulder.

"I would advise you," he said, very softly in my ear, "to concentrate on the work in hand."

It was a warning, without any doubt. He left me sitting bolt upright, his words ringing through my head.

The best antidote for fear, as for many other emotions, is work. I busied myself unnecessarily with the few dockets on the board, writing up elaborate reports on the backs as they were retried. Gradually the trembling left my body. I became calmer and able to think more clearly. Why had Bertie let me escape from him? Not that I wasn't very grateful but his sudden manifestation of mercy was not in accordance with my idea of the murderer. And if Bertie wasn't the murderer, who was he? Then I remembered the suggestion that I had made that afternoon on the golf-house veranda. Was he an accomplice? The one who was directing the movements of the killer, who was in his turn managing the whole business from the outside?

No, Bertie was no murderer. Otherwise he would have removed me quickly as I stood hunted against the wall of the cloakroom. He knew that I had been searching Mac's locker with some ulterior motive. Not that I was any better off for doing so; rather, I was in a worse position now that Bertie's suspicions were aroused. I sighed despairingly, leaning back in my chair with my feet thrust out in front of me. Where else could

Mac have hidden that docket? My eyes wandered restlessly down the boards to where the girl Jameson was filing her nails, and chattering to the Hobart telephonist.

'What on earth do you find to talk about at this hour?' I thought irritably, turning my head to survey the rest of the staff. My glance swept the end of the room, and I saw the sortagraph standing large and untenanted in its corner.

I gazed at it speculatively, and at the filing cabinets beneath. That was where Mac had stood on Saturday night. I could almost see her efficient hands picking up the dockets that fluttered along the revolving belt, and the quick frowning glance she gave them before placing each one with rapid accuracy in its correct receptacle. Before I knew what I was doing, I had pulled my plug out of its socket and had darted down the room.

"If you want to hide a needle, you put it with a whole lot of other needles," I muttered under my breath, reaching for the last file.

A quick upward glance told me that Bertie had gone out of the room again. The others were engrossed in their own affairs. I was safe for a while; time enough to run through Friday's and Saturday's dockets. Although my search was hurried, I was certain that I had not missed anything that might be a message from Mac. Once again, I felt that hopeless, bitter disappointment. My sudden inspiration had seemed so reasonable, and the sortagraph so exactly the place where Mac would have chosen to hide her message.

I stopped short in my slow walk back to my position. Mac might have filed the docket earlier than Friday. That meant it would be amongst those tied together with string and dumped in the basement storeroom. My mind flew back to the evening I met Mac, when I was too excited about my discovery of the hidden door to question her activities. She had just come out of the storeroom, and there was a smudge of dirt below her left cheekbone as though she had put one grimy finger to her face while she thought deeply. That had been an old trick of Mac's. I remembered the would-be casual way in which she had answered me when I asked what she was doing.

"Just hunting around for a docket," were her exact words. But were they to put me off the scent? Had Mac gone down to the storeroom to look for something quite different? The place was full of old bundles of used stationery, and as that day was Friday, surely she wouldn't have filed away her message so soon.

Unless—My brain stopped dead, then groped itself back still further to the beginning of the whole tragedy. Compton! I'd almost forgotten her. She was the cause of the second murder. It was something that Mac had discovered about Compton's death that made the killer strike again.

Mac's statement! What was it she had said again? She had seen Compton going down in the lift with a docket in her hand? No, not that. There was something else; another docket, the one that I had seen Compton poring over in the lunchroom that Wednesday while I ate my cold sandwiches, and then later still on the roof. Compton had filed it herself, muttering under her breath. Mac had caught her words. "That'll fix it," Compton had said.

No one had attached any importance to those words. They seemed meaningless at the time. I knew now that Compton had held in her hand an important document, for the sake of which someone had killed her.

That was why Mac had been acting so strangely. She remembered that docket later, and the careful way in which the late monitor had filed it personally. It was Compton who wanted to hide it, not Mac. She went down to the storeroom in the basement to look for it. But had Mac found it? I shut my eyes tight, trying to capture the scene that had taken place between us. She had not been holding anything in her hand, because if I had noticed that they were grimy, I would have seen it. What frock did she wear that day? She had slept with me the night before, and had gone straight from Mrs. Bates's boarding-house to work, looking cool and fragrant in that printed silk dress with pouch pockets set in the skirt. Mac must have slipped the docket into one when she heard me exploring for the second exit.

I tried to remain calm in the face of my new discoveries, and to put myself in Mac's place. What had she done with that docket? Had she put it back with the others, or taken it home to study it more closely? When the murderer searched her room, was that the evidence he was after? Surely Mac would have realized that something like that would happen, and— what was it John Clarkson had said? Mac would have insured herself against losing it. Perhaps she kept it in her handbag, or concealed about her person. She may have done what Dulcie Gordon did. If so, I knew where that docket was, and it was safe. Once again, I saw Mac's room with the drawers pulled out, and the upturned wastepaper basket with its contents scattered around the room. I felt myself smoothing out those crumpled sheets of pale blue notepaper, and saw each one starting with Clark's name. That was why Mac had found it so hard to write that letter. She was insuring herself by telling someone else what she had learned. Someone whom she knew she could trust.

Without a second's hesitation, I put on my headphone and called the Windsor Exchange to give Clark's number, praying wildly that the sleeping draught had not taken full effect on him yet, and that he would answer my call. If Mac had posted a letter to Clark on Saturday that meant that he would receive it in the morning's mail. But if the killer had reached the same conclusion, he would be waiting outside Clark's flat to get that letter first. I must get hold of Clark to warn him.

"They're not answering, Central," Windsor's voice said boredly.

'You dumb cluck!' I thought, 'If you only knew how important it was to get that 'phone answered, you'd snap out of it."

"Keep trying, Win.," I ordered curtly. "If you raise them, get in touch with Margaret Byrnes in the trunkroom."

"O.K.," she answered lightly.

I dropped my head into my hands, thinking hard. If Clark had taken that dose, he wouldn't awaken for hours; perhaps too late. Glancing at the clock, I saw that it was now 2 a.m., and speculated on trying to reach either Inspector Coleman or the Sergeant.

"They wouldn't love me if I dragged them out of bed at this hour to tell them a theory," I thought with grim amusement. "The best thing that I can do is to slip down to the basement, and see if Mac re-filed that docket. Then I would have a legitimate excuse to rouse them."

Bertie sat at his desk once more, his head bent over papers. I threw him a cautious look, and called gently to Jameson: "Come on Adelaide 5."

She set up the line on her own board by opening a key and tapping out 35 on her dial.

"What do you want, Maggie?" said her voice in my ear.

I glanced at Bertie again, but he hadn't lifted his head as the lines clicked loudly in the silence of the trunkroom. "I want to sneak out without Bertie seeing me. Come up here, and change positions with me. I have more chance of making a dash from the Hobart board."

Jameson turned her head to watch me curiously. "What's the idea? You've just come back from relief." But she arose carelessly, and sauntered towards me swinging her flex by the plug.

"You're a pal," I told her fervently. "There's no work to do. You needn't worry that I was trying to put one over you. See you later."

I sat on the Hobart board for five dragging minutes, but still Bertie did not move.

'Now's your chance,' I muttered, watching out of one corner of my eye as he lifted his telephone and called out a number. Quickly and silently I slipped from the chair and sped behind the delay board to the door opening on to the back stairs. My telephone was dumped on the first step and I took the others in flying leaps.

One would have thought that after my narrow escape with Bertie in the cloakroom, I would have disdained any further adventures that night.

I must confess to a one-track mind. All thought of Bertie, outside wondering if he had already missed my presence, had left me. I wanted a docket from the basement storeroom, and nothing would stop me until I got it. How I expected to recognize it as the one Compton had filed just before her death never entered my head. It was sufficient to say that I knew what I wanted, and even the uncanny half-gloom in the basement caused by the street lights shining through the glass bricks failed to deter me.

I heaved a sigh of relief as the storeroom door opened under the turn of the handle. Thank heaven, it was not locked! The little matter of finding the key would have been most irritating. Even the light went on. I felt that luck was with me as I surveyed the shelves that lined all sides of the room before starting on my search. I found the bundle labelled Wednesday, February 11th, without any trouble, and sank down on to my knees tearing at the string.

Mac said that Compton had filed a docket before she went on relief, so I turned to the bottom of the pile and picked out those timed from 9 p.m. to 10 p.m. Moistening my forefinger, I went through the dockets, but each one appeared a genuine call. None of them held either the signature of Compton or Mac. It was only on glancing through them a second time that I noticed that one had been completed at 5 p.m. I sat back on my heels slowly. Was it an error that a call, connected five hours earlier, should be amongst those of a later hour? Then the calling number leaped to meet my gaze. I stared at it fascinated, unable to believe what my senses told me. It was the same number that I had rung from the power-room with Dan Mitchell. A man had answered that call. A man whom I had identified with an armchair golfer in Riverlea club-house that very afternoon.

Was this the docket that had cost two lives? Had Mac found it, and purposely placed it in its wrong place to avoid detection by the killer? Or had she done so hoping that it would catch the eye of the right person, in case something happened to her before she could reclaim it? It looked innocent enough. But for the number, I would have passed it over. What had Sarah Compton learned about Mr. Atkinson that made her file his call so carefully? Something very grave indeed that would send her to her death. I turned over to the back in a puzzled fashion.

"I'm blowed if I can see anything odd about it," I said aloud, about to rise to my feet.

Before I got both feet to the ground, the storeroom was plunged into darkness. My heart stood still with a terrible fear. Was it Bertie again? Would he let me go this time? Not in my wildest hopes did I expect to get out alive from that room. I could hear someone breathing lightly, and got cautiously on to my other foot, still holding the docket in my hand.

In those few seconds before I heard footsteps approaching me very, very slowly, I thought of a million things. I must do what Mac did. I must hide the docket again. When I am dead, Clark will look for it. He knows.

The footsteps came on. I backed away quietly, my fingers ever feeling for a hiding place, and encountering nothing but bundles of dockets. With a sudden inspiration, I slipped one out of a pile, jamming the docket I held into its place. I continued to creep round the wall. Where was that door? If I could reach it, I would have a chance. Even if it was to open it and scream. Someone might hear me.

Suddenly I could stand the sound of those footsteps and soft breathing no longer. I rushed like a mad woman through the blackness, sobbing under my breath as I banged my fist along the wall in a desperate search for the door. But it was no use. The last thing I remembered was a feeling of triumph as the dummy docket I held in my hand was torn from my grasp.

CHAPTER X

It was very annoying to recall later that I had used precisely the same words as Gloria Patterson when she recovered from her faint. But I had some excuse, as I found myself lying on a hard bed in a room of dazzling whiteness, clad only in a knee-length robe that tied with strings around my neck.

A thin, boyish face studded with freckles bent over me. For one moment I thought it was Sergeant Matheson, until Charlotte's candid remark floated gently into my brain. "Either they've come back very quickly, or else Charlotte couldn't have been seeing too well," I said resentfully. Those freckles worried me, until my eyes travelled over his white-coated figure.

"You're not a policeman, after all!" I exclaimed in triumph. "You're a doctor."

The boy's face crumpled into an attractive smile, that revealed rather buck teeth. Sergeant Matheson had a nice, even grin.

"Not quite," he said modestly. "I'm only a medical student. You had an accident, and they brought you to hospital."

"Who are they?" I demanded, my mind still on Sergeant Matheson. I was going to ring him about something; drag him out of bed for a joke.

"A Mr. Scott brought you into the casualty ward. There was a young lad with him, whom he called Dan."

"Dan Mitchell," I nodded, pleased to be able to remember something. "Was it Bertie who hit me?"

The embryo medico turned my head gently, and started to plaster some evil-smelling ointment on to my forehead.

"I asked you a question," I said reproachfully. He shook his head, smiling, and turned away.

I scowled. "Like that, is it? Where are my clothes?"

He came back quickly to force me down on the bed. It didn't require much effort on his part as I sank back with a groan.

"You're not leaving here for a while," he told me firmly. "Try and get some sleep."

As I opened my mouth to protest, a hypodermic was flourished warningly before my face. "See that! If you don't shut up, I'll give you a plug of dope that will make you sleep. Now turn over, and off you go."

"The room is too light," I grumbled, rolling over on to my side obediently.

When I awoke later, the whiteness was even more glaring. The sun filtered through the frosted windows, and fell in a pattern on the starched coverlet of my bed. While I was studying it in a bemused fashion, a nurse came into the room holding a tray aloft.

"Cup of tea?" she snapped, placing one on my chest at the same time, and whisking off before I had opened my mouth to thank her. The hot liquid felt grand as it flowed down my parched throat. Very warily I raised myself on one elbow. There were half a dozen other beds in my ward, and I grimaced in a friendly fashion to the blowsy-haired woman opposite.

"Feeling better?" she asked.

"Much, thank you. Were you here when I came in?"

"This is my second week," she replied cheerfully. "I stopped a car down town, and didn't remember anything else until the doctor was taking the stitches out of my head. What happened to you?"

"I'm not too sure," I replied, feeling the dressing on my forehead gingerly.

"You made enough row when they brought you in. I knew you couldn't have been hurt much."

"Oh," I said, interested. "I was talking, was I?"

The woman folded the bedclothes in an embarrassed manner. "Of course, I didn't listen to what you were saying. It was about 3 a.m. when they brought you in, and the wards were asleep. But you kept calling out to someone called Clark. They had to put you in another room. You were waking everyone up," she finished in an injured tone.

The woman seemed inclined for conversation as she sipped her tea gustily. I asked her how she came to get run over, and let her ramble on about car drivers' manifold iniquities as I lay back to think. I could remember going down to the basement to look for a docket, but somehow I couldn't fit Bertie in. Did he hit me, and then cart my senseless body off to hospital with the assistance of Dan Mitchell? No, that was wrong. I couldn't see the person who knocked me out. I could only hear that horrible breathing and those creeping footsteps. It couldn't have been Bertie. What happened about that docket? I looked down at my clenched hand, and then opened it slowly. There were one or two tiny spots of paper on the damp palm. I laughed triumphantly.

The patient opposite raised an aggrieved face. "It wasn't funny, I can tell you," she remarked. "The doctor told me that it's a wonder I'm still alive."

"Sorry," I replied. "I was thinking of something else. Go on."

The murderer didn't get away with the right docket. I had swopped it with another in the darkness and foiled him. How angry he would be to discover his mistake, and that it needed a harder blow to penetrate the skull of one Maggie Byrnes. I closed my eyes hard in an attempt to remember every detail. Someone had turned out the light in the storeroom just as I was about to rise, holding the docket on which was inscribed that number that I had allocated to Mr. Atkinson, broker and golfer. Was it he who had struck me down in the darkness? Was that the reason that I could in no way identify my assailant. Supposing that Bertie, after finding me at Mac's locker, rang him and told him of the danger in which they stood. He could have directed Mr. Atkinson to the door opening from the lane, and arranged that I could have been sent to a nice quiet spot to be finished off. Furthermore, if Bertie knew what I was searching for in the cloakroom and had seen me at the files below the sortagraph he might have guessed that my next move would be to continue my search in the basement. Once he saw me leave the trunkroom, he could have advised the murderer as to where I was heading. What would be a better place in which to eliminate me than the lonely, soundproof storeroom? Evidently Mr. Atkinson was so eager to get that docket out of my hand that he did not worry whether he killed me or not. I felt my forehead again. Perhaps he had no suitable weapon to hand, so hurried was the need to stop me, and used his clenched fist.

The fact remained that he didn't get the correct docket. Even if he had, there was always that letter that Mac posted the day of her death. I glanced around the room for a clock, but there was none in sight. I waited until my blowsy-haired friend took a breath, and cut in.

"Have you any idea of the time?"

"It would be about 8 a.m. Do you know that when doctor examined me yesterday, he told me that it was a miracle that I was alive?"

"Yes, I know," I replied. "You told me before. How do I get hold of a nurse or someone? There doesn't seem to be any bell near my bed."

"Just tap on the wall. The pantry is next door, and someone will hear you."

I banged with my fist. Presently a nurse came running in. "What's the trouble?" she demanded, looking down the ward.

"The young lady over there wanted you."

She swung round. "I'm just preparing the breakfast trays. You'll have to wait until the right time."

I looked at her puzzled for a moment before light dawned.

"I only want my clothes," I said firmly. "Where are they?"

The nurse gave me a sharp glance. "Never mind. You're not to get up until the doctor sees you."

I lay back in a turmoil of impatience, biting at my lip. It was essential that I got out of the place, and got hold of Clark. If the murderer had learned of that letter Mac had written, he might go armed to Clark's flat to intercept it. I shuddered, visualizing a short struggle for the letter between the two men, and the sharp sound of an exploding pistol before Clark staggered and crashed face downwards. That must not happen. I couldn't bear to see another twisted figure lying in a pool of blood. I banged hard and urgently against the wall and waited a few minutes, but no white-garbed nurse appeared in the doorway.

"What's the matter, dearie? Can't you wait any longer?"

"No!" I shouted, throwing off the bedclothes, and slipping to the floor. My appearance must have been ludicrous, to say the least, with my long legs bare to the knee. I didn't care. Things were desperate. With a swimming head I managed to negotiate my way to the door, and clung there panting as the nurse came hurrying in, bearing two breakfast trays.

"What on earth do you think you're doing?" she asked angrily. "Get back to bed."

I shook my head, and demanded weakly for the nearest telephone. "I must make a call; in fact, two calls," I added, remembering Charlotte. The poor darling would be out of her mind if she knew that I was in a hospital.

The nurse dropped her trays on one of the beds, and advanced with both arms outstretched. "Come along now."

But I clung to the door defiantly. "Please, nurse," I begged. "You've no idea how important it is that I make those calls."

She slid one arm around my waist, and half-pulled me across the room. "Don't be so foolish," she scolded. "You're in no condition to go rushing about. I'll call whatever people you want and give messages. Climb up into bed again."

I clambered up, and sank down breathlessly. It was amazing how weak a crack on the head could make one.

"Will you ring up at once?" I pleaded.

She handed me a pencil and block from one of her capacious pockets. "Write down the numbers, and the messages you want sent. I'll do it as soon as I've finished with these breakfast trays."

"No, ring them right away," I insisted. "Nurse, you've no idea—"

"All right," she cut in peevishly. "I'm glad you're not a patient of mine for long."

I gave her a warm smile, writing quickly. "Like the rest of your profession, you're an angel in disguise. Here you are."

The woman in the bed opposite remarked to the ward at large after the nurse had gone: "Well, I must say that some people haven't much consideration. Do we have to wait for our breakfast while Nurse Williams makes telephone calls?"

"You don't happen to mean me?" I asked gently. "I'm sorry about delaying everyone's breakfast, but since there are two trays at the foot of your bed I don't think you need worry."

She snorted indignantly, and, not attempting to take my advice, folded her hands with a martyr-like expression on her face.

The nurse came back again. I watched her eagerly as she handed around trays. Finally she came to where I was biting my fingers in feverish anxiety.

"No luck with the first, but your mother said that it would be all right."

"What about Mr. Clarkson? Wasn't the number answering?"

Nurse Williams shook her capped head as she propped me up with pillows. "The girl at the Exchange was terribly rude. She said that she had been trying all night, and not to worry her again. It was the first time that I'd used the 'phone this morning, let alone called that number."

'That must have been the girl I spoke to last night,' I reflected. 'Clark must have taken those deadly pills. He might sleep all the morning and miss the mail.'

I surveyed the sausages before me without interest. What could I do now? Someone must be there to get that letter; someone I could trust. Charlotte? No, I wasn't going to let her run any risks of meeting an armed murderer. I pushed the tray aside, and called to Nurse Williams again. "Get me the police."

She turned round slowly, her mouth open. "Have you gone mad?" she burst out, after swallowing once or twice.

"Get me the police," I repeated stubbornly, "or I'll run out of the hospital like I am, and shout until I find one." I made a move as if to get out of bed again. It caused her to come hastening back.

"Now, look here, dear," she said in the kindly, reasoning tone that nurses seem to keep for refractory patients. "Just you eat your nice breakfast and wait for the doctor. Maybe he'll let you go home."

"It's not a nice breakfast," I said childishly. "I loathe sausages, and I want the police."

My friend across the way spoke up patronizingly: "That's exactly what I said, dearie. Find me the police. I want to give them my side of the story. Those car drivers think they can get away with anything."

Ungratefully, I glowered across at her, thinking: 'I bet it was your own silly, damn fault you got run over.'

I gazed up at Nurse Williams in what I hoped was an appealing manner. "Couldn't you make just one more call?" I coaxed. "Ring Russell Street Police Station, and ask either Inspector Coleman or Sergeant Matheson to come and see me at once. No, wait a minute, it'll be too early for them to be at the office. You'll have to look up their private numbers."

"I am not going to do anything of the kind," she returned. "I've got another ward besides this to give breakfast to. Then I've got to sponge down the patients, and tidy up before the doctors arrive. And you're asking me to spend my time at a telephone."

It was no use. I couldn't make her realize that my request was much more important than washing people unless I gave her all the facts; not that she'd believe me if I did. I tried to stay patient until the doctor arrived. Maybe he would discharge me from the hospital. The sausages tasted like leather. I managed to swallow some buttered toast and another cup of tea, glancing now and then at the clock and praying that the morning mail was not delivered at the flats where Clark lived until late.

At a quarter to nine, I was presented with a bowl of water and two towels, and instructed how to wash myself in bed.

"I'll be back later to do your back," said the nurse, moving off to sponge one of the more incapable patients. I surveyed the water distastefully, but set about the job, trying to keep in mind the instructions. The bowls and towels having been removed and the ward swept and dusted, the door was thrown open for the doctor. He came in with a retinue of medical and masseur students, and began the round of the beds. When they came to mine, the doctor turned to the curious group around him and said: "There is nothing of any medical interest in this case."

I felt like a butterfly squirming on a pin as he stepped forward to take my pulse.

"Well, young lady?"

"Very well, thank you, doctor," I retorted, and heard a snigger from the group. "I want to go home."

"All in good time. How's the head?"

"Just fine. Would you mind telling that dumb nurse to bring me my clothes?"

He shook his head gravely. "I want you to stay here until midday at least. Then we'll see how your temperature is."

"You haven't got a hope in Hades," I replied. "Once more, where are my clothes?"

"You're a very curt young lady," said the doctor reprovingly. "What's the matter with you?"

"Nothing," I shouted. "That's why I want to leave."

"Very well," he said, signalling to the others to move on. "I'll write out a discharge. Nurse Williams," he called. She came hurrying over, glancing at me suspiciously. "Find this young lady her clothes. She can go home."

"Certainly," she replied, so promptly that I gave her an offended look.

When she returned to dump my belongings at the foot of the bed, I remarked gently: "I think that you're glad to get rid of me."

"I am," she snapped, "and the next time someone hits you on the head, I hope that they make a better job of it. Good-bye."

I climbed gingerly into my clothes, trying to avoid the dressing on my forehead. My head still ached intolerably. It wasn't until I strolled automatically to the nearest mirror that I realized that my handbag was missing. Loss of make-up was a minor matter in face of the fact that I was without a penny. One can't do anything in this world without money. I was prepared to sit down helplessly when I remembered the calls that I had asked Nurse Williams to make. I bade a fond farewell to my friend in the bed opposite, and made my way to the entrance of the hospital. There I found a small room partitioned off by a counter. A girl sat at a large switchboard manipulating plugs and cords.

"Hullo," I said. "I think I know you. I work at Central." She glanced at the plaster on my head curiously. "Just a disguise," I explained hurriedly. "Your name doesn't happen to be Doris?"

The curious look deepened. "That's right. Who are you?"

"Margaret Byrnes. Could you trust me at that board for a while?"

She looked at me doubtfully. "Margaret Byrnes?" she queried.

"Maggie," I said suddenly on an inspiration.

"Oh—Maggie. Sure, come right in. But if you only want to make a call, I'll put you through on the public telephone over the way."

"Thanks very much. As a matter of fact, I had an accident last night and I haven't got any money." I gave her the number of Russell Street Police Station. She raised her brows, but made no comment. I went across to the P.T.

"Inspector Coleman or Sergeant Matheson," I requested. "It's very important," and waited.

"I'm sorry, but they are both very busy. Would anyone else do?"

"No," I said firmly. "Tell them that Miss Byrnes wants to speak to them."

There was another pause, and then a click, and a slow voice said: "Miss Byrnes? This is Police-Officer Roberts. What is it you want?"

"Your superiors," I retorted. "I've got something very important to tell them."

There was another silence. I could see Roberts scratching his head in perplexity.

"I've got strict instructions not to disturb them, even for the Commissioner himself," he pronounced in his slow voice. "Wouldn't I do instead?"

"Wait a minute while I think."

His heavy breathing came over the wires as I speculated on what was best to do. Time was getting short, and it was imperative that someone should be at Clark's flat as soon as possible, in case he was still under the influence of the sleeping drug. Blast those two policemen and their high and mighty way in which they were not to be disturbed.

"Yes, you'll do," I said at last. "Listen carefully, Police-Officer Roberts, or whatever it is you call yourself."

"You can call me plain Roberts, Miss, if you like."

"Many thanks. It'll save time. Can you leave whatever it is you are doing, and come down to the Royal Melbourne Hospital? Don't start asking questions as my head is nearly splitting already. Just come. I'll be waiting for you at the main entrance." I rang off without giving him time to demur.

"Thanks, Doris," I called, putting my head out of the box. "Will you give me a line to Windsor now?" But Clark's telephone still remained unanswered. I hung up slowly, beginning to feel uneasy. Surely he couldn't still be asleep.

The first thing I asked Roberts was whether he had any money. After a moment's hesitation he took off his tall helmet and produced several five-pound notes from the crown.

"That should be enough," I remarked dryly. "Now go and hail that taxi. I want to get to South Yarra in a hurry."

Roberts seemed in no way surprised at my high-handed behaviour. He must have been used to girls demanding his escort, so unchanged was his phlegmatic expression. It was only when we were bowling swiftly down town that he asked in a disinterested fashion: "What hit you, Miss?"

"The murderer," I retorted. "But I can't explain now. There isn't time," and I leaned forward to give the taxi-driver some directions.

Roberts did not open his mouth again until we drew near the block of flats where Clark lived.

"What are we going to do?" he asked.

"See if Mr. Clarkson is all right," I replied grimly. "I have been calling him all night, but he doesn't answer his 'phone. I also want to have a look at the contents of his letterbox."

Roberts seemed a trifle shocked. I hastened to explain my reason for wishing to interfere with the King's mail. He nodded solemnly as the taxi swerved around a corner into South Street. The driver muttered under his breath as he pulled the wheel sharply to dodge a car parked on the wrong side of the street.

"I'd like to report the swine who owns that car," he said. "I nearly crashed into him."

I had a good look first to see whether it was the one Clark usually drove, and suggested that as one of his passengers was a policeman he go right ahead.

"That looks like the owner getting in now," I began, as a man came hurrying out of the flats. My heart leaped in excitement. "Don't stop your engine," I commanded. "Let me get out; then follow that car. Roberts, you stay here and detain that man when you catch him."

"But, Miss!" he protested.

"Do as I say," I said fiercely. "It's vitally important."

I wrenched open the door and jumped on to the pavement. "Quickly. He's headed for town."

The taxi-driver waved to me in a reassuring manner as he swung the taxi round again and sped after the car. I watched them turn the corner, Roberts leaning forward with both arms resting on the front seat. Evidently his blood was up.

The group of mail-boxes caught my eye as I ran for the stairs. As I opened Clark's my heart sank. There were two letters, but neither bore Mac's writing. We had been beaten after all. Clutching them in one hand, I flew up the stairs and pounded on the door. There was no answer. A woman in the flat opposite put her head out. I asked whether she had seen or heard Mr. Clarkson that morning. She shook her head, eyeing me curiously as I banged at the door again. When I was just about to give up, the taxi still containing Roberts stopped at the kerb.

"Did you get him?" I cried, running to the edge of the stairs, and leaning over the banister.

He made no reply until he joined me outside Clark's door. "He got away; dodged down a side street." I thought that he looked a trifle disgusted.

"Mr. Clarkson hasn't answered his door either," I told him, troubled. "What will we do?"

Roberts gave the lock one keen glance, and drawing out what looked like a large hairpin told me to stand aside. Presently there was a click. He turned to me saying simply: "I can usually open them."

"Clark," I called from the doorstep. But there was no reply. I walked cautiously along the hall to the closed door of his bedroom. I said his name again, but the only sound that came to my ears was the steady tick of the clock standing in the hall. Swiftly I threw open the door and walked in, Roberts close on my heels. Clark was lying face down across the bed, clad in the clothes that he had worn the previous day at golf. Even his feet were still shod in rubber-soled brogues.

"John," I whispered, staring at his back. Was it my imagination, or was there a movement of breathing? Roberts strode quickly over, and put one hand on his shoulder, My heart leapt again as I saw Clark stir. Raising himself on his elbows he stared for a moment in a dazed fashion at the policeman, and then sank back.

"Come on, sir," said Roberts, shaking his arm. "Wake up." He helped Clark to sit up. His eyes were dull as he stared across at the door where I stood, nearly sick with relief.

"Maggie?" he said. His voice was thick. I went swiftly across the room, and knelt on one knee before him to look up into his face.

"Are you all right?" I asked, choking a little.

He nodded. A shadow of a smile came into his eyes. "Those damn pills," he said hoarsely. "I took three of them. They certainly work."

I laughed with the sheer joy of finding him alive. "Get under a shower at once," I ordered. "I'll make some coffee. Hurry, Clark. There are such a lot of questions I want to ask you."

Glancing down, he saw the two letters that I still clasped in my hand, and tried to take them from me with fumbling fingers. I disengaged myself gently, and rose to my feet.

"Later," I said. "Roberts, will you help Mr. Clarkson while I am in the kitchen?"

Clark did not seem surprised to find either of us in his flat, but accepted the situation as if it was quite normal. I put it down to his dazed condition. If I had felt it was my second time on earth after taking two sleeping tablets, what must Clark be like after a triple dose? I heard the shower running as I made coffee and toasted some bread. By the time I had loaded a tray and carried it into the lounge-room, the two men were waiting, Clark's dark hair gleaming wet under the sunlight that streamed through the unopened windows. I poured out a cup of strong black coffee and gave it to him in silence, passing on to throw open the windows. The air outside was humid, but at least it was better than the close atmosphere that pervaded the flat. As Clark drank his coffee, Roberts stood quietly against the wall holding his helmet in his hands, his countenance still unmoved. I watched a brighter look come into Clark's eyes as he ate some of the toast. Presently he glanced up, trying to grin in his old way.

"What have you done to yourself, Maggie?"

I glanced over his head to a mirror hanging on the wall, and gasped in horror. I had had neither comb nor make-up with which to lessen the effect of the plaster strip on my forehead. Even my dress was crumpled and dusty.

"What happened to your head?" Clark asked swiftly, setting down his cup and coming to stand near me.

"It's a long story," I replied, pushing him gently into a chair, and seating myself opposite. "Sit down, Roberts. By the way, Clark, do you remember Roberts?"

"Just. You were with Inspector Coleman at the Exchange, weren't you? What are you doing here?"

"I brought him," I interrupted. "I thought that something had—I mean I was worried you didn't answer your phone. I've been trying to get you all night from work."

"I didn't hear it," Clark replied. "All I remember is taking those damn tablets, and feeling so wonky that I lay down on the bed. The next thing that I knew was Roberts shaking me. Why did you ring me, Maggie? What has happened?"

"I remembered Dulcie Gordon," I explained. "When I was in Mac's room after it had been searched, I found a lot of notepaper torn up. They were the beginnings of a letter that Mac had been trying to write to you. I wondered if she had posted a letter to you, explaining everything. Clark, I think she had. Only that man got here before us and took it out of your letterbox."

"What man?" he demanded. "Take it quietly, Maggie. I can't think too well, yet."

"Mr. Atkinson. We saw him drive off just as we arrived. Roberts followed the car, but he got away. Clark, he must be the murderer."

"Atkinson! Don't talk nonsense. How can he have killed Compton and Gerda?"

"If he had an accomplice working in the Exchange, he could have come through that door I told you about. I think that that is what he did last night."

Clark looked up, his eyes sweeping my face and coming finally to rest on the ornament on my forehead.

"Did he do that?" he asked in a low, hard voice. "Maggie, are you sure that you're all right?"

I nodded happily, and told him about the discovery I had made in the basement storeroom, and the subsequent events that led up to my precipitous appearance in his flat.

"Will you be able to find that docket again'?" he asked dubiously. "Atkinson might have had another search, when he saw that the one he snatched from you was the wrong docket."

"He might have," I acknowledged, "but it was about two in the morning when he knocked me out. Bertie and Dan Mitchell must have found me soon after, as I was in hospital before 3 a.m."

Roberts spoke slowly: "Excuse me, sir, but I think I'd better ring Headquarters and get them to pick up this man."

"Certainly! You'll find my telephone around that door. I wonder how Bertie came to find you, Maggie?" Clark said, as we heard Roberts dialling in the hall.

"He'd had his eye on me all night. I searched Mac's locker first, and he caught me. I was terribly scared, but he didn't say a word until I went back to the trunkroom. Then he came up and said in a horrible voice that it would be better if I kept my mind on switching. Clark, could he be the person who was working with Atkinson?"

"His behaviour is suspicious," Clark agreed, "but what I can't understand is why you think that Atkinson committed the murders. What possible connection could he have with Sarah Compton, and—and Gerda?"

"Mac was removed because she discovered something about Compton's death. She either guessed or knew who the inside person was. As for Compton, we all knew what type of woman she was; always prying into other people's business. Supposing she found out about some shady deal that Atkinson was up to, and threatened blackmail?"

Clark frowned, but made no reply. Outside in the hall, I could hear Roberts's slow voice saying with monotonous regularity: "Yes, sir," and "No, sir," and finally "Very good, sir," as he hung up.

"Sergeant Matheson is coming right away. I have orders to keep you here until he arrives," he announced from the doorway.

I got up to gather Clark's cup and plate. "I won't run away," I promised, backing into the swing door that led to the kitchen. Clark followed me leisurely.

"I never knew how domesticated you were, Maggie. What a good wife you'll make some lucky man!"

I grimaced, trying to disguise the sudden flush that crept into my face.

"Don't say that. With my unpowdered skin, it makes me feel worse. Where are your tea-towels?"

Clark pulled open the drawers, one after the other. "Damned if I know! An old woman usually comes in every day to do for me. Wait a minute, Are these what you want?"

"Yes, they're correct. You can use them while I wash these dishes. Why didn't she come in today?" I asked, pouring hot water into the stainless-steel sink and soaping vigorously.

"She has every second week-end off," Clark replied. "I wonder why that flat-foot friend of yours is coming here?"

"To cross-examine us," I answered cheerfully. "Are you sure that that's all the dirty plates?"

"Stop being so energetic. You make me feel worse."

"Head and tongue like cotton-wool?" I asked knowingly. "What on earth possessed you to take three tablets? I found two more than adequate."

"I wanted to make sure," he replied, following me back into the lounge-room. "I wish you'd sit down, Roberts. You've no idea how sinister you appear, standing near the door like that. You need have no fears. Neither Miss Byrnes nor myself feel any desire to make a getaway."

Roberts compromised by perching on the arm of the chair nearest the door, only to rise again as the bell pealed.

"He'll go off you when he sees you without lipstick," Clark warned me. It was nearly more than I could stand. "Hullo, Sergeant. Welcome to my humble abode."

"Good morning, Mr. Clarkson. You've got a very nice place here," and his eyes wandered appreciatively over the room. They came finally to me, seated with my back discreetly to the light.

"Good morning, Miss Byrnes. I believe you met with an accident last night."

"My, how the news gets around! When did you learn about it?"

Clark motioned, him to be seated, and he chose a straight-backed leather chair, staring full into the sun. I wondered why he was not more careful, if he freckled easily.

"There was a report on my desk when I came in. Mr. Scott had telephoned early this morning."

"Bertie!" I exclaimed incredulously. "The cheek of the man. It was he who hit me; or at least he had something to do with it."

The Sergeant raised his brows inquiringly. "What makes you say that?" he asked.

I told him the same story that I had related to Clark, preceding it with my new discovery, in the shape of Mr. Atkinson.

Sergeant Matheson glanced at his henchman. "Was this the man you rang Headquarters to pick up?"

Roberts replied cautiously. Evidently, years of association with criminal inspectors had taught him not to commit himself. "It is, if the young lady is talking about the same man as the one she told me to follow this morning."

"What description did you give them?"

Roberts half-closed his eyes. "About six feet, fair-haired, driving a blue sedan, number 68,749," he rattled off.

Sergeant Matheson wrote it down in his notebook and, tearing out the sheet, handed it to the policeman. "'Phone these further particulars through. Would you mind, Mr. Clarkson?"

"Go right ahead," Clark replied, waving his hand. "I'll send my next quarter's bill in to Russell Street."

The Sergeant's face remained expressionless. I felt annoyed at his lack of humour.

"This docket you found, Miss Byrnes? I understand that it will be quite easy to trace?"

"I don't know on which pile it will be, but it will be the first; that is, if Mr. Atkinson or one of his associates didn't remove it later."

"In that case I won't trouble you to come into town. If you don't mind me saying so, you look very off-colour this morning. I advise you to go home to bed."

I felt Clark shake gently beside me, and dug my elbow into his ribs.

"Just one other matter before I go," continued the Sergeant. "Mr. Clarkson, are you certain that Miss MacIntyre wrote a letter to you before she died?"

"There is a possibility," Clark admitted. "The theory is Miss Byrnes's, not mine."

I hastened to explain the torn-up sheets of notepaper that I had found in Mac's room. "Mac might have remembered Dulcie Gordon and imitated her. After all, it would have been the safest way."

"That's all very well," said the Sergeant irritably. "The best move would have been to tell the police."

"Did you look in your own mail this morning?" I asked pointedly.

"No communication was received from Miss MacIntyre," he replied, rising to his feet. "That's all for the moment. It only remains for us to trace this man Atkinson, and see what he has to say for himself."

Clark got up to escort him to the front door, but I remained where I was.

"By the way, Miss Byrnes," he said casually from the doorway, "if you care to come up to the Exchange this afternoon, you can see those statements. Inspector Coleman will be in his usual room. Good-bye."

I heard his light steps going down the brick stairs outside, followed by the heavy plodding of Roberts. Presently a car drove off.

"What statements?" Clark asked, coming back. "Maggie, you're to go home at once. You look fit to drop."

"So the Sergeant observed," I retorted. "Will you come in with me this afternoon? You remember how there were eight people left on the floor after that awful game of yours. It is their statements that I want to read."

Clark stood directly in front of me, looking down.

"Can't you drop out of the business now, Maggie? You're killing yourself. After all, it is a police job."

"As long as no one else does the killing, I don't mind," I remarked grimly, and suddenly stretched myself, yawning. "I'm tired, but I seem to have been in that state for the past week. Have you ever got that way when your brain feels stretched to its limit, and liable to snap at any minute?"

Clark looked troubled, "You're heading for a breakdown." I got up swiftly, and had to cling to the edge of a table as my head swam suddenly.

"Nonsense!" I replied. "I'm not going to rest until they find out who killed Mac. And that's final. Can you lend me some money? My handbag is still in my locker at the Exchange."

"I'll get you a taxi," declared Clark, and ignored my feeble protest. "You'd never get home without one. Does your mother know what has happened?"

"Not yet," I confessed. "I phoned from the hospital to say that I was delayed in town. I suppose she'll shriek when she sees the lump on my head. Will you call round, or will I meet you at the Exchange?"

"The invitation wasn't issued to me," Clark pointed out. "But I may come in, even if it's just to annoy Sergeant Matheson. Don't bank on it, as I have a few things to do in town."

"Why should your being there annoy him?" I asked indignantly. "After all you did for them on Saturday night?"

Clark shrugged. "He has a nasty look in his eye whenever he speaks to me; in fact, he reminds me somewhat of your psalm-singing landlady."

"Well, if I don't see you this afternoon, I will to-night. I suppose I'd better work. It may take my mind off things."

I found Charlotte attacking Mrs. Bates's zinnia bed with a dutch hoe, and called out to her in a cheerful manner that I was far from feeling. She dropped the hoe, and came running over the lawn.

"Maggie Byrnes, where on earth have you been?"

"In hospital," I replied. "Do you mind if we go inside. The sun is making me feel a bit sick."

My mother gave the dressing on my forehead one troubled look, and guided me upstairs to her own room. It was cool there.

"On to the bed," she commanded, making a nest of pillows, "and no talking until you've had a rest."

"Don't you want to know how I came to be in hospital?" I asked, baffled at her lack of curiosity.

"I already know. That nice Mr. Scott rang me this morning. As a matter of fact, he caught me under the shower. Shall I pull down the blind?"

"Did you say nice?" I asked incredulously, raising myself on one elbow. As if it wasn't bad enough to be told by your Senior Traffic Officer that your mother was a remarkable woman, without her more or less reciprocating his sentiments!

"I thought that you'd have been home ages ago," she scolded. "When I rang the hospital, they said that you'd left. Where have you been?"

"At John Clarkson's flat," I said, suddenly very weary. I felt that it was almost impossible to go into lengthy explanations just then. "Let me rest a while, and then I'll tell you everything."

"I'll call you for lunch," she promised, tip-toeing out and closing the door quietly behind her.

I clasped my interlocked fingers against my forehead, trying to still the tight throbbing pain that seemed my whole world. Presently I fell into a restless doze that only increased the feeling of fatigue when I awoke. Charlotte was very sweet and understanding, but it was necessary to keep myself tightly curbed to avoid answering her questions irritably. I had given her the barest outline of my adventures, and, not unreasonably, she was dissatisfied with it. But my brain felt incapable of deducing and theorizing just then. After a while she forbore any more questions and left me in peace. However, she protested strongly against my decision to go into the Exchange that afternoon for the purpose of examining the statements.

"You are knocking yourself out," she remarked, as she followed me into my bedroom while I got dressed. "What do you hope to get out of it?"

"The murderer. The person who killed Mac. Charlotte, please be patient. I promise you that I'll go to bed for a week after everything is finished."

"But the case may go on for months," said my mother despairingly. "You'll never stand the strain."

I paused in making up my face, and noticed that the hand that held the lipstick shook slightly.

"I can and I will," I said stubbornly, finishing the outline of my mouth. I leaned forward to survey the bruise on my forehead in the pink-tinted mirror, and remembering my attempt at a new coiffure in the golf-house cloakroom the day before, I combed my hair forward loosely so that the lump was partly hidden. It was ridiculous how different my face looked; the new hairdo seemed to alter the contours and features.

"If ever I want to disguise myself I'll remember this way," I said to Charlotte, drawing her attention to my hair. She surveyed it critically.

"It doesn't suit you," she announced. "You look like that Patterson girl." Which remark was really rather extraordinary in the face of an incident which happened not very much later.

＊ ＊ ＊ ＊ ＊

It occurred going up in the lift at the Exchange, when I was caught in a crowd of mechanics coming on the afternoon shift. I got far back, knowing that they would get out before me. After a half-hearted glance to see if Dan Mitchell was amongst them, to thank him for what he did the night before, I dropped my eyes to the floor. Not that I actually knew what it was, but he may have been able to throw some light on the identity of the person who had hit me. Leaning against the wall of the lift with my head sunk wearily, I wondered in a vague way why Bill hadn't given me his customary greeting. Had the police interviewed him, and told him that it was I who had laid information against him? I watched his one hand manipulate the lever that brought us to a standstill outside the eighth floor. It was odd how one noticed people's hands. They seemed so much more to blame for acts of violence than their brains. Was it just that one hand, now sliding open the doors to let me get out, that was responsible for two deaths?

Bill spoke very quietly as I came forward. His words made me stop to look down at him in amazement. He was fiddling with the shutters on the board in front of him, and his head was turned away as he said sternly: "I am going to tell the police, Gloria. It is better to do so than to let them find out for themselves."

I stood there speechless, one foot on the floor of the lift, the other on the eighth floor landing. Presently he glanced up, and his plain, pleasant face became suffused with a dull colour. Was it anger or embarrassment? Even in spite of my bemused state of mind, I was sure that it was the latter.

He said confusedly: "Miss Byrnes? I thought you were—that you were someone else." His laugh was unnatural and without mirth.

I made some noncommittal reply, and stepped out. The doors closed sharply behind me and the lift descended, leaving me standing still dazed on the landing.

The whole incident only took a few seconds, but in that time I had learned that Bill knew Gloria well enough to address her by her Christian name, and that he shared the knowledge that she had held secret for the last few days. Would his mistake make him change his decision to go to the police; the fact that he had taken me for Gloria, and thereby letting something slip that was meant for her ears alone, weaken his determination? I could tell the police what happened myself, but how far would that help, if Bill suddenly refused to talk?

The two men were seated in that same hot, little room, as if they had never left it since that first terrible night of Compton's murder. Inspector Coleman rose as I entered, and beyond a quick glance at the plaster half-hidden by my hair, made no comment on the nature of the accident. Evidently he had no desire to waste time, as he knew that Sergeant Matheson had taken down all particulars concerning my adventure in the basement. However, it was he who told me that Dan Mitchell was responsible for getting me to hospital so quickly. Dan had slipped down to the basement to get something from his locker, when he noticed the door of the storeroom ajar and the figure of a girl sprawled across the threshold. I must have fallen against the door when the unknown assailant struck.

"We haven't succeeded in tracing this man Atkinson," said the Inspector. "When a squad of plain clothes men went down to the office where he conducted his business, they found it picked clean. He must have been warned that we were on his tracks."

"Did you find that docket?" I asked eagerly. It was put into my hand without a word.

Although I scanned it carefully, my decision was as before. It seemed a perfectly harmless piece of paper, recording a call to Sydney to a man called Brown.

"Can you make anything of it?" asked the Inspector hopefully. "I am afraid that we have to confess ourselves baffled. What is it about that docket that made the killer so anxious to have it in his own hands?"

I turned it over, and read the telephonic code on the back. Mr. Brown had been rather elusive. First of all, his number was engaged then not answering, and lastly he wasn't in. Nearly the whole of the back of the docket was written on. I turned back to see if the call was finally completed, and saw something very odd indeed. It was such a small thing. It puzzled me until I realized what a tremendous significance it held.

"I *can* make something out of it," I told them. Slowly, trying to keep the excitement out of my voice. I placed the docket down on the table and inspector Coleman came to look over my shoulder.

"See these," I said, pointing out the remarks made in our own telephonic code. "Mr. Atkinson had a great deal of trouble trying to get hold of a man called Brown in Sydney. When his 'phone was not engaged, it was W.D.A. That means that the wanted subscriber's number is not answering. When the phone was answered, Mr. Brown himself was not in—P.P.U., which is particular person unavailable. Mr. Brown was unavailable for a long time according to this side of the docket, but," I continued, turning it over and putting the tip of my forefinger under the time that the call was booked, "this call was recorded at 4.58 p.m., connected five minutes later, and completed at 5.6 p.m."

"You mean that if the remarks on the back are genuine, the call couldn't have gone on in that space of time?"

"Exactly," I replied, not attempting to keep the triumph out of my voice. "Furthermore, someone must have seen to it that his call went to the top of the pack. The delay on the Sydney lines at that time of day is always well over an hour. Mr. Atkinson was a very privileged man indeed, if he didn't have to wait for that hour."

The silence that fell was intense.

"Whose signature is that?" asked the Inspector presently, indicating the number at the bottom of the docket. It was then that I received one of the many shocks that the whole affair dealt me. At first, I couldn't believe my eyes. But there it was in black and white.

"It's—why, it's my own," I stuttered. "But that is not my writing. I know nothing about it."

"Are you sure?" asked the Inspector gravely. I fairly boiled with rage at the nerve of the person who had used my numerical signature on a docket that the police regarded with suspicion. Then I saw the twinkle at the back of the Inspector's grave eyes, and relaxed a little.

"Wait until I get my hands on whoever was responsible for that docket!" I exclaimed darkly.

Inspector Coleman returned to his chair, taking the docket with him.

"I hope that you never will," he said, and his voice was grim. I remembered his first description of the man for whom they were hunting and shivered. The memory of those stealthy footsteps that stalked me down in the blackness of the store was still vivid.

"This man Atkinson," I demanded. "What exactly is his business? Mr. Clarkson could only tell me that he was a broker. Beyond having heard one or two whispers as to his method of dealing, that is all he knows."

Inspector Coleman did not look up as he answered. "He is a broker," he agreed suavely, "but the term covers a varied amount of business interests."

"That is what I said," I remarked eagerly. "But have you found out any particular one which would connect him with someone in the Exchange?

This man Brown in Sydney, for example. What is his business?"

The Inspector searched amongst his papers, his face expressionless. "He is also a broker."

I glanced from him to Sergeant Matheson who was sitting quietly by his side, puzzled. But as soon as I met his eyes, they dropped and he fidgeted with his notebook.

The Inspector drew out a long single sheet, and tossed it across his table. "Those are the statements, Miss Byrnes. I believe you said you wanted to see them."

I picked up the paper automatically, still frankly bewildered. "But—" I began.

"Have you got those reports, Matheson?" asked Inspector Coleman. "Don't worry about us, Miss Byrnes. Just go on with your reading."

"I'm not worrying," I snapped, feeling balked. Why had they suddenly shut up like clams when I asked them about Mr. Atkinson? I turned my attention to the paper in front of me. Quite obviously, I was being fobbed off. The statements were all bald and uninteresting. Probably it was my bemused state that hindered me from reading between the lines, but it appeared that each statement was covered by a strong alibi.

In the first three, signed by Bertie, his wife, and Miles Dunn, was the declaration that they were together for the whole time that they spent on the eighth floor.

As Bertie himself had issued the order that no one was to use the trunk-room floor on Saturday night, the only way he could explain to his guests the working of the new automatic boards was to take them to see the dummy that was kept in the telephonists' classroom. They all declared that they had got there about 9.15 p.m. and had spent no more than a quarter of an hour before returning directly to the danceroom. They had neither seen nor heard anything of a suspicious nature.

The only interesting point that I gleaned by comparing the three statements was that they lost sight of each other soon after their return.

Gloria's remarks only covered about three lines. I was full of admiration for the person who made the précis. She had gone up to the eighth floor for the purpose of checking up on the supper arrangements, but had not stayed more than a few minutes. She did not mention having spoken to Mrs. Smith, and it was that omission that put me on my guard. There was something fishy about Gloria and the cleaner-woman. It hadn't needed Bill to draw my attention to the fact that they were withholding some information from the police. It also seemed that they shared the same knowledge.

The four remaining statements held little interest, although I noticed Dan Mitchell's name amongst them. I glanced through the paragraph which concluded with his signature. He and his partner had used the back stairs from the roof, and walked through the length of the eighth floor to follow another couple by way of a joke. The unfortunate pair they had been shadowing were the newly-engaged couple Clark had congratulated at the commencement of his alibi game.

"They tell me precisely nothing," I said flatly, flicking the sheet across to the Inspector with the tip of one finger and feeling indignant that Clark's good work had been used to no avail.

Inspector Coleman picked it up, holding it at arm's length to regard. "I am not so sure," he replied musingly. "There are one or two possibilities."

"Beyond the fact that Mr. Dunn lost sight of Mr. Scott and his wife immediately after their return to the danceroom, I can't see them."

"Mr. and Mrs. Scott also became separated," interpolated the Inspector gently. I did not miss the significance in his voice in spite of my glowering reflections as to the way they had wasted the result of Clark's invention. I made a mental note not to let Clark know how his effort to help Mac had been of no material use after all. How bitter he would be, on top of his failure to get hold of her letter ahead of Mr. Atkinson.

In the midst of these reflections, Sergeant Matheson was called to the door by a knock. I heard the voice of my friend Roberts.

"Here's Mrs. Smith now, sir. Will you see her?"

Inspector Coleman glanced up quickly. "Bring her in. Sit down, please. No, not in that chair; the one facing me. Perhaps if Miss Byrnes wouldn't mind moving over a little?"

"Certainly," I replied, shifting my chair against the wall, and regarding the Inspector with renewed interest. Just as I was beginning to feel disgusted with his methods, he had introduced what I considered one of the most important figures of the case. The elusive Mrs. Smith!

I studied her closely for perhaps the first time, and saw a middle-aged woman of the type that doesn't attract undue attention. She was fairly tall, with dark greying hair and a heavily lined face, set now in a sullen expression. She wore the white overall which was usually the dress of the women who attended the cafeteria. It puzzled me slightly, as hitherto she had always been on the cleaning staff. By lucky chance, the Inspector remarked on it after taking her name and address and making a few routine inquiries.

"Mrs. Smith, I believe that your position in the building is that of a charwoman. How did it happen that you worked in the cafeteria kitchen on the night that Miss MacIntyre was found murdered?"

I saw her fingers interlock as she muttered her reply defiantly. "Mrs. Dobson asked me to. She hated these dance suppers. She always got in a bag."

These were the first words she had volunteered since her entry. As soon as she spoke, a blinding light swept through my brain. The shock of sudden mental sight made me forget my position as an onlooker. I got up from my chair and stood leaning over one corner of Inspector Coleman's desk. Mrs. Smith looked up at me in surprise, and then her eyes flickered once or twice fearfully. I think she guessed her mistake.

"You were a telephonist at one time," I declared.

"I don't know what you're talking about," she whispered.

"Yes, you do," I insisted. "Only a telephonist would use that expression 'in a bag'."

I straightened up and faced the Inspector. "For months now, ever since the first time that I heard this woman speak, I have been troubled by a sense of familiarity about her. Now I know. It was not her appearance that I recognized, but her voice. Only a trained telephonist has that type of voice. You can pick them out of a crowd."

"Is this true, Mrs. Smith?" asked the Inspector quietly.

Out of the corner of my eye, I saw Sergeant Matheson look up suddenly from his writing. His eyes met mine, and I think the same thought struck us both. But I was not to be done out of my triumph.

"Smith," I repeated. "Smith! Was that what Charlotte meant? Show me your notes, Sergeant."

Inspector Coleman expostulated a little. "Really, Miss Byrnes! I am conducting this inquiry."

"Just one moment, please, sir," begged Sergeant Matheson. "It was Millicent, Miss Byrnes."

I turned back to the woman, who cowered now in her chair. "Is that your real name?" I asked, holding her eyes. She nodded. "Does the name Irene mean anything to you?"

"No, no," she almost screamed in reply. "I don't know what you're saying. What right has this girl to ask me questions?"

"None at all," responded the Inspector dryly. "But she seems to be succeeding where we are not, so I suggest that she carries on. Well, Miss Byrnes?"

I grinned at him warmly. He was certainly behaving like a sportsman in the face of my audacity.

"Just one other matter, before I explain what I'm driving at," I said, fumbling in my handbag. I was forced to empty the contents on the table in order to find what I was looking for. The two men watched me, and once Sergeant Matheson dived under his chair to retrieve my rolling lipstick.

"This," I said, holding out my hand to Mrs. Smith. "This belongs to you, doesn't it? You dropped it in the cafeteria kitchen, when you crouched behind the counter to overhear what I was saying to Dulcie Gordon. Oh, no, you don't," I added, closing my fist quickly, and tossing a short indelible pencil in front of the Inspector. He picked it up with a broken-off exclamation.

"Too bad you lost it just then," I went on. "You had to find another one to write that anonymous letter I found pushed under the door of my locker."

The woman covered her face with her hands and began to whimper. Perversely, I began to feel a brute, and cursed the soft streak in me. Then I remembered the reason for my bullying and stiffened. What did this woman mean to me? It was Mac's death that I wanted to revenge. Whoever fell in my path was of no importance, in comparison with discovering Mac's killer.

"You'd better own up," I told her shortly. "You gave yourself away when you made to take that pencil. Who are you, and why did you write those letters?"

Mrs. Smith raised her tear-stained face. It was contorted with anger, and her eyes were full of hate. "Damn you!" she choked. "Damn you to hell, you prying smart alec! You'll get what she got. You're just the same; poking into other people's business. And won't I laugh when I see you dead, all battered and the blood streaming out of your face! I'll laugh, do you hear? Laugh!"

She was horrible to listen to, before Sergeant Matheson closed her mouth with his palm. I shrank trembling into a chair.

Mrs. Smith spluttered and clawed at his hand, but the Sergeant didn't release his grip. His face was very grim as he looked down at his victim.

Inspector Coleman said sternly: "Will you be quiet? Or must we lock you up until you cool down?"

Her eyes darted around the room. I flinched as they rested on me for a moment. Gradually the flush went out of her cheeks, and she made a sign with one hand. Sergeant Matheson removed his.

"I'll tell you," she said quietly. "But first, I'd like someone to be here."

"Your lawyer?" asked the Inspector, and she gave him a startled look.

"I don't need a lawyer, I didn't kill those women." Inspector Coleman folded his hands on the table in front of him, and watched her dispassionately.

"I didn't!" she cried shrilly. "Don't look at me like that. I swear I know nothing about the murders. I only wanted Bill here."

I covered my eyes with one hand. It had been inevitable, of course. Bill was mixed up with her somehow, but I had shrunk from the direct truth. Roberts was called in, and came back presently with the liftman. Bill stood in the doorway, his grave eyes, usually so bright and laughing, going slowly from one to the other. I couldn't meet them when my turn came.

"Milly!" he said, coming forward. "What has happened? Have you come to your senses at last?"

"That girl has found out," she replied grudgingly. "I suppose that I'd better tell the police now."

Bill took a chair quietly, facing me from the opposite wall. It was hard trying not to look up, but I dared not read the reproach I knew would be in his eyes.

"I am Millicent Smith," the woman began in a low, unsteady voice. She seemed calm now, and I felt very thankful. Outbursts like the one that had fallen on my head were very wearing to the nervous system. "But I did know Irene Smith. She was my sister."

She paused. My brain slipped ahead, fitting in various facts and different incidents. I longed to speak, to ask her questions that would cement the theory that I had evolved in my brain, but one brief glance at the Inspector made me hold my tongue. He would brook no interference at this stage of the game.

Mrs. Smith went on: "We were both telephonists here, many years ago. Sarah Compton was too. Irene was only a year older than me, and very attractive, while I," and her lips twisted a trifle, "was always plain. No one ever noticed me. In fact, very few realized that I was Irene's sister. She and Sarah became very friendly. But it didn't last when Dan Patterson appeared on the scene. He was only a mechanic, but he was one of the best-looking men I have ever seen. Irene and Sarah both fell in love with him. That was what made them quarrel. He chose Irene, and they got married before he sailed overseas to the war. Sarah did everything she could to stop their marriage. She was mad with jealousy." Here Mrs. Smith raised her head, and I saw a little smile flicker around her mouth. "She needn't have hated Irene so much."

"I told you that Dan was a very attractive man. He was spoilt by all the attention that the girls at the Exchange gave him. Everyone more or less fancied themselves in love with him, Irene included. I think that the only one who really did love him was—myself," Mrs. Smith dropped her head, and I had to lean forward to catch what she was saying. "I used to stay with Irene while Dan was in camp. One week-end he got unexpected leave when my sister was in the country staying with friends. He was very upset to find her away. I think he realized then that I was in love with him. But he didn't care for me. I was there in his home, and he was bitterly disappointed to find his wife gone.

"He went overseas before he knew what had happened. Irene was wonderful to me. She had always protected and mothered me. She promised that when my baby arrived she would adopt it and pass it off as her own. Dan and the rest of the world would never know. But Sarah Compton found out somehow. It has always puzzled me how she did.

"Irene died from influenza before Dan came back from the war, leaving me in her home with the adopted baby who was really my own daughter. Then Sarah wrote to Dan, telling him the true facts of the story. I never saw him again. He wrote once, giving me the deed of the house, and now and then money would arrive, but I never knew where he was. He said that if he received any communication from me, he would tear it up before reading it.

"After a while, when my little girl went to school, I got work again, as a domestic. I dared not go back to Central, fearing that Sarah had spread the story around. Strangely enough, she had not. She was biding her time until the proper occasion arose, and she could revenge both Irene and myself." Mrs. Smith paused again. The silence of the room was only broken by the scratch of the Sergeant's blunt pencil. Her voice was hard as she continued.

"The time came when my daughter started work at the Exchange."

"Is Gloria Patterson your daughter?" asked Inspector Coleman quietly.

She nodded. "You see, Irene had adopted her legally, so her surname was that of her father. When Gloria started at the Exchange, I obtained a position as a charwoman to keep an eye on her. It was Bill who recognised me after all these years, but I knew that he would not give me away."

Inspector Coleman turned his head, his brows raised inquiringly.

"I was a mechanic with Dan Patterson," Bill explained, "and went overseas with him. He received Sarah's letter on the boat coming home, and told me what had happened. He got off the boat in South Africa."

The Inspector returned his gaze to the woman in front of him. "You say that the liftman was the only one who recognized you. What about Miss Compton?"

"I don't think she did at first. Of course, she knew who Gloria was. Anyway, she made no move to attack me openly, but started to play a cat-and-mouse game with my daughter. Gloria told me, and I swore that I'd never let Sarah Compton break up my life again. You see, had Dan not heard that Gloria was my own daughter, he probably would have married me.

"I wrote to Sarah, asking her to meet me one day so that I could beg her not to give Gloria away, but she did not reply. Not once did she come openly to me. If I tried to catch her alone, she would look blankly at me and walk away. I got desperate, and eventually confided to Bill the state of affairs. The lift was his idea, really. Knowing Sarah the way we did, we realised that she would never be able to withstand her curiosity. On Wednesday evening I hid myself in the lift cabin. I knew the shift that Sarah was working, and that she would probably use the lift at some stage or other if I waited long enough."

Mrs. Smith glanced at me. "This girl was with her. I saw them on the roof together, and heard her say that it was time to go back to the trunk-room. I waited until they were nearly at the stairs before I showed myself. I wanted Sarah to see someone, and come up later to investigate. As soon as I heard the power starting, I opened the trap-door in the cabin and dropped a letter through. It contained a warning that I hoped would further induce Sarah to come back."

"And did she?" asked the Inspector swiftly. I sat up tensely, conscious of an approaching climax.

"No," muttered the woman, and her face became sullen again. "I waited for hours, but she didn't come."

The Inspector's voice was as smooth as silk as he asked: "You didn't see her again?" Mrs. Smith shook her head.

"Then how is it," he demanded loudly, "you could give us an accurate description of what Sarah Compton looked like when dead?"

Millicent Smith was an awful fool if she hadn't seen that coming, She gasped and her eyes widened with fear.

"You saw Miss Compton when she was dead in the restroom," declared Inspector Coleman. Her mouth formed words noiselessly. Her eyes never left the Inspector's face.

Bill said slowly: "You'd better tell them, Millicent." But still she made no reply, and Bill went on: "When Sarah Compton failed to go up to the lift cabin, Mrs. Smith decided to go and look for her."

"What time was it?" demanded the Inspector.

"I asked her that," Bill said with a troubled frown, "but she didn't know. It must have been after 11 p.m., because she said that the floor was deserted, and I know that there is usually a staff coming off duty at that time."

Inspector Coleman turned to me. "You and Miss MacIntyre worked the late shift, didn't you?"

"That's right. We were delayed in the trunkroom until about ten minutes after the hour."

Bill looked at me puzzled for a minute, before he said: "That was why Mrs. Smith missed you. Do you want me to go on, Millicent?"

The woman croaked out something unintelligible.

"Her search for Sarah naturally took her to the cloakroom," continued Bill, "She saw her lying on the floor of the restroom and was terrified, especially as she realized that she had no business being in the building at that hour. She hurried down the back stairs and out of the building without raising the alarm."

"Did you see anyone?" asked the Inspector.

Mrs. Smith shook her head. "I heard voices coming up the front stairs. That was why I used the back way."

'That was Mac and myself,' I thought. 'Therefore it must have been after eleven when you found Sarah.'

Inspector Coleman asked: "Does Gloria Patterson still live with you? Was she in when you got home?"

A look of deeper fear came into her eyes. "I don't know," she replied. "But I am sure that she was. I didn't want to upset her, so I didn't look in her room. I swear that Gloria knew nothing about it until I told her in the morning."

I nodded, satisfied. So Mrs. Smith was the aunt with whom Gloria lived. No wonder she could tell me where the murder took place when she came to see me the following morning.

Inspector Coleman reached for his brief case, which stood against one leg of his chair. He opened it and, extracting a creased piece of paper, passed it over to the woman in front of him.

"You have already confessed to writing anonymous letters," he remarked. "Is that one of yours?"

Mrs. Smith unfolded it slowly, a look of bewilderment coming into her face. "No," she replied in a low voice. "I know nothing about it."

I guessed. rather than saw. that it was the one that I had suspected Dulcie Gordon of writing.

The Inspector frowned down at his clasped hands. "Mrs. Smith," he began. "I have to warn you that your position is very unsatisfactory. You have no alibi, either for the murder of Sarah Compton or Gerda MacIntyre. Moreover, you have confessed a motive for desiring the death of Sarah Compton."

"I didn't kill her," she whispered. "I swear that she was already dead when I saw her."

The Inspector ignored her desperate defence. "Did Miss MacIntyre ever approach you during the days between Miss Compton's death and her own?"

"Only once," she replied quickly. "She came up to the kitchen last Saturday night. It was to ask me something about the supper arrangements."

"The murder was committed not far from where you stood," said Inspector Coleman grimly. "Do you still say that you heard no outcry?"

Mrs. Smith hung her head without a word. I felt my body becoming more and more tense.

"Mrs. Smith," went on the Inspector. "Does the name Atkinson convey anything to you?"

"I know no one of that name," she muttered. "Why do you ask?"

"That," returned the Inspector coldly, "is my affair. Perhaps you will be able to help us on this point. Will you give us a fairly accurate description of Dan Patterson?"

"I can't remember," she replied, and her breath came in pants.

The Inspector turned to Bill without a word.

"He was tall; over six feet," Bill said. "Straight features and fair-haired. I think that his eyes were a blue-grey."

"Thank you," said the Inspector. "Would you know him again if you saw him?"

"Yes," replied Bill quietly. "He has the mark of a shrapnel wound on his left arm."

Inspector Coleman thanked him again. He made a brief sign with his hand to Sergeant Matheson, who arose.

Mrs. Smith's voice rose to a scream. "What are you going to do? Where are you taking me?"

I closed my eyes to shut out the sight of that ravaged face, but I could not stop the sound of the Sergeant's voice, repeating that monotonous formula "—and anything you say will be used in evidence against you."

"I didn't kill them!" she shrieked, hanging on to her chair. "You're arresting an innocent person. Bill! Tell them I didn't."

"Be quiet, Millicent," he said sternly. "Pull yourself together. You are only being detained for further questioning because you have no alibi. Go quietly now, and I'll do all I can to help." He helped to lead her from the room.

I stayed where I was, spent and weary, and slumped in my chair. It was all over. They had found Mac's killer, but somehow I didn't feel as jubilant as I should. A hand touched my shoulder.

"Maggie!" I opened my eyes, and saw John Clarkson looking down at me. Tears of sheer exhaustion started to pour down my face.

"They sent me to find you, Maggie."

"They've arrested Mrs. Smith," I started to explain incoherently. "She's Gloria Patterson's mother. They think that Mr. Atkinson is Dan Patterson."

"Hush!" Clark put a hand on my mouth. "Come and get some air, Maggie. You'll feel better."

"Not on the roof," I shuddered. "It reminds me of Sarah. This was about the time when I saw her there on the day she was killed."

Clark drew me to my feet. "Nonsense. Come and I'll give you something more pleasant to remember."

"I want to go home," I said forlornly.

"No, Maggie," he insisted. "Come upstairs for a little while. You're in no fit state to go home."

I allowed myself to be led up the back stairs to the roof. The air was still and hot. The north wind had dropped, and the sky was banked with heavy black clouds.

"It will change soon," said Clark. I nodded eagerly in anticipation of a cold wind that would bite through my thin dress, and the heavy drops of rain which would fall on my hot body. A low growl came out of the south.

"A thunderstorm!" I said excitedly. "Let's wait for it."

We leaned over the rail of the parapet as the sky grew darker above us, and watched the heart of the city waiting for the elements to disturb the furnace of heat. The buildings were shrouded in the gloom of the approaching storm. Directly below me lay the dump-yard where they had found the buttinsky that had killed Compton. I shivered, and glanced involuntarily over my shoulder to where the lift cabin stood black against the sky.

"What is it?" Clark asked quickly.

"I was thinking of Sarah Compton," I replied. "That dump-yard down there reminded me of the way in which she was killed."

"Don't think," he said, and I searched for his face through the gathering darkness.

"It was odd the way a buttinsky was chosen for the job," I went on presently. "You know, somehow it strikes a familiar chord in my mind. Like the time I saw Sarah lying on the floor of the restroom. It was almost as though I expected it."

A flash of lightning lit Clark's face palely and another clap of thunder sounded, but still the rain held off. The air was wet with humidity, and my clothes were beginning to cling to my body. I stared musingly down to where the yard was now a black well.

"Very odd," I said half to myself. "I wonder if that is what I have been trying to remember all these days."

I felt Clark's shoulder touch my head as he stood directly behind me.

"What are you talking about?" he demanded, and his voice sounded harsh in my ears. "What is it you remember?"

"I don't know," I confessed, smiling up at him, "but it is something about a buttinsky. If I thought hard and long enough, maybe I'd remember all. Gosh! That was a beauty!"

A jagged fork of lightning split the southern sky, and its accompanying thunder sounded closer.

"It won't be long now," I remarked, glancing at the set white face above me. Was it a trick of the light, or did I see faint beads of perspiration clinging to Clark's upper lip? When he met my gaze, he placed his hands either side of me on the railing, hemming me in completely. There was something odd and intense in his eyes that made my heart skip a beat, and then continue at a harder pressure.

"Margaret!" he began, I thought his big body trembled, and felt sorry for him. Surely it was not going to be hard for him to say. I laughed softly and encouragingly. Clark's hands left the rail and gripped my waist.

"Don't laugh, damn you!" he said, between clenched teeth. His body shook again, but this time it did not stop. I knew something was wrong then, when the grip on my flesh tightened and the big man behind me trembled violently. I struggled to escape.

"What are you doing?" I panted. as I felt myself lifted from my feet. "John, have you gone mad?"

His laugh was a horrible sound. "I'm doing something that I should have done days ago. Let go that rail. It's no use, Maggie. I knew that you'd remember sooner or later."

But I clung on tighter than ever. The thunder crashed down again. My ears were filled with a sudden roaring, as though the thunder was continuous. The next flash of lightning lit a face which I was not to forget for many years.

Somewhere in my brain a voice was saying over and over: 'Clark! He's mad—he's going to kill you.'

But it couldn't be Clark who was trying to loosen my grip on the railing, tearing and biting at my knuckles. It was an animal. A mad, raving beast. I heard my own sobbing breath, and felt my tired muscles weakening at every second, while the stranger who was pushing me over the parapet grew stronger and stronger.

The days rolled back before my eyes during those desperate seconds, and I remembered my imaginary fall through the glass of the basement. There would be no crash of glass this time; only a dull, sickening thud as my body would hit the scrap-iron that filled the yard below. My world was one of thunder and lightning, and a sea that seemed to sweep up to my very feet. I was so tired, so very weary of waiting for the end. I let go the railing and sank slowly, wafting here and there like a feather, into the blackness.

CHAPTER XI

'Complete mental exhaustion,' they diagnosed, charitably vague. But I thought that I knew better, and complained to Charlotte of the iron bars at my window, and the handleless taps in the bathroom.

"I know, darling," she sighed, "but it was the only place the doctor could get you in. You know how things are nowadays."

I looked at her straightly. "Tell me one thing," I demanded, "and I don't want any quibbling, or beating around the bush. Have I gone mad?" I noticed for the first time that my mother's eyes were heavily ringed.

"No, Margaret," she replied gently. "They thought you might be for a while, but you're not. All you've got to do is to have a complete rest, and soon you'll be well again."

I grinned, trying to dispel the mist before my eyes. "That's one thing out of the way," I said, ticking off items with my fingers. "How long have I been here?"

"Five days." My mother got up to re-arrange the phlox that she had brought with her. I stirred restlessly in bed.

"Stop pretending to fix those flowers," I ordered, and she glanced over her shoulder. "Come and sit down. Now listen, Charlotte, if you want me to get well, and believe me I've had enough of this place already, I must know what has happened. The doctors have told me nothing but a string of medical phrases that might mean anything. As for the nurses! They call me 'dear' in voices you could sharpen an axe on, and their eyes never leave my movements. Do they think that I'm going to bite them? I certainly feel like it sometimes."

Charlotte laughed suddenly, and came to sit on the edge of my bed. "I knew they were wrong!" she exclaimed joyously. "They only let me in on the condition that I made no mention of the Exchange. I told them that I knew my daughter better than they, and that the first step to regaining your health would be to give you the true facts."

"Silly fools," I smiled at her. "Go on."

Her face grew grave again. "It's liable to hurt you, Maggie."

"I know," I replied, dropping my eyes to the counterpane. "Clark?"

"Yes. You loved him, didn't you?"

I turned my head on the pillows, and stared through the bars to the brilliant sky. "I thought I did,' I said dreamily, "but somehow I don't feel as bad about him as I should now. It's funny, Charlotte, but I never dreamed that he had a weak streak until that day at the golf-house when he clung to me."

"You fell in love with the romance woven about him," she suggested gravely. "Love is not like that, Maggie."

"I suppose not," I agreed, and a short silence fell between us.

"Where is he?" I asked presently, turning my head to look at her. She made no reply, but her eyes were full of sadness.

"Dead?" I queried and nodded gently to myself. "It is better so. Poor Clark, I still can't understand how it happened. I thought that I'd let go the railing."

"Sergeant Matheson followed you up on the roof. He suspected him all the time."

"The Sergeant?" I repeated, frowning. "Do I owe my life to him?"

"Yes, Maggie."

I waved my hand to another group of flowers. "Those came from him. It took me a while to work out who he was. Get the card and read it."

Charlotte rose obediently and stood with her back towards me, the piece of pasteboard held between her forefinger and thumb. She remained so a longer time than was necessary to decipher the scrawled message.

"Well?" I said impatiently.

She turned round slowly, "It must have given you a shock," she said.

"Not really. I'd only called Clark by his Christian name once or twice. Mac was the only one who used it regularly. Give me that card again." I studied the name engraven on it—John P. Matheson—before turning it over. On the back was written: "May I come and see you?"

"Have you got a pen?" I asked my mother on impulse. "Or a pencil would do."

I crossed out the message and wrote "Please come." I signed "Margaret Byrnes" with a flourish.

"Will you post this to Sergeant Matheson?" I asked Charlotte. "Don't put it in your bag, or you'll forget it."

"I'll hold it in my hand until I find an envelope and stamp," she promised with alacrity.

"I wonder how he came to suspect Clark," I said musingly, as Charlotte slipped the card between her glove and palm.

"Several facts seemed to point to him, but I'll let him tell you himself."

I sat up with a jerk. "You thought that it was Clark too!" I exclaimed. "Why?"

Charlotte put out her hands in a helpless gesture. "I don't know exactly why. It was Mrs. Bates who first put me on to it. She remarked on his eyes."

"His eyes?" I repeated in astonishment. "What had they to do with suspecting him of murder?"

"They were brown," she replied simply. "I never yet have been able to trust anyone with brown eyes. Neither has Mrs. Bates."

"I only hope that you didn't tell Sergeant Matheson," I remarked. "I don't think that he holds much brief for feminine intuition."

"It is very well in its right place. It caused me to discover the truth about Mr. Scott."

I looked at her curiously. "What did you say to him? He was very loud in his praises of you. I was beginning to be afraid that his intentions were dishonourable."

"I considered that the story he gave about coming into the Exchange to keep a clandestine appointment was very weak indeed. I told him so. Surely there are heaps of other places to conduct such meetings. Anyway, he buckled at the knees, so to speak. I suppose I took him by surprise. It was then that I received the first hint of what was going on."

"And what was going on?" I demanded wearily. It appeared that I had been the only one in the dark.

As Charlotte opened her mouth to answer, a nurse rustled in bearing a glass of some repulsive liquid that I was coerced into swallowing four times a day.

"How are we after our first visitor?" she asked brightly, closing my fingers around the tumbler. I supposed she thought that I might try balancing it on one foot, the fool!

"We are very much better," I retorted. "It's a pity that a few more aren't let in."

She wagged one finger roguishly. I longed to throw the glass into her face. "Now, now! You know doctor's orders. Complete rest and no excitement. Say good-bye now, Mrs. Byrnes."

I protested violently, but it was no use. Nurses seem to have wills of iron.

"Don't forget that card," I whispered, as Charlotte bent to kiss me, "and come again soon."

I had to wait another two days before learning the answer to the question that I had asked Charlotte. Two days, which I spent wandering around the grounds of the rest home, nearly tearing my hair with impatience. I tried talking to my fellow inmates in order to pass the time, but gave up in despair after a long session with a white-haired, regal-looking woman, who told me some astounding stories about the life of Louis the Fifteenth, at whose court she had displaced La Pompadour as the royal favourite.

It was during the afternoon of the second day, when I was sitting in the garden staring moodily at nothing, that my special attendant came across the grass, followed by Sergeant Matheson. Her face bore an expression of professional sagacity as she reached for my pulse.

"Between seventy and eighty," I declared, looking warily past her to the Sergeant. He had made no sign of recognition and I had seen a warning flash in his eyes.

"We are doing very well, doctor," remarked the nurse, tucking in the rug that I had kicked off in a fit of petulance. "Very well indeed. This is your new doctor, dear. Doctor Ingram has been called away for a few days."

"How do you do?" I said coolly. "What did you say his name was, Nurse?"

The Sergeant pulled up a garden seat, and spoke with professional briskness. "Matheson is my name. That will be all now, Nurse, thank you. I'd like to be alone with the patient for a while." He dropped his voice to a confidential murmur, and the nurse, after nodding once or twice, hurried away. As soon as I saw her disappear into the house. I began to laugh softly.

Sergeant Matheson glanced nervously over his shoulder, "Hush! Someone might be watching. You have no idea the trouble I had to get in. If they knew my real profession I'd be thrown out quick and lively. How are you feeling?"

"Rotten, thanks. No one will tell me anything, and I'm nearly sick with curiosity. I asked for a newspaper one day, but they said that they'd all been destroyed. The doctors are worse; all pulse-feeling and medical terms. I really will go mad if I don't find out exactly what happened."

He laughed and sat nearer. "I'd better hold your hand," he suggested. "Maybe if anyone sees us, they'll think that it is part of my famous cure. I got your note."

"Thanks for the flowers," I replied gruffly, "and for saving my life."

"Don't mention either. They were both very small deeds. You are still very nervy, I see. Your fingers are jumping all the time."

I made an effort to draw my hand away, only to find it clasped the stronger.

"Who wouldn't be?" I retorted. "I'm not used to holding hands with strange men, especially married ones. What would your wife say if she saw you now?"

"Nothing," he grinned, "because I haven't got one. Where on earth did you get that idea?"

"A girl I know told me. Did you know that you had three children as well?"

"How ghastly!" he remarked blankly. "She must have mixed me up with Inspector Coleman. I know he has several. It wasn't that Patterson wench who told you all these interesting facts, by any chance?"

"Never mind," I replied, wrenching my hand away at last. "You're not here to talk about her, even though you did have two dances running with her."

"Only for professional reasons. What do you want to talk about?"

"Don't be tedious," I replied. "You know very well. And don't look at me as if you're scared I may crack up under the strain. I know it was Clark."

"I don't want to upset you," he said apologetically. "You see, I thought that you were—"

"I wasn't," I said crossly. "Get on with the story. Was the Inspector pleased with solving the case?"

"No, he's in a foul mood because the killer escaped."

I think that it was then that I realized how little Clark had meant to me. "Escaped!" I exclaimed fearfully, glancing around expecting to see that face, lit so horribly by lightning, lurking amongst the trees and shrubs.

"He escaped from justice," Sergeant Matheson hesitated, eyeing me warily.

"Go on," I said.

"When he saw that the game was up, he did what he was trying to do to you. Threw himself over the railing."

I covered my face with my hands for one minute. "Was he killed outright?" I asked, my voice muffled.

"No. We got a confession from him before he died, two days later. It was rather—grim."

Slowly I uncovered my face, and lifted my eyes to the sparkling sky. The wind and the trees, and the lone sky-lark circling overhead, reminded me of those days when we strode side by side down the fairways, Clark, Mac and I. How happy those days had been! Or were they, when all the time I waited for Clark to choose between us. Did he know then that he would murder Mac and make an attempt on my life? Had he made his plans as he looked laughingly into our eyes?

"Mr. Atkinson," I said abruptly. "What has happened to him?"

"He was arrested the day before Mr. Clarkson died. He was more to blame than the person who actually struck the blows at the two women."

I looked at him curiously. "Inspector Coleman seemed loath to discuss him with me," I remarked. "Who was he?"

Sergeant Matheson grinned in a teasing fashion. "A broker."

I let out one foot to kick him on the shin, amazed at my own familiarity. His manner was reminiscent of the day he took me to tea before we quarrelled. An atmosphere of contentment pervaded between us.

"He was," Sergeant Matheson assured me, rubbing his leg. "Atkinson bought and sold a certain commodity—secrets. As you once observed, the term broker can cover a number of affairs; in Atkinson's instance, rather nefarious affairs. The man ran an amazing show. Business secrets, social—anything he could lay his hands on was used. Contracts and estimates in the commercial world proved worthless overnight as the result of a rival party learning of them. The latest Society scandal became known to the world despite every precaution to keep it quiet. Another branch of Mr. Atkinson's activities was the trading of this country's defence secrets."

"Espionage?" I raised my brows sceptically. "Surely—"

"Don't delude yourself. More spying goes on between wars than during them. We'd had our eye on Atkinson for some time, but he was too clever to let us have any proof. As soon as we knew he was connected with the murders at the Exchange we had a fair idea what was going on."

"But, Clark? Where did he come in?"

"He was in Atkinson's pay; had been for some time, in fact. What could be a better place in which to pick up incriminating information about people and learn defence plans than the Trunk Exchange? Mr. Clarkson held a key position. I should say he was at the beginning of most of Atkinson's business deals."

I said: "It is a wonder he didn't set up a rival concern." I spoke in a flippant manner, mainly to hide the hurt that the tearing down of the rosy veil was causing.

"Atkinson, to give him his due, had amazing executive ability. His was the ultimate responsibility. Mr. Clarkson probably felt it was safer to leave things to him. He was waiting to learn certain instructions from Atkinson when Mr. Scott paid his surprise visit to the Exchange. Not only did their sources of business come from the lines, but they also used them to transmit certain information to their agents in the various states. To avoid detection that night, Mr. Clarkson had to find another telephone other than in the trunkroom."

"You mean that Clark was the mysterious caller in the restroom?"

"He was. But he didn't know that you were there. He thought that you'd be asleep in the dormitory and took the precaution of locking that door."

Suddenly I remembered Clark when he stood staring out of a window of the trunkroom, and the way his lips stirred as though he was repeating some phrase over and over. I mentioned the incident to Sergeant Matheson.

"He was probably memorizing his instructions," he suggested. "A code, originated from your telephonic one, was always used. That was where Mr. Clarkson made his fatal mistake. We had Atkinson's telephone under constant observation, so he had to pass messages to Brown himself. Brown was the head of the New South Wales bunch. He wrote one down on the back of the docket bearing the record of the Atkinson call, and Sarah Compton noticed it. Either she actually heard Clarkson using the Sydney line, or observed the same odd feature that you did, namely, that although the call had been completed at once, the remarks on the back signified that it had been delayed. Anyway, she took it away with her to study."

"Clark had tea with her that night," I nodded. "He probably knew she had it."

Sergeant Matheson leaned back in his chair, half-closing his eyes. "Do you remember what you told me about that time on the roof? You came upon Miss Compton playing 'peepo's' as you put it."

"I remember," I replied slowly. "I wondered at the time if she was going mad."

"The following night you showed us over the trunkroom and explained, amongst other things, the standard phrases used on the lines. There was one that stuck in my mind. Particular person unavailable. Or, as you telephonists put it, P.P.U."

"I follow what you mean," I said, snapping my fingers in annoyance. "What a fool I was! Of course, that was what Sarah was saying, not that idiotic 'peepo.' I suppose she was trying to decode the message. Did she realize that Clark was mixed up in espionage work?"

Sergeant Matheson shook his head. "I don't think so. Mr. Scott said that she was still in ignorance when he met her in the observation- room later that night."

"Bertie must have had some idea of what was happening all the time," I declared. "He had aged a great deal in the last few weeks. Of course, after that absurd yarn he pitched to Inspector Coleman, I naturally put it down to the fact that Compton must have been blackmailing him. What on earth possessed him to say what he did?"

"Probably it was the first thing that came into his head," said the Sergeant. "Don't forget that Mr. Clarkson was present at that interview. Mr. Scott couldn't show his hand even to us."

"Do you mean to say that Bertie knew it was Clark all the time?" I asked in amazement.

"He had a fair idea. You see, it had to be someone fairly high up on the Exchange staff, who could use an Interstate line without arousing any attention."

"And I thought that he was the murderer!" I exclaimed faintly. "My opinion of him had dropped to zero."

"So did we for a while," grinned the Sergeant. "He was a good actor."

"How did you first come to suspect Clark?" I asked in a low voice, breaking the silence between us.

"I was prejudiced from the start of course," he replied, and I looked at him inquiringly. "I think the first hint I got was when I read the report that the wireless boys took over the air from the car in which he drove you and Miss MacIntyre home the night of Miss Compton's death. It came out in the course of your conversation that he had been alone in the restroom for several minutes. You were in a faint, and Miss MacIntyre had gone to ring up the police. In itself, it was not suspicious, but the fact that he omitted it from his statement made me wonder."

"But why should he want to be alone?"

"To answer that question properly, I will have to deal first with the mystery of the locked door."

"Please do," I said gratefully. "If there was one thing that depressed me more than another with its unreasonableness, it was that damned door. Why was it locked?"

"To hide the weapons," was the prompt reply. I stared at him in a dazed fashion.

"There were two buttinskys," explained the Sergeant. "One was used for the actual murder. The other to throw the police off the scent and on to Mr. Scott's trail. Mr. Clarkson tried to make a scapegoat of the Senior Traffic Officer. Once we got on to the espionage part of the story, we would immediately look for someone high up—one of the Heads, as you put it—who could be Mr. Atkinson's accomplice. You don't appear to be listening very closely," he added in an injured voice.

"I've got it!" I shouted. Sergeant Matheson again glanced towards the house nervously. "For days I have been searching for a reason for what Clark said when he tried to push me off the roof. Now I know. I saw him with a buttinsky in his hand. No wonder he was concerned when I told him that there was something nagging at the back of my mind! That was it. When I escaped from the lift where Sarah Compton was reading that anonymous letter, I ran right into him. Clark must have taken a buttinsky out of one of the power-rooms. It registered itself on my unconscious mind as odd, although not unusual, that he should have one with him out of the trunkroom. I was just starting to remember it when I noticed the dump-yard from the roof, and mentioned it to Clark."

"I wish that you'd remembered days ago," said the Sergeant peevishly. "It might have meant the saving of a great deal of time, not to mention Miss MacIntyre's life."

I winced at the mention of Mac's name, and bent my head to hide the sudden rush of tears to my eyes. Sergeant Matheson's hand closed over mine warmly.

"I'm sorry," he said simply. I shook my head, unable to speak for the tightness in my throat.

"Would you like me to go?" he asked, making a move to rise.

I twisted my hand under his and gripped it urgently. "Please go on about the door," I said, managing a rather watery smile. "I won't be able to sleep to-night unless I know."

"The door! Yes, of course. Mr. Clarkson had to have somewhere to put both buttinskys. They are not over small, as you know. He evidently feared that his locker might be searched at some time or another. Also he wanted to form a bait for Miss Compton. According to you, she was the first on the scene at untoward happenings in the Exchange.

"He may even have planned to kill her earlier, but Miss Compton had made an appointment to meet Mr. Scott in the observation-room for the purpose of showing him the docket. He decided to leave it until such time when Mr. Scott was either in or near the building. Before Compton kept that appointment she made a shrewd move by duplicating the docket and filing it. Whether she knew that her life was in danger or not, I don't know. I cannot help but be thankful that she did duplicate it. In order to make the docket appear as normal as possible, she even filled in the operator's signature, choosing by some extraordinary chance your own number. Perhaps she had it in mind, as she had just been querying a call with you. Then she took the original down to show Mr. Scott. He knew at once the significance it held, but he didn't want the fact that espionage was going on in the Exchange spread around the building. He merely pooh-poohed Miss Compton's suggestions as to its meaning, and told her to forget all about it. She was a little disappointed by his lack of interest, and made no mention of the duplicate she had filed. In fact, it was very lucky that Miss MacIntyre, not realizing the importance, told Inspector Coleman about it."

"Was that why Mac was killed?" I asked hesitantly.

"One of the reasons. But I think what really signed her death warrant was the fact that she could break Clark's alibi."

I leaned forward eagerly. "That is what I can't understand. The three of us had cast-iron alibis. How could he murder Compton in the restroom, and yet be in the trunkroom at the same time?"

"Mr. Clarkson had his plans timed down to the last possible minute. The first thing he had to do was to get the door of the restroom unlocked. This was accomplished by placing the key where Miss Compton could find it. He probably put it in her handbag some time during the course of the evening. This acted as a further bait. When she saw the strange key, her first impulse would be to find out if it was the one missing from the restroom door. Having once opened the restroom, the sight of two buttinskys lying side by side in a conspicuous place would hold her there until such time as Mr. Clarkson could slip out, unobserved by you and Miss MacIntyre. You yourself told us that a busy telephonist has neither the time nor the inclination to watch what others are doing. He was very lucky, of course, as things went according to his plan. First of all, Miss Compton found the key and went to satisfy her curiosity; secondly, the lines were exceptionally busy that night."

"Did Mac see him leave the room?"

"She didn't actually see, but she heard the noise of the back door opening near her position. At the time she didn't bother to look up, but later when she heard Clarkson say that he had been in the trunkroom the whole night, she began to grow suspicious."

"So that was why she behaved in such a peculiar fashion. Why didn't she tell the police if she knew Clark had no alibi after all?"

Sergeant Matheson looked at me oddly. "She was in love with him."

"But a murderer!" I exclaimed. "In her position, I would have told you quickly enough."

"I am relieved to hear you say that," he said with a faint smile. "It gives me proof."

"What proof?" I asked, puzzled. He shook his head, still smiling.

"I still can't understand it," I went on. "Thinking back, I can remember the telephone ringing on the Senior Traffic Officer's table. It stopped after a while. I presumed that Clark had answered it."

"He had hoped that one of you would notice that 'phone. That was part of his alibi. After he had killed Miss Compton and taken the docket recording Mr. Atkinson's call from her handbag, he rang the Senior Traffic Officer's number on the restroom 'phone for a few seconds and then hung up. He left both buttinskys hidden in the restroom, and went quickly back to the trunkroom."

I nodded. "He helped me with the switching. When I saw him at the other end of the boards, I merely thought that he had been too busy before. Clever!"

"But for Miss MacIntyre's ears being too sharp, he would have succeeded in getting away with it. Incidentally, that was another matter that helped us to get on to his tracks. Inspector Coleman observed that the majority of telephonists, Miss MacIntyre included, wear their headset on the left ear. That meant that her uncovered ear was nearer the door."

"It's a pity he didn't choose the front door," I remarked. "I doubt if I would have noticed his exit."

"There was no chance of anyone seeing him on the back stairs. Although, as a matter of fact, someone did. Gloria Patterson mentioned something about a masked and hooded figure stealing along the corridor, but she had plunged herself so deeply into a maze of mendacious statements that we took no notice. We thought it was only a cover for herself."

"Masked and hooded!" I snorted.

Sergeant Matheson laughed. "It wasn't an exact description perhaps, but Clarkson probably did make some effort to disguise himself."

I was inclined to be derisive until the Sergeant interrupted me quietly. "Mr. Clarkson carried a light raincoat over his arm as he was leaving that night. Do you remember it?"

"Certainly. He shared the opinion of many that the wind might change and that it would rain. Nearly everyone arms themselves with a coat of some description when that north wind starts to blow. I have often come to work dressed for the summer. By the time I have finished, it is like the middle of winter."

Sergeant Matheson spoke in an off-hand manner. "The Weather Bureau issued a warning that we might expect a heat-wave that very morning. No, Miss Byrnes. When Mr. Clarkson decided to bring a raincoat with him, I think he had two other reasons in mind. Firstly, to use as a possible disguise; don't forget that the corridor is very dimly lit at night. The appearance of someone draped in any sort of covering from the head to the knee would present a very sinister picture to a vivid imagination, such as Miss Patterson possesses. The second reason, and probably the primary one, is that Mr. Clarkson needed something in which to carry the bloodstained buttinsky away with him. What could be better than the deep pocket of a waterproof coat?

"What he did, once he got rid of Miss MacIntyre, who went downstairs to ring Russell Street, was to remove both buttinskys from their temporary hiding-place. The one that he had used for the actual murder— that is the one that you saw him holding earlier that evening—he put into his coat pocket. The other he threw out the window, after running the tap over it in the lunch-room opposite, in order to give the impression that we leaped at so readily; namely, that the murderer had endeavoured to wash away the bloodstains before hiding it in the dump-heap. These things would only take a few seconds to accomplish. Again luck was with him, inasmuch as you collapsed. He could hardly have sent the two of you to call the police."

"He must have felt rather terrible when you started questioning," I murmured, forever putting myself in the other fellow's place. "It's a wonder that he stood the strain of pretence for so long. Afterwards, he took us home to his flat for a dose, as he called it."

The Sergeant's voice was grim. "He had an object in doing so. He wanted to find out how much you and Miss MacIntyre knew."

"Mac showed her hand immediately. She never could deceive anyone. At the time I thought she was only worried about her own position in the case. It's a wonder Clark didn't kill her before Saturday."

"He was planning to, but two things stopped him. He knew Miss MacIntyre's feelings for him, and tried to persuade her to join him in his enterprises. Either he didn't want the risk of another murder on his hands, or he was soft-hearted where she was concerned. Then Dulcie Gordon committed suicide, and he felt more or less safe. You were the main trouble. You insisted that the police decision was incorrect and started the ball rolling again."

"He wasn't much of an actor either," I remarked thoughtfully. "I could tell he didn't believe that Gordon was guilty. No wonder that he tried to dissuade me from continuing my inquiries! I never dreamed he was the murderer. Rather I favoured Bertie or Gloria. No, not Gloria; but I thought she knew more than she would admit."

"Miss Patterson believed that Mrs. Smith had killed Compton," declared the Sergeant. "That is why she fainted when you told her that the identity of the anonymous letter-writer and the killer was one and the same."

"I didn't say that exactly," I protested.

"That is the impression she received," he replied dryly. "She came to see me yesterday, wanting to know if she could sue you for making such a libellous statement."

I sat up with a jerk. "I hope you told her to go to hell."

"No," he replied, smiling faintly. "I said that she required the services of a solicitor, not a policeman. But you needn't worry. No sane man would accept such a case, especially from such a client as she would be."

I sank back, muttering darkly about what I'd do to her when I got my hands on her. They were brave words, but when Gloria did come to see me a few days later, I felt that the effort to impress her misdoings on her was more than I could manage. She arrived dressed in baby blue and flashing a deep sapphire on her left hand, which I ignored out of sheer unpleasantness. She remarked with wide-eyed innocence on the nature of the place.

"Poor Maggie! How terrible it must be for you. I mean, realizing where you are."

"Not at all," I assured her. "It's just like being at the Exchange again. A veritable home from home. Do you know, Gloria," I went on confidentially, "that there is even a patient here who reminds me of you. What more could I want?"

"Very funny!" she said on a high note. "I'm sorry I came now."

"Don't say that, Gloria," I said reproachfully. "I'm always delighted to see you. To whom are you waving all the time?" Her left hand fluttered down to her lap.

"I'm engaged," she said crossly.

"Are you really? Who's the unlucky—I mean, my heartiest congratulations."

Gloria gave a small, self-conscious laugh. "You should say best wishes," she corrected. "It's not the thing to congratulate the girl."

"Sorry. You must excuse my ignorance in such matters. To whom are you engaged?"

"The American I told you about. He comes from Virginia. His people are immensely wealthy. They own tobacco or something," and she went into a score of details. I listened to them with only half an ear.

"Auntie pleased?" I interrupted presently, watching her closely. She paused open-mouthed in the middle of a description of her proposed trousseau.

"She hasn't met him yet," she muttered, without looking at me.

There was silence. She began to fiddle with the blue leather handbag on her knee. Once she glanced up as if to speak, but lowered her head as she searched for a powder compact. I gave her no help.

"Maggie," she burst out suddenly.

"Yes, Gloria?"

"You won't tell anyone, will you?" Her eyes filled with tears. "I don't know what I would do if Schuyler found out."

"Is that his name?" I asked in astonishment. "His people must be rich indeed to be able to afford to call their son that. The poor boy!"

"Oh, Maggie!" Gloria said, between a sob and a laugh. It was the first evidence I had found of a sense of humour in Gloria.

It moved me to say impulsively: "You needn't worry. I'll never tell anyone that you're a—"

"Maggie!" she interrupted, looking deeply shocked.

"Well, aren't you?" I asked reasonably. She bent her head into her hands. I welcomed the appearance of a nurse to put an end to visiting hours. Gloria bade me a tearful farewell, and I shook her hand, hoping that she would be very happy with Schuyler. She seemed satisfied then that I would hold my tongue.

* * * * *

The following day I had another visitor from the Exchange. John Matheson had already got me started on what he said was the true story of the Trunk Exchange murders, and I glanced up, annoyed at being interrupted, as the nurse entered my room.

"Still at the letter writing?" she asked brightly. "You must have loads of friends."

"I am a very popular girl," I assured her.

"You must be;" she returned, giving me a sharp look. "A Mr. Scott has come to see you. He is waiting on the side veranda."

I went down to meet Bertie, filled with what can only be described as mixed feelings. Here was a man for whom I had had nothing but the highest regard. Then something happened that aroused my dislike, and my opinion of him had dropped to nil. But it had been my own fault. I had confused his business personality with his private life. I considered that as an ordinary man, his code would be as rigid as his behaviour as Senior Traffic Officer of the Telephone Exchange. Then I learned that Bertie was none of the despicable things I had thought about him. Indeed, he had sacrificed the respect of his fellow men for a deeper and more worthy motive. That he had recognized my sudden distrust, I was certain. Therefore it was with some trepidation that I made my way to the side veranda.

He was sitting on the extreme edge of a deck chair. It was remarkable that it did not overbalance as his feet did their perpetual dance-step. Seeing him twist his hat around and around in his hands, I realized with some relief that he was just as nervous. His lips moved slightly, as though he was rehearsing his part in the forthcoming interview.

"It is very kind of you to come and see me," I said, seating myself on the edge of the opposite chair, and drawing the folds of my long housecoat together.

"Not at all, not at all," he replied, standing up with a jerk. He must have known that he still seemed ill-at-ease even in that position, and sat down again.

"How are you?" Bertie demanded with that forced smile which men seem to keep for the sickroom.

"Fine, thank you. I didn't go out of my head after all. The doctors were disappointed," I added dryly.

He looked very unhappy. "I'm sure that there wasn't the slightest possibility, Miss Byrnes. You've been remarkable, simply remarkable."

'A true daughter of my mother,' I thought to myself, as Bertie began to cough and fidget. I was about to start commenting on the weather when he said abruptly, not meeting my eyes:

"I want to apologize to you, Miss Byrnes."

"Do you?" I asked in a dazed fashion. I had thought that the hoot was on the other foot.

"Yes, I do," he insisted fiercely. "My behaviour was scandalous, and

I am very, very sorry. I should have known better, but at the time I was suspicious of everyone. I hope you understand what I mean?"

"I think I do," I replied cautiously, "but I'd be glad if you'd explain a bit more."

"Certainly, certainly," said Bertie, coughing again. "It was your—er—friendship with Mr. Clarkson that made me apprehensive. You see, I thought that the pair of you were working hand-in-glove, as it were. Whenever anything untoward happened, you always seemed to be together. That was why I decided to work that Sunday night in his place. I hoped that I might be able to find out what part you were playing. When I found you at Miss MacIntyre's locker I considered that my worst fears were justified."

Bertie arose, and walked to the edge of the veranda. Without turning around, he said gruffly: "I need hardly tell you, Miss Byrnes, that I was most upset. I had always considered you as a young lady of the highest integrity."

I stared in amazement at his dumpy little figure, silhouetted against the sky. So that was why he had let me go unharmed from the cloakroom! The warning that he had issued was not prompted from any sinister motive, but from his desire to release me from Clark's toils.

"I thought that you were mixed up in the murders yourself," I burst out.

Bertie spun around. His pince-nez slipped down the length of its chain as his brows rose in an astonishment that must have been equal to mine.

"Dear me!" he said blankly. Then I saw a twinkle appear in his eyes, and as a broad grin lit up his face, I suddenly began to laugh.

"How amusing!" he exclaimed with his odd little chuckle. "We seem to have been at cross-purposes, Miss Byrnes."

"When you started apologizing to me," I said, wiping my eyes. "I wondered what on earth you were talking about. It was I who should have been doing the apologizing."

"Not at all," he repeated, seating himself again. But this time he lay back at his ease, crossing his short legs. "May I ask what made you think that I committed the murders? I presume that is what you did think?"

I nodded. "I'm afraid I did, and for just the same reason as you suspected me. You always seemed to be on the scene when anything happened. The night Miss Compton was killed, you entered the Exchange in the most suspicious way." I hesitated, glancing at him for a brief moment. "Although you gave an explanation of what made you return after your usual working hours, that explanation only increased my suspicion. I thought maybe that Compton was blackmailing you. She had tried to with others, you know. My theory was that you killed her, and made your escape by that door down in the basement."

Bertie placed the tips of his fingers together, and inclined his head gravely. "Quite feasible," he announced. "To concoct such a story as I did about that meeting was most abhorrent to me. Apart from soiling your ears with sordid facts, I never did like telling untruths. But at the time I had no option. Mr. Clarkson was there as well as you. In fact, Mr. Clarkson's dramatic defence rather amused me. There was no better way in which he could have made worse my already uncertain position. I knew he was guilty but I had no proof, and I had been warned to use the utmost discretion in handling the situation. Time was with Mr. Clarkson, and he used it to put me in the most suspicious light possible."

"About what were you to be discreet?" I asked.

Bertie glanced sideways at me, a dubious look.

"I know that Mr. Clarkson was mixed up in some espionage game," I said encouragingly. "Sergeant Matheson told me."

Bertie seemed relieved. "If the police told you, I suppose that there is no harm in my telling you what I know. Over the space of several months many well-known people, not the least among them a high Defence official, have approached the head of the Telephone Department concerning information that had leaked out over the lines. You may have observed the way the secrecy line has come into more frequent use just lately. I had instructions to employ it for every call of a confidential nature."

I nodded. That secrecy line had certainly been working overtime.

"Mr. Dunn called for my assistance in tracing the person who was at the root of all the trouble. As I have told you, he warned me to go carefully as the good name of the Department had to be protected. There was also the fear that our man might slip through our fingers. It was impossible to go to the police. They would have immediately started inquiries at the Exchange, and that was the last thing that we wanted to happen.

"Checking up on my staff's activities was a very difficult job, and one that was most distasteful. It meant putting all the outward phones in the building under observation, and even going through the lockers in the endeavour to discover who the person was."

My mind flew back to that game of solo I had played in the restroom. I could hear the girls' indignant voices as they protested against the continual spying.

"After a while," Bertie went on, "I came to the conclusion that the person must be fairly high up on my staff. A monitor, or even a traffic officer. Strangely enough I thought of Mr. Clarkson almost at once. But it wasn't until I overheard a certain remark that I had anything to go on. It was passed by a person who had recently been at a party Mr. Clarkson had given at his flat. Perhaps you were there too?"

I nodded, and felt that weary feeling creeping through my brain again. How could I forget the sight of Clark playing the debonair host in the middle of his charming flower-filled apartment. He had come to us for help.

"Look here, you girls," he had said. "What about coming and poking weeds into vases before the show. I don't know how to arrange flowers."

I could see the broad mixed bowl on the window sill against the chintz, and Mac standing back, her small dark head on one side, as she surveyed her handiwork with grave concentration. I jerked myself back to the present. What was it Bertie was saying? Someone was wondering where Clark got his money; how he managed to run a flat in South Yarra on a traffic officer's income?

"That's funny," I said aloud. "I used to speculate on the same thing. I presumed that his parents had been well-off."

"He was a member of a very exclusive golf club, too," Bertie continued. "It was always a source of surprise to me, until I made a few inquiries. I discovered that his name had been put up for election by a man called Atkinson."

"Atkinson!" I repeated, almost yelling the name. "So it wasn't a coincidence after all."

Bertie surveyed me anxiously. "I am making you excited. Please be calm, Miss Byrnes, or they'll make me go."

"No, they won't," I replied firmly. "You're staying until we thrash things out."

Bertie chuckled again, like a playful conspirator. "That's exactly how I feel about anything unpleasant. Get it off your chest, and then forget all about it. Where was I?"

"I'd just taken over the conversation," I said, smiling at him warmly. He was a lamb, after all. "Did you know about Mr. Atkinson?" I demanded.

"I had been furnished with the names and telephone numbers of several persons who were suspected of being connected with the affair. He was one of them. As soon as I realized that there was some link between him and Mr. Clarkson I knew that I was on the right track." Bertie paused, and I noticed that the twinkle had faded from his eyes.

"Everything was going well," he went on presently. "I had only to wait for such time when I could catch Mr. Clarkson red-handed, when Sarah Compton started to interfere. Poor woman! She thought that she was acting for the best, but really she was just an infernal nuisance. I tried to head her off, but she kept coming to tell me that something wrong was going on in the Exchange. It was only a matter of time before Mr. Clarkson would realize she was on his trail. I became desperate," Bertie stopped again, and I wondered why he looked so sheepish.

"I even had recourse to a trick I have never done since my schooldays," he confessed. "I sent her an anonymous letter, warning her to mind her own business."

"So that's how that letter fitted in!" I exclaimed, remembering the third note Inspector Coleman had handed me to read in Compton's room. "It had me puzzled."

"Even that did not work," Bertie went on regretfully.

"I should think that it would only increase her curiosity," I told him. "The mere fact that she kept it proves that."

"She was a very foolish woman," said Bertie, shaking his head. "Her inquisitiveness caused her death."

"In spite of all her faults, she was proud of the Telephone Exchange," I declared slowly. "I think that she would have done anything to protect its reputation."

Even my own defence of Sarah Compton did nothing to dispel the feeling of angry bitterness that filled me when I remembered the unhappiness and destruction she had left in her wake. Had she not started prying into matters that were really none of her concern, Clark would not have had to kill her. Not only Mac would have been still alive, but also Dulcie Gordon.

By a great effort I had managed to write a short note to Gordon's people. It was an unpleasant task, and one that I considered was more than amply rewarded by the grateful reply that came by the following mail. They thanked me for the description I had given them of what I knew of Dulcie's last days, and also for the way in which I had befriended their girl.

Far from being satisfied with their letter, it did more to augment that guilty feeling that I was responsible for Dulcie's death. Certainly I had achieved what I had sworn to do. She was totally exonerated from any suspicion of murder; but what comfort was that now, when she was dead by her own hand? Compton was more to blame than I, by her wicked exploitation of the simple country girl not overladen with brains. Poor little unsophisticated Dulcie, with her easily aroused timidity and concern for her family. Rather than face what she imagined would be shocked and disappointed parents, she had chosen to commit suicide. The principal emotion I felt when I thought of Gordon was regret. But the slightest remembrance of Mac made me clench my hands in the endeavour to beat off that old feeling of horror I had known so well in the first days of my breakdown.

One lonely, hot night, when sleep was playing the coquette, I got up to pace the floor of my narrow room and pondered on every incident that brought Mac to her death. It was easy enough now to slip facts and incidents into their correct places to make a whole picture, which contained as its central figure a small, dark-haired girl lying dead in a pool of her own blood. It was like working out a jig-saw puzzle when you already knew the answer. Mac's secretive manner and haunted eyes were both explainable now I knew the secret she had been hiding. If she had loved Clark so completely, and it was obvious that she had, what an agony of indecision she must have experienced. Either she had to denounce Clark, or keep her guilty secret for his sake. Mac must have known the probable result of her foolish choice, but she was willing to risk even that.

I could only guess at what time and how she arrived at that decision. The day after Compton was killed, she had clung to me trembling with fright and begged to be allowed to spend the night with me. Then Dulcie Gordon wanted to speak to me, and I sent Mac home armed with my latchkey. Although Dulcie had kept me a considerable period, I had arrived at my boardinghouse before Mac. What had she been doing in that time? No one would ever know. My idea was that Clark had followed her. Perhaps at first they talked about everything but what was uppermost in both their minds. But Mac could not pretend for long. She told him what she knew and promised to hold her tongue. Clark went one step further by proposing that she joined forces with him.

"Money!" I could hear him saying persuasively, and almost see the greedy light in his eyes. "We could make a lot of money, Gerda."

Little Mac, always as straight as a die! What did she do? She twisted her hands, and her fine eyes filled with untold agony as her innate honesty fought with her loyalty to Clark. I could hear her begging for time in which to think it over, and then see the hurried glance at her watch.

"I must hurry. Maggie mustn't suspect anything, John."

But even the story she told me of the tram stoppage did not deceive me. We came near to quarrelling, and that was the beginning of the shadow that grew up between us. I did not see Mac as a friend again until I found her dead, and read the message that she had tried to convey in her last consciousness; an appeal for my help to discover her killer. In the basement that late Friday afternoon we had been as casual acquaintances; perhaps not even that. We had been strangers, suspicious and jealous of each other.

Mac had held in her hand proof of the espionage taking place in the Exchange—the docket that she had found in the basement storeroom. Was it then that something stronger than her distorted loyalty to Clark stirred her? Did she pace the floor, as I was doing now, while her conscience battled against her own desires? If she continued to protect Clark, the espionage would go on. Her own life would be safe from him personally, but the lives and well-being of countless numbers of her fellow country-men would be in jeopardy.

She tried to put the responsibility on to others, making inquiries amongst the other girls who worked late on the night of Compton's mur-der. Officially the case was closed, but there was a chance that someone on the late staff had seen or heard something that might prove important. Mac's prompting might assist them to remember and to tell the police. I don't think that Mac succeeded in her idea. She may have learned about the masked and hooded man from Gloria Patterson, but placed no depen-dence on the police taking notice of Gloria. The responsibility was still hers. It was then in desperation that she came to me. That she had not done so before was probably because she was afraid that I might emulate her attitude towards Clark.

Meanwhile, Clark must have been watching Mac closely. Her obvi-ous devotion to him was a small thread on which to rely for his safety. He knew the type of girl Mac was, and must have wondered how long her fearless, honest character would stand out against his persuasions. To make certain that her plea for time to consider the situation was not an endeavour to double-cross him, he searched her room for any possible evidence that she might be holding against him. He may have seen those letters I had found later and guessed that Mac had decided at last. He may even have received a complete note from her warning him that she was going to the police. The latter was more probable. It was like Mac to play fair and give him a chance to escape. She didn't realize that Clark would stay where he was until she saw him that night at the charity dance. Having warned him she felt almost happy. On duty in the trunkroom that night she regained some of her former spirits. The other telephonists said that her behaviour had been normal. She had passed some flippant remark about dancing with Bertie. But when she saw Clark still at the Exchange, she knew at once that her life was in danger. There was only one thing to do—get in touch with Russell Street.

Clark had made his plans earlier. This time it was not difficult to arm himself with an alibi. As Inspector Coleman said, there was no better op-portunity to commit a murder than at a crowded dance. But Clark played safe. He arrived at the Exchange at about 8.30 p.m. that evening. His first move was to prepare a line in the power-room from the microphone in the danceroom to a vacant channel in the Trunk Exchange. Having done this, he made himself as conspicuous as possible, dancing with several different girls and always placing himself near the entrance to the hall between items where all could mark his presence.

All he had to do was to wait until Mac saw him. He knew that her first thought would be to get to a telephone, and outside the trunkroom the only line she could use would be either the one in the restroom or the public telephone in the old building. In her need for haste, it was more likely that Mac would make for the restroom. Everything went according to his reasoning. Mac came off duty, prepared to go and change in the cloakroom near the danceroom. She must have paused a moment to look into the hall and exchanged a few words with Charlotte before she actually saw Clark.

I could visualize the carefree smile fading from her lips and her small hands clenching themselves into balls as she realized what his presence meant. She hurried upstairs to the eighth floor, quite oblivious of the fact that Clark, observing her reactions when she caught sight of him, interrupted his dance with me under the pretext of amplifying the dance music to the trunkroom for my benefit. He ran up the back stairs to stop her from using that telephone in the restroom. But Mac managed to dial out the first numerals of Russell Street Police Station, automatically using a pencil instead of her finger as is the custom of most telephonists.

I did not pause to imagine the scene that took place then. But Mac must have known what was going to happen, despite the fact that Mrs. Smith still swore that she had heard no outcry. The only conclusion at which I could arrive was that the shock of the sudden and fearful realization that she was going to die froze all sound from Mac. Having satisfied himself that Mac was dead, Clark made quickly for the trunkroom. It only took a minute to complete the connection of the line which he had already erected.

I don't know whether the immediate discovery of the second murder or whether the game he organized when I told him the news were part of his plan, but both served well to establish his own security. He admitted being absent from the seventh floor, but the time that elapsed during his absence was sufficient only to erect the transmitting line to the trunkroom.

When Bertie learned that another murder had been committed and saw the way in which Clark was stage-managing the affair, he was helpless. The only thing he could do was to stand by, and hope that Clark would make some slip that the police would seize upon. Observing the way I acted under Clark's instructions, he began to suspect that I had had some part in the scheme. Most reluctantly, he set about trying to trap Clark through me. He decided to work the dogwatch the following night in order to watch my actions closely.

I gave him the slip when I managed to leave the trunkroom without attracting his attention. It was so soon after our brush outside Mac's locker that he did not think that I would attempt anything further that night, especially after his warning. I considered that if Bertie remained in the trunkroom, I would be safe to continue my search for the docket in the basement. Little did I know it was imperative for Clark to find it before me. Here Clark played safe again. He informed me of his intention to take the sleeping tablets Charlotte had given him. He may have had a look for the docket, and failing to find it, waited until I arrived on the scene in the hope that I knew more of its whereabouts than I told him.

I don't think Clark meant to kill me then. He had lost his nerve after Mac died, and although he could not regret having murdered her, he was genuinely upset at what he had done. His one desire was to get that docket and to destroy it before I had time to work out its significance. He knocked me out with his clenched fist, and snatching what he thought was the correct docket out of my hand, left the building by the door leading from the basement passage into the lane.

Before Bertie had time to mark my absence, Dan Mitchell had gone down to his locker for cigarettes and nearly tripped over my senseless body, lying half-in and half-out of the storeroom. He rushed upstairs with the news that yet another murder had taken place. After ensuring that I was still alive and rushing me to hospital, Bertie was completely bewildered. Here was a girl, or a young lady as I suppose he phrased it, considered by him as a likely accomplice in a couple of murders, who had been knocked on the head by someone whose intentions could not have been lawful. Bertie could only shake his head and come to the rather dubious conclusion that I had taken his warning to heart, and had quarrelled with the person directing my actions, refusing to do his bidding, and that that person had struck me down in frustrated anger.

When John learned of our mutual suspicion, he laughed uproariously.

"What's so funny?" I demanded, nettled. "You thought it was Bertie, too, until I put up a case against the liftman." Bill had been another of my visitors. It was only when he was announced that I knew the reason why his surname had remained such a dark secret. He brought me the first nectarines from his garden. In an unspoken bargain, we discussed everything but the Exchange.

John's laugh was so infectious that I could not help joining in, although I don't know what amused me. It was the first time for days that I had done so, and the sheer relief of being able to laugh again made it hard for me to stop.

"I thought it was you, too," he gasped presently. I went off into another spasm of mirth. A nurse put her head out of a window and called across the lawn to where we sat.

"Are you all right, Miss Byrnes?"

I controlled myself with difficulty. "Quite, thanks," I replied hurriedly, fearing that John might be ordered to go. She merely grunted and pulled the window down with a bang. I wondered who was the happier that I was leaving the following day, the nurses or myself.

The sight of the nurse must have sobered John too. He was quite serious as he explained: "You seemed to know too much. Whenever Inspector Coleman asked for your opinion on any matter, your answer was too prompt and exact to be healthy. Then there was your obvious dislike of Sarah Compton, and the hint that she had been interfering in your affairs."

"It would be rather foolish of me to admit it if I had killed her," I remarked.

"Not at all. Many's the person who has tried a double bluff and got away with it. Moreover, you could present us with theories before we had time even to get facts. When we checked up on them, they were found to be amazingly accurate; for example, the second exit to the Exchange."

"Do you mean to say that you doubted every word I spoke?"

John grinned. "Definitely. You never trust anyone in our game; not even your best girl. That was why I was absent from the dance-hall the night of Miss MacIntyre's death. I was crawling around the basement looking for your secret door."

"So that's where you'd got to!" I burst out.

He looked at me quizzically. "What did you think I was doing? Flirting with Gloria Patterson on the roof?"

"Of course not," I replied, trying to look dignified. "I wasn't in the least interested in your actions. Go on with your explaining."

"That's about all. Let's stop discussing crime, and talk about something pleasant for a change. Whenever I come, you spend the whole time asking questions."

"It's your own fault," I pointed out. "It was your idea that I should write a book. Is that really all, or are you trying to spare my peace of mind?"

For a while John made no reply. He got up and stood at the back of the long cane chair in which I sat. By tilting my head, I could see his face, grave and unsmiling.

"Not quite," he said, "but I don't want to hurt you, Maggie."

"If it's about Clark, go right ahead," I said fiercely. "I'm sick and tired of people eyeing me askance whenever his name crops up."

"Good girl!" He touched my hair for a brief moment in an approving fashion before resuming his lounging position in the chair opposite.

"We shall discuss the relations between you and Clark dispassionately.

The idea did come into my head, but briefly I assure you, that you killed Miss Compton because she was attempting in some way to break up your friendship. Miss MacIntyre was murdered because you were jealous of the hold she had on Clark's affections."

I smiled a little, but it was an effort. "You sound like a third-rate love story. Purple passion and the like."

"I told you the thought was only a passing one. But apart from that side of the question, you did appear to know Clarkson very well. As soon as Mr. Atkinson appeared on the scene, I began to wonder if your relations with Clarkson were for business purposes instead."

John drew out a small, red-covered book from an inner pocket and gave it to me. "I couldn't help noticing that nearly every second day held some mention of him," he said apologetically.

I flipped over the pages of my diary containing my notes on the case. After a moment's hesitation, I held it out to him. "Would you mind taking it away with you and destroying it?" I asked in a low voice. "I don't think I could bear to keep it."

"No, not yet. I want you to glance through it after I've gone."

John seemed so insistent that I tucked the book down the side of my chair. To break the silence that had fallen between us, I asked, without caring much about a reply: "Why was Mr. Atkinson at Clark's flat that morning?"

"He wanted to question him about how much you knew. He had seen you with Clark too many times. Men like that cannot afford to trust even their accomplices. Atkinson paid the rental of the flat and possessed a latch-key, so he was able to enter without arousing the attention of the neighbouring flats."

"Then Clark did not really take the sleeping tablets?"

"Oh, yes. He took them as a precaution as soon as he arrived back from his tussle with you. He knew you would get in touch with him as soon as you were able, and wanted to appear as though he had not left his flat. Mr. Atkinson learned that we were on his trail from some other source. You'd be amazed at the enormous organization he used to manage."

I don't think that there is anything more I have to add. The pattern seems complete now that all the smaller, but just as important, pieces have been fitted into place. Oddly enough, what I considered was the central figure of the picture seems to have changed. Perhaps because of what I read in my little red-covered diary when John had gone.

I sat there in the flickering shadows of the beech tree for some time before I remembered it, my mind wandering for the last time over scenes of violence and unhappiness, suspicion and misery. Presently I slipped my hand down the side of the chair and drew the book out curiously. It seemed lighter and thinner to hold. On opening it, I found that all the pages had been torn out up to the present date. I turned the first leaf wonderingly, and my eyes fell on a few words written in a sprawling hand in the space allotted for the following Saturday: "'Varsity versus Brighton Rovers at Teachers' College field. I'll call for you at 2 p.m."

Blasted cheek was my first impression. Then I gazed at the words speculatively. Perhaps it might be fun to watch a basketball game, after all.

THE END

CPSIA information can be obtained at www.ICGtesting.com
Printed in the USA
LVOW07s0322150415

434384LV00002B/2/P